DELIVERANCE

A Novel

By

Samantha Schinder

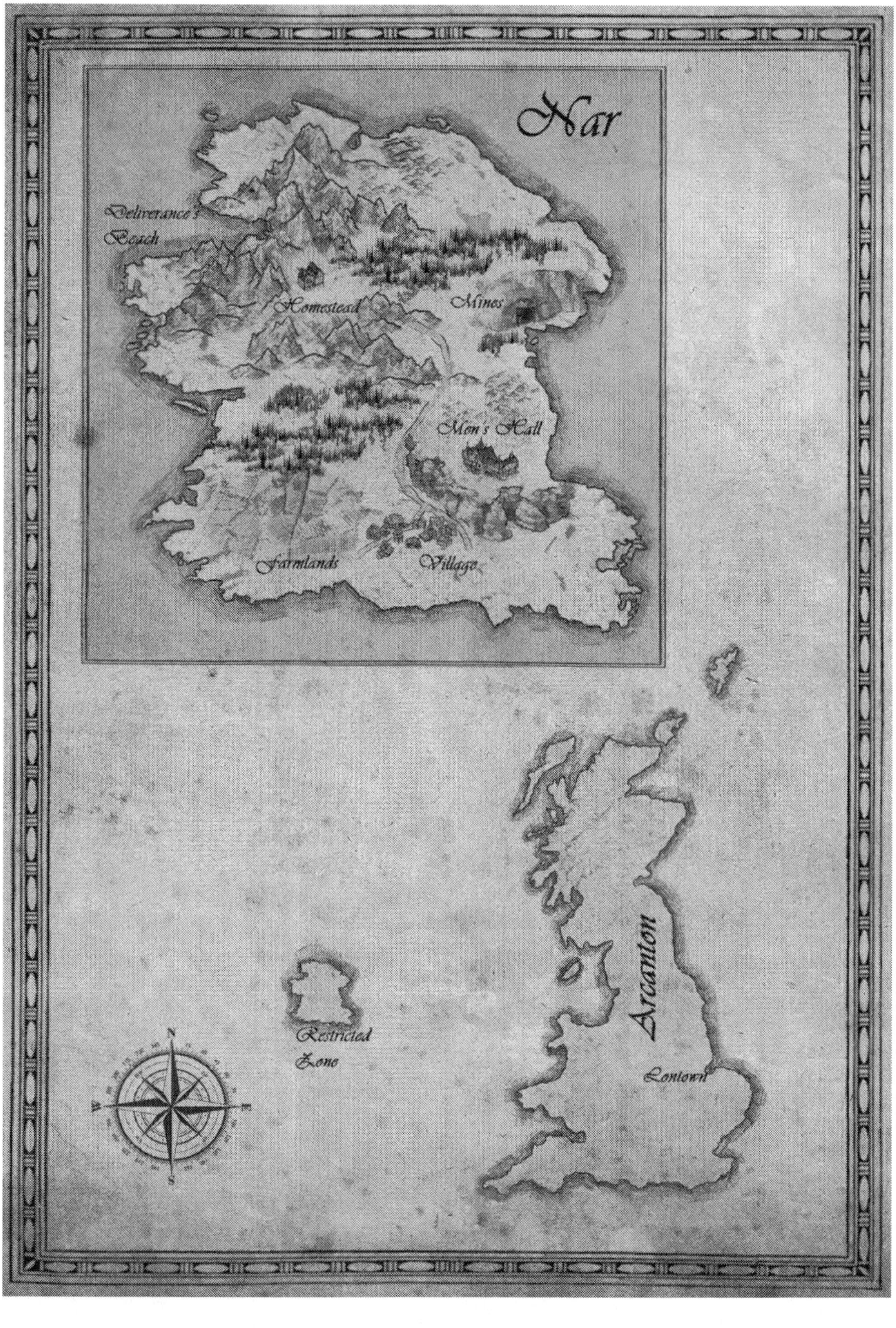
Nar
Deliverance's
Beach
Homestead
Mines
Mon's Hall
Farmlands
Village
Restricted
Zone
Arcanton
Lontown

Dedicated to independent souls

TABLE OF CONTENTS

CHAPTER 1 1

CHAPTER 2 11

CHAPTER 3 19

CHAPTER 4 33

CHAPTER 5 47

CHAPTER 6 55

CHAPTER 7 71

CHAPTER 8 95

CHAPTER 9 101

CHAPTER 10 115

CHAPTER 11 129

CHAPTER 12 145

CHAPTER 13 163

CHAPTER 14 169

CHAPTER 15 185

CHAPTER 16 193

CHAPTER 17	205
CHAPTER 18	215
CHAPTER 19	233
CHAPTER 20	249
CHAPTER 21	255
CHAPTER 22	267
CHAPTER 23	275
CHAPTER 24	283
CHAPTER 25	297
CHAPTER 26	309
CHAPTER 27	315
CHAPTER 28	321
CHAPTER 29	339
CHAPTER 30	345
CHAPTER 31	353
CHAPTER 32	369
CHAPTER 33	381
CHAPTER 34	389
CHAPTER 35	397

NOTES	401
ACKNOWLEDGMENTS	403
AUTHOR BIO	405

Samantha Schinder

In this world there are powers and empowerment. Deliverance had never known power, the ceded gift bestowed upon a soul, but she knew empowerment — that hard won, delicious sliver of self-given skill. Here in the winter-softened wood, in the trundles of billowing snow, was the seat of her empowerment. Her silent kingdom.

Her falcon eyes zeroed in on her quarry, barely discernable to the unschooled eye. A quivering tuft of fur just out of balance with the still line of the white pines. She slowed her breathing, willing her pulse to quiet as well. This was the hard part. She never liked what came after, the taking of a life to feed another life. It would stick in her gullet for hours to come, that irrepressible guilt unavoidable when life demands the death of another. She blew out one more breath. With a resounding thwack the arrow sung through the air, into the snowshoe hare's stilling heart.

Deliverance paced her breathing as she struggled through the thigh-high drifts of snow toward her quarry.

On the other side of the island, another woman's breathing was just as ragged, in the same pursuit of life. She screamed, clutching the hands of her village sisters. A new soul was poured in a sluice of blood and terror at the unknown into this world. The new mother caught her harried breath as she rested back on the birthing bed, veins receding over dappled, glistening skin.

"It's a girl!"

Cries of the new infant breached the thick warmth in the midwife's quarters. She took her first breaths of this foreign stuff called air.

The village women gathered around the new mother and placed the protesting, writhing bundle into eager arms. They joined hands, invoked the gods, and began the sacred naming.

"Those who came before us, and those who will follow,
Heed the calling of this new sister,
Though she is young, she will grow.
Let her grow to glorify the gods
And to please the village."

The new mother waited anxiously, silently with bated breath.

"We invoke the Naming God to place upon this daughter,
her Gift. Mother, what shall she be named?"

A pause. Then very carefully, as to not disrupt the powerful magic humming through the room, the mother announced: "Wisdom."

The village ladies clasped eyes with one another, nodding, appreciating the gift this daughter would bear. With hands intertwined they raised their arms, a crown of limbs around mother and new daughter and spoke, "Let her be named Wisdom."

The humming took a crescendo and then, with a breath, faded into the ambient atmosphere. It was done. The girl was named. She would be Wisdom. For this life she would bear the almost supernatural gift of wisdom. When choices were difficult, she would have uncanny discernment. When the way was unclear, she would be able to see the path. When others lacked judgment, she would supply the answers. Wisdom was her name, and it was now her innate gift.

On the far side of the island, another girl, nearing womanhood, trudged through the drifts with her glassy-eyed hare dangling over her shoulder. Her name was Deliverance, but no one knew her gift.

CHAPTER 1

Deliverance

"The oldest and strongest emotion of mankind is fear, and the oldest and strongest kind of fear is fear of the unknown."

~ H.P. Lovecraft

Deliverance tossed open the oak door to the sleepy cottage. Swirls of frothy snow trickled at the edges of her fur-lined parka, sneaking into the warmth of the firelight. She removed her rabbit-skin cap and discarded it on the rickety reed woven chair next to the door, allowing her dark waves of hair to spill out over her snow-coated shoulders.

"Ah, you've returned, daughter. You had good sport," the woman crouching at the fireside commented, nodding at the dangling prey.

"It's not sport. Bringing down this hare was hardly diverting," Deliverance replied, kicking off her calfskin snow boots and trudging over to the large, knotty table. There, she plopped her prize onto the section reserved for meat preparation.

"And yet, daughter, you are secretly enthralled with the skill it takes to accomplish such a feat." Her mother stood and set the spoon she had been using to stir her pot on a rest on the sooty hearth. Cat, short for Catalyst, was a willowy, older version of her daughter, with rich, thick hair and haunting green eyes. Those eyes were adept at assessing situations, including her daughter's various moods.

Cat was right. Deliverance did feel a certain thrill at her capacity to make her mark, yards away, accomplishing shots that most men on the island could only dream of and perhaps boast falsely. It was not the kill that enticed her, but the precision of it and the independence it provided her and her mother. They needed very little from the villagers on the island. This was opportune, as their little homestead was settled far on the other side of the island from the main village. Cat and Deliverance preferred to keep to themselves.

Today would not be one of those days they could bide by themselves, though.

"'Tis good you were able to make your mark, daughter. The hare's blood is the last ingredient I need for the Fishmonger's wife's tonic," Cat remarked, reaching out to procure the dangling prey from her daughter. She adeptly slit the hare's neck vein over her cauldron already bubbling with a noxious brew. A gelatinous river sprung from the hour-dead neck and splashed into the concoction below.

Deliverance attempted to ignore the odor emanating from the pot and plopped down by the fire to warm her tingling limbs.

"Do not get too comfortable, daughter," Cat said, stoppering a little cobalt glass bottle with the odious substance meant for the Fishmonger's wife. It would help ease her gout, especially with the small, luminescent puff of magic swirling in the midst of the hare's blood, St. John the Conqueror's root, willow bark, and the slew of other herbs Deliverance did not have the patience nor the proclivity to name.

"Yes, I know. We must away to market today." Deliverance grumbled, laboriously pulling herself from her comfortable chair by the hearth. Secretly she thought perhaps the ninnies in the village could wait a day or two for their precious remedies, especially considering their ungrateful, snide treatment of Deliverance and her mother, whose skill as a healer and chemist they all had to thank in some way or another. But her mother was an indomitable force, and so she went to saddle the ponies.

✳✳✳

"A whole sixpence! Really, I do not know what your mother is thinking charging such for a simple tonic!" The cartwright's wife, who was the Fishmonger's wife's sister, sniffed, eyeing Deliverance with barely disguised disdain.

"I had to spend the entire morning hunting for a hare to complete the spell. That is time I wasna spending mending the broken fence in our corral or chopping wood, or doing any of the other tasks it takes for us to survive," Deliverance replied pointedly, not letting the woman's refusal to meet her eyes bother her.

"Yes, well, I suppose this time. My sister does need her tonic." The cartwright's wife relented, picking the six pence coin from her satchel and placing it on the makeshift wooden table Cat and Deliverance had set up for their market stand.

Deliverance was accustomed to the women not handing her monies directly. They treated her like her strangeness might be contagious. That was the due for someone whose name was so obscure as Deliverance. They always thought their whispers went unheard. They did not. *Odd little thing. Pretty but weird, just like her mother. I mean, what does her name even mean?*

When she was younger, and the girls in the village, as girls are apt to do, were rude to her, Deliverance would fervently wish her mother named her something like Fire or Hex. Even Karma would have been useful. To be fair, almost all the women in the village possessed impotent names themselves, their mothers choosing gifts such as beauty or piety. Names such as Bella, Prudence, and Patience abounded. The Abbot's wife selected names for her girls such as Chastity or Temperance.

The only other girl whose name gift was a rarity chose this moment to appear beside Deliverance's stall. There was no missing Effie in her fiery brilliance and brightly colored stockings. She was a splash of color in the dullness of village life.

"Are ye not going to hand the lady her payment?" Effie's musical voice came hard as a dagger. The cartwright's wife hesitated. "Because it twould be rude and we both know ye would not want to be un-neighborly, Constance. Your husband is always saying how friendly you are. I havna seen him in a while...perhaps I shall make it a point to catch up with him?"

The threat in Effie's words was plain. Sputtering, the cartwright's wife picked up the six pence coin lying on the scarred wooden stand and plopped it into Deliverance's waiting palm. With that, the woman snatched the blue bottle from the stand and scurried off before any further insinuations could be leveled.

"Ye didna have to do that, Effie. I would have gotten paid all the same," Deliverance remarked but softened it with a smile, as she knew her friend had her best interests at heart.

Effie spat. "Ye canna give those heifers an inch. Otherwise they twould walk all over ye. Ye would think it would be the men that try to trounce ye, but the women be just as bad. Maybe worse." She shook her head in disgust. She'd endured as much ridicule from the folk of this island as Deliverance — if not more — that was certain.

Name gifts were meant to be prudent and a blessing. While Deliverance's name was a bafflement and enough to label her an outcast, Effie's was a downright curse. Her mother had died in her childbed. She had not been lucid enough to understand the village women were performing the naming rite because when prompted for a name; instead, the woman had uttered a crass curse word and then fallen dead. The village women, staring in shock at one another, could not undo the naming ritual once the mother had spoken, and she could not be roused to right the wrong. Only a mother could reword the name in the ritual. And so, everyone called the girl Effie...and Effie, growing up motherless and in need of love, had become seductively skilled in the physical arts. The names were prophecies of what would come.

"Come on, now, love," said Effie, clapping her hands together. "It's cold as the Horizon's twat out here. Let's go to the tavern and get some mulled wine!"

"Alright. I'm done for the day here. I'll just close up and leave a note on the stall for my mum. She's visiting the new babe, Wisdom, to check on her health," Deliverance allowed, pulling down the canvas to cover the stall and tying it off against the bitter wind.

The tavern was a moldy building, which started out as a modest plank structure, then grew, like a cankerous blight in additions. Now it spilled in mismatched sections throughout the mucky street on which it was built. Inside was as dark and musty as one would expect from such a place, but the hot wine was decent and the food was naught to complain about. Besides, there were many nooks and crannies one could squirrel away in for some privacy. It just so happened Deliverance's and Effie's favorite spot by one of the many hearths tucked in a corner was occupied by some of the village boys. But with a flick of Effie's wrist, the boys willingly relinquished the corner.

"Oh, and Darren, bring us some mulled wine from the bar, would you, Love?" Effie commanded one of the retreating youths, who happily obliged her whim. Although Deliverance noticed the barmaid, Industry shoot them a scathing look of jealousy and suspicion as she filled the order for the young man. Darren hastily returned with two steaming mugs of mulled wine, thick with cinnamon and nutmeg. With a word of praise from Effie, the boy's ego was duly caressed.

"Now, Deliverance, love, let's talk about how those daft village women are treating ye. Ye canna just let them walk all over ye like ye do," Effie started in on her, and Deliverance took a generous sip of her sweet concoction. "Take it from me. If ye let them an inch they will drag ye a mile."

Deliverance thought Effie was powerful, the way she held sway over men. Men dictated much of the life in the village, hence Cat and Deliverance's preference to abide far away from their prying eyes and commanding edicts. But Effie held court and they attended eagerly. Sometimes when she and Deliverance would steal away for a quiet lunch on market days, Effie would bid the baker to impart on them loaves free of charge, or whatever group of workers to surrender the best spots under the shade trees so she and Deliverance could sup there. A glance from Effie was enough to silence a protest from any man in the village. While it was not outright power through authority, it was power all the same. There was power in a name.

Deliverance found herself drowning out Effie's chatter as the warm fire and low lighting lulled her into a semi-stupor. Outside the small mullioned window a magpie pecked at the worm-rotted windowsill, sending Deliverance into a daydream of days past.

Deliverance

Sixteen years ago

The bird master who maintained the aviary had always reminded Deliverance of a hoot owl, with wavy eyebrows and eyes enlarged by the too-big glasses perched upon his generous beak. Once, when Deliverance was a little girl, she wandered away to spy on him, entranced by his secret sept of messengers. As she crouched in a corner, unconcerned with the bird droppings and dust of the aviary—as children often are—she spied on the old man shuffling about his business. He measured careful scoops of seed for each of the birds, a red-tailed hawk, a large clucking brood of pigeons, and a visiting albatross from a faraway land called Icasus. As he was huffing about, sending up little puffs of dust from the floor, a sleek black and white bird landed on the windowsill.

"Ah!" The old man cackled, reaching over for the bird hopping at the beam of the large window opening. Rivulets of particles danced in the waning slant of light. Deliverance realized she had been playing spy far too long and would soon be missed by her mother. But the arrival of the new bird riveted her attention. She let out a small gasp, as excited by the prospect of news as the bird master.

"Ye can come out now, ye there," the old man croaked, not turning in her direction, but obviously meaning Deliverance. "Ye have been spying on me for a while. Must be stiff from sitting so still." The old man was right—her knobby knees were aching from remaining in a crouch so long. Reluctantly, she stood and wandered over to the bird master, expecting a rebuke for trespassing.

Instead he cackled. "Ah, it seems the King and Queen of Torrendia have welcomed a baby girl into the world." Deliverance nodded solemnly, not wanting to draw the old man's wrath. She wondered what the baby girl would be named, what her gift would be.

"You like birds, little girl?" the bird master inquired, finally focusing his bespectacled attention on her. His eyes were magnified like bugs beneath a looking glass.

Deliverance nodded, drawing a little circle in the dust with her toe, as bashful children are wont to do. She did not want to gaze too long at the curling hairs emanating from the bird master's nostrils. She wondered if all old people grew longer nose hair or if just men did.

"This one here is a Magpie. The Magpie is one of the smartest creatures on the planet. They say they can recognize their own reflection in a looking glass. What do ye think of that, eh?" asked the bird master, carefully depositing the magpie in a spacious coop. It shook its feathers out, settling itself on its new roost.

"I know," Deliverance said, finding her girlish voice. "Sometimes one will come to Mamma with a message. She told me how intelligent they are." She recalled wanting to stroke the spot on one of the bird's wings, like a dollop of fresh cream on the oily black feathers.

The elderly man frowned. "Cat should not be getting messages firsthand. 'Tis not for women to receive such information unvetted by the Men's Hall."

Deliverance stared up at the man, horrified eyes rounded, realizing she must have said something she shouldn't have.

He grimaced, opened his mouth like he was going to say something, then closed it again and sighed. "Ye best keep that little tidbit to yourself. Sometimes it's best if certain things are kept silent. Do you understand, Deliverance?" He finally bade, chiding the little girl and then shuffling her out of the aviary. "Your mother will wonder as to where ye be. Off with ye."

It was not until Deliverance was much older that a fuller understanding of what had transpired in the aviary that day would dawn on her. Some concoctions take time to brew.

CHAPTER 2

Deliverance

Present Day

"Honestly, daughter, if your head was any cloudier, I would ask ye to rain a bit on my posies to keep them from wilting," Cat called Deliverance back into the here and now. They were up to their elbows in lanolin, shearing the sheep, and Deliverance had still managed to wander off in her own mind. How she could do so in the midst of all the stinking grease and bleating, she could not rightly fathom.

Deliverance asked her mother as she returned to her shears, "Why is it all the gods are men?"

Her mother smartly replied, "Because if they were women they would be goddesses."

But Deliverance was in no mood for her mother's vagaries. "I understand the linguistic nuance, Mother, but not the cultural one." She stared at her mother with a look that allowed no idling.

Cat sighed and put down the wooly beast she had been pruning, and wiped the sweat from her lined brow. "Which gods do we most often call upon?" she asked patiently.

"The Hunter God and the God of Horizons," Deliverance replied.

"Yes, and do you know why that is?"

This time Deliverance had some difficulty answering. "Well, the Hunter God provides us with game and helps us to live through the winter…and the God of Horizons…I don't know. Lives in the sky?" It had not been a subject she had pondered much. On the solstices and proper eves, she had dutifully gone through the motions of the rituals with her mother, alone by a bonfire on their stretch of beach. But the reasoning had never really occurred to her.

"Daughter, you were born with a good mind. Use it more often," her mother chided. But she softened the blow by explaining, "The Hunter God is not just our chosen because of survival. When you are alone in the woods, pursuing your prey, the world is your own. He allows you to move with the grace of a cat, the stealth of a wolf, and the precision of a hawk. You are the predator. This is empowering, daughter. Women so often are the prey."

Deliverance mulled this over, turning the idea over in her mind, exploring its edges and finally accepting it. "But what of the God of Horizons? I never even hear the Abbot mention that one."

Her mother smiled, secretly, indulgently. "Well, the Abbot is not in possession of all the world's knowledge, now is he, daughter? There are more things in heaven and earth than are dreamt of in your philosophy."

Deliverance smiled. "Those are beautiful words. From whence do they come, Mother?"

"From none of the tomes in the Abbey vaults, daughter. The God of Horizons is the god of infinite possibilities. Not only does he rule the skies, but he watches and sees all that happens beneath it. And as to your question about goddesses, who is to say how a god views gender? Perhaps the God of Horizons is indeed a goddess? It is not for us mortals to know or say. We just do the best we can."

Best they could was exactly what Deliverance and Cat did with their lives, and they did quite well. It was a happy existence, she and her mother amongst the towering pines and rocky crags of their homestead. Deliverance loved the little cottage growing out of the mountain, as if the cottage were fighting to emerge from the boulders. The walls were lined with paintings and weavings handed down from generation to generation of Cat and Deliverance's family—always a mother and a daughter, then for a time a grandmother, a mother, and a daughter, until the universe reverted once again back to the duo of mother and daughter. Two of everything existed in their sphere—two wooden bowls, two kiln-fired mugs, two knotty chairs by the hearth. There was one bed, which Deliverance shared with her mother, and one dinged, iron tub for bathing. But these were exceptions to the rule of two that seemed to overtake the tiny abode.

"Now," Cat said, again interrupting Deliverance's reveries, "pick up those shears or I've a mind to use mine on that curly mop of yours!"

✸✸✸

"Tell me the lore, again, Mother," Deliverance said, hugging her cup of mint tea close, huffing in the warm steam.

"How many hundreds of times have ye heard it, Daughter?" Cat laughed into her own cup. They were relaxing by the fireside after the long day of sorting and cutting wool.

"I know…it's just. I have been thinking a lot lately," Deliverance began, but did not know how to finish her thought.

"And when are ye not thinking, daughter o' mine?" Cat quizzed her, but soon relented, settling back to retell the story.

"In the time of your grandmother's grandmother's grandmother's mother, and perhaps some mothers more, the island of Nar was uninhabited," Cat began, falling into her rich storywinding voice. "The Kingdom of Nar existed in the Outside, connected to many other nations and kingdoms, some of which we still receive news of via raven today. The Queen of Nar was reported to have been a great sorceress, without a name gift, as they did not exist yet, but possessing many other gifts. She used them to control the King of Nar and impose her will on the entire kingdom. The queen was evil though, and was said to have had a

Deliverance

great disrespect for men. She often made them dance like puppets for her in her court. She took their voices and made them howl like monkeys or made them fight amongst themselves unwillingly." Deliverance had also heard darker versions of the tale, in which the queen had done other unspeakable acts to the men of her kingdom, the tales mostly emanating from Effie, who had a sense of the darker side of life and a great many connections to powerful men with access to information in the village.

"Nar was the only kingdom in the world to produce sorceresses," her mother continued. "As you know, men were incapable of magic of any kind even in that ancient time. The queen's voracious appetite for evil soon closed all its political doors with the surrounding kingdoms. No one wanted any part of what the alien, merciless queen had to offer. Then, the King of Nar, in an act of desperation, reached out to the queen's only living relative, her elderly aunt who was on her deathbed, to aid him in reining in the reigning queen. The aunt, as her dying magical act, ripped her niece's power from her soul. But as with many magical acts, there had to be counterbalances, prices paid.

"The king, in his desperation, agreed to the aunt's terms. In exchange for taking the queen's power, the power had to be distributed elsewhere. And so the gifts of the queen were filtered throughout all the females in Nar. But the king and the other men would have some recompense against the abuse of powers as the females, with such diluted magic, could only possess one gift each. The gifts would be determined at birth with the Naming ceremony, which the aunt prescribed, scribbling out the incantations in ink on papyrus to later be preserved, copied, and kept in the vault of the God of Names in the temple run by the Abbot on the island. If a mother were to name an infant something overreaching, say Dominus, or Reina, well…an infant is a delicate being. Many do not make it long past the birthing. Ambition can be deadly."

Deliverance nodded at this, knowing this wisdom to be truth.

"With the aunt's last breath, the curse alighted across the kingdom, sapping the queen's power from the marrow of her bones and scattering it across the land. The other kings in the surrounding nations, having heard of the queen's seized power and subsequent execution, converged on Nar once again. They convinced the King of Nar to move his people to a faraway island for the good of the rest of world. Even though the women were far less powerful than the queen had been, they still possessed unnatural abilities, which had to be contained. And thus came the Great Migration to the Island, and here we been ever since."

To Deliverance's knowledge no one had ever tried to leave the island. Had reaching the Outside been attempted, she probably would have heard about it. Effie knew everything that went on in the village, and so, by proxy, did Deliverance. No one ever discussed elsewhere…the Outside was an academic concept having no tangibility in their minds. In any case, she was not sure how one went about leaving an island or how they got there in the first place. That knowledge was kept strictly confidential in the vaults of the Men's Hall and the records kept in the Abby's vaults.

Still, her daydream earlier in the week whilst visiting Effie had conjured questions about the great looming Outside. Especially weighing on her mind was how did they manage to get here in the first place? Magic? Some gargantuan bird? It seemed incomprehensible and yet intrigued her.

"Are ye satisfied now, daughter o' mine?" Cat laughed, reaching to stir the pot of stew bubbling over the fire.

For a moment, so slight Deliverance could have imagined it, Cat seemed to hesitate, as if she had something more to say. But Deliverance nodded because she knew even if she prodded, there would be no more answers tonight. Cat was often a guarded book and Deliverance cherished these telling moments but knew if she pushed for more, the book's cover would snap shut.

CHAPTER 3

Deliverance

"**G**ods' teeth! Do you have sheep's wool stuck in your head, girl?" Deliverance exclaimed one overly warm summer day. She squinted her mossy green orbs up at the sun and wondered if the God of Horizons was delivering just a little too much sun that day. Any more and they would roast like plucked chickens.

"It's not as daft as it sounds!" Effie defended herself, pointing a corner of her generous salami sandwich at Deliverance. They sought their usual shady refuge under the massive oak outside the town square in the brunt of the afternoon. The corner of the browned bread reminded Deliverance of the honeycombs she had just harvested the other day. It was the same shade of amber.

"You think I'm royalty!?" Deliverance snorted, the incredulity dripping from the gesture.

"Well, not royalty anymore. We don't have royals no more. Not here anyways. But used to be. Royal descended," Effie explained, mouth full of masticated pig.

"Right...whatever would give you such an addlepated notion?" Deliverance demanded of her friend, amused all the same at the imagination of the girl.

Effie tossed her burnished auburn curls over her shoulder and with mock importance stated, "I am a lady of the night. Men tell me things. Things they would never tell their wives. I can suss out a string of information like a badger can find a mound of juicy gob-worms."

"Lady of the night? Where in the Fades did you hear such a term? Not that it is not fitting," Deliverance said, changing the subject, although she knew for a fact that Effie conducted her business at all hours, not just the eve.

"The carpenter. He reads a lot in the Men's hall. He said it's a real title for my job description," Effie explained. Everyone knew Effie was a harlot. She insisted it suited her and took to the trade not long after her body took the shape of a woman's. She earned her keep and more besides. Deliverance was told once by the Abbot's wife that she should choose better company, but Deliverance wondered if the woman was simply jealous of Effie's freedom. Of all the women in the village, the Abbot's wife was the most constrained, doomed to a life of servitude to that sniveling man of gods.

"But it's not the carpenter that told me of the lore. It were the butcher," Effie continued, not to be dissuaded from her intended mission of convincing Deliverance she was some kind of royal offspring. Deliverance wondered briefly if every man in the town had been in Effie's bed, and made a mental note to supply her with more tonic to ward off any illness. She did not need to contract the baker's wife's unfortunate bout of warts…

"He said in one of the stacks there was a book that said that the aunt was spiteful of the King of Nar, who brought us here in the Great Migration for being too weak to contain her niece himself. And so, as part of the curse ridding the queen of her power, she made all the queen's daughters indifferent to men. And the king's line would forever be daughters, no sons to console and be comforted by, so he would die lonely."

"And so, you think…I am indifferent to men?" Deliverance raised an eyebrow.

"I'm just saying that ye and your mother and her mother and her mother's mother have all lived out there in that little cove on the other side of the isle…for generations…with no men. I mean, there must have been a man…men…at some point. For Hunter's sake, you did not just spring from your mother's forehead!" Effie babbled on, indifferent to her friend's grimace. Deliverance too had had no inkling in all her 23 years from her mother from whence the other half of her being came. It was a sore subject with the young woman. "All I'm saying is that the curse was supposed to make the royal line indifferent to men, or that's what the butcher said he read in the book. That they would be odd and separate, having no need for the regular social conventions of the people."

Deliverance mulled over this thought, but it seemed…off, like a puzzle box with too few pieces. It was true she had never had any friendships with anyone other than Effie. It was not as if she did not notice the young men her age in the village; she simply did not need them. Her life was replete without the complication of adding pheromones and sex and the power trips that came with interacting with the awkward other sex. It was a precarious business interacting with men. Deliverance left it to Effie, who was naturally inclined to handle that business.

"And what of this book, this insightful tome which the butcher just so happened to alight upon?" Deliverance asked, finishing her sandwich and taking a swig of cider from her waterskin.

Effie twisted her mouth. "You know, he did comment it was odd, the book was rather new. Most of the lore books have been collecting dust in that blasted mildew-ridden Men's Hall for generations. But this one was neater, with a newer cover and tighter binding. Or maybe he was reaching for information. By that time, I was almost done with him, and he knew his time with me was short," Effie commented as an afterthought.

Deliverance noted that even though Effie's customers paid her, she dictated the length of time and terms in which they could keep her company. Effie had truly made a racket of her gift.

***

Deliverance thought she had dismissed Effie's frivolous notion from her mind, until later that night when she found herself asking her mother about it as they had their wine by the hearth.

"Do you think it's possible?" Deliverance asked, always just slightly too hungry for information about her origins.

Cat smirked to herself, although Deliverance caught her smug expression and raised her eyebrows expectantly. But as usual, Cat was just as agile at dodging her daughter's dogged inquiries about their lines' complicated name gifts.

As always, Cat measured her words carefully before speaking. "I suppose it is possible, daughter. It would explain our proclivities, giving us rhyme and reason to our society. Rather convenient, is it not?"

It was rather convenient, Deliverance noted, but if the men wanted to take it as further reason to leave them the Fades alone, then she was all for it.

"That Effie girl, though, needs to be careful in her mining for information. The society on this isle is never kind to a woman who wields power…of any kind," Cat said, closing the subject for discussion.

✳✳✳

It was not a fortnight later that Cat's prediction proved tragically accurate.

Deliverance was occupied sharpening her axe, sparks leaping from the spinning stone wheel like fireflies darting in the glade, when her mother came stomping back into the homestead. Deliverance did not raise her eyes from her task. It was still late summer, but the solstice had long past and the days had begun to wane. It was as if the winter were pulling all the energy it needed to sustain itself just a bit ahead of the event. The onset of colder weather was never quite predictable on the isle. It would not do to be without enough wood for the harsher months. Deliverance prided herself on her axe swing. She had rippling muscles beneath her homespun tunic and could put away enough wood easily for herself and her mother. She swung, and sweated, and stacked all the daylight hours, pausing briefly for refreshment but not needing much respite. Physical strength meant independence, and that was something she prized above all. She mused her grandmother, aptly named Independence, would approve had she not passed onto the side of the Fades. Perhaps she could still approve from her spot amongst the Fields in the afterlight of the Fades, if such a thing were possible.

Once her axe was honed again, Deliverance planned to continue her war on the felled pine logs littering in the yard. But Cat had other plans for her daughter's attentions.

"Girl, have ye not heeded a good word I just said?" Cat chastised her impatiently. It was only then Deliverance realized her mother was ranting. For Gods' fury, she was just trying to prepare them for winter's coming. What in The Hunter's name was she chattering on about?

"Apologies, Mother. I could not hear you over the grinding stone," Deliverance said, halting her peddling on the foot wheel. The fireflies died with the smile in her greeting, when she caught the look on her mother's face. Something was terribly amiss. "What's happened?"

"What's happened is that Effie could not keep her fury-fated mouth shut. Gods' teeth!" Cat swore. Deliverance felt a pit growing in her stomach. Her mother rarely swore.

Deliverance set down the axe and swiped the glistening condensation from her brow, leaving a darker stain against the beige of her spun tunic. "Tell me what's happened."

"I know Effie must have felt something for that Tobin boy, the young one, them both being orphans. She must have felt duty-bound to protect the lad, him only being but twelve, but oh, she's gone about it all wrong. It is not going to end well for her," Cat stammered, shaking her head. She related the story in pieces Deliverance had to mash together like the dovetail joints of a wood project. Her eyes widened as she listened, and she felt like she might be sick.

Apparently, Effie had come upon the Abbot in a compromising position with Tobin, the prepubescent orphan boy. She'd snatched the tearful child back behind her and with a clawing slap, ripped her fingernails across the Abbot's cheek. It was an outrage. Sodomy was highly forbidden in Narisi culture, and with one so young…it was a dangerous charge. But with the claw marks evident upon the Abbot's visage, there was bound to be a scene.

Deliverance didn't have to speak for her mother to know she wanted to help her. Effie was her one and only friend — she couldn't lose her over this.

Wordlessly, she and her mother hastened across the isle on the backs of two of their larger ponies used for plowing. It was the fastest way to the village.

"Had I been there, I would have counseled the foolish girl to take a different path," Cat muttered as they rode. "I would have advised Effie to shuffle Tobin away and use the information as blackmail against the Abbot — write off her lashing out off as a fit of "swooning" or feminine irrationality. No, instead, Effie will be swept in front of a village tribunal for questioning. She will be called hastily by the Abbot before Effie could use her gift to influence the outcome. In the Abbot's mind, as a man of authority, his will is predestined to be delivered. Effie sealed her fate when she pointed her finger and named the man a sodomite, a molester of young boys."

It was not the jarring plodding of the pinto pony's trot that grew the massive knot in Deliverance's stomach. By the time the ponies bumped into the main stretch of the village, everyone had already congregated in the Great Hall in the center of town, collocated with the Abbey. Cat and her mother had to jam elbow to wrestle their way into a position in which they could see the proceedings. Dusk was beginning to fall, but the hall was bright, humming with activity when the world should be beginning to fall asleep.

Effie was held at the front on the dais to the left of the center pulpit. The Abbot had positioned himself next to, but not upon, the pulpit at the front of the hall. During the winter months, long tables were erected in the hall to serve as a gathering spot for the village, a place to share banquets and company. This happened only on special occasions, though; the men preferred to cloister themselves away in the Men's Hall, receiving and vetting news and doing whatever it was they did in the hall. The women, in turn, kept to the Women's Hall, preferring its sanctity and comfort. The tables had been shoved to the sides of the hall,

Deliverance

although several villagers took to standing on them to gain a better point of view.

Effie stood defiantly with her pointed chin aloft, her russet locks cascading down her back like sea serpents. The Abbot, for all the seriousness of the charges levied against him, did not seem concerned. Instead he stood with his hands clasped, a self-satisfied smirk alighting his pinched features. It was incongruous with the raw, crimson lash marks dug into his cheek.

Deliverance and her mother pushed farther forward, until Effie was able to see and meet their eyes. Only then did Deliverance see a small faltering in her friend's bravado. But it was gone as soon as it appeared, snatched into the overwarm ambient air.

They must have missed the formal accusations, Deliverance realized. "What's happening?" her mother whispered to the baker's wife, Dolce, who was squashed next to them in the crowd.

"She accused Abbot Richard of…terrible things. Heinous acts with the Orphan Boy Tobin," Dolce whispered back, not taking her eyes off the scene at the front of the hall.

"And what of the boy?" Cat hissed. "Where is he?"

"They took him up front to question him, but he would not say either way. Just stared at the ground like he was possessed by daemons. Would not even respond to his name. So they questioned him louder, and then the boy pissed himself. He just stood there in it as the puddle grew on the floor. They ushered him away after that. He looked up once at Effie and that was all the human things he did. Right unnatural." The baker's wife clucked her tongue like a fattened hen. Deliverance briefly wondered if hens could get genital warts, but then cast the irrelevant thought from her mind.

"It was as I told ye," Effie proclaimed, fists clenched. She had dug her heels in and was hankering for a fight. Deliverance knew the hot nature of her redheaded friend well.

The Reeve, who was also the head Fishmonger, looked distinctly uncomfortable at the pulpit, having to undertake these delicate proceedings. He mopped beads of sweat from his generous, trenched brow, not bothering to re-pocket his handkerchief. The humidity caused by the closeness of the crowd in the room caused little half-moon fog clouds to form on his reading spectacles.

"Yes, right…well," he stammered, seeming unable to find something to do with his hands. At last he simply dropped them to his sides. "At this point in the proceedings, we must call the accused to make a statement on his own behalf. Abbot Richard?" The Reeve looked relieved to relinquish the pulpit stand to the Abbot, although traditionally an accused had to stand on the other side of the pulpit from the accuser. Yet Effie was occupying the accused's side of the pulpit, on the left, not the accuser's, on the right. Odd, thought Deliverance.

The Abbot took the stand with ease, having spent every End Week's Day blathering on about the God of Names and occasionally touching on the other gods briefly, from his usual pulpit at the Abbey adjacent to the hall. He did not appear phased in the slightest over the grotesque accusation Effie had levied against him. Deliverance did not like this one bit.

They lived in a society where, though the women had small, magical name gifts, the men tightly controlled all. They ruled and directed and held sway. Women like Effie, with all her swagger and secrets, and Cat and Deliverance in their independent lifestyle, were oddities. Most were like dutiful Chastity, the Abbot's daughter, who prayed and swept and hardly uttered a peep. Her head was perpetually bent in homage not to gods but to the other half. Deliverance shuddered at this. She much preferred her little cottage and her goats and her sometimes enigmatic mother over these lording, pedantic men.

"It is perfectly normal..." the Abbot began, although his words caused a stir. Surely, he did not mean this gross behavior with the young boy. That was evil embodied, not normal. The pastor of his flock would not endorse such behavior, but all were quelled when he continued, weaving his plot like a snake through the rushes, "It is perfectly normal to accuse someone of something even more heinous when one is caught in an act of immorality. Indeed, it is natural for someone to attempt to defend herself in such a way after being discovered."

Discovered? What could he possibly mean? Was he not the one on trial? The Abbot was skilled at manipulating crowds, whereas Effie only swayed individuals. Crowds were another beast. And the Abbot was a professional.

"Yes, to strike out and fabricate lies. These are the feminine recourses to avoid due punishment. So I was not surprised by

Miss F***'s actions." The Abbot paused for gasps because he'd used her traditional Name, the curse uttered by her delirious mother before her passing in childbirth. "She, being an orphan, has lacked for a mother to set an example and a father to lay discipline. Indeed, she must be dealt with leniency because of her troublesome upbringing. After all, we are not a harsh people. We often overlook the predilections of our neighbors, which may be slightly unorthodox, because we are magnanimous."

What on earth was he getting at? It had not gone unnoticed by Deliverance the Abbot had managed to turn the discussion around into some kind of counteraccusation against Effie.

"And so, we must look at Miss Amity with this in mind as we discuss the true nature of events here," the Abbot preached. A murmur arose through the crowd. Deliverance shook her head. What in the Fades did Amity have to do with any of this? Amity was, as her name gifted her, an amiable girl, but slow in nature. She still had not quite grasped the concept she had been named in the proceedings as the crowd turned their attention to the pie-faced girl.

"Now Miss Amity, as her mother so graciously name gifted her, is the most accommodating amongst us. So, when Miss Effie made advances upon her..." The murmur rolling through the crowd became thunder. God's teeth, Deliverance thought. "...Amity graciously tried to avoid the unwanted and unnatural attentions of the harlot. But of course, being as pugnacious as she is, Miss Effie would not take no for an answer, and thus I discovered her trying to force her lesbianism upon Miss Amity.

Therefore, in a desperate act to save her own skin, she made up these ridiculous accusations against me, the witness to her disturbing, criminal behavior."

Effie's defiance flattened like embers doused with a bucket. Her blue eyes widened in dismay. Hastily, she shot a glance to Deliverance and held her gaze for a moment, before returning her now unsteady attention to the magistrates of the proceedings.

There was no quelling the crowd at this point. The hall erupted in chaos as the Reeve tried ineffectually to bring order several times before giving up and adjourning the session until the morrow. Effie, in shock, was led out the side entrance in shackles, shame raining upon her as the crowd hurled insults. "UNNATURAL WHORE!" "LESBIAN DAEMON!"

Deliverance hissed at the young teenage girl next to her, who was hurtling insults at the top of her screechy lungs, to stop her foolishness. "Ye aught to be ashamed of yourself, Levity. You of all people should be able to discern the true nature of what is going on." The girl, abashed, stopped her yelling and disappeared into the raucous crowd.

"Come," Deliverance's mother commanded, grasping her hand and pulling her through the crowd. When they emerged a wall of cool air smashed into them, belaying the torpidity of the angry hall. "We must be gone."

"Be gone?" Deliverance protested, snatching her hand from her mother's, who was leading her toward the ponies waiting in the village paddock for their return. "Are you mad? We have to go to Effie. She must be so frightened! We must help her!"

Cat turned on her daughter in an instant, snapping, "And we will. But now is not the time, daughter. We must be gone from this place for the moment. It will do Effie precious little good if we are in shackles beside her. Come now."

Deliverance glanced from side to side, but her stomach deflated as she realized her mother was right. And so, they fled into the fallen night, the God of Horizons obscuring their trail.

CHAPTER 4

Deliverance

"But we are going to help Effie?" Deliverance demanded, seeking assurances from her mother as they rambled into their homestead later that night. The moon overhead expended precious little light, hanging in the sky like a fingernail. The ponies were eager to return to their pasture lean-to and picked up their modest pace accordingly.

"Hush, child. I am thinking," Cat replied, danger flashing in her eyes. They remained silent as they slid the halters off the ponies and released them to go whiffle the backs of their compatriots and shift through the leftover hay.

Back inside the cottage, Deliverance could not gain an easy position. The nervous energy within her would not allow her to sit, and so she paced, picking up this task and that, only to leave it half finished in a wake of more pacing. Cat sat silently, hands clasped, staring at the small fire she had stoked in the hearth.

Finally, Deliverance could bear it no longer and burst out, "Well, what in the Fades are we going to do?"

"Tis' a delicate situation, daughter. Effie put herself in a precarious place accusing one of the most powerful men on the island of such an unforgivable act. They will converge upon her now she is in a weak stance," said Cat stiffly, still staring into the yellow, licking flames of the fire.

"What will they do to her?" Deliverance asked, the lump in her stomach from earlier in the night refusing to unknot. To her knowledge she had never seen a woman publicly punished. If she were found to be in transgression, a woman's husband would surely handle the task at home. There were very few cases in which women on the island of Nar warranted notice, much less punishment. Although Effie did not have a man to rein her in. Nor did Deliverance and Cat.

"If she is lucky, she will be given labors. Although I am not certain she will be," Cat replied grimly.

Deliverance's eyes widened in shock. Labors were harsh toils sentenced upon men caught in crimes such as thievery. The men were sent to the island mine to labor for metals, without pay and with very little sustenance. The handful of other men who worked the mine as a trade were stingy with rest, water, and food. In Deliverance's time, only a few men were sentenced to labors, one for thieving, and several others for violently brawling. They had not fared well during the labors, emerging emaciated with bouts of scurvy. Deliverance was not sure Effie could survive labors long.

"Wait, you said if she is lucky? What else could possibly be worse than labors?" Deliverance asked, panic rising in her gullet.

As far as she knew, the worst sentence that could be levied was labors, varying only in degrees of time to be served.

Cat leveled a stare at her daughter. "They could put her to death."

Deliverance gasped. "Surely not! God's teeth! How is it even possible to think such a heinous thing?" Did the Narisis even have a historical precedent for such brutish, crude law dealing?

"Daughter, I think you will find people are capable of terrible deeds when power hangs in the balance. Effie, unfortunately, has more power than most here think a woman aught. The chance to dispose of the threat of her may prove too great."

Deliverance felt the energy drain from her body as she plopped into her chair beside her mother's at the hearth. What a horrendous thought!

"Surely the people would not tolerate such a sentence!" Deliverance exclaimed. She could not imagine the butcher, the baker, the blacksmith, the cartwright…any of the village men she had known since birth could be capable of allowing such a deed to take place in their midst. It was unspeakable.

"You are naïve, daughter, if you think they are contemplating anything less than labors or death," Cat asserted staunchly, her eyes haunted. "Effie has been allowed to be as she is because her name gift, though a travesty, is sacred. But how long did you think she would be allowed to carry on, wielding power over men so?"

Deliverance had no answer to this. She understood Effie's difference as fundamentally as she understood her own. But she knew Effie's differences were on parade in front of the village, whereas hers and her mother's were tucked away out of sight and out of mind. They would go the whole winter sometimes without seeing another soul. Effie, however, plied her trade and gift right in the epicenter of the island. She was at the center of the fire fed by human interaction. Though Deliverance and her mother were on the outskirts of that fire, they could still be burned.

At the end of their conversation that night, Cat forbade Deliverance to venture away from their part of the island until she could conjure a solution to Effie's problem. "Stay here, girl. I must think on this," Cat issued her edict. "People will hate that which is different. Unfortunately, daughter, now is not the time to draw their ire upon us for also being so," she added before the discussion was closed, for the night was aging and they both were numb with weariness.

※※※

It was several days before Deliverance could stand the waiting no longer. Her mother had made discreet inquiries at the village each day as to Effie's status, but so far no movement had been made as to a verdict or sentencing. So late on the fourth night, Deliverance silently slid out of the bed she shared with her mother, careful not to wake her. As Deliverance tiptoed to the door, however, the formerly slumbering form called out in a crackled, sleepy tone, "Where are you going, daughter?"

Fades. Deliverance had never lied to her mother beyond the childish years of tall tales and excuses for ripped hems and skinned knees. But tonight, when she said, "Just out to deliver the water," she did for the first time. She was not going to pee, but to abscond with one of the fleeter of foot ponies. She had to see Effie.

Deliverance paused at the door, as if frozen in place by her deceit. But the lump that was her mother's form in the warm, indented bed merely said, "Alright."

Deliverance breathed out a sigh of relief the moment she made it out the door, pausing only to roust her favorite pony, Torrent, a little black mare with a large attitude. The pony was quick but slow to tire and blended in with the night. Deliverance wrapped a dark cloak over her own shoulders and took off across the island.

The fingernail moon had faded into a New Moon, leaving precious little light to reveal Deliverance and Torrents as they trotted along. The night enveloped them in her velvety embrace.

Torrent did well lightly picking her steps despite the dark of the night. Deliverance made good time to the edge of the forest, where she alighted from her pony and left her tied under cover of the trees. The gaol was not far from here. Deliverance thanked the gods it was not directly in the center of town. She only had to steal by a few outbuildings and a couple window-darkened residences before she came upon the shanty that served as a gaol on the island. It was not much more than a lean-to, as there was not much use on Nar for a gaol. Penances or labors were sentenced quickly, leaving a place to hold prisoners only a temporary necessity. The lean-to was covered and one side of it was timber bars looking out toward the forest.

Effie was huddled with her arms clasped around her knees in the outside corner of the gaol, but sprang to her feet when she spied Deliverance making her way to her.

"Deliverance, what are ye doing here? Are ye daft!?" Effie hissed, looking around in case they were to be caught.

"I had to come see you. To at least try to provide some comfort. What you did…it was brave. And it was just," Deliverance said, clasping her friend's hands through the bars.

"God's teeth, it was stupid none the less. I think I only traumatized the poor boy more," Effie replied, shaking her head in anger at herself.

"Maybe so, but at least the village will keep a closer watch on Tobin," Deliverance said, searching for the spot of bright sun in the dismal situation.

"Aye. Let's hope for that then. The damn chicken-lickers have not yet given me a sentence. It is right chaos every time the Reeve tries to hold court. I cannot decide if this is a good omen or poor," Effie said, blowing out an exasperated sigh. She was not one to be kept in a cage. Her crimson locks looked like flames about to burn their way out into the freedom of the night air.

"Perhaps my mother can threaten to withhold remedies if they do not give ye penance," Deliverance said.

"Deliverance, I love ye, but you and your mother need to stay as far from this situation as possible. You will only get yourselves caught in this Fade-loving mess. Besides...penance? For what? Damn male-driven cockamamy. I have wronged no one," Effie declared defiantly, the clear blue in her eyes shining with a dangerous gleam. She was itching for a fight, Deliverance could tell.

"I know that. I'm so sorry, Effie," Deliverance replied, feeling a wave of melancholy rush over her at her ineptitude to aid her friend in her hour of need.

"Just… if I do not get a chance to see you again—" Effie started, but Deliverance balked. "No, no, I am not giving up hope. I just know it may not turn out well for me. I just wanted you to know, I never did anything with that pie-faced Amity."

"Oh, Effie. I know," said Deliverance. "It was just the Abbot trying to save his hide."

"There's only one I've ever loved, and it's never been her," Effie declared fiercely, locking eyes with Deliverance. Then, suddenly Effie's hands snaked through the bars and caught Deliverance's face, pulling her close. Effie gently, but fervently, pressed her lips to Deliverance's for but a moment, and then released her.

Deliverance's mind spun. She tried not to appear shocked. The idea that Effie might love her had never occurred to her outside the bounds of friendship. Whenever Deliverance had the rare thought of carnal love, it was vaguely male, but having not real form or function. Even at twenty-three she hadn't given love in that capacity, and much less marriage any real thought. It had always been her and her mother. Effie's lips felt foreign and out of place, but she was desperate to not hurt her friend by revealing how jarring the experience was for her. Perhaps if she had more time to adjust? Briefly, she wondered what it would be like if Effie used her magic gift—what it would feel like for that green light to flick across her fingers as it must when she took a lover and used her gift.

"It is alright, Deliverance," said Effie softly, her eyes full of understanding. "I know ye. I know ye aren't the same as me in that. I just wanted ye to know…to know someone loves ye…that I loved ye. Just in case I do not get the chance to tell ye again."

What was it Cat used to say about unrequited love? "Thy self thou gavest, thy own worth then not knowing, Or me to whom thou gav'st it else mistaking; So thy great gift, upon misprision growing, Comes home again, on better judgment making."

Later, when Deliverance had the chance to ponder, she would wonder if there were more like Effie on Nar. After all, the women and the men were all but segregated. Who would one fall in love with, but those with whom one spent the most of their lives? For Effie, the men were but fodder for her magic, a means to an end, and sometimes obstacles to be transformed instead into tools. Deliverance alone was her solace, her friend and confidante. Although Deliverance did not necessarily feel sexual love toward Effie, why should she not love her? What an honor it was that Effie had the courage to tell her, to bestow such a gift upon her.

Deliverance

Deliverance would not get the chance to relate this sentiment to Effie, however.

"LOOK THERE! WE CAUGHT HER IN THE ACT!" A screeching yelp rang out in the darkness. Voices descended around them, closing in.

"It weren't Amity at all!"

"It were that strange, giftless Deliverance girl!"

"Cat's daughter!"

"It isn't right, them living out there by themselves all isolated. They become unnatural that way, being self-sufficient. Look at the abhorrence it spawns."

Effie's eyes flashed to Deliverance's in panic. "Go! Run!" she hissed, flinging herself back against the lean-to, as if by breaking physical contact, she could force Deliverance to react faster. Deliverance, despite her growing fear, locked eyes with her only friend for just a moment longer before dashing off into the night.

She collided with her mother at a full sprint near the tree line. The bobbing torchlights in the village were just now converging upon the gaol. One of their ponies, the sorrel, was tied next to Torrent and Cat made an *oomph* sound as Deliverance barreled into her.

"God's teeth, girl! Can you not heed instructions one whit?" Her mother cursed, collected herself and pulling her daughter back toward the ponies. They both lithely swung onto their ponies' backs and cantered deeper into the forest. They could not afford for one of the ponies to falter and break a leg in the darkness, but they dared not go too slowly either.

"I had to see Effie!" Deliverance protested as the thicket pulled at the edges of her cloak and leaves and the horse's mane whipped her face.

"Ye had to do nothing, daughter. You wanted to. And now you are forcing my hand. Those men are not going to stop until they have their satisfaction. For men, all too often, that is either total submission or blood. I cannot see them being satisfied at any charade of submission we might play nor us bearing it."

"What will we do?" Deliverance cried, the impossibility of escape in the tiny island weighing more heavily by the moment on her shoulders. As they rounded the last bend to their homestead, her mother did not slow, however, and kept heading toward their beach cove. Far off in the distance, the baying of the hunt master's bloodhounds could be heard, sending a shattering chill down Deliverance's spine. There would be no outfoxing those noses, and they only had a small lead on the long legs of those voracious hounds.

At the top of the ridge, her mother alighted from the sorrel, swinging her legs in an arc over the pony's neck. She beckoned for Deliverance to follow her down to the water. "Hurry!" she said. The climb down to the pebbly beach was steep, but both women knew it in their sleep. Once upon the beach, the sliver of moon was more than enough illumination. It bent its silvery beams off the round stones creating a lattice like crocheted lace upon the shores.

Deliverance

"Come, daughter! Quick! We haven't much time!" Cat bid her daughter urgently.

Her mother did not stop at the beach but led her along it past the tall crags that marked the end of the cove. In the towers of rock there lay an almost indiscernible passage through the rock spires. Beyond them lay a smaller alcove, mostly encased in a cave whose depths were not visible. Cat flicked her flingers and a greenish spark gave rise to a flame on a torch. She must be certain they would not be found down here if she were risking the light, Deliverance thought. But for how long could they hide? Would they not eventually be found? Was it not inevitable? And then what? The thought of being caged like Effie…like an animal…made Deliverance's soul howl like the banshee spirits. The light from the torch showed the cavernous alcove to be relatively deep, twisting under the mountain into which their home was built on the other side. Perhaps they could sustain themselves a while here?

"Help me, daughter!" Cat commanded, rushing into the alcove around the first bend. Inquisitive, and heart still pounding from their harried flight, Deliverance followed. Past the bend lay a curious hulking shape, like a hollowed-out rind of a melon. Upon closer inspection, Deliverance saw it was made of wood. What an oddity! Could it be a shield of some kind?

Cat started dragging the shape with a thickly twined rope, one of the many attached to the object. She gestured for Deliverance to help her, and so she took up a hold alongside her mother, dragging the hulking weight across the sand. Her mother did not stop at the water's edge, but kept tugging the large shape into the surf. Oddly enough the object began not to sink, but to float.

"What in the Fades are you doing, Mother?" Deliverance demanded, hands burning from the exertion of dragging the thing and the ropes, which left little indentations in her palms.

"Get in the boat, Deliverance!" her mother ordered. What in Hunter's name could she be on about?

"Boat? What is a boat?" Deliverance asked...although surely she meant this large wooden melon. Her mother wanted her to mount it like a horse?

"This!! Daft girl!" Her mother all but screamed, gesturing for her to climb inside. She tossed a canvas bag inside the "boat" and held out her hand to boost Deliverance in. Surely it would sink! But she trusted her mother, as enigmatic as she was, and so she took her hand and allowed herself to be hoisted like a sack of grain into the "boat."

Miraculously, it did not sink. It merely bobbed and remained afloat.

"Listen to me, Deliverance. You need to find Lord Asher...Doctor Asher. He can be found at the University of Oxdale. Find him!" Cat instructed urgently.

"Who? What?" Deliverance cried, an uncertain panic welling in her chest. Her mother ignored her for a second, rooting around in the sack, which appeared to be full of waterskins and dried provisions, and came up with a circular object. She fiddled with it, glancing skyward for a moment, then handed it to her daughter. Then she found a small metal box and flipped a clasp on its surface. It began to make a curious blinking light. Satisfied, Cat tucked the box away again and returned her focus to the round object.

"Keep this arrow here pointed at this mark. The prevailing winds should take you straight to land. When you find land, find Doctor Asher," Cat said, clasping the circular object into Deliverance's shaking hands.

"Don't be silly! Are you not coming with me!?" Deliverance cried. The panic was an animal clawing up her throat to escape.

"I cannot, daughter. I have to see to this mess here. Doctor Asher will know how to help." Cat pointed at the bobbing torchlights appearing on the ridgeline. "Go! You haven't time, daughter. May the God of Horizons show you the way. I love you, Deliverance."

With that, Cat pulled one of the ropes and a large sheet of canvas spread overtop the "boat," held aloft by the unwieldy tall pole sticking out from its almost middle, like a spoke in a broken wagon wheel. Deliverance hoped it was supposed to look that way. The God of Horizons whispered, and a wind caught the canvas sheet, and to Deliverance's dismay it whisked her out into the open water more quickly than she could have imagined. The canvas sheet was like an oiled parchment bird's wing, cupping the air and pulling it under its folds. The melon rind slid through the lapping waters like a knife through soft cheese. Her mother's form grew smaller on the beach and the ominous torches made their way down the path to the sand.

"No!!!" Deliverance wailed, holding her arms out toward her mother, who was already out of reach. She looked down toward the water, but it was dark and deep and she knew she was already too far out to swim back to shore. But she couldn't leave her mother! What in the Fades would she do when the torches found her?

What in the Fades would Deliverance do now that the great sea was engulfing her little floating melon? No one had ever left the island, to her knowledge. Was it not suicide out here in the salty unknown? And what of her mother's cryptic instructions? Surely, she would not…and yet that must be what she had done. Catalyst had sent her only daughter, encapsulated in this foreign and improbable object called a boat, into the great Outside.

CHAPTER 5

Deliverance

Much to deliverance's surprise and relief, the rind-boat stayed afloat even when the waves of the sea rocked her skyward, only to pull her wrenchingly back down. It was as if she was a riding a bucking pony in a slowed state of time. As the night drew on, Deliverance caught herself dozing and awoke with a start as the bruise of dawn crept upon the horizon. The God of Horizons dawned a new mask once more, shedding the velvet of night and pulling on the promise of sky's quickening.

A squirting growl in Deliverance's stomach prodded her to rummage through the sack of goods her mother had hastily slung into the vessel. In it she found several waterskins, dried fruits and meats, and the curious box her mother had fiddled with before casting her out to sea. Its blinking eye continued to wink at her, like a mirror flashing in the sunlight. As she gnawed on a stringy piece of venison jerky, she fiddled with the curious box. Its lines were curiously smooth—finer workmanship than their blacksmith generally was able. She wondered what magic fueled the firelight in the box to continue its curious flashing pattern.

After a while she set the box aside and began to fiddle with other items—the ropes of the boat, the canvas of the sheet propelling her along with the wind, and the circular object she checked often to ensure it still lined up the way her mother showed her.

Her mother…why had she not also climbed aboard the boat? Surely it could've stayed afloat in the water with just her mother's slight weight added. Was it in allegiance to Effie, to try to help the girl? Deliverance pondered this option, letting it sift through her mind like a colander sifting beans, and finally discarded it. Her mother seemed fairly indifferent to Effie, even though she and Deliverance were friends of a sort. Her attachment to Effie was no more than a passing interest in her daughter's friend. So why sacrifice herself to the villagers who were sure to chance upon her eventually?

The sun crept steadily into the sky as Deliverance tinkered with the boat. She found the boat had a sort of tail with a handle, which she could manipulate to cast the boat slightly in either direction. It would come in handy if the little circle object stopped lining up just so.

Sometime around midday it became apparent shade would be a necessity to hide from the God of Horizon's fierce overhead glare. She fashioned a sort of tent from the sacks stored on the boat and extra twine, not daring to fiddle with the large canvas sheet propelling her forward just yet. As she tucked herself away from the burning rays, she pondered this Lord…Doctor Asher? What sort of man was both a lord and a doctor? She had no concept of what doctors were, really, except for the tales told of the Outside. From what she understood they were healers, something like Cat. But they could not possibly use magic to heal, so Deliverance was not sure what use they would be beyond the brewing of teas and mixing of poultices. She was vaguely aware that a lord in some of the Outside was considered a sort of nobility. How and where that fit into the world, she had no idea.

As she pondered the Outside, she was struck with a sudden fear. The men in the village, whose job it was to relay information from the Outside, often told stories of marauders and pirates. They were evil, hungry men who stole from the weaker, raping and pillaging. More than once as a girl, Deliverance had wondered if it was just a scare tactic to keep anyone from wandering too close to the beach. It was an idle threat to her, as she and her mother spent many a night conducting rituals on their own beach to the Hunter God and the God of Horizons. Her tacit ignoring of the men's tales now struck her as perhaps unsound. What if pirates were real? What if they were abroad on the very same waters she was now cast adrift? The thought left her queasy, and the unrelenting sun did not help.

She wondered how long she would remain drifting until she made landfall. And when she did, how would she go about finding this Lord Asher? Oxdale University…that must be some sort of place. It sounded like a place of learning of some kind but she had never heard of it in the tales of the Outside related by the men. They were often too fascinated with the wars of this kingdom and that, marriages and exotic women, and only expounded upon that which grabbed their fancy. It was only when they were deep in their tankards that the women could pull other information from them, but by then the related details were shoddy at best, in slurred curses and misremembered statements.

Deliverance yearned for Effie's counsel. If anyone could remember such a place as Oxdale being mentioned, it would be her. She would be able to coax all the needed details from the men about Lord Asher and this place where Deliverance was supposed to find him. But Effie was back in Nar, most likely about to be sentenced to labors…possibly alongside her mother for aiding in her escape. She was branded now like Effie. Even though Deliverance felt a certainty in her that she was not like Effie in her apparent sexual affinity for women, she did not find she minded being labeled alongside her friend. If the villagers were so ignorant as to paste a label across the bosom of her friend, then she too would wear it proudly. Who cared what they thought, the ignorant, lousy lot of them? They were only trying to supplant Effie because she held a dangerous amount of sway over too many of the men.

But Deliverance knew Effie would not use her power for anything other than the good of her friends and her fellow women. She was not a conniving person, nor ill intentioned. She often brought meals to those in need, helped new mothers with their housework with naught in return. This woman deserved no condemnation. The indignity of it singed Deliverance's mind with fury. Now her mother, too, was implicated in the whole mess.

Deliverance

With a growl, she flopped back on the pile of grain sacks and cast an arm over her eyes to block the sun. Her mother was an exacting woman. She would not have told Deliverance to find this Lord Asher person if she did not know he could aid her situation. There was nothing left for Deliverance to do but to find him and beseech him for help.

God's teeth! What did she know of the Outside? For all she knew they did not even speak her language, Anglish. She pondered this thought, chewing on her salty, chapping lips. No, they must at least some speak Anglish because the bird messages received by the Bird Master could be read by him and the other men. It was not likely the men all knew some strange tongue and kept it from the women. Otherwise Effie would have tickled it out of one of them by now. Even her mother occasionally received the rare messenger bird in the form of a Magpie, the oily black with a dollop of cream. Although she tried to conceal the fact she got messages, Deliverance doubted her mother could conceal knowing an entirely separate language.

No, there would be someone who could understand her...if she ever saw someone. As the sun slid across the sky, Deliverance was beginning to question whether or not she would find a person, pirate or not, Anglish speaker or no, ever again. She was the smallest kernel of corn bobbing in this vast pot with no other soul in sight.

The God of Horizons built his empire and tore it down three times as Deliverance swayed along in her little rind in the great salty water-desert. She conserved her food and water the best she could but was soon desperate for moisture. Her tongue gathered the vestiges of dew in the morning from the canvases, hungrily sucking the fresh water from the grimy tarps. Her lips became swollen and craggy and her skin ached with the rays of the sun, sloughing off even though she hid from its gaze under the tarps during the day, pulling the sleeves of her homespun linen, divided skirt shift as far down as she could to cover herself. She prayed for rain even though she was afraid too much would fill her rind and cause it to drop to the bottom of the sea.

In her feverish state, she began to hallucinate. Images of her stony cottage home, emerging from the side of the mountain danced across her crusted eyelids. She daydreamed about her time running through the forests on her and her mother's side of the isle. There she felt as agile as a cat, as stealthy as a fox, flashing through the trees. Her days were spent in a feral freedom only granted to, aside from her mother, who shared her taste for stretching her limbs amongst the limbs of the trees. Deliverance would run, and jump, and climb, and swing until her heart could veritably leap out of her chest. She would careen through the brush, feeling the winds sweep through her locks just to taste the feeling of almost-flight. Pining for those moments, for the solitude of her forest, the manes of her wooly ponies, and the arms of her mother, Deliverance tossed and turned.

As she slipped further into a feverish state of dehydration and hunger, the curious box continued to blink.

✲✲✲

Deliverance

Deliverance startled awake at a huge whooshing sound. Her rind-boat plummeted as did her gut, and she felt the spray of salt water across her prone face as a large shadow enveloped her boat. She was too feeble, she found, to sit up, and the shadow soon vanished. Had she had another fever dream? She thought perhaps her mind was playing tricks on her again. She had seen both Effie and her mother earlier, riding ponies across the waves as easily as if they were cantering on the grassy fields outside the villages. But the images blinked away if she tried to focus her bleary eyes too closely on them. She remembered once as a child babbling about a dark-haired man in a fever-dream before her mother's healing potions and a flick of her green fire cooled the fire of infection burning in her. These mirages had the same ethereal feel. Perhaps she was also imagining the whooshing sound. She shut her eyes and was beginning to drift back into the corners of her mind again when a smaller shadow encompassed her face.

Squinting, she looked up to see the outline of a man against the backdrop of the sun high in the afternoon sky. She must have been passed out firmly, for she never felt his boots drop onto her small boat nor the boat bob to compensate for his added weight. She groaned and tried to move but found her limbs uncooperative.

"Jesus Christ! You look like something out of a renaissance festival!" A deep, masculine voice with an odd lilt became paired with the shadow outline in the sun. She tried to reply but all that came was the rasping of her windpipe.

"Right…sorry it took so long to find you. We weren't expecting a distress call, Cat…oh. No. You are certainly not Cat. You are far too young. Bloody hell. What is going on? Christ, you're in no state to answer. Let's get you fixed up then, up you go." The musical voice spouted nonsense at Deliverance and the shadow man changed angles so she got her first view of the owner of the odd voice. He seemed to be pawing at her, lifting her limp form. How strange, she thought.

A pair of deep brown eyes assessed her from a square, chiseled face of a man of perhaps late twenties to early thirties. A messy spray of black hair jutted out from his head like the spikey tufts of down pulled from a cattail. Before Deliverance went unconscious completely, her last thought was, pirates are really quite handsome.

CHAPTER 6

Deliverance

The sands sifting in her brain slowly abated, their ringing and raining slowing as she regained awareness. She allowed the pins and needles to trickle out of her fingers before flexing them slightly. As her thumbs brushed the fabric of her bed, Deliverance became all too aware that this was not her bed at all. The linen was much too fine, almost alienly so. With a rushing gasp, her eyes flew open and she struggled to sit.

"Hey there. Easy does it," came the familiar voice again. The pirate materialized out of the shadows.

Deliverance was in some sort of cabin, but the swaying let her know they were still very much out at sea. A curious torch lit the room with more light than a fire normally would shed, but still left the corners of the cabin shrouded in darkness. She pushed herself up to lean with her back against the wall and regarded her captor. The nearness of him caused a wallop of panic in her heart, which she hoped was not betrayed in her face.

He edged closer, hands outstretched in supplication as if to show he rendered no threat. Deliverance tested her voice but found it stolen by the salt and the sea.

"Here, have a glass of water," the pirate offered, filling a clear, glass vessel with liquid from a delicate urn perched upon a wooden stand. Deliverance accepted the drink without touching the man's hands, her own trembling slightly. She noticed he had curious designs in ink crawling up his forearm, revealed by his lifted sleeve as he stretched to hand her the glass. Very pirate-like indeed, Deliverance thought. Well, pirates were notorious for having information. Perhaps this scoundrel would know of Lord Asher. Deliverance drank thirstily, coughing at first as her throat accepted the moisture anew.

When her thirst was slaked, she cupped the glass to her and tucked her legs, still clad in her salt encrusted divided skirts, beneath her on the soft bed. She regarded the pirate with a wary yet assessing gaze. He seemed amused by her perusal of his features. Now that she was in this situation, her fears had no purpose in her survival, and she must set them aside.

"Feeling better, are you?" he asked. She did not answer but merely nodded, waiting. Deliverance wondered how Effie would go about drawing the needed information out of the pirate, but then set aside the idea. While Effie did not necessarily have to use her sexual prowess to obtain information, the merest hint or suggestion from her was enough to cause men to fly to her aid. Deliverance did not have an ounce of that gift. She did not have the slightest clue as to how to begin to converse with this thief of

Deliverance

the seas, much less turn the conversation to her advantage. Oh, how she missed Effie…and her mother for that matter.

"Yes, well, sorry about all that. It took us a while to navigate out here. We were not expecting a distress call. In fact, I'd be very curious to know how all this precipitated," the pirate said, after pausing a moment. He reached over and pulled up a chair beside her bed so that he sat facing her, the construction of which was a curious mix of metals and wood.

"Did I call out in distress? How could you have possibly have heard me?" Deliverance asked curiously, letting the suspicion in her voice be plain.

"Did you…? Your beacon was on…and the state we found you in…well…" the pirate stammered, obviously not knowing what to make of her.

"Beacon?"

"Oh, dear Lord."

"Lord…yes, that is the person I am seeking! Lord Asher. Do you know of him?" Deliverance asked, eagerly sitting forward.

The pirate stared at her, confounded. Perhaps there were limits to knowledge of pirates after all, Deliverance thought. This one seemed very strange. Perhaps touched in the head a bit despite his handsome face.

"Do I know Lord Asher? Bloody hell. You have absolutely no idea, do you?" the pirate exclaimed, looking at her in wonderment as if she were some sort of oddity.

"We are not acquainted, pirate. But it is him I seek." Deliverance sniffed, annoyed at the man's obtuseness.

"Pirate...? You think I am a pirate..." the pirate stated slowly, a large grin blooming across his attractive face. It made him seem almost wolfish in nature.

"Well...are you not?" Deliverance demanded, perturbed. To this the man, most curiously, burst into raucous laughter. When she did not join in, he attempted to smother his amusement, but scarcely succeeded.

"Of sorts...I am a sort of pirate, I suppose," the sort-of-pirate admitted. "My name is Jack. Jack Quentin. At your service, madam." He extended a hand from his inked arm. At least this was a mutual gesture Deliverance understood.

She took his hand in hers and was about to reply with her own name.

And then flames shot from the tips of her fingers.

❋❋❋

"FADES!" She shrieked in alarm.

"CHRIST!" He yelped, ducking just in time to avoid singing the tops of his tufty hair.

"What is going on?!" she cried, as he reached for her hands to point them into the center of the room, obviously attempting to keep her from lighting the bed, and herself, aflame.

Deliverance

"Just relax!" he commanded, a firm grip on her hands—miraculously, because they must've been white hot.

"Relax?! THERE ARE FLAMES SHOOTING FROM MY FINGERS! WOULD YOU RELAX?" Deliverance screeched. The pirate...Jack... shook her hard enough to make her teeth clatter up through her arms.

"Watch," he commanded her again, and then slowly released one of her hands, leaving the remaining one firmly affixed to her flaming ones. With his free hand, he flicked his fingers nimbly in front of her face and the green light of magic sizzled into a burst of small, controlled yellow flame. Then with a snap, he extinguished the fire.

Impossible! Deliverance was dumbfounded. Apparently, she was surprised enough to loosen her focus so that the flames pouring from her own hands tempered slightly. With a breath, she managed to allow the fire to wink out completely.

"What.... what just happened?" she stammered unsteadily. Jack the Pirate's one hand remained firmly atop her two, as if he were not entirely sure she would not attempt to burn his ship from bow to stern.

He did not reply right away. Instead, when he finally met her eyes, his were full of amazement. "So, it is true. Fascinating!" he exclaimed. And then, becoming more aware of himself, he removed his hand swiftly from hers.

"What in the Fades is true? Do you mind telling me exactly just what in the Gods' teeth is going on here?" Deliverance demanded, her nerves worn to their absolute end. Had her name gift finally surfaced? It could not be so…Deliverance certainly was not code or a foreign tongue for Scorch-the-Pirate or Burn-down-Things. Her mother would have a care, as independent as she was, to not name her something so…volatile. So dangerous.

"Yes…sorry. You must be so confused. My apologies. Here, why don't I give you a tour of the ship and I will do my best to enlighten you as to what I think I know, and what I do know? And perhaps, my lady, you could do the same for me." He stood and proffered an arm.

Deliverance blew out a breath and decided it would be good to get out of this stuffy cabin and see where the God of Horizons was at this hour. She stood and took his arm, careful not to touch his tattooed skin, lest that odd occurrence with the fire should happen again. Stealing a glance at her free fingertips to make sure they were indeed not on fire, Deliverance followed the pirate from the bedchamber up to the deck of the ship. There her breath was yet again stolen from her.

The sheer immensity of the ship was difficult for her brain to conceive. One could've had a pony race, several ponies thick, on the top deck with room to spare. And the ship itself…the ship was made of metal! How in the Fades were they not sinking? Deliverance wondered, staring in awe at the massive cylindrical stack in place of where her own ship's tiny mast would have been. Billowing clouds spewed from the tops of the stacks, up into the horizons. Jack led her along, weaving through crates and men scurrying about this task and that, then showed her to the front stern of the vessel. Deliverance could barely breath as Jack gestured for her, his eyes full of wonderment at her wonderment, to step up and take a hold of the handrail. As she did so, she began to grasp exactly how fast they were moving, and it dizzied her.

"How...?" she started to ask, staring at the white caps of the waves shooting past them, the v-shaped front of the ship cutting a frothy arc in the water due to her immense speed.

"How... well steam, actually," Jack replied, although not adequately enough.

"Steam?" she asked, trailing off. It was all so bewildering. She had never moved so fast in all her life! The wind whipping at her tresses filled her with a heady sensation. This pirate's ship was truly something to behold.

"Yes, well, you heat something hot enough and you make steam. Steam makes pressure, and the pressure pushes things forward...it's physics really," Jack said by way of explanation that was really no explanation.

"Physics...is that like magic?" she asked, turning around to take it all in. Her green eyes must have been like huge glowworms in the briny light. The salty air had a tendency to make her eyes luminesce.

"Yes...er. Kind of. Magic is a gift one possesses. Physics is like magic everyone can use," Jack tried to explain, feebly gesturing. He cupped a long-fingered hand behind his neck and looked up at her, apparently struggling to find the words.

That reminded her. "And you! How are you a man?" She spun on him, demanding, an accusing finger wagging in his face.

"How am I...what? Oh. For Christ's sake." He sighed, throwing his hands up now. "You aren't used to seeing men with magic, are you?"

Deliverance paused. Men with magic? Was there such a thing? She shook her head.

"Yes, well. Here in the world—in the Outside," Jack said carefully, "men and women both have magic."

"Yes...but your name is Jack."

"Yes."

"Shouldn't it be something like Fire Manipulator Man?"

"Oh, ah. Your name curse."

"Excuse me? Curse? You mean our name gifts?" Deliverance put both her fists upon her hips. This confusion was growing wearisome.

"Yes...gift. Curse. Often the same thing, depending on who you ask. We do not have those out here. We are left to develop our natural gift, whatever it may be."

Deliverance stared at him in askance, so he continued, "As we grow up...become more adult, our magical gifts reveal themselves. Many are like me, elemental...earth, wind, water, or fire. We can build or manipulate our element. Some...some are mind gifts, such as thought-reading, or some have the power to sooth with touch, or to take memories. Some can heal people. Some, God help them, can intuit the future, although it is rare to do so with any clarity."

"And men have these gifts too?" Deliverance asked, fascinated.

Jack nodded, bringing his hand forth and alighting a small flame. He allowed the fire-orb to dance along his fingertips, jumping from one finger to the next in a playful fashion.

"That's so odd," Deliverance exclaimed, reaching forward to touch the orb with her own fingers.

Jack extinguished the flame in a green crack of light before she could burn her fingers. He laughed, white teeth flashing in the sun. "Hah. It must seem quite feminine to you, I would imagine."

Deliverance looked up at him. Oddly enough, he was right—it did seem strange for the greenish light to be emanating from the hands of such a masculine figure. She had never in all her days imagined a man manipulating power so. So, in the Outside, everyone had a gift…and it came to them naturally. It was not decided for them at birth by a tribe of village women. How utterly strange.

"Does this mean…does this mean I also have a fire gift?" Deliverance thought to ask, as she and Jack walked along the boardwalk around the edge of the ship. The size of the vessel was still dizzying to Deliverance, so she clasped the pirate's elbow companionably, hoping he would not notice how disoriented she was and use that information to his advantage.

| 63 |

"No…at least, I don't think so. It is hard to say," he said, casting a glance at her, assessing. "It is clear you are Narisi."

"And what do you mean by this?" Deliverance asked.

"Narisi women…they are said to be able to take on the powers of whomever they touch. The last research done on your island was well over two decades ago, but it seems the affliction is still in place," Jack explained, as they walked in stride.

As they came upon the galley way, a group of men parted for them, curious expressions alighting their faces. The man in the center who'd been commanding their attention until that moment was a scraggly bearded older man with hair wrapped in a bandana coiled in grey snakes reaching past his shoulder blades.

"Ah, Finley!" Jack exclaimed, raising a hand in greeting. He brought Deliverance over to the man with the snake-hair, who looked upon Deliverance with merriment dancing in his grey eyes to match his grizzly visage.

"Jack, sir! I see your rescued maiden is up and well," the man stated with a merry slap on Jack's back. Despite Jack's generous height, this man dwarfed him. Deliverance decided he was very pirate-like with his swarthy features and craggy skin. Even his leathery trousers and loose shirt reminded her of something she'd heard described in a tale.

"None the worse for the wait, I believe. Deliverance, this is Finley, the captain of this ship. Finley, this is Deliverance," Jack said by way of introduction.

Deliverance

Deliverance did not miss a beat, putting on a pretty smile, the way Effie might have done, and dropped a small curtsy. "Pleased to make your acquaintance, Captain Finley," she said, but her mind was riveted elsewhere. She hadn't told him yet, unless it had happened while she was half-delirious...so how on earth did Jack know her name?

✳✳✳

Jack showed Deliverance almost every inch of the colossal vessel, from the steam rooms to the control and guidance tower. It was dizzying, the sheer size and complexity of it all. It even had a name, the *Daedalus*. She wanted to run her fingers along the greased clockwork gears in the engine room, powering along in fluid mechanical motion, but Jack warned her not to get too close. Machines could be dangerous as well as fascinating. Much like people, Deliverance thought, casting a glance at her pirate captor. She was waiting for the right moment to suss out exactly how he knew who she was, but as of yet, the moment had not arisen. Be patient, Effie would have said, your instincts will tell you when the moment is right, when the man is distracted or off his guard. Then you can wheedle information from him slowly like a line of ants carrying off granules of sweet sugar.

The moment came over dinner in Jack's private quarters. Deliverance had not entirely figured out where Jack lay in the command structure of the ship. He seemed to be in a position of authority, given the richness of his living arrangements and his freedom to move about the ship. And yet, Finley was very clearly the captain. This was added to her list of information granules to target and carry away from this Jack Quentin fellow.

She gazed distractedly at her wine glass, ruby glob swaying from side to side.

Jack cleared his throat. "It must all be so daunting for you…being at sea for the first time. Seeing the ship. It will only get more overwhelming as our journey continues."

Deliverance eyed him across the table. "I am not easily dissuaded from a task at hand. Although I admit, the idea of such large…containers floating on the sea is a mind-boggling concept for me. However, I am adaptable."

"Good," Jack replied and spooned a bit of stew into his mouth. Deliverance noticed he spooned away from him, in the proper table etiquette manner the ladies in town would insist upon…odd for a pirate.

"So, you intend to take me to Lord Asher then? At Oxdale?" Deliverance questioned, digging into her own stew with a bit more lust than was appropriate. She was starving though. As she looked up, Jack gave her a nodding gesture as if to say, "by all means, dig in." He did not seem to be a judgmental fellow up until this point, but he did stare at her as if she were some sort of oddity.

"Mister Quentin, you are staring while I devour this meal. I admit I am famished but need you watch me so?" Deliverance rankled.

Deliverance

"Oh, I am sorry," Jack said quickly, his cheeks reddening a bit. "It's just fascinating, is all…to meet one of you. A Narisi, especially a woman. No one has left that island for centuries…well, save for a few exceptions. We do not get to see such a person firsthand often. It is truly unique." He cleared his throat. "Forgive my rudeness."

"Are we really all that different?" Deliverance asked after a gulp of water and a sip of wine.

"I think you will begin to understand how vastly so as our journey continues," Jack replied, leaning back in his seat and pursing his fingers to his lips, considering her. Deliverance was distracted again by the strange tattoo symbols running up his forearm.

"Are those pirate symbols?" Deliverance asked, indicating his tattoos.

At this he barked a laugh. "No, although I can see how you would think that. No…these are from my former military days. Each is a unit I served with in the Arcanton-Plaedes conflict. Fire-breather brigades. A past I have put behind me in career but not in memory."

Deliverance arched her eyebrows. "So, you took to pirating instead?" There was much to this man who mysteriously knew exactly who she was.

"Hah! Well at the moment you could say that is fairly accurate, yes." He laughed, a sparkle dancing in his dark eyes. Deliverance thought his spikey wayward hair reminded her of one of her roosters back home, and she felt a sudden pang of longing for home.

"Please do explain what caused this unusual exodus on your part?" Jack asked of her.

"You cannot read minds as well, can you?" Deliverance asked in return.

He chuckled. "Alas no, we are only granted one gift or ability. Mine is great for lighting gaslight lamps but not so much for discerning the minds of ladies."

"My friend...Effie. She saw one of the powerful men on the island, the Abbot, do something untoward," Deliverance began, unsure of how much language was common between them and so trying to explain as simply as possible. "However, it went badly for her and they accused her of an unnatural gender proclivity...when I went to go talk with her I was accused of being in collusion with her. So, my mother and I fled. I did not know of this boat vessel she had hidden in a cove on the island. I was certain she would have fled with me, but she pushed me out to sea and did not climb aboard herself. I do not know why. I wish I knew why..." Deliverance's voice became froggy with emotion. She stopped to compose herself. She prided herself on being level headed. Tears would not do.

"Ah...so Cat may be in trouble, then?" Jack asked, concerned.

"Yes, she may get sentenced to a work camp if she and Effie cannot twist the people to their favor...how...how do you know

Deliverance

my mother's and my name?" Deliverance blurted out. So much for waiting for the right moment.

Jack hesitated. "That is a conversation I think is best left for Lord Asher to handle. I would not want to overstep my bounds. But I will try to help you as much as I possibly can. That includes navigating the world outside of your island. I imagine it will be somewhat of an eye-opening experience." He was obviously fascinated with her, or her people perhaps.

"I am adaptable," Deliverance replied, squaring her shoulders. Self-sufficiency had served the women in her family for generations.

"Good. I imagine you must be exhausted. We will begin preparing you for what is to come tomorrow. I have arranged for clean sheets on the bed over there," Jack said, indicating a comfortable looking inset bed against one wall. When Deliverance blushed, he quickly added, "I will take a hammock with the crew. Or I can put one there in the corner if you would be more comfortable with me as your chaperone...the crew is fairly well disciplined, but I will understand if you want me close by."

"You...oh. I see. Yes, that...might be nice," Deliverance stammered, cheeks heating. She had never shared space with a man before. The only close proximity she had ever had with men had been occasional town gatherings or meetings.

Jack must have sensed her hesitation, because he wiped his hands on his napkin, stood up, and said, "Right, I will give you your privacy to clean up. There is water and soap over there on the stand and some fresh clothes. They are men's clothes but close to your size I would think. Just hang a towel on the handle of door outside when you are comfortable and I will return."

Deliverance stood too and watched him retreat with the door clicking shut behind him. She was eager to cleanse the salt and grime from her skin. There was not much to be done for her tangled mess of hair…how curious a pirate should be such a gentleman. She did admit she might feel more at ease with him guarding the door. She was not sure why—he was a total stranger, who obviously had many secrets. But her intuition guided her to trust him.

On the knotted pine nightstand was a pitcher of water, a soft, downy towel, and both a bar of soap and a curiously liquid soap smelling of fir trees and rain. Deliverance stripped off her ruined shift, her leggings, and her boots, and cleansed herself as thoroughly as she could. Under the nightstand she found a comb and attacked the tangles in her mass of dark curls. Once they were reasonably rinsed and tamed, she donned the soft, oversized man's tunic and tiptoed over in her freshly washed bare feet to hang the towel on the outside of the door. Then she allowed herself to collapse onto the fresh bed, which was curiously softer than any she had ever felt. The materials were foreign to her, but pleasingly plush.

She vaguely registered the door click open and Jack stretch a hammock in the opposite corner of the room. Dreams overtook her before he even dowsed the light.

CHAPTER 7

Jack

While he waited for the girl…the woman…to clean up, he paced the gangway of the ship. It was not a wholly large vessel, but it suited his purposes. As he paced, he worried. His governess had often scolded him, good naturedly, for this habit of his. But like many of the fire-graced, he had pent up energy that needed regular expulsion.

The girl…woman. He was not prepared at all for the Narisi signal to go out, much less to find someone other than Cat adrift on a small dingy, apparently for days out at sea, having run out of provisions. The girl could have died before they reached her. There were those who would have preferred it so. This thought gave him an unpleasant yank at the bottom of his stomach.

He paused, grasped the railing with his hands, and stretched. The situation must have been dire for Cat to cast her daughter out to sea in such a way. Narisis had been conditioned with a carefully crafted narrative to discourage any sort of seafaring. It was a credit to Deliverance's courage that she had maintained thus far, delving into the depths of the unknown and remaining as undaunted as she seemed. This whole world must seem so incredibly foreign and as of yet she had only seen a sliver of what they called "The Outside." How would she react when Jack was obligated to drag her into the full force of it?

He blew out a breath and stretched his eyes heavenward. Out here, swaying rhythmically to forces far larger than himself, life seemed so much simpler. Shale, indigo, onyx...lapping and overlapping as far as his mortal eyes could attempt to grasp, shattered only by the impossible sieve of sky, peppering the dome overhead with small pinpricks of light. The depths of sea and stars were vastly more formidable than his insignificant will that one was simply left to render themselves to the mercy of Mother Nature and her infinity. Often, in his actual life, he felt the same way. He would much rather submit to the will of the Sea than the will of those far craftier, nebulous forces who governed Arcanton. Even in Mother Nature's cruelty there was logic...justice even. This was not so for the world manufactured by man, more often than not.

He was not an overly religious man, although the battlefield tended to make even the least pious into believers. He might be tempted to dust off some of that Episcopalian inspiration in the next few days. He would need some Divine intervention of some kind...angels or saints or whatever it was those priest-types prescribed. The task at hand seemed insurmountable. Hundreds of years of precedent and a cruel world were formidable enemies.

Deliverance

Letting his hands fall from the railing, and taking one more swig of briny sea air, he decided he would simply have to tackle the situation one day at a time. Having no reference point really to how Deliverance would feel about sleeping on a ship full of men, he'd offered to sleep near the door if it gave her a sense of security. After he made the offer, he'd kicked himself. Of course, he was yet another strange man to her. What he knew of her life on the island, which was probably more than most, was that the girl had lived alone with her mother her entire life. But Deliverance seemed grateful for his offer, hesitating slightly as her situation on the ship reeled across her face like a picture show. She was not accustomed to hiding her thoughts, this one, Jack thought. He often frequented circles where everything was a game of nuance and subterfuge. The girl's innocent candor was refreshing. She'd accepted his offer to sleep by the door. That much seemed to be an indication she at least trusted him a modicum more than the rest of the strange men on the boat. That was something at least.

She was asleep by the time Jack ferreted a spare hammock from the berth below, the washcloth hanging like a shroud from the knob of the great cabin. He slung his hammock in the corner nearest the door as quietly as he could, but it became apparent the girl was in a deep sleep already. Elephants would not wake the poor thing…elephants. What on earth would she make of them? As far as he knew the largest creatures on the island were the stocky ponies they bred for farm work and carting.

He flicked off the overhead lights, then hesitated. Allowing a small illuminating flame to bloom at his fingertips, he crept over and studied the girl. He did so as stealthily as he could. It would not do for her to stir and find her "pirate" lurking near her bunk. So he kept the light low and studied her from as close as he dared to venture.

She was beautiful. Not beautiful in the way the society ladies of Arcanton were beautiful—all ruffled and painted and girdled and plucked. She was as natural as the tides, her dark hair billowing out in waves like volcanic glass. This was a woman who had never seen a beautician's parlor, the powdery machinations rampant in Arcanton's capital Lontown. And yet her skin, despite her harsh lifestyle of sowing and reaping on the island of Nar, was as alabaster as fresh cream. Her mother, Cat, was known to be a beauty as well, famous for her luminous green eyes. Her daughter must have inherited well from her mother.

A small snore escaped from her parted lips and Jack snapped himself out of his reverie. He too would need sleep to navigate the difficult task set before him. It was Providence that he happened to be out scouting in the area when her unique distress beacon showed on the ship's radar. He shuddered in his hammock as he thrust the thought of what would have happened to Deliverance had someone else picked up her signal and found her first firmly from his mind. Within minutes, he too had entered into a deep sleep.

✷✷✷

Deliverance

There had been three once upon a time...but only the vaguest of memories could touch the third. Then it was two. Always two. But somehow a nagging sensation made Deliverance want to remember three again. But that was never how it was. It was always grandmother, mother, daughter then mother, daughter. Grandmother did not arise from the grave...and yet the sensation of a third could not be quelled. It was brief, only for a short time. But the idea of a third, nebulous and obscured, could not be shaken from the back reaches of her subconscious. But this could not be. There was never a third until there was a babe, but this third felt nothing like an infant. She did not have an infant. Who was this third trapped in the vestiges of her memory?

Deliverance awoke with a start. Jack the Pirate was still snoring softly in the hammock he must have hung after she fell asleep last eve. Her mouth was full of cotton but luckily the pitcher still had some water left and she rinsed the film from her teeth. There was a tube of something set beside the pitcher. "Toothpaste," Deliverance read quietly, frowning. Why on earth would anyone want to paste their teeth? Perhaps Jack thought she had dentures? That was an odd assumption. She maintained her dental hygiene well with mint, alcohol, and twig brushing. Maybe they had no concept of dental cleanliness in the Outside and had to paste their teeth back into place?

She set the odd-shaped tube aside and regarded the slumbering pirate. In his sleep, he appeared younger, more peaceful. Awake, his fire current was almost visible in his quick, energetic mannerisms, in his eyes. Lashes fluttered over the dark, intelligent eyes Deliverance knew to be resting underneath. He was older than her, she decided, although perhaps not by much. If they aged so terribly in the Outside that they required teeth pasting, he could be perhaps close to her own age of three and twenty. If he were Narisi, she would guess him closer to thirty.

He must have sensed her watching him because he startled awake. He stared at her a beat before regaining his wits. Then he swung his legs over the side of the hammock and rubbed the sleep from his visage.

"Good morrow," Deliverance said tentatively. It seemed Jack the Pirate was not a spry awakener.

He grunted and shuffled around murmuring, "Coffee." Good, at least they had coffee, Deliverance thought, aching for the hot, black liquid. She and her mother farmed and gathered the beans that grew at the very top of the island mountains. The roasted smell wafting in Deliverance's direction gave her a pang of homesickness. She wondered what had become of her mother and Effie and what they might be filling their day with today. Hopefully menial farm tasks and not the dreaded work of miners.

"Here you go, love. This is coffee," Jack said after several minutes of fidgeting with a contraption that looked like a kettle.

"Thank you. I know what coffee is. We drink it often at home," Deliverance responded, gratefully accepting the smoothly potted mug. A master maker must have thrown this mug, as it had little by way of lumps or abnormalities. She marveled at its smooth texture.

Deliverance

"Ah that's right. I forgot how diverse your agriculture is on that little island. Quite a wonder," Jack said, pouring and mixing a mug for himself. After a beat he said, "Sorry it's instant. Not the best stuff but it will get us by for now."

Instant? Deliverance understood this adjective for the coffee because it had been prepared instantly. She wondered if Jack heated the kettle with his fire gift. She sipped the steaming liquid. It was bitter and slightly off-putting, but after a couple drags, not bad.

"Cream or sugar?" Jack asked her. He must have been half asleep because the creamer he offered was not even liquid…it looked like he had mixed up flour with creamer.

"Black is fine, thanks," she responded, not wanting to draw attention to his sleepy error. He poured some for himself, inhaling the steam as if to steel himself for the day ahead. After a few sips he walked out of the cabin brusquely, then returned within a few minutes.

"They'll have breakfast brought up," Jack said by way of explanation, then plopped with ease into the window bay seat on the far side of the cabin. He regarded her in an assessing manner. Gesturing to the open portion of the cushion beside him caused the heat to rise in Deliverance's cheeks. She had never spent so much time in close vicinity to a man. His speech and reactions were entirely foreign to her. He seemed…conciliatory? Not domineering and abrupt, the way Narisi men were with the village women.

"It's alright. I don't usually bite," Jack joked, noting her hesitation. Deliverance squared her shoulders and then ascended into the seat as well, although backing up to put as much space between them as she could. "Perhaps you could help enlighten me better by telling the tale of how you came to be adrift in the sea once more?"

As she retold the tale, this time in as much detail as she could recall, she picked at the pale blue threads of the bench cushion. It reminded her of the morning glories that used to snake their way across their pasture fences, the buttons in place of their centers.

When she got to the part about Effie's proclivities, she reddened further, but stared at Jack in a defiant way, warning with her eyes.

"Though she be…different, she is still my fast friend. I would defend her to the last," Deliverance declared, daring Jack to counter her.

Jack's response was unexpected. "Damn shame how utterly backward that island has remained. Being tried for being a lesbian? It's unconscionable! But then again, loads of things are unconscionable on Nar…" He looked up at her and added, "From what I understand, at least."

"How is it you know so much about our island?" Deliverance inquired, suspicion creeping into her tone.

Jack shrugged nonchalantly. He seemed to know he was treading in awkward territory. "I have made it my business to study it and learn what I can about it."

Deliverance

How odd, Deliverance thought, that a pirate with no business on Nar would choose to inform himself thus. Perhaps he meant to raid it in the future. That was a terrifying thought. They had never had visitors other than the messenger birds in their entire history…at least not that she knew of, anyway. A raid would be disastrous. The village was wholly unprepared for an assault by sea. Perhaps she'd better not give him more information than she needed to get him to deliver her safely to Lord Asher.

Jack seemed to read her thoughts. "I pose no threat to Nar, Deliverance. Of that, I can give you my word."

Deliverance let this promise sift in her mind, before accepting its truth. However untrustworthy pirates were, her instincts told her this one was good to his word. And she had well-developed instincts to be wary of men.

Another thought struck her. "In the Outside, women…preferring women is not a crime?"

Jack snorted, but seeing she was serious, explained, "Good Lord, no. Well, I can't speak for all the countries in the Outside. There are a few who remain…backward. But in Arcanton it isn't an issue. Even some of our elected officials are of that persuasion. Men preferring men, women preferring women…some preferring both or none or whatever. It is not something we care about much."

Deliverance thought of the Abbot and his abuse of the poor orphan boy Tobin…was that?

Jack, again seeming to read her thoughts, added, "Of age, of course. Consensually."

"Oh," Deliverance replied, relieved. "And that age is...?"

"18. In Arcanton at least. Consent applies even within a marriage as well," he added.

"How interesting! On Nar, well, once a woman is wed, the husband dictates when such activities occur. Some men, from what I understand from Effie, are gentler than others, more considerate. She often plies her trade to give some of the wives a break from those duties," Deliverance related, eagerly at first, but then blushed when she realized she was discussing such a subject matter with a complete stranger. Another question popped into her mind. "Are you...? Do you prefer men? Is that why you can do magic?"

Jack, startlingly, broke out into a deep laugh. He guffawed for a time before wiping his eyes and realizing he owed Deliverance an answer. "No, I most definitely prefer women. Like I said before, magic is not limited to one sex, or sexual persuasion if you will, in the Outside. Everyone comes into their gift on their own in childhood. That reminds me..." He stood and strode to the armoire in the room. He rummaged through its contents for a while before producing a pair of black leather gloves.

"Where we are going, it is best, for now, that most people do not recognize you for a Narisi," he said, handing her the soft, kidskin gloves. They were beautifully tooled, thin, and they stretched over her hands as she donned them. Deliverance wondered why Jack would have a fine set of ladies' gloves in his cabin, but decided she had no right to ask.

"I had picked these up for my kid sister as gift, but her hands are yet too small, I believe," said Jack. It was slightly annoying how he could deduce her thoughts. Perhaps that was one reason Cat had kept themselves secluded on their side of the isle. No, Deliverance decided, this man was entirely different from the ones she knew on Nar.

"It should stop any unplanned for fires, at any rate," Jack continued.

Ah yes, this was clever. Although Deliverance did wonder how it might feel to absorb other gifts. Would it be immediate like her encounter with Jack? Was it through her hands or all of her skin?

"It is something I would like to study a bit though, if you don't mind," Jack said, eyeing her gloved hands. "There is not much known about the Narisi female's curse or how it manifests. We thought perhaps it would have died out over the generations, although your little performance the other night would indicate otherwise."

He sounded rather scientific for a pirate, but Deliverance was curious herself.

"Do you mind?" he asked, extending his hand toward hers. She nodded and allowed him to gently pull the glove from her right hand. Thinking better of it, he pulled the second one off as well. "It would not do to have the ends singed off. Would defeat the purpose of the disguise."

He gracefully perched next to her and said, "I am going to touch your hands again. This time, remain calm. Slow your thoughts. Believe inherently you have control."

Deliverance stilled her mind, breathing the way her mother taught her for meditation rituals, slowly, evenly. Like before she took a shot, in the woods of her home, before felling game.

He placed his larger palms on top of her outstretched ones, carefully. They were warm over hers, and at first she felt nothing but the physical sensation of touch. Then slowly, like grains of sand sifting, green light began to trickle from his palms to hers. No flames leapt out, however. Just the tickling sensation of the magic sinking through the layers of skin upon her work-worn palms.

"Ok now carefully, take your left hand away and try to light a flame…a small one. Barely a candle's size. Keep calm as you do so. If it goes out of control, I will douse it. There is nothing to fear," Jack instructed, his dark eyes locked on her green ones. In their reflection, Deliverance could see her eyes were glowing as she absorbed his magical gift.

She followed his instructions, slowly lifting her left palm, then turning her hand over. At first the flame flared when she thought of fire, but quickly she was able to mentally wrangle the flame into a small, barely illuminating ball of light. She broke her gaze with him to marvel at the orb floating just above her palm. How utterly transfixing!

"Now I am going to take away my other hand, and we will see if the gift remains with you," Jack said evenly, calmly. Slowly, he lifted his other hand, but the orb did not dim or snuff out. "Now let's see if I still have the capability to use my gift or if it transferred entirely to you."

They both looked down at his hands. Palms still up, a twin light orb blossomed first in his right hand, then danced to his left, a juggling act.

"Fascinating," he breathed. "I feel like my gift is still full strength. It's like it's been copied or mimicked by your magic."

"This is…amazing," Deliverance exclaimed, breathless with the magic coursing through her system.

"Your eyes have stopping glowing as well, but the fire remains strongly lit in your hand. I wonder how long you will retain this copy of my gift?" Jack mused, absorbed in his scientific observation.

"I'm not sure. I suppose we will have to test it at several intervals to see if it is still present," said Deliverance.

"Let's! It might come in handy if we have to pretend you have a gift at some point. Arcantons do not normally display the name gifts Narisis impart on their girls…at least not naturally. There have been some abominable experiments on changing gifts throughout history, but… well that's a discussion for another time. Chastity… Temperance… these aren't the sorts of gifts you would find in the natural world. Usually it is something simple like bending an element or growing things, sometimes mental gifts or physical ones. Nothing so esoteric as the ones chosen on Nar."

"Yes, Deliverance is a gift-name I have yet to figure out," Deliverance admitted. "I often have wondered if my mother was addlepated with birth pains when she selected it. I seem to have had no magic up until this point. And this magic was merely mirroring yours. It is not mine."

"Yes...Deliverance is a bit of a mysterious choice, although I am sure Cat had her reasons," Jack allowed.

Deliverance's eyes narrowed. "How do you know so much about my mother?"

Jack put up his hands in placation, saying, "I have not met her in person. But I think that is probably a question best left for Lord Asher. Let's work on extinguishing the flame, so that we can have a better understanding of your control."

Deliverance quelled her urge to demand further information and focused on the task at hand. They worked on extinguishing and relighting the little orb of fire floating in Deliverance's palm until she felt confident she could do so without coaching.

"Excellent. I thought perhaps it might be much more challenging to teach you. Children usually grow into their gifts as their gifts grow, if you see what I mean," Jack said, and Deliverance nodded. That made perfect sense. As the children matured, so did their powers. "This is most promising," he added, although Deliverance did not know to what end it might be promising. In the back of her mind she wondered how long it would take the *Daedalus* to reach Lord Asher.

By this time the sun had shifted high overhead, and Deliverance was beginning to feel cooped up in the cabin. She had not spent so much time inside since last winter. The thought of winter drew her mind to her animals. She hoped someone was caring for them and she hoped most of all that someone was her own mother.

"Shall we get some air? I should explain the next phase of our journey soon, as it will be taking place this evening if the charts are accurate," Jack said, standing and stretching. Deliverance looked away as his shirt slipped up, revealing a taught stomach. Life at sea must have its physical advantages, Deliverance thought abashedly.

She followed him out of the cabin after donning her gloves, up the metallic staircase and out onto the open-air deck. It was still foreign to her to see so much metal surrounding them, despite the cabin's furnishings being wrought in masterful woodwork. When she was a child, she used to spy on the smithy, watching the blacksmith pound away with his hammer and forge. It was a wonder to watch him meld metals, forming something stronger than either of the parts, and then bend them to his will with the white, searing heat. It was a little like magic, although she never would have insulted the blacksmith by saying something was feminine about his work.

Being aboard this ship made Deliverance feel like she had shrunk to the size of a fairy and landed softly like ash in one of his metallurgic works. There was something alive about the ship as it broke through the whitecaps, causing a spraying wake. It was like those strange creatures she would glimpse far out at sea from the top of the seaside ridge during the autumn season…whales? Yes, whales. She knew alive things could not be made of metal, but even so, the ship reminded her of the elegant seafaring motion of those beasts. Perhaps it was a physical bond between creatures and things adept at navigating the sea.

"Ah Finley! The weather seems good for it tonight, yeah?" Jack said, raising a hand in greeting and heading off to talk to the captain. Deliverance followed more slowly, savoring the tang of the salt air. She used to sit amongst the sea oats at home and pull the sea air in great inhalations, like a drink for her lungs, although she knew not yet what she was thirsting for.

"Aye, should get you back before anyone knows you're gone," Finley replied, slapping Jack on the back heartily. His impressive grey dreadlocks shook as they dangled like Spanish moss.

"Good man!" Jack returned the gesture by locking their arms. They must sail together frequently, Deliverance thought as she sidled closer. Finley was rather pungent, although Deliverance tried not to notice.

Jack turned to her and clasped his hands together. "Alright, let me explain what is about to happen as best I can." He reached out and took her gloved hand, indicating she should follow him from the quarterdeck to the upper deck. There, men were busily carting loads of what looked like canvas material onto the deck of the ship in a systematic manner. Shouts of instruction volleyed back and forth between the men as they worked to move the heavy, massive cloth.

"It is of the utmost importance we enter into Arcanton undetected," Jack began. This made sense, Deliverance thought. Pirates would not want to announce their whereabouts or have to pay taxes on the goods they plundered or whatever it was that happened when one sailed into a port. She honestly did not know for sure, but could only guess. "And this is how we do it," Jack said, gesturing to the piles accumulating before them.

She frowned. "Are you going to…cloak the ship in that?" Deliverance asked doubtfully, pointing at the canvas with the toe of her leather boot. This plan seemed…ridiculous.

Jack paused, then threw his head back and laughed. He had a pleasant, rolling laugh, Deliverance thought. Like the heaviest bells pealing in the Abbey.

"No, although it would be rather funny to try to sneak into port that way." He laughed. "These are…how to explain it…large air containers. In a few minutes, once they are battened down, we are going to inflate them with hot air and the hot air will cause these sacks to expand and lift the ship from the water."

She blinked at him. "Lift the ship from the water?!"

"Yes, it seems quite daunting when I say it, but it is a rather fun experience. You will be fine," Jack reassured her, then added with a bit of a wicked glint in his eyes, "You can hold onto me if you like."

Deliverance cleared her throat and raised her chin. "Thank you for the kind offer, but I can handle whatever comes without dissolving into an ineffectual sop."

He chuckled. "Alright then."

Just then, a shout rang out to Jack from Finley across the way. "Care to do the honors, mate?" he called.

Jack winked at Deliverance and bounded over to the captain, who was standing in front of a large, cylindrical tube. It was made of shiny material, like metal, but somehow flexible.

With a flash of green, Jack ignited his fire gift. Green light seemed to crack and shimmer off his entire body, growing with some intricate manipulation of his hands, and he sent the flames pouring like dragon's blast into the tube, which connected to the underside of the canvas. Deliverance gasped for a second—he was going to light the whole Faded ship on fire! But after a pause it became clear the canvas was not catching fire, but holding the hot air. Deliverance watched with abated breath as the canvas expanded rapidly, inflating and then miraculously lifting from the deck of the ship. The ropes attached firmly to the canvas monstrosity began to creak and strain as the heaving sack of air ever expanded.

Then, impossibly, the ship itself groaned in protest, a loud mauling bellow as it lifted from the salted sea. Showers tumbled from the sides of the ship as it climbed, cubit by cubit, into the air.

Deliverance, in her excitement, ran to the edge of the gangway, grasping the railing to watch as the ship detached itself from the sea. She was not expecting the lurch as the ship settled fully under its hot air sails, and found herself thrown against the railing, clambering for purchase.

"Careful now," Jack warned as he caught her firmly in his arms.

"Ooof, sorry. I was just so overcome. I had to see it!" Deliverance exclaimed, delight brimming in her voice. They were flying!

"Yes well, best stay toward the insides of the ship for now until we find some smooth air. Going overboard at this point is quite a lot more traumatic than when we are in the water, if you see what I mean," Jack said, nodding at the whitecaps growing smaller as they climbed. He righted her, and somewhat reluctantly dropped his arms from around her.

"Don't they need you to keep the fire going to keep the ship afloat?" Deliverance asked curiously, entirely distracted by the events at hand to pay any mind to Jack's attractions.

"Nah. They have a mechanical fire going under it now. They just like to see me light it because it's a neat trick," Jack replied good-naturedly.

"Oh, so they can pilot the ship with the everyone magic...physics?" Deliverance asked. "I would have thought maybe someone with an air commanding gift would be needed for such a task."

"No, just simple science. Well, I suppose it is not that simple. But yes, it is accomplishable through engineering. Besides, it would take someone with a hell of an air gift to lift an entire ship," Jack explained.

Deliverance thought he must have a hell of a fire-gift to produce such a raging blast from his person. On Nar even the women with the strongest gifts were barely a spark compared to the great conflagration she had just witnessed. It was terrifying and yet awe inspiring.

Just then Finley strode over, clasping Jack's hand in some sort of complicated handshake.

"Impressive as always, Jack my man. The crew always gets a kick outta that!" Finley exclaimed with his crusty ale voice. "Not many firebreathers could do what Sir Jack here can do. Takes a damned talent. Crew always marvels at it." He elbowed Jack in camaraderie. Jack cleared his throat, looking uncharacteristically embarrassed. "Oh Jackie boy, I keep telling ya, it's nothing to be ashamed of."

Jack scowled. "The gift comes with some unpleasant memories, Finley. But enough of that. Let me take Miss Deliverance here and finish explaining how events will transpire this evening."

Finley shook his head with an emotion Deliverance could not quite put her finger on…regret, perhaps? Pity? She did not have time to ponder this interaction though, as Jack was tugging her along to the…what did they call it? Oh yes, poop deck. Very odd term. There were no privies there.

Deliverance

"That was quite the show, Master Quentin," Deliverance said. She absentmindedly tugged at her own gloved fingers. Could she do that?

"Yes, let's take a peek and see if you still retain my fire-gift," Jack prompted, noticing her fidgeting. He pulled her away from prying eyes and nodded to her. She removed her gloves, pulling them with her teeth to get them started shimmying off her fingers. She took a breath and focused the way Jack had taught her before, below deck. A small green crack alighted in her palm and became a dull candlelight glow, she grew it taller for a second, but then as diligently as she concentrated, the flame snuffed out. She could not relight it, try as she might.

"Hmm, seems your imprint of someone's gift lasts only a few hours. Or maybe it is based on the strength of that person's gift. More experimentation will shed more light on the matter, no pun intended," Jack noted, then caught her gaze. "With your permission, always, of course, m'lady. There will be no atrocities under my watch."

"There were atrocities…before?" Deliverance asked carefully, not sure how to broach the topic.

"Mmmm, yes indeed. Much of history is littered with actions our forebears would deem unrighteous. There were periods in time, not just in Arcanton but throughout the world, when this leader or that got it into his or her head they could meddle with the forces of magic. There were periods of purging people with certain kinds of magical gifts. Others in which scientists sought to control which gift a child could develop and to magnify some gifts while wiping out others. It's rather a complicated, messy business. Once we are settled in Arcanton, I can lend you a few books to read if you are curious — oh, blimey. I mean, that is…can you read?" Jack bumbled.

"What? Of course I can read!" Deliverance cried. What kind of ignorant woman did he take her for?

"Well, it's just from…studies, we have noticed a propensity for Narisi women to be kept from learning. Even basic literacy," Jack said sheepishly.

Oh, he did have a bit of a point. Most of the girls in the village could not read or could only do basic sums. Deliverance had taught Effie to read herself when they were both girls. Cat had always insisted she be educated, and yet at the same time told her to mask her education when around the rest of the villagers. When Deliverance was old enough to understand, Cat explained the main islanders believed women reading was untoward and there was no reason to draw unnecessary attention to themselves.

"My mother," Deliverance said, her voice catching, a mariner's knot in her larynx. She cleared her throat and began again, "My mother, Cat, always insisted I learn to read, although reading material was scarce. I never knew where she obtained the few volumes we had, although at odd intervals she'd manage to produce a new one here and there."

"Right, Cat would have insisted such. She seemed so determined you be different. At least from her correspondence. I wondered if perhaps she meant for you to blend in more and not focus on such things," Jack explained without really explaining at all. How on earth could he fathom what her mother intended for her? Deliverance was not even sure herself what her mother had intended her future look like.

CHAPTER 8

Jack

Watching Deliverance's eyes light up as the ship wrested itself from the briny sea amused Jack more than he cared to admit. The girl had come alive with excitement rather than the fear he had expected. Hopefully that remained the case into the night. They had some difficult maneuvering to do to get themselves into Arcanton undetected. It was best for everyone, especially Deliverance, if they remained undetected. Good thing his little clandestine forays outside of the Republic allowed him plenty of practice in such matters.

Deliverance let out a gasp, suddenly, as she leaned far out over the water in her enthusiasm to watch the ship lift higher into the air. The railing, however, was slippery with salty sea and she'd lost her balance—she was about to topple overboard!

"Christ! Whoa there," he said, jumping forward to wrench the girl back from the railing. "Careful, now." His heart thudded in his jugular.

"Sorry," she said with a smile.

He shook his head as she turned back toward the water again, thankfully not as close to the edge this time. She'd nearly given him a bloody heart attack. Being responsible for her, which unfortunately destiny seemed fit to shackle him with, was going to be a difficult task but he was determined to keep her safe.

It was not that she was stunningly beautiful in a way he had never seen before, not like the trussed-up hens strutting about the high society of Arcanton's elite. No, it was that she was unique... scientifically unique, he meant. One of a kind. Someone who could hold the key to unlocking secrets and perhaps even doors. Shackles, even? There were many who would not protect this woman if they knew about her but would use her or worse. He simply hoped Lord Asher would be willing to help. He thought he would be...but with that man, one could never know exactly what he might do.

Jack wrenched himself from his unpleasant reveries and set himself to the task at hand. He motioned for Deliverance to come follow him as he took her to the lazaret. There he pulled out several large, what probably looked to Deliverance like knapsacks.

"This is a parachute," Jack began.

"Para-shoot? Is that a bird we are going to fell? I do not see any other quarry up here to shoot."

The girl never ceased to amuse him. Earlier he'd had to explain that toothpaste was not glue for teeth, but rather for maintaining their cleanliness. She seemed dubious about it, but after sniffing

Deliverance

it, admitted it did smell rather like the mint and alcohol regiment they used on Nar.

He could not manage to stifle a chuckle. "No, it's rather like the canvas balloons above our heads only made for a single person, or in our case, a double set of people."

"It does not look like a balloon. It looks like a pack," said Deliverance, reaching to poke the knapsack. Jack swatted her hand away gently.

"Ah ah, no touching. For professionals only," Jack chastised her playfully, then explained, "When I pull this handle here, a curtain of strong cloth comes out and slows our rate of fall so that we can land safely. The ship is cloaked in a sort of camouflage paint that avoids radar…well that avoids detection and we turn our beacons off once we enter Arcanton airspace."

"Like the one in my boat?" Deliverance asked, looking at the knapsack skeptically.

"Yes, exactly so. We coast in at an altitude that will not draw too much attention but is still high enough for us to leap out and use our parachutes to make it safely to ground. Unfortunately landing this behemoth, cloaked though she may be, would draw far too much attention even at night. So Finley and I have been running our operations for years this way and it's worked like a charm." Jack smiled, more than a little proud of his scheme. It was rather brilliant if he did say so himself.

To her credit, Deliverance did not question him as to why they needed such a covert entrance into Arcanton. She was an intuitive woman and seemed to see the benefit in remaining undetected. He was also glad he did not have to explain the specifics of why; it was such a massive subject it made his brain cramp trying to think of how to explain to her all the issues and ramifications of her even being here. He just prayed to God Almighty he had a solution. He was pretty sure he did...but pretty sure was not a certainty.

"So when it is nightfall, and we are over the area you want to land, we are going to leap off the ship, and use this...parachute to get to the ground intact?" Deliverance said, her desire to tinker with the packs evident on her fae-like face, but so far she was showing admirable restraint. Jack himself had not been able to resist tinkering with the rigs and learning their ins and outs at the drop zone where he learned to skydive back in his military days. The mates used to tease him he would be a master rigger before long. But that was years ago. Many of those men were not amongst the living anymore. Jack shook his head. Best not dwell on those bygone times.

"That's precisely it!" Jack exclaimed approvingly. Quick study, this girl.

"Can I have my own parachute?" she asked, looking longingly at the rigs.

He grinned a large, shit-eating grin at her. Ballsy one, she was. "Hah! No, not this time, love. I would rather you make it to the ground in one piece. So unfortunately, you have to ride strapped to me. But don't worry, I have done it a few times." A few thousand times.

Her face fell a bit, so he added, "But perhaps eventually I can teach you how!" This returned the honey and sunshine smile to her lovely face. Jack chided himself, internally, for making far-fetched promises. But he found himself like a dog begging for biscuits, looking for ways to brighten that smile. He was such a dolt.

"Come along now. I need some more coffee. This fire-breather is out of fuel I'm afraid," Jack said, proffering his arm to her. She took it without hesitation. Secretly it pleased him she was so willing to accept his company. He had expected a Narisi woman to be more fearful of men than Deliverance seemed. They lived in such a backward society. But then again, she was Cat's daughter. If she shared any of her mother's rumored personality, she had some piss and vinegar in her veins. Or maybe she just rather liked him.

No, he ought to stuff that thought away somewhere in the darkest reaches of his mind where he could not muse on it. Such thoughts were dangerous.

CHAPTER 9

Deliverance

She was so excited she could hardly stand it. Her cheeks flushed with anticipation. Not only was she flying on the airship, but she would get a chance to fly through the air, in and of herself! Well, sort of... strapped to Jack, anyway. It was the closest thing to becoming a bird she could fathom.

Back home, Deliverance would sometimes run as swiftly and agilely as she could through the forests near their homestead, weaving through the pines, each stony foothold memorized. She could feel the drumming of her heart as she pushed longer and harder, peeling through the countryside with all she had. And when she finally spent the last of her energy, she would drop into a bed of rushes at the top of the ridgeline by the sea, letting the sun recharge her. Her rattling breaths would match the rustling of the sun-warmed grasses surrounding her collapsed form. And she would gaze at those seafaring birds, floating high aloft the waves, resting nimbly on thermals, as if they could nap there; it was so natural to glide that way. She would study those avian athletes as she recovered her breath, a pleasant ache in her muscles falsely promising that next time, if she ran just a little bit harder, she too might take flight.

So how fascinating it was that people on the Outside did such things and did them often! They had a set system for doing this parachuting. Jack explained a bit about it to her. It was a sport called skydiving. There were different types of parachutes and the knapsacks were called rigs. The large cloth wings that would come out of the rigs were made of a fabric she had never heard of before, something strong called nylon. Jack showed her how one could pilot the chute, turning for and aft, like the wing of a bird, using his hand as an imitation of the parachute. Apparently, this required some skill, as did balancing in the air during the fall. Jack described different "disciplines" of skydiving where people would jump together in large groups or do complicated sky dances. He said the air benders, if they were strong enough and practiced enough, could stay in the sky longer and do more complicated routines. He started to tell a story of an air-gifted friend of his, but seemed to think better of it, and changed the subject. The man did not like to dwell on the past much. Deliverance speculated it had something to do with his military history scribed on his body in those intricate tattoos snaking up his arm.

But she was determined to find out as much as she could about this fascinating Outside world, which, like the seabirds, had previously been beyond her reach. Now it was a jump away…literally.

Her eyes stretched to the reaches of the canvas inflated over their heads, at the deepening bruise of the sky, at a seagull coasting below them, marveling.

"There are more things in heaven and earth, Horatio, than are dreamt of in your philosophy," she breathed.

Jack snorted, arresting Deliverance from her daydreaming. "What is so funny, pirate?" she asked him playfully.

"You just quoted Shakespeare. I find it very odd you do not know about toothpaste and yet you are versed in famous literature," Jack said, eyeing her in an amused manner. One of his eyebrows cocked up asymmetrically on his rugged face. He had grown a shadow across his face, denoting a beard yet to grow in thick and dark. What would the storywinders in the village call him…swarthy? Yes, perhaps swarthy was the word.

"Shake Spear. Is he a warrior?" Deliverance asked, turning to run her hands across the railing of the gangway, not wanting to miss the last of the sunlight. She knew it would be dark before they came into view of Arcanton and its capitol, Lontown. She still wished she could see it, though.

"Hah. Of sorts. He was more of a warrior of words. The pen being mightier than the sword and all that," Jack replied, bemused.

Deliverance shook her head. What an odd expression. Anyone with any sense knew a sword could do a lot more damage than a quill. "So, he was a writer?" she said. "My mother used to quote portions of that play to me. We did not have a written copy of the actual work though, so she would recite from memory. We had a couple books but not many. It was not for women to own such items, although not much of anyone ever bothered us in our little corner of the isle. I thought perhaps the words came from some orator before the exodus to the island—a play from the time before, or perhaps she'd heard one of the storywinders in the village tell the tale."

"He was actually from Arcanton. One of the most famous playwrights in our history in fact," Jack replied. "He wrote a little bit after the Narisi exile though."

Deliverance would have wondered what her mother was doing in possession of such knowledge from the Outside but she had become aware in the past couple days her mother was much more than met the eye. The mysteriousness of Cat's connection to the Outside nagged at Deliverance's mind. What had her mother been hiding?

✷✷✷

There was a flurry of excitement before the hush. Men rushed to accomplish last minute duties and tie up loose ends before the sun dropped below the weighted horizon in a flash, leaving indigo and violet in its wake. Deliverance had not moved from the deck of the ship, pacing along the gangway and attempting to steer clear of the bustling crew. Jack had disappeared for a spell, also claiming last minute details to attend to.

Deliverance alternated between watching the horizon, still not being able to pick out any hint of land, and watching the scurrying men tie down ropes and toss dark covers over cargo. She considered the matte black paint of the boat, deciding it was adapted well to being inconspicuous, though she confessed she had no understanding of what Jack meant when he explained about ray-dars. As best she could tell, it was something akin to how a bat finds its prey, they being the insect and the Arcanton dock authorities being the predators. She swallowed quickly, her huntress nature feeling unease at becoming the hunted. The unease was coupled with the lingering doubt that a nefarious pirate could possibly have a connection with a Lord of station such as Lord Asher, but she felt she could trust Jack despite these concerns.

She hoped so.

A shrill, undulating whistle settled itself across the entire ship, and suddenly there was silence. Deliverance felt Jack slip into the space next to her, indicating with a finger to his lips their covert entry to the Republic of Arcanton had begun. It was eerie how the hustle and bustle fell dead, only a light breeze and the waves below them daring to peep a sound. There was hardly any moon, which aided their clandestine entry. The moon would have traitorously revealed their looming silhouette.

Deliverance could tell by the sounds of the water beneath them they had crested the shoreline and were floating over land, but the pitch-blackness of the night made it impossible to make out any features of the city below. From what she understood they would float by various drop off points throughout the city, ones that had a large open space with landing and contacts waiting to squirrel the sky intruders away quickly before they were detected. Jack and Deliverance's drop off point was one of the last.

Jack grasped her hand in his, and warmth radiated up her wrist. She had learned to control the fire gift response in her, and so nothing alit at the contact. Nothing visible anyway. Deliverance shook her head, clearing it of useless thoughts of attraction cluttering her attention. He folded her leather gloves into the palm of her hand.

"Best put these on, love. We don't want you to get too wrapped up in the moment and forget to control your gift mimicking. A burnt parachute sounds less than appealing," he whispered in her ear, the downy curls there tickling her lobes. She nodded in agreement and slipped on the supple gloves, pulling the fingers down so she had full mobility. After doing so, he towed her along to the main deck where the crew was gathered.

Men in various assortments of readiness adjusted straps, checked gadgets, including red light headlamps, and practiced pulling, arching backward in an odd, uncomfortable looking way. Deliverance had learned earlier this was the position they would have to assume in the air to remain stable and not flip or spin out of control like a leaf in the autumn falling from its branch.

Jack ventured over and tugged on straps, checking this and that on his crewmates' rigs. He slapped shoulders, shook hands, and gave an occasional hug to his fellows as he went. She could see why all the crewmates respected Jack. He was concerned for their safety. He looked out for them. It was an admirable quality.

When he returned to her, he considered her for a moment, then spun her abruptly and rather forcibly so her back was to him and grabbed her hair. She had to stifle a gasp at the suddenness. Then, with gentleness despite the terse motions, he wound her waist-length dark hair into a single braid.

When she looked over her shoulder questioningly, he admitted, "I have a little sister. She likes...used to like to have her hair braided. Also, I can't have that wild mess whipping me in the face as we descend." With that he tucked the braid into her shirt collar. Deliverance nodded in agreement. It made sense.

After that he slung a larger looking rig over his shoulders and fidgeted with it for a while before helping her into a harness, this one for obvious reasons lacking a parachute behind it. He attached his rig to hers with her back to him, and they shuffled forward to the opening in the railing Finley had popped free for them. The other jumpers thus far had catapulted themselves over the railing with salutes and grins, gravity sucking them away in a blink. Deliverance could almost not believe how they were there one second and gone the next.

When they neared the gateway, Jack cinched the straps connecting the two of them securely. Deliverance could feel the press of his solid, reassuring body behind her.

"Stand or sit? Sometimes sitting is easier to swallow," Jack murmured. Deliverance tried to eye him but found she could not shift enough to give him a look.

"Stand," she whispered back and could hear his faint chuckle in reply. They inched forward to the edge, blackness stretching out before their feet. Deliverance's heart began to race. There was nothing between them and the pit of nothing before them.

"Cheers, Finley. Until next time!" Jack whispered to his captain, then squared with the opening. Deliverance in front, and Jack close behind. "Ready?" Jack asked in her ear.

Deliverance, despite the adrenaline coursing through her veins like the water in a mill grist, felt a huge grin blossoming across her features.

"Always."

With that, they launched.

Deliverance's stomach lurched, but not as much as when she dove from the cliffs on her and her mother's beach. It was not the drop that was overwhelming but the noise. The wind ripped across her body, singing like a banshee, all consuming. At first she found it difficult to breath, but then realized all she had to do was to inhale and exhale as she normally would. The wind pealed across her cheeks, causing indents and her eyes to water. It was shatteringly cold, but it did not matter in the slightest. It seemed like an eternity. Deliverance almost wished it would last that long. They were flying, hanging aloft in the sky like night birds!

Too soon, Deliverance felt a rattling jerk, her feet flying up in front of her face, although it was too dark to see them clearly. And the noise ceased. She felt Jack shuffling around behind her, and then the canopy tilted forward slightly and picked up speed.

Deliverance

They turned slowly one way and then the next, finally pulling up again before dropping back into a steady flight speed. Jack had explained before he would do that to check the steering and that all was well with the canopy.

Her heart was still pounding with excitement, though her breathing remained, she proudly noted, fairly steady. The silence enveloped them, wrapping around their limbs and their eyes, singing a faint lullaby in the breeze through the risers of the rig.

Jack risked a whisper to ask, "You okay?" She nodded fiercely and grinned. Even without the moonlight, her white smile was visible. He flashed a hearty one back. His hands found her gloved ones, and guided them up into the steering toggles. With his larger ones overlapping hers, he helped her turn left, then right. She had to stifle a squeal of glee. Who would have ever have thought this was even possible? That she, Deliverance, the girl with no gift, would be flying? It was truly astounding.

Jack flashed his glowing altimeter and switched on his red headlamp, indicating they were starting their pattern to land. Below them, perhaps a little less than 1000 feet, two large lights switched on, illuminating a swatch of open farmland. Carefully, Jack guided them in a rectangle and swooped into the lights. Deliverance picked her feet up, making herself a ball as she was instructed previously and they slid unceremoniously to a halt. The lights flicked off again, and Deliverance felt she was again alone with Jack, although she knew there would be another person close by operating the lights.

They reclined back for just a second, catching their breath, relishing the shared moment. Carefully, Deliverance lifted a gloved hand behind her, searching for Jack's face. When she alighted upon his cheek, she strained her neck backward and pressed her lips to the other cheek. The stubble there prickled and she smelled his sea and pine scent. His hand came up and touched the one on his face, laying his overtop hers as though to say, *stay there*. She could not. It was as intimate as she had ever been with a man. She had to break the contact, breathless. But a small flicker of joy deep inside her was glad she did not let that singular moment pass unmarked.

"I say, are you alright, Senator?" A voice came from the direction of the switched-off lights, further breaking the moment. Jack coughed behind her and began fumbling with the straps that bound them together.

"Yes, Stevens, just a moment," he replied hastily, ducking his head and fiddling with the last of the attachments. Deliverance stretched after she stood, freed of the constraints. Suddenly, she was blinded by a flood of light.

"Put your hands up!" The same voice that had spoken before commanded. Deliverance cast around, confused. "Put your hands up or I will shoot!" Fades! The man had a bow!

Erratically, Deliverance spun around looking for an escape route before Jack piped up.

"Stevens, for Christ's sake. She's with me. And you don't own a gun." He sounded slightly perturbed, wrestling with the

Deliverance

mounds of swishing fabric, but did not give the armed man the slightest care.

"Oh! Oh, very good, sir! Sorry about that... I may not own a gun, but I got this illuminating taser from Mrs. Potter." The voice came again and the lights shut off in a scramble.

"Jesus, put that taser away, man. You'll bloody likely shoot yourself. And come help me with this!" Jack ordered, stumbling toward a large wagon-looking contraption.

It was sleek and shinier than any paint she had ever seen, with the bright lights affixed to the front. After wrestling the tandem rig into the backside of it, Jack glanced up at her and took in her wonderment.

"Oh...this is an automobile," he said, gesturing at the wagon.

"Aught-to-mobile?" Deliverance tried.

"Something like that, but we really must hurry, otherwise all this subterfuge and clandestine-ness will be for naught. Come along," Jack said as he shuffled her into a seat near the back of the aught-to-mobile.

The man, Stevens, Deliverance assumed, climbed in the front and grasped a round wheel while Jack piled in beside her.

"To the hideaway!" Jack ordered, although Steven must have thought him tongue in cheek because the older man rolled his eyes. Deliverance could see it in the mirror affixed to the front window. With a roar, the aught-to-mobile sprang to life and

| 111 |

Deliverance gave a start. There were wild animals enclosed in the front of this carriage!

Jack noticed her widened eyes and took her hand. "It's alright, love. It's supposed to sound like that…well, mostly like that. It needs a new muffler." Deliverance looked at him quizzically as they sped away.

"I imagine you've never moved so fast in your life. Is it disorienting?" Jack asked, studying her, almost scientifically, as if he could catalogue her reactions for further research.

Deliverance put her other the hand to the transparent glass next to her and peered out at the world zipping by. It was disorienting. She wondered what type of animals were contained in the front of the carriage to cause them to move with such speed.

"Yes…but I like it. It's fascinating," she admitted, not taking her eyes off the landscape whizzing by. If she could drink it all in, she would. It was difficult to see anything in the dark, although she gathered when they had traversed from countryside into more populated areas. Strange gas lamps began to illuminate the road, which had transformed from a normal, rocky path to something altogether strange and smooth. Someone had painted symbols on the smooth road and occasionally another aught-to-mobile monster would whiz by them in the opposite direction at a dizzy speed.

Occasionally, Deliverance caught Stevens eyeing her through the mirror in the front. She tried not to stare back into his watery grey eyes, which, although wary as he regarded her, seemed kind enough. He was wearing some sort of dark jacket and waistcoat, but no hat, although the weather seemed a bit chilly. Involuntarily, she shivered.

"Stevens, can you turn the heat up, old chap? Thanks," said Jack, although Deliverance did not know how they would light a fire in the contained space. Miraculously though, hot air began to blow forcibly on them through tiny vents in the ceiling and floorboards.

"There, is that better?" Jack asked her, looking torn as to whether or not to slide over and provide physical warmth or not, but then evidently decided against it when he met Stevens's eyes in the mirror. "Yes, alright. We will have a family meeting post haste when we arrive at the manor, but until then, Miss Deliverance…er, well I suppose you do not have a last name do you?"

Deliverance shook her head. "No, if someone has a last name on Nar, it is because it is their job. Mother and I do not have official stations or titles."

Stevens gave a walloping exhale, spitting toward the windshield, and began to cough. Jack had to reach around and pat the elder man on the back to help him with the fit.

"Sir, I…" Stevens began, clearly concerned, but Jack interrupted him with a hand up.

"No, this can wait for the family meeting. But Miss Deliverance, may I present to you Edward Stevens, my manservant? Stevens, this is Miss Deliverance." Jack gave perfunctory introductions, unphased.

"Pleased to meet you?" Deliverance tried.

"Yes...um. The pleasure it all mine, Miss. Yes..." Stevens replied then trailed off, turning his attention back to the road. A worried grimace had affixed itself to his visage, trailing deep crevices in the man's face.

"Don't mind him," Jack said to Deliverance. "He has my best interests at heart. Has since I was a boy. Is a bit of a worry wart, though." Deliverance heard a very faint grunt of protest from the front seat but nothing else followed it.

CHAPTER 10

Deliverance

As they ventured into more populated areas, the illumination grew brighter. Deliverance could see outlines of large, stone-built homes, some all smashed together in a row. Tall metal rods held the not-flickering lamps over the streets and their curious signs and symbols. It was odd how still the light was, having no life like flame normally has. Occasionally, she caught a glimpse of a group of men wearing coats similar to Stevens' traveling together on the lip of the roads, or a woman in a cloak curiously attached to a dog with a rope. She wondered if the woman was alright or if she was mentally ill. She decided even if she was, the woman's clothes were fine enough—she probably had caretakers looking after her. Although, she hoped they knew their charge was wandering the streets at night being led by a dog on a string, or that at the very least, the dog knew where they were going.

She was amazed at how far they had to travel before entering the sector in which Jack's "manner" was located. There were so many people all crammed together in this city, and yet the structures were more enormous than anything she had ever seen. Perhaps they enjoyed living so close to one another if the monstrous structures provided some privacy?

After what seemed an age, they turned onto a cobblestone street. Here the homes became statelier and imposing, and the roads were lined in gardens. The change in street material caused the aught-to-mobile to bounce slightly, disrupting the alien smoothness of the journey thus far.

"Shall we pull around back, Stevens?" Jack asked, shifting impatiently in his seat, as if to survey for possible onlookers.

"'Fraid everyone is awaiting you at the front, sir." Stevens replied as they pulled up to a large, wrought iron set of gates. A scrolling Q was rendered into the blackened metal and the gates creaked open after Stevens pushed a button on the ceiling of the aught-to-mobile.

"Bloody hell. Well, Deliverance, it seems you are about to get inundated with attention. Don't worry, it's just the family. Are you ready?" he asked, turning to stare at her intently. She nodded, with a nervous lump in her throat. What would this family be like? Would it be like the ones in the town in Nar, like the Butcher's, where there was a father, mother, children, and perhaps some grandparents if they survived? Or would it be like Deliverance's own—a cobbled-together threesome of her, her mother, and Effie? Jack had mentioned he had a little sister. Were there others? What would they make of her?

Her racing thoughts were interrupted as they pulled through a circular drive in front of the main entrance to what Deliverance assumed was a "manner." She never thought of houses having manners or lack thereof, but it must've been some sort of idiomatic expression. There was lots she would have to learn. Large pillars propped up a roof over the area in which Stevens pulled the aught-to-mobile to a halt. Jack sprang out of his seat and swiftly came to her door, opened it, and proffered his hand to take hers. Inhaling deeply, she reached out and allowed him to help her from the carriage.

A large, double-door entrance sprung open, billowing warm light out into the night and reaching them. Jack firmly guided her along with him into the entrance of the "manner" and chaos erupted.

***

Deliverance was inundated with cheerful sounds from the host of people converging on them. They seemed to be wearing uniforms of some sort, the women wearing black and white ensembles and the men wearing similar ones, but not in skirts.

"Welcome back, Senator!" A kindly old lady greeted Jack, pausing to wipe her hands on a frilly apron encircling her modest, high-collared dress.

"Mrs. Potter!" Jack began but was interrupted by a high-pitched squeal, the kind only prepubescent girls could make.

The sea of people parted slightly and a blur of fabric attacked Jack, leaping at his chest. Deliverance took a step back and took in the reunion. A girl, about twelve or thirteen if she were guessing in Narisi age, wrapped her arms tightly around Jack's midsection. Jack's eyes, for his part, were afire with affection as he returned the embrace.

But it was so odd. The little girl had no hair. None atop her head, none where her eyebrows aught to have been. If this was the fashion in Arcanton, Deliverance thought, maybe the women were more practical than Jack had made them out to be. She could see definite advantages in the girl's choice of haircut, although it seemed hard to maintain. No more difficult than her wild, unruly mess of curls though, she thought ruefully, and then became uncomfortably aware that not only was she a grimy mess, but everyone had stopped talking and was staring at her.

Jack cleared his throat and announced, "Everyone, this is Miss...pardon, Lady Deliverance. She will be staying with us for the foreseeable future. Please prepare her a guest suite and see to it her needs are met." He stopped talking but everyone did not seem to notice. They continued to stare at her. Deliverance fidgeted uncomfortably.

It was the girl who broke the standoff finally. She came up to Deliverance with a bright smile upon her bald face and dropped a curtsy in front of her. Deliverance did the same, not sure of the protocol but deciding mimicking would be the best way to get along for now. The girl held out her hand, beckoning Deliverance to take it.

"I'm Eleanor!" The girl introduced herself effervescently.

Deliverance

"My name is Deliverance," she replied. The girl giggled and clapped her hands, evidently pleased. She cast her attention to her older brother.

"You naughty rascal! I cannot believe you did not let me in on this!" The girl chastised Jack, although he returned her enthusiasm with a quizzical stare. Deliverance stared back and forth between the two of them, one dark head and one shiny. Jack had not known when he had set out on his voyage he would encounter her, so what was the girl implying?

"Yes…I did not?" Jack said, unsure.

"It has been one hell of a wait. No, do not tsk tsk me, Mrs. Potter for language. It is the truth! But now I will finally have a sister in law!" The girl clasped her hands in glee and excitement, and Jack had a coughing fit.

Oh no, Deliverance thought. They thought…

"Yes…this is my…fiancée. My fiancée, everyone. She is just in from… the Southlands, so please excuse her if she is not familiar with our customs. I am sure you will help her and make her comfortable," Jack managed, although his voice squeaked uncomfortably with the lie.

Deliverance remained quiet. It was as good a subterfuge as any, she supposed, if he meant to keep her Narisi origins a secret for now. The household seemed to accept this answer with ease and started to break away into a flurry of activity.

"Please, Deliverance, come with me. We shall retire to the drawing room and you shall tell me all about yourself. Jack, she is so pretty! No wonder you fell for her!" Eleanor babbled as she started to lead Deliverance off.

"Er...Stevens...Mrs. Potter? Can you accompany us to the drawing room as well? We need to have a family meeting....we REALLY need to have a family meeting," Jack said weakly. Deliverance wondered how stressful it would be on him to maintain such a fib as their cover. She had not considered he might already have someone else—another woman, already in his life. What would happen to his personal affairs if that were the case? What a pickle she had put him in!

Once all five of them were ensconced in an elaborate room evidently deemed a "drawing room," Jack shut both of the carved wooden doors behind them and flipped the latch. Stevens and Mrs. Potter were gazing at him expectantly, although Eleanor seemed keen to pull Deliverance over to the fire to chat. Jack rested both of his palms on the closed doors, leaning forward and taking a moment to compose himself before turning to face them.

He clasped his hands together. He began by calling Eleanor's attention back to the here and now, although it was clear the girl would rather be happily enveloped in a tête-à-tête about wedding plans and getting to know Deliverance. She stuck her lip out in protest at her brother seizing her attention away from her new playmate.

"Yes, so...I lied," Jack admitted meekly. Mrs. Potter cluck-clucked, sucking wind through her pursed lips, although she did not seem surprised. "It seems my antics may have caught up to me. I was out, as you know, on one of my data collection missions

Deliverance

when we received a distress beacon from a very old registry. It was the informant frequency from Nar. So we followed it and came upon a primitive sailboat, adrift with no wind and out of provisions…and in it, Miss Deliverance."

Stevens gasped. "Are you saying, Senator, that Miss Deliverance is…?"

"Um, yes. That is what I am saying. She is Narisi. In fact, she is Cat's daughter. Apparently, there was an emergency and Cat sent Deliverance out to sea with the distress beacon activated to avoid imminent danger. It was all very sudden," Jack explained.

Mrs. Potter sank into one of the ornate looking chairs and began absently running her fingers along its finely embroidered filigreed fabric.

Jack looked at her. "I could not just leave her out there!"

"No…no, of course not," Mrs. Potter replied quietly, obviously shaken. The elderly woman's face had taken on an ashen shade.

"Wait…" Eleanor interrupted, catching on. "So…she's not your fiancée?"

"No, although that is a brilliant cover. Good job, Eleanor. I hadn't thought of a decent cover story until you did," Jack replied, not seeming to notice his sister's utter disappointment.

The girl seemed to deflate in a flounce of lace and crinoline beside the hearth. A pouting lip wormed out to complete the picture of utter dismay. Deliverance almost hated to let her down, but the truth was important. She hoped they would not have to keep up this ruse long and she could reach Lord Asher without too much difficulty. It would not be necessary if the entire household had not seen them enter, but Deliverance imagined the staff would talk and rumors would spread. She was beginning to understand Jack was a lot more influential in society than a pirate...Fades, no, they had called him Senator! How had she missed that point? God's teeth, he was part of the top tier of Arcanton's government!

Finally, Stevens broke the silent mulling of the group, clearing his throat. "Well, it certainly seems ill advised, sir, to bring an actual Narisi woman into Arcanton...but it cannot be helped now. We must find a way to proceed as carefully as possible."

Deliverance piped up. "Why is it so precarious—my being here?" It could not have been all that odd for people to travel in the Outside. Their storywinders told them often of epic odysseys in which heroes or even regular folks would embark on journeys.

Mrs. Potter fielded her question. "That, my dear, is a very complex question. The simplest way to answer it would be the rest of the world—the Outside, as you call it—is afraid of what the Narisi women may be capable of."

Deliverance's brow furrowed. "I do not understand. We are an island of farmers, weavers, potters, and the like. We have useful capabilities, but they are simple. Our women are, well, quite ordinary. The men do most of the power wielding on Nar."

"Ah yes, but then they have no magical power still, do they?" Mrs. Potter countered.

"No. It was not until recently that I understood that…well, that men could also have magical gifts. The men on Nar lack them entirely," Deliverance answered.

"Yes and this is because…?" Stevens led her.

"Well, I don't know. They've never had them, as far as I know. Just the women," Deliverance replied.

"And has your gift shifted since you've left the island?" Stevens interrogated her.

"I…well yes, I suppose. I did not have a gift before. Ours are bestowed at birth by our mothers. My mother…well, she is an independent sort and selected a rather odd name for me. Deliverance. It does not have any logical meaning I can think of, and it has never manifested itself into any magic sparking gift I could see." After a pause, she added, "Although once I was aboard the ship with Jack, he showed me…oh."

The reality of it hit her like a hammer. He'd showed her she could shift her gift to match anyone's. But why would that matter? It only lasted a couple hours anyway. It was not as if she were actually stealing their powers.

"Oh indeed," Mrs. Potter finished. Deliverance was starting to get the impression Stevens and Mrs. Potter were quite the team. In fact, Jack had referred to them as family in stating he was calling a family meeting. Deliverance wondered if they were related by blood distantly or if Jack simply had an affinity for them.

She studied their faces and builds. Mrs. Potter had watery grey eyes, large, although sagging with age. There were pink pockets just visible above the rim of her lower eyelid. She must have been at one time a beautiful woman, plainly, Deliverance determined. Years had thickened her waist, giving her a matronly air. She was decidedly shorter than Jack and of even height with Eleanor. Her high collared dress, though impeccably clean somehow reminded Deliverance of dusty, old curtains, though why, she was not certain. She was neat as a pin. Her steely grey hair was gathered into a succinct bun and her leather shoes were carefully spit shined.

Stevens, who had only a few wispy salt and pepper strands of hair combed evenly across his scalp, was of a lanky build. He was the kind of man who seemed as though someone had stretched him and through sheer lean muscle had snapped back into the shape of a man. He had kindly cerulean blue eyes beneath generous brows, which hung lower when the man sunk into deep contemplation. They did not seem to be of close relation to Jack, but one could never really know. The seamstress and the shoemaker back on Nar were both brunettes and yet had a brood of churlish redheaded boys, each of them more flame-touched than the last.

Eleanor's relation to Jack, however, was evident. The curve of their high cheekbones, the darker, olive tone of their skin, and their intelligent coffee-colored eyes framed in thick lashes were almost identical. Eleanor's chin was more delicate, her figure much slighter than Jack's solid frame, but the resemblance was uncanny. Had she had any hair, Deliverance would have guessed it would be the same shiny raven as Jack's.

The girl seemed to have revived from her bout of disappointment. She sat up straighter on the embroidered chaise she had plopped down on earlier.

"Does that mean I...?" Eleanor began, but Jack cut her off with a gesture of his hand.

"No," he replied curtly.

"But..." she protested.

"No. Not yet anyway."

"Not yet? So that means I can then? Eventually?" Eleanor pleaded. Deliverance was lost as to what they were discussing, her eyes bouncing around the debating figures in the room. Obviously, it had perked the girl up though.

"Miss Eleanor, you know the doctors said..." Mrs. Potter began, reaching to fuss over the girl. Eleanor shrugged her off.

"But that was months ago! I am getting better!" she retorted in an exasperated tone.

"Better is not fully recovered, young lady," Mrs. Potter countered sternly, withdrawing from her efforts to fuss over the girl. Jack cast her a reproving stare, and Eleanor relented.

"Yes, Mrs. Potter. I know you only want what is best," the girl grumbled reluctantly. Deliverance was starting to see the family dynamic at play here, with Stevens and Mrs. Potter taking pseudo guardian roles, especially over Eleanor.

Jack, in the meantime, had snapped his fingers and lit the hearth, bringing some warmth into the room.

"Central heat is still a bit drafty in these old houses, I'm afraid," he said by way of explanation to no one in particular.

Deliverance did not know where exactly the center of this palatial house was, but she was certain they were not anywhere close to it, and yet it was still quite cozy in the drawing room. She supposed it was named a drawing room after the easels and pots of paints and charcoals strewn about one corner of the room. But it also contained a rolling bar stand and luxurious seating around the fireplace. Paintings displaying a dizzying array of styles and tastes adorned the walls, including some portraits Deliverance could only assume were of family members. Sweeping drapes in rich fabrics matched the tasteful, elaborate furnishings. Even the flooring was ornate, with patterns worked into the wood. Ornate was exactly the word Deliverance would use to describe the whole ambiance. Imagine decorating even the floor one walked on! What opulence they had here.

And yet Jack, despite his regal features, seemed somewhat out of place here. It made no sense considering he must own the property. And yet he seemed more suited to the pirate ship than this decadent setting. Perhaps it was the fire in him.

Eleanor piped up again, zeroing in on Deliverance with an assessing gaze. "So when—?" she began but was cut off. The poor girl seemed to be forever interrupted.

"It has to be controlled…scientific. We cannot simply go about it here in the privacy of the manor without documentation," said Jack, turning to gaze at the fire, as if the dancing flames in the hearth would aid in his machinations.

"But would that not mean exposing her, milord?" Stevens asked hesitantly.

"It will all have to be aired out eventually, Stevens, but we must do so with the utmost care so that we get the outcome we seek. That is paramount. We cannot go about this business willy nilly," Jack said in a calculating manner, eyes moving as he seemed to be cataloging variables in his mind.

"Ok, excuse me. Pardon my ignorance, but what in the Fades are we talking about?" Deliverance burst out, finally not being able to withhold her curiosity and apprehension any longer. They all turned and stared at her as if they had forgotten she was in the room.

They all began talking at once.

CHAPTER 11

Deliverance

"Fades? Oh wow, she has the customs and everything!" Eleanor exclaimed gleefully while Stevens began a discourse on something to do with their parliament. Mrs. Potter seemed more concerned with maintaining Jack's reputability in society due to his duties. Jack simply apologized for leaving her behind in the conversation. It came out in a jumble of words Deliverance could not quite sort through.

It was Eleanor who broke through the cacophony and silenced everyone. "Why, they mean to use my gift to help you!" she said. "I am a healer, but not of the physical. My magical gift is quite a bit more rare. I did not have a chance to use it more than a half dozen times before...before my treatments began, and it became too dangerous for me to use magic."

Treatments? Ah, so the little girl must have been stricken with an illness. Perhaps that was why she lacked hair — an illness, Deliverance thought with clarity.

"Anyway," Eleanor continued. "My gift is to fix other people's gifts."

"What she means is that she heals magical maladies. Magic is a part of us. It sits in our blood, working through our circulatory system. So, like anything physical, it can get sick or be injured. Eleanor is able to sense that which is ill in someone's magic system and heal it," Jack explained with greater clarity.

"They literally did not know what was wrong with my gift. Like, I never manifested any spark for the longest time. They thought my growth was stunted or something," Eleanor chattered. "But then one day I shook hands with a man at the hospital and boom! There it was!"

Jack cleared his throat. "Yes, it was rather unexpected. It is a little unsettling to see her gift in action."

Eleanor stuck her tongue out at her older brother. "Whatever. They didn't know what was wrong with the man. They thought he had some rare form of Parkinson's but in reality his magic was short-circuiting. I figured it out!" she declared proudly.

Deliverance nodded. She did not know who Parkinson was or why he was diseased, but she assumed it was grave. It made sense magic, being tied with the corporeal body, could also become ill. It was fascinating there was such an array of magical gifts that a brother may breath fire and a sister could heal the intangible.

"Yes and you did a fine job, Miss Eleanor, but you know what the doctors said," Mrs. Potter interjected.

The girl rolled her eyes. "Yes…that I am not supposed to use my gift until I am fully recovered. But I should be off restriction soon! I've finished the courses of treatments and they say the cancer is gone!" she protested.

"Just because it is in remission does not mean your body is fully recovered!" Mrs. Potter replied. It was evident the elderly woman was used to caring for the brash young woman. She took the girl's protests in stride.

"Agreed," Jack interrupted, and clearly his word was final. He sidled over to his sister and put an arm around her thin shoulders and plopped a kiss upon her crown. "I cannot have any risk to my best girl, can I?" She smiled up at him begrudgingly, although Deliverance could see the adoration shining behind her façade of indignation.

"Could I at least just check to see if I can detect anything? Please? It won't mess anything up and I can do it again later under other circumstances. I promise I won't mess with anything!" Eleanor pleaded with her brother. Jack met Deliverance's questioning eyes.

"I suppose…I admit I am curious myself. But in the end, it is all entirely up to Deliverance what she wants to be done," Jack answered levelly.

Deliverance returned their abated glances with a quizzical one. "I am not sure I entirely understand what you mean," she admitted.

"She wants to see if she can detect your magical malady," Jack explained.

"Magical malady?"

"I…have a magical malady?"

"Yes, or illness…a genetic condition if you will."

"Oh…so I'm sick?" Deliverance finally asked with trepidation.

"In a sense, yes," Jack said gently. "All the people of Nar are."

"Everyone on the entire island!?"

Jack took her hand and pulled her onto a seat with him on one of the numerous lovely sofas in the room. He kept a hold of her hand and clasped his other on top in a comforting gesture.

"Yes, I am afraid that may be the case. It has been that way for hundreds of years."

"I still don't understand. How could you possibly know?" Deliverance stammered, trying to wrap her mind around it all. Her entire island was…sick? Was it dangerous? It could not be if they had thrived for hundreds of years without noticing it.

"It's rather a large source of academic study and political debate here, actually," Jack began, but Eleanor cut him off.

"Jack's main platform as a Senator is Narisi rights," she informed Deliverance proudly, as if Deliverance would be impressed by this knowledge. She might be if she had any idea what it meant.

Deliverance

"Eleanor, that's not important right now." Jack scolded his younger sister. He turned to Deliverance and continued, "A little over seven hundred years ago, the people of Nar were stricken by a magic plague. This was before their pilgrimage to the island — the Exodus, I believe you call it." Deliverance nodded for him to go on. "The plague rendered men's magical abilities completely inert. We are not entirely sure if they are dormant or if the plague completely eradicated the magic from their bloodstreams. The women, however, were affected a little bit differently. Their abilities began to shift...to change. Not much was understood at the time about the plague other than the women's abilities became erratic and it seemed they could steal or mimic others' powers. You have to understand — adults grow into being able to control their abilities, and when adult women suddenly had their gifts shift and change, it caused mass chaos. Women who had previously been healers accidently burned down whole villages when they touched a fire breather. Thoughts were unknowingly stolen from people by women who were unaware their gift had shifted to a memory-eating. A lot of people died. And many more feared what they did not comprehend or know how to control.

"And so the King of Nar at the time was confronted by the other world rulers and threatened with exile to the island of Nar, in order to save everyone else and to keep the plague from spreading. The king agreed to go without a fight only if the other rulers could find a way to rein in the destruction the Narisi women were waging. He did not want to exile his people to an island and have them consume themselves in magic death. His queen, Queen Arwen the III, had not yet been stricken by the plague, and provided an avenue to help contain the plague on the island. She was a powerful sorceress and some say the king himself, powerful in his own right as a lightning-bringer, was jealous of her craft. Queen Arwen agreed to contain the women's abilities by bringing down the naming curse onto the women of Nar once they reached the island. It was Arwen's last act as a sorceress, as the naming curse blighted her own power at the same time it took all the other women's. She is considered a heroine in Arcanton historical texts. And so the women of Nar have been rendered almost magic-less, save for the gift of their name at birth. It was not until modern day, in recent studies done by the University at Oxdale, that they learned the women on Nar still retained the genetic markers of the plague. We knew from crafted interaction with the male leadership of Nar that they remained magically inert. But it was not until Oxdale undertook controversial research that we understood the women would…well, do what you do, once they left the confines of the island."

"You mean, mimic and change gifts?" Deliverance asked, after pausing to take it all in. Jack nodded grimly.

"I could probably fix her," Eleanor broke in pertly.

"That we do not know," Jack replied with a warning look in his eyes.

Deliverance's mind was racing. She was sick? They were all sick? But people had lived full lives on Nar for hundreds of years…it was not life threatening, at least. The more she pondered it though, the more she realized it did not matter if they lived full lives—they did not live the lives they were born to live. The unfairness of it hit her like a branch to the forehead.

She stood up with a shot, ignoring the looks she garnered from the others in the room, and went to pace by the windows. Seeing the outdoors, she reasoned, might help to calm her turbulent mind. But the folds of opulent fabric in the curtains and all the curious straight lines of the groomed garden outside only served to frustrate her more…to inundate her more in the foreign. Until she saw the stars. The same stars Effie and Cat would be seeing on Nar…if they were not relegated to the mines. The God of Horizons was still at work, turning the world slowly, and so she must turn along with it.

"Master Jack, you must realize what a shock this whole ordeal must be for the young woman!" Mrs. Potter was saying to Jack when Deliverance brought her attention back to the room before her.

"Pish posh. She's been handling everything up until now with the constitution of a soldier!" Jack replied. He didn't seem to be dismissing Mrs. Potter's sentiment, but rather boasting about her bearing.

"Still, it will be best to introduce her slowly to what the world is now…or what it is outside, rather," Mrs. Potter cautioned.

"Yes, I suppose," Jack relented. "So, you and Eleanor will have your hands full for the next few days while I try to track down the elusive Lord Asher."

"He is elusive?" Deliverance interjected curiously.

"Erm...he is...eccentric. His proclivities include ranting and disappearing into his world of study and research like a hermit. Oh, and also drowning himself in Scotch," Jack said dryly.

"Jack got assigned to work with Professor Asher when he showed his intent to support Oxdale's research in the Senate," Eleanor informed her. "He did not find Professor Asher to be...effectual."

"He's bloody barmy," Jack corrected her. Eleanor rolled her eyes at her brother as if she, a lady, could not use such course language. Mrs. Potter tut-tutted at him as well. "But, he has a lot to answer for, and I shall thoroughly enjoy sticking him in the hot seat."

Hot seat!? Deliverance glanced at Jack, visions of a man strapped to a chair and Jack roasting him like a pig dancing across her vision. No, it must be an expression, she decided. No one else seemed remotely alarmed, and she did not peg them to be deranged.

"So," Jack announced, clapping his hands together in anticipation for whatever schemes were circulating in that active mind of his, "while I do that, Eleanor and Mrs. Potter, see that Deliverance is brought up to speed and also well concealed."

Mrs. Potter regarded Deliverance with a sharp eye, as if assessing all the work she had ahead of her. "It will not be an easy task, sir," she said.

"Which is why I am entrusting it to you. Family can withstand anything, right Mrs. Potter?" Jack came over and put an arm around the elder woman's shoulders.

Deliverance could see any protests melt away and be replaced with unadulterated pride in those slate grey eyes of hers. "Leave it to you, to use my words against me," she muttered, although good-naturedly.

"Right, so that's settled then," Jack said. Deliverance had the distinct impression Jack had been charming his way out of the bunch for most of his life. For him, it was never a question whether they would support him, even if he brought a strange Narisi woman home and expected them to hide her. It struck her that perhaps he often pulled antics, and that could be another reason they took the situation in relative stride.

"Can I at least see if I can detect anything in her?" Eleanor broke in, not having given up her previous quest.

Jack paused, evidently thinking a million steps ahead into whatever plan he was machinating in his mind. He sighed. "Yes, I suppose…but NO tinkering!" he warned.

Eleanor's demeanor brightened like a gas lamp. "Yay! Okay, let me see. Miss Deliverance…can I just call you Deliverance?"

"You may if I can call you Eleanor…it reminds me of a friend…from home," Deliverance said.

Eleanor seemed pleased with this arrangement and beckoned her to come stand in front of her. The girl also stood, although she only came up in height to Deliverance's throat. Deliverance had always been a tad taller than the other girls on the island. Her mother would always correct her when she referred to herself as ogre-ish in those awkward early teen years. You are *lithe*, she would insist, replacing the bad self-image with the good.

"Ok, now remove your gloves please," Eleanor instructed, but added, "Oh, those are exquisite though."

"They were actually meant for you. Your brother was going to gift them to you," Deliverance said, although she didn't really want to distract the girl if she needed to concentrate.

Eleanor waved a hand. "You shall need them more than I in the coming days. Now place your hands, palms facing down, lightly atop mine. Remain there, and do not move." She proffered her own delicate hands, palms upward in front of her expectantly.

Carefully, as though reaching to touch a skittish colt for the first time, Deliverance lowered her hands to Eleanor's waiting ones. The girl closed her eyes in concentration, her eyes shifting beneath silky eyelids. They remained like that for several moments before Eleanor's eyes slammed open, wider than Deliverance thought could be possible for a human—and they glowed effervescent green, beaming from her bulking sockets. Deliverance, in her efforts to remain absolutely still, became aware the girl seemed to be getting taller. But through her peripheral vision she saw the girl was not growing…but floating. The heels of her feet lifting from the floor until just the tips of her toes remained in contact with the parquet floor.

Then as suddenly as it began, it dissipated. Eleanor touched back to the ground, her eyes fading to their normal coco, righting themselves in their sockets. Deliverance quickly removed her hands.

"Told you it was disturbing," Jack said wryly. Eleanor seemed to snap right out of her trance and yet again poked that pink tongue out in his direction.

"Oh no, it's not that. I just did not want to absorb her gift," Deliverance said, not wanting to be unkind to the girl whose gift was actually quite uncomfortable to see.

"Oh, you wouldn't have. I blocked that from happening. I learned to do that as one of the first safety steps in curing magic illness. It's like…magical hygiene, I suppose," Eleanor said matter-of-factly. Then she turned to Jack. "You saw it right?"

"Yes. You light up like a ghoulish jack o' lantern," Jack confirmed. Deliverance decided whoever Jack was, his lantern must be absurdly creepy.

Eleanor turned her attention back to Deliverance, not rising to her brother's bating. "That means," she said to her, "that there is a detectable malady in you. Otherwise nothing would have happened. My gift only activates when there is something to fix."

Deliverance nodded, her stomach deflating a bit. So, it was true then. She had some sort of affliction.

"I was prodding at the edges of it though…it's hard to explain in words exactly how I go about doing it. But I could see a good picture of it in my mind. If I were allowed to…" Eleanor reasoned, although Jack cut her off with a warning stare. "Yes, okay fine. I'm just saying I think I can fix it, given a chance."

Jack beamed. "That's my girl. I knew you had it in you...but one step at a time. There is more at play here than just remedying one woman."

"I know," Eleanor said while the others in the room agreed as well. The girl seemed to inflate under her brother's praise. She must hold him in high regard, Deliverance thought. They all seemed to, in each other in return. It was a reassuring thought that perhaps she was amongst trustworthy people. It imbued her with a small flame of warmth that although she was marooned in this alien world, she was surrounded by people of character. Deliverance had learned from a young age to be critical and assess the character of those around her and trusted her gut in this.

"Right well, it's late and there is much to do," Jack said finally, drawing their "family meeting" to a close. "Remember to keep what you say about Deliverance from prying ears." They promised, and stood to go about the rest of the night.

"Mrs. Potter, I think the Green Room for Miss Deliverance," Jack instructed Mrs. Potter, after giving Deliverance an assessing look. Deliverance turned away. She was not used to such intense study, especially not from a man. Not from one she respected or felt any sort of affection for anyway.

"Very good, sir," Mrs. Potter said and turned to collect Deliverance.

"Oh and set out something for her to wear. I intend to take her out early tomorrow morning. Something she does not need help getting into but will disguise her well," Jack said and turned to start discussing plans with Stevens.

"Master Jack, is that wise?" Mrs. Potter asked, looking at Deliverance apprehensively.

Jack turned back to her, but instead of being peeved, as the men on Nar might have been had their orders been questioned, he seemed cheerful. A mischievous glint flitted across his eyes. "Frankly, I do not care how prudent it is. Deliverance has been deprived of the world for long enough. I intend to show her all I possibly can of it." With that he broke into a satisfied grin and bade the ladies good night.

Deliverance wondered if he enjoyed thwarting whatever powers that be. She suspected that might be the case and that he derived great enjoyment from doing so.

After leading her through a dizzying array of hallways bedecked in artwork and paneling, Mrs. Potter led her to her room.

"It is to your liking, Miss?" the older woman asked as she drew the curtains and starlight filtered into the room. The windows overlooked a massive garden, and Deliverance could hear the babbling of the tile-and-stonework fountain below chortling a song to the night sky. She wandered over to the feature wall, green like the name of the room, and ran her fingers along the velvety filigreed vines, emerald atop a field of the same green her basil plants obtained in the height of summer when their leaves were plump with sun.

"Very much so. It is much fancier than I am used to..." Deliverance replied, then added, "My favorite color is green. I wonder how Jack knew that?"

Mrs. Potter clucked as she set about turning down the mattress and doing various other tasks about the room. "My Jack, he is a thoughtful boy. And quick as a whip." She pulled some plush looking fabrics from the armoire. "He'll talk his way into knowing just about anything he wants to know without you even realizing you told him, that one."

Deliverance nodded. This seemed an accurate assessment of him.

"Now, through here is the bathroom," Mrs. Potter said, tapping a switch on the wall, which lit up an adjacent room. Deliverance was starting to become used to how they illuminated their houses here. It seemed quite efficient. "You probably do not have indoor plumbing?"

When Deliverance gave her a quizzical look, she nodded. Plum-ing? Plum trees inside? There were not any trees in the tiled room only...oh. A commode...inside. How unhygienic.

Mrs. Potter must have seen her looking distastefully at the pot and gave out a hearty ha-ha! "Oh my. Do not worry. It is quite sanitary. Just pull this lever here when you've completed your business," she said and demonstrated. Water swirled through the bowl and down its gaping mouth. Interesting. Deliverance

Deliverance

wondered where the nastiness went once it had passed through the mouth. Best not dwell on that, she decided.

"And here is the shower," Mrs. Potter announced, showing her a room within the bathroom encased in glass. There was a glass door to the shower and various metal knobs and such. Mrs. Potter demonstrated how to use each of the knobs and handles.

"Amazing," Deliverance breathed. They had a waterfall inside their house! After questioning Mrs. Potter some more, who remained patient and affable despite her torrent of questions, Deliverance discovered that not only did the manor house have many of these waterfalls, but most everyone had at least one in their home in Arcanton. How very useful…and yet Deliverance still wondered where the muddy bathwater would go once it seeped through the cheese-grate looking sieve in the floor. She reasoned it could not simply just go down, otherwise all the rooms under her would be soaked.

"Do you need me to help you? I do not mind. We are both ladies," Mrs. Potter kindly offered. "I used to have to help Miss Eleanor when…when she was ill. And when she was still a babe too, of course. It's not something I bat an eyelash at."

"No, I think I can manage," Deliverance decided. Mrs. Potter gave her a button to press should she require further assistance from her tonight.

As she turned to go, she mentioned over her shoulder, "Oh, and Miss Deliverance?"

"Yes ma'am?"

"Here it is customary to shower daily."

"Daily?"

"Daily."

CHAPTER 12

Deliverance

After a few moments, Deliverance decided indoor plumbing was magical in and of itself, even if it was not actually powered by magic. It was odd at first to get used to the waterfall being so warm. Mrs. Potter explained most people enjoyed a hot shower. The waterfall in the alcove by her and her mother's homestead was frigid even in the dead of summer, its source being mountain snowcaps. It took some time to soap her hair with the various creams Mrs. Potter showed her, but the result was luxurious. She smelled like a flower, rather than the squeaky smell of lye mixed with earthy lavender, like their baths at home. Arcantons must like not smelling like people but rather…flowers or fruit. She supposed there was some merit in it. The men on Nar did not smell particularly good if they were ripe for a bath, but she did not have to deal with their odor much other than a few nasty wafts here and there selling her wares in the town square. Effie, though, she would appreciate the miracle of indoor plumbing, especially in her trade.

Deliverance stood under the waterfall long after the rivulets of dirty water turned clean. Finally, she stepped from the glass enclosure in a cloud of steam. Having shut off the water faucets, she dried herself with "towels." At home they used linen sacks, or if the weather was warm, the power of the sun. Towels were fluffy and a bit like drying oneself with a baby lamb…without that baaing.

Her worn garments had disappeared from the spot on the floor she left them, although they left a ring of sand on the marble floor in their wake. On the chair lay a simple shift made of some soft, tightly woven foreign fabric Deliverance was not familiar with. She ventured into the main bedroom chamber and tested out the bed. It was pillowed and far more giving than any bed she had ever slept in. Actually, she had only ever slept in her own bed at home since before her sea adventure, or occasionally out under the stars on a pleasant night in the soft pine needles or tall rushes. Despite all its plush virtues, Deliverance found it hard to get comfortable. After throwing open all the curtains and tinkering with the windows to let in some fresh night air, she began to relax. Finally, curled in a small corner of the overly large bed, she was able to find peace.

She must have sunk into a deep sleep because it seemed like only moments before she felt a strong, warm hand gently prodding her shoulder. There was something about his smell, the lingering of sea and pine, that told Deliverance it was Jack without opening her eyes. She did not want to open her eyes.

Deliverance

"Hmmf," she groaned and flipped over. She heard a small chuckle but tried to ignore it.

"Come on, sleepyhead. I have things to show you." His voice came. She sighed and cracked an eye open at him. The sun was not yet up.

"Do you never sleep?" Deliverance moaned, righting herself in bed.

"Not when adventure awaits," Jack said, cheerfully tossing various garments from the chair onto the bed in front of her. She assumed Mrs. Potter had left them out. She sat up a little straighter. Adventure sounded good…and what was that smell?

"And here is a little incentive to get dressed," Jack said, handing her a mug of steaming coffee. It smelled divine.

"My hero," Deliverance said, inhaling the aroma from the heady vapors. He chuckled again and left the room swiftly, so she could get dressed. True to her word, Mrs. Potter had selected clothing she could don herself, although she had to figure out what order the various skirts went in.

She gave it a try then called Jack in, who proceeded to laugh out loud and tell her to try again. Deliverance reversed the order of the skirts and called him in again.

"Better…I think. Although I must admit I am no expert in these matters. Here, take this. It will be chilly at this hour," Jack said, and pulled a heavy, green velvet cloak around her shoulders. She stood still as he fastened it at her throat. "There, I think we're ready."

"Where are we going?" she asked, as they descended the main staircase and wound their way out the back of the house toward another outbuilding.

"That, my darling, is a surprise," Jack said impishly and led her inside. It was a stable for the aught-to-mobiles. Although they were eerily silent. Her stables at home were always filled with snorts, stamps, whinnies, and all the other sounds that made a barn come alive.

Jack helped her into the front seat of one of the aught-to-mobiles and got in the other side.

"Um," Deliverance said. "The gate is still closed." The large door in front of them was still shut. Jack must have forgotten to open it before taking the reins…the wheel, of the mobile.

"Oh, haha. Right!" Jack exclaimed, and with a click of a button, the gate started to pull itself open. He awakened the mobile with a twist of its key, and away they went.

The morning was just beginning to grow into the sky as the God of Horizons began to shift his cloak. The black of deep, resting night was making way for royal, promising blue. Through the headlights, Deliverance could see them winding through the city, but it was still too dark to make out much of it besides that which the curious not-flickering street lamps illuminated on their posts. The sheer scale of the buildings and variety of architecture as they whizzed by awed her. They passed several spacious parks, lit up with lamps and fairy lights. On their edges perched stately manors and what Deliverance would call castles. She craned her neck to see up the largest clock tower she had ever seen, which really was not saying much as the largest and only one she had ever seen was the one in Nar's town square. It was only four stories high at the most. It was slightly frustrating to try to take in all the sights in the dark and limited by the windows of the aught-to-mobile, but she suffered silently. Jack, for his part, drove smiling silently to himself.

After they crossed a thick river obscured by the dark, Jack whirled the aught-to-mobile to a screeching halt and hopped out. He rounded the vehicle, popped her door open, and pulled Deliverance to her feet. The wind left her as she took in the gigantic wheel in front of them. There were hardly any people around this early in the morning, and the structure seemed, although gaily lit with lights brighter than Deliverance had ever seen, asleep.

"Come along," Jack said as he brought her closer to the behemoth monster. "It normally does not run at this hour...but well, I called in a favor."

Affixed to the wheel were numerous translucent pods, taller than a man and the size of several hog pens.

"You don't mean we're going into those...bubbles!?" Deliverance said, pulling back, suddenly a little apprehensive.

"It's perfectly safe, I assure you," Jack said. "I'll be right there. Just like I was on our skydive."

Deliverance shook her head as if to clear it. Of course, he was right. If he could go into one of those little pods, then so could she. Cautiously, she edged her way into the waiting bubble-room.

It had begun to move slowly, rotating along the massive wheel, but its motion was so slight she relaxed a bit.

"Does it go faster?" Deliverance asked, venturing to the edge of the pod after glancing over her shoulder at Jack to ensure it was okay for her to traverse near the windows.

"Nope. It is actually quite tame compared to some of our previous endeavors," Jack replied, joining her by the edge of the window.

"Look! The sun is rising!" Deliverance cried, as they rounded the bottom of the massive, spoked contraption and began to rise themselves. The God of Horizons donned peaches and vermilions as he discarded his indigo night robes. The illuminated palaces along the sluggish river below them began to glow of their own accord, although the clock face of the giant clock tower still shone an eerie cat's eye yellow despite the rising sun. She was transfixed. The enormity of the scene alighting before her eyes stole the very breath from her lungs. It was not until Jack reminded her to breathe that she realized it. They climbed higher as the sun pulled itself into a full orb on the horizon. The city was absolutely massive and it was beginning to wake.

"There are no other people in the pods," Deliverance remarked, not peeling her eyes from the city unfolding before her. Who knew anything like this could exist in the world?

"No, I called in a favor to get them to run the Ferris Wheel for me. I wanted you to see the world…I want you to see the whole world," Jack said, not watching the scene, but watching her. He seemed to be deriving as much pleasure from watching her take in the Arcanton capital of Lontown as she was taking it in.

"Can we see Nar from here?" she asked, her hand on the glass making small ghosts.

"No. This is just a small piece of the world. But I would show you the whole thing if I could," Jack said gently, eyes never leaving her.

For a moment, Deliverance slid her eyes sideways and assessed him. "You must be pretty important to call in favors such as this… Senator."

At this he coughed uncomfortably. "Not nearly as influential as I would like to be and far more in the public's eye than I would like to be as well. I see you caught my title."

"Yes, I do not know much about Arcanton, but I do know it is a Republic and the Senate is the highest level of lawmaking in it," Deliverance replied. "Are you not too young to be a Senator?"

"I am 27. And no, unfortunately things in Lontown, like much of the world, depend on where you were born and who you know. Which is entirely unfair and yet so is much of life. For better or worse I was born into a position where I could affect some good. After some prodding in my younger years, I realized it was foolish not to make use of what God granted me."

"You were in the military before?" Deliverance asked, still absorbing the scenery, but keen to also absorb everything she could about this mysterious pirate-turned-senator.

"Aye. I was a bit of a rebellious sort in my younger years. Did not want much to do with the status and wealth I was born with. As soon as I was old enough, I enlisted in the Arcanton Republic military and was sent to a fire breather brigade. It was not until I served a few tours and life had knocked some sense into me that I began to understand it was not necessarily what I wanted out of life that mattered, but what those around me needed. The Plaedes-Arcanton conflict was...brutal. Most of the men were there out of necessity to feed their families and the government was not making enough efforts to actually win or end the conflict. Around the same time Eleanor fell ill, my brigade was nearly wiped out in a battle, save for three of my men and I. I was offered a chance to gain an appointment to the Senate, and was going to turn it down, but it was my sergeant's dying wish that I take the appointment." Jack cleared his throat, choking down the emotional memory. "He knew Eleanor needed me and that I, unlike so many of them, actually had a chance to affect real change. He told me the fight was not necessarily always on the field of battle. That stuck with me ever since."

He fell silent after this revelation and regarded the skyline. They had reached the pinnacle of the wheel. Deliverance's mind was also wheeling, not from just the immense sights but the depths of the man next to her. There was so much she wanted to know. She reached over and covered his hand, resting on the metal railing, with her own. At first she could feel his power wanting to leap into the capillaries of the undersides of her fingers, but she blocked it, and soon it became natural...just two hands joined in comfort.

After a while, a niggling thought itched in the back of Deliverance's mind. The shape of the skyline seemed...familiar somehow. It could not be possible. She would have remembered seeing a painting or sketching of such an immense city if it were in any of the few books she had seen on Nar. But something about the colors and the dramatic sweeps of the bridges...

"My glass globe!" Deliverance exclaimed.

"Come again?" Jack asked, frowning.

"My glass globe...it was a small trinket I had back home on Nar. It was a small glass orb about yeah big on a pedestal. When you would shake it, little fake snow would flutter around the fairy city inside...*this* fairy city," Deliverance said, pieces starting to click in place.

"So you're saying...you had a snow globe of Arcanton?" Jack asked incredulously.

"Snow globe? If that is what you call such a thing, then yes. I have one. It is stowed away in our floorboard cache where we keep our books and other items we do not necessarily want the menfolk of Nar knowing we have," Deliverance said. In her mind's eye she could see the rough, knotted pine boards and the small catch in the seam where they would pry them up. In it, their treasures—the couple books she and Cat had in their careworn leather covers, some heirloom lockets and brooches, paper and quills for her mother's messages, some curious flags or other knickknacks Deliverance had been warned not to mess with, her mother's herbal physick grimoire, and among the bits and bobs,

Deliverance's snow globe. She could not remember how she had come to possess it. Perhaps it too had been an heirloom?

"That is rather an odd possession for a Narisi woman," Jack said, affirming what she was thinking. How on earth had it come into their care?

The city awakened as they descended. Steam dirigibles, smaller than the ship they came in on, dotted the sky over the city. Automobiles, Deliverance learned from Jack earlier, not aught-to-mobiles, piled up like worker ants along the twisted streets and the muddy, sluggish river reluctantly tugged vessels of every size in its brackish waters. There were several pedestrians about as Deliverance and Jack alit from the Ferris Wheel and returned to his car. Car was another word for aught-to...no, automobile.

As they came down the ramp, Deliverance spotted a woman more unusual than she had ever seen in her life. The woman, not much older than her mother, had an elegant carriage, fine silks clinging to her skin, and beautiful high cheekbones. But her skin seemed to be burnt. Deliverance could not help but stop and stare. The woman did not take any notice of her in return but was fussing with a baby pram as she ambled down the pathway. No, her skin was not burnt. It was glowing with health...it was simply the color of burnished ebony. Her hair hung in intricate braids that wap-wap-waped along her back as she pushed her baby carriage along, like tiny fishing net lines, except built for ensnaring glances rather than fishes.

Jack coughed beside her, breaking her trance. Very slyly, he reached up under her chin and closed her gaping mouth. "It's rather bad form to stare, love," he said with a smile.

Immediately Deliverance colored in embarrassment. "I...oh. Sorry. It's just I have never seen anyone so beautiful before," Deliverance murmured, ashamed of her poor manners.

"Yes, from what I understand, Nar is quite ethnically homogenous," Jack replied, not unkindly. He seemed to understand her faux pas and take it in stride.

"Most everyone has blond hair or brunette, or sometimes even red. There is no one such as that woman. Is she...born that way?" Deliverance asked curiously, sneaking another sideways glance at the foreign woman.

"Yes, quite. And you will find the world is made of people of all shapes, sizes, and colors. Traditionally Arcantons were like Narisis. But in the past several hundred years, our demographics have expanded both because of friendly relations and some misguiding colonial efforts. We've had dark times, unfortunately, when people of color, or people with darker skintones like that woman, were oppressed or enslaved even. We have since reformed, or at least the vast majority of society has, but we are not proud of that piece of our history. It is part of my job as a man of law to make sure that does not happen again," Jack explained as they took a jaunt on the path beside the river.

"I can't imagine," Deliverance exclaimed.

"Can you not?" Jack answered, his tone indifferent, but his look seemingly baiting.

"I do not know what you mean." Deliverance replied.

"Can you make law?" Jack asked.

"What, here?"

"No. On Nar. Are you eligible to make legal decisions?"

"I...no. I suppose not. The assembly is made of men. They select their representatives at the Men's Hall. I know not of their procedures," Deliverance replied, unsure.

"Okay. Well then can a married woman on Nar own property then?" Jack asked, going a different direction.

"Well...I suppose she would not have the need to. Her husband would be in charge of whatever property there was in a marital union," Deliverance replied again.

"So, if you were to marry, all your possessions would really be your husband's?" Jack asked, following a line of logic Deliverance did not see the end of yet. She nodded. "So, really all you own, you own because you are either not married or exclude yourselves from society?"

He was right. Cat and Deliverance had reign over their homestead because it was just them and they kept to themselves. Effie had some freedom, but she had to wheel and deal for it, and owed a large portion of whatever she came by back to the Village Common.

"What of punishments? Who decides those?" Jack asked again.

"In the village? The Reave and sometimes a council selected from the Men's Hall," Deliverance answered, starting to feel an uncomfortable truth revealed before her.

"Ah…so men again. What about marriage then? Does a woman select her husband?" Jack interrogated.

"Don't be daft! No, a father does…although usually with his wife's council." Deliverance protested.

"Ah, with his wife's council…but he has the final say though then?" Jack ferreted out. She nodded again.

"Reading?"

"Discouraged for women."

"Trades?"

"Only with the husband's permission and only a select few like seamstress or baker's assistant."

"And your gods?"

"They're…all male," Deliverance admitted, resigning to something she could never quite put her finger on until now. Inequity.

"So, let me get this straight. You cannot vote. You cannot hold offices of power. You can only own property in a limited capacity. And you cannot even read for the most part," Jack enumerated.

Deliverance nodded with a lump in her throat. When he put it so blatantly it seemed entirely and horrifically unfair.

"Sounds to me like you do know a thing or two about oppression then, wouldn't you say, my love?" Jack made his point as they ambled along. Deliverance nodded gravely. It seemed so simple. How had she not thought about it until now?

She fell silent as she contemplated this, coupled with the surroundings. The river below became more congested as the morning drew on and the crass cries of boatmen mixed with seagulls and motorists' horns. Two-wheeled contraptions whirled by them on the promenade, weaving around pedestrians in an assortment of dress. Many were decked out in suits for the men, or ornate multi-layered dresses not unlike the one Deliverance was wearing, for the women. But occasionally she would see both men and women in plain pajama-looking clothing or long white jackets, which Jack explained meant they probably worked in medicine or science. The men with rougher looking pants, tool belts, and shiny, bulbous hats were construction workers of various sorts. Deliverance used to feel odd wearing her leather pants back on Nar. Women did not usually wear such things, but they gave her greater freedom of motion in the forest and were better for farm work, and so she bore the stares of the village people if they happened upon her in such garb. Here there were so many people in such an array of dress that no one looked sideways at a woman in pants…or a man in a dress, even. Jack did mention the man in a dress was wearing something called a kilt, but still, Deliverance decided it was quite progressive.

"What about women here?" Deliverance asked finally, deciding to end her brooding and find out more about Arcanton instead.

"They are all different. They are wives, mothers, sisters. But they are also university professors, doctors, lawyers, and politicians. Our senate is full of women representatives," Jack said.

Deliverance thought of Effie. "What about…women who like other women?" She couldn't quite believe what he had said on the ship about Arcantons being so accepting.

Jack glanced at her and for a second Deliverance thought he might say something untoward, but unexpectedly he asked, "Why, are you…?"

"What? Oh—no, I don't think so at least. The reason I asked is because of my best friend, Effie. She…is like that from what I gather. It's one of the reasons we're in this mess, I suppose," Deliverance said.

"No, we're in this mess because the men of Nar have their heads stuck up their arses and have had them firmly affixed there for several hundred years. If you ask me, they feel really inadequate because they've no magic themselves," Jack replied. "But to answer your question, like I said before, it is something that is allowed here. Women marrying women, or vice versus, men marrying men. We try not to discriminate based upon skin color *or* what you like to do in the bedroom. At least that's the idea of it. What we strive for. It may fall short sometimes in reality. But that's the job of a senator—to help society become more open and progressive."

Deliverance had colored a little at the mention of the bedroom. After her friendship with Effie, she was well aware of the mechanics of what went on there...she just had never had the inkling of wanting to find out in the first person. It was not the sort of thing one discussed openly on Nar...only behind closed doors if your best friend was a whore.

"Well we had best be back. Mrs. Potter is having kittens that I brought you out here, but frankly I refuse to shutter you up like a caged animal. This is the world, and I mean to show it to you as best I can!" Jack announced. "However, she might neuter me if we are not back in time for breakfast, so in the interest of any future little Jacks that may occur, let's get back to the manor."

Deliverance smiled at his wit and they hurried back to Jack's parked...car. Driving back in the daylight was eye opening. Lontown was whirring with activity on the ground, in the sky, and on the water. The only stagnancy was in the stately architecture and looming towers, providing constant in all that action.

Jack and Eleanor's manor—which he referred to curiously like a human, with the name Hathaway—was even more resplendent in the sunlight. Creeping, luscious vines snaked along brownstone terraces and multi-paned windows reflected the brightness of day. The buttresses and lines of the imposing house were softened by the healthy primrose bushes blossoming about the grounds and the trickle of garden fountains.

Jack pulled the car around the side but did not park it in the garage. Instead he tossed the keys to a teenage-looking boy in the bricked driveway and gave him some instructions about oil changes? Perhaps cars needed their nappies changed like babies, Deliverance pondered.

"It's a glorious morning and I'm ravenous for breakfast!" Jack said to her cheerfully as they entered through the main doorway. "We're back in time that Mrs. Potter should not be too peeved."

His gay, carefree smile, however, rapidly slid from his brow as he spotted two figures loitering in the foyer.

CHAPTER 13

Deliverance

"Damn, we should have come in the side entrance. At least then we'd have had some warning…maybe we can still sneak away," Jack whispered, grabbing Deliverance by the arm and attempting to steal away before they were noticed.

"Jack!" A decidedly shrill female voice broke across the space. "Dear Cousin Jack! Is that you? It is!"

"Damn damn damn damn," Jack swore under his breath, then plastered on a broad ostentatious smile and spun around to meet the two figures. "Aunt Claude. Cousin Caroline. How…unexpected to see you."

Jack gave the two women pecks on each of their cheeks in obligation after closing the distance. They were a younger and an older version, one just a tad greyer and more wrinkled than the other. They were trussed up in layers of rustling skirts, with buttons and lace in intricate patterns. Each had pristine kidskin gloves lined with careful buttons and a fluted, folded parasol, in one hand. Deliverance could see some family resemblance in the brown eyes and dark hair, but these women were not blessed with Eleanor and Jack's graceful cheekbones. Their faces looked pinched, awkwardly nosed, and perhaps a tad anemic. While Jack's hair was lively and shiny, both of these women had frizzy curls teased into elaborate styles, which looked heavy and uncomfortable.

"Yes, I suppose it would be," the elder said, drawly sniffing, "since you never call or write."

"I was traveling, Aunt. You know I must often for work," Jack answered. Deliverance noticed he did not invite them in for tea or to sit and chat. He merely talked with them in the hall. She wondered if that was rude in Arcanton or normal.

"Well, we were going to come over to discuss with you an overture on the part of Senator Ribald, but your other news must simply take president!" exclaimed the younger—Caroline, Deliverance assumed. Both sets of beady eyes zeroed in on her like birds of prey. They stared at her expectantly. She stared back.

"Oh...um. Yes. Aunt Claude, Cousin Caroline, this is Deliverance...my fiancée. Deliverance, this is my lovely Aunt Claude and her even lovelier daughter, Caroline...Great, now that that is out of the way, there's a lot to do before the Senate session so you'd best be off. Love to you," Jack said and attempted to rush them out the door.

"Jack Quentin!" Aunt Claude chastised him. "Do not be base!" Jack deflated as his aunt built ballast. "The last we heard from you, you were single and the most eligible of Arcanton were waiting expectantly to see who you might take a fancy to...and now you've just come back from a trip and...well this! A fiancée! From the Southlands of all places! Really, Jack!" The elder tut-tutted like a cranky hen.

"Everyone at the club was really quite put out, Jack." Caroline sniffed, eyeing Deliverance like she was a satchel she might purchase. "Still, she is quite lovely." The girl fingered Deliverance's sleeve as she said it, considering her. Caroline's bottom lip poked out like a fat earthworm. "I myself enjoyed the intrigue. Tell me, dear, are you pregnant?"

At this both Jack and Aunt Claude had a coughing fit.

"I...what? No!" Deliverance answered, her cheeks heating with indignation. Jack recovered from his fit and grimaced, his face pained. Deliverance could tell these were not some of his favorite people.

"Pity. That would have made for some intriguing gossip. When's the wedding date? I may just say it anyway if it's close. Would cause a right stir!" Caroline chattered.

"Caroline!" Jack barked. "You will do no such thing!"

She sighed at her cousin, but acquiesced when her mother seconded that order. "You're no fun, cousin. At least say you'll come to the ball. We're hosting the debut this season. I am sure many of the girls making an appearance were hoping to catch your eye, but you should still come and bring your fiancée. It will be such fun to watch their disappointed little faces!"

Jack's eyes started to gleam as though he was about to break down. "I, like everyone in Arcanton, exist merely for you amusement, cousin," he said sarcastically.

"What your cousin so inelegantly meant to say, was that when we heard the good news, we wanted to come by and congratulate you, and also extend our invitation for the ball in felicitations," Aunt Claude said, eyeing her daughter with resigned disenchantment.

Jack traded glances with Deliverance. He looked panicked. He must need an excuse to refuse the invitation, Deliverance thought. What if… she started to work up a fake cough. She gave a couple chuff chuffs into her gloved hand and looked back at Jack. He looked at her uncomprehendingly. She tried harder, with a little more volume. COUGH COUGH COUGH.

The two women's gazes snapped to her, regarding her strangely. Jack, having finally caught on said, "Oh, right. See, we will have to send our regrets because obviously, Deliverance is ill."

HACK HACK HACK. She gave a couple chest deep wallops in there for good measure. When they looked unconvinced, Deliverance hocked some phlegm in the back of her throat for the coup d'état. A couple flecks of spittle flew across the foyer and speckled the wallpaper. They stuck there like glistening beetles.

After a couple beats, Aunt Claude said finally, "Well. There is that… lucky for you the ball is not for another week. We shall see you there, nephew."

Deliverance

As they turned to leave, Aunt Claude stopped and said in an exaggerated whisper behind her hand to Jack, "And get the girl a cough suppressant, for Christ's sake!" With a whirl of satin and hairspray, the interlopers left.

After Jack shut the door firmly behind them, his shoulders began to shake. At first, Deliverance thought he, himself, was taken with a coughing attack. But when he finally turned toward her, she could see he was not coughing, but laughing.

"Bloody brilliant!" he cawed as the laugh roared out of him. Tears threatened to stream down him face as his chest was wracked with bellowing, wheezing laughs.

Deliverance too began to laugh. It was rather ridiculous. "But it didn't work. They're still expecting you!" Deliverance managed between gasps. They had both slid down the walls into sitting positions, not being able to keep standing and laughing at that rate at the same time.

"That, my darling, will be our penance for witnessing that brilliant display. Besides it's a week away. I'm sure we can figure out a suitable cover story and get you up to speed enough. It might be fun to dance, quite literally, underneath all their noses," Jack replied, hugging his aching ribs.

"We're really not supposed to be here then? Narisis?" Deliverance asked.

"Perhaps you're not supposed to be here, but you ought to be."

CHAPTER 14

Deliverance

"Jack, who is this Christ person everyone keeps referring to?" Deliverance asked over breakfast. Eleanor had joined them and was sitting next to her, watching her every move.

"Oh how novel!" the girl piped, but quieted when Jack shot her a look.

"He's like one of your gods," Jack answered.

"Oh? You have different gods here?" Deliverance asked, although she had been expecting something like this. One of the few treasured books she and Cat had stored in their floorboard cache was a thick volume called Odysseus. Deliverance read the book, cover to cover, several times, absorbing the Plaedian masterpiece. When she learned Jack served in a conflict against Plaedes, she felt a tinge of sadness that Odysseus's society should find itself on the wrong side of a war.

"Yes, the Narisi gods are only really still acknowledged on Nar. In the Outside we have many other gods. Some worship one, others many. Christ is one of them," Jack said.

"What are your gods like?" Eleanor asked, poking at her eggs. They had taken on a gelatinous sheen due to her inattention.

"Well there is the main god we are supposed to worship, the God of Names or the Naming God. He is the definer of the female power. The Abbot has us pray to him to give us judicious work and to help us retain humility…but there is the Hunter God and the God of Horizons, as well as several lesser spirits like the merpeople and the fae…Mum and I prefer the Hunter God and the God of Horizons, although we keep this fact to ourselves and our rituals to our side of the island," Deliverance explained patiently to the younger girl.

The younger girl mulled this over before asking, "And what are the Hunter God and the God of Horizons like? I suppose the Hunter God brings you good luck in hunting and good aim? Something along those lines?"

"Yes, you would be correct in your assumption. He is my personal favorite. He also bestows grace and stealth, agility, and cunning. In depictions he is lithe and blends into the backdrops of wherever he is painted. He represents independence, which is why I like him best. Now the God of Horizons is less concrete. He is change—change of the time of day, change in the sky, change in stars, change in the seasons. He is depicted as a glorious god shedding skins or robes and donning new ones as time marches on. He is also fate and serendipity," Deliverance told her.

"How fabulous and intricate! Why does your…Abbot? Why does he prefer you worship the God of Names?" Eleanor asked, the keen interest sparking in her intelligent eyes.

Before Deliverance could answer, Jack snorted and broke in, "Because the so-called God of Names represents power limitation. The male half of the island has to keep their thumb over the female half somehow in their impotent state."

Deliverance opened her mouth, then shut it again. She had been ready to protest such a harsh depiction of her fellow islanders. But perhaps he was right? The thought left a sour tang in her mouth.

"Tell me of this Christ," she said instead.

"Well, he was a man but also the son of God. He was born a little less than three thousand years ago. The Plaedic-Romanis butchered him and when they did that, supposedly he took away sin and made it possible for humans to enter into heaven," Eleanor expounded.

"That is a rather truncated version," Jack quipped.

"And heaven is like…the Fields in the Fades?" Deliverance asked, noticing the girl enjoyed having her attention in conversation. She blossomed like a begonia in the spring sun when she could voice the ideas rolling around in her sharp mind.

"Yes, I suppose they would be similar. Many religions have a heaven or Fields-like place associated with them," Eleanor replied. Ah, so Eleanor was astute to the world around her too, drawing parallels across cultures.

"A man who was butchered does not seem to be a powerful icon," Deliverance commented, curious although not wanting to insult their god if they believed in that one. She remembered Jack might.

"Yes, I agree your Hunter God seems more awesome and powerful. And yet, it is not necessarily the image of the man himself but the great waves his life has caused since then that are a testament to his power," said Eleanor. "Whole dynasties, revolutions, advancements in science, terrible wars and hard-won peace—these are all byproducts of this one man-god's existence."

Deliverance was amused by the girl's savvy. Brains ran in the family, no doubt. "I shall have to learn more about him then. And does your brother dictate what god you must worship?" she asked.

Eleanor snorted. "Not bloody likely. I may take up your Hunter God if it pleases me."

"Eleanor, language!" Jack chastised her, finishing his meal. It had been a pleasant affair in the sunny dining area, which Deliverance understood was for informal meals. Fresh mums dotted the table in cut glass vases, and cinnamon hung in the sunlight beaming through the room-height shuttered windows. "Now I have to see if I can track down Lord Asher, and I have a few other political errands to attend to while I am out. I am leaving Deliverance entrusted to you and Mrs. Potter, Eleanor. Remember you have a job to do!"

Eleanor nodded sagely. "You can trust me. We will get her squared away!" the girl promised seriously.

"I know I can, monkey. I must be off." He plopped a kiss atop his sister's head and looked to Deliverance. He hesitated, but then grasped her hand and kissed it as well. "I shall see you lovely ladies later this evening!" And with that he was out the door.

Deliverance's cheeks warmed slightly at the gesture. She was not expecting that.

"It is okay to blush. My brother can be charming when he wishes…it just is not very often he wishes it!" Eleanor said with a bit of a smirk. She jumped to her feet. "Come along, we are to meet Mrs. Potter in the drawing room."

✸✸✸

Eleanor brought her to the same room they had the family meeting in last night, but promised a proper tour of the grounds at a later point that afternoon. Mrs. Potter was in the room, busily arranging a series of objects on a tabletop.

The morning sun leaked through the windows like shafts, ensconced on either side by an outlandish amount of fabric for drapery. Deliverance thought the valances looked a bit like some of the seashells that used to wash up on her beach.

"Good heavens!" Mrs. Potter exclaimed once Eleanor had shut the doors firmly behind them. "Jack cannot go a day without attracting trouble!"

Eleanor sniffed. "To be fair, Aunt Claude and Cousin Caroline are rather like bloodhounds. Once they catch a whiff of upward mobility, they are dogged. Hah, get it?"

"Buzzards, more like," Mrs. Potter grumbled.

"Aunt Claude and Cousin Caroline are not our favorite people," Eleanor explained as she began demonstrating the various ways a lady should sit on a piece of furniture. Deliverance mimicked her whilst listening. "When Mummy and Daddy died, they were about as cold and distant as you could get. They certainly were not any help. It was Stevens and Mrs. Potter who stepped up and helped Jack take care of me. He was only fifteen at the time. I was two, still in nappies."

"I am so sorry, Miss Quenton!" Deliverance replied, a lump forming in her stomach, both of sympathy and empathy, as her own mother was most likely at risk at this very moment. It sent a restless chill down her veins.

"Please, call me Eleanor. Jack does. It's okay. I do not really remember them, but it was quite hard on Jack. I wonder if in part he ended up joining the Republic military because of it. Although I think mostly it was to spite Aunt Claude. She and her slimy husband Reginald ferreted out Jack had an inheritance to come into when he turned 18. They figured it out when he was 17, and suddenly began fishing around for ways to become executors of Jack's estate before he came of age. Everyone was expecting him to start university at Oxdale that autumn, but instead he pulled a fast one on everybody and joined the military, as an enlisted man no less! Normally people from our social standing might choose to become officers, but he did not want to wait long enough for Aunt Claude and Uncle Reginald to weasel their way into our inheritance. Besides he said it would do the Quentins good to have some association with the real world. Jack is a firm believer in the common man. The regular bloke, if you will."

Deliverance now understood why Stevens and Mrs. Potter were family and Aunt Claude and Cousin Caroline were simply odious attachments. Eleanor had switched from sitting posture to standing posture, although she seemed rather pleased with Deliverance's carriage, and so moved on to Mrs. Potter's table. Laid out were various cutlery, as well as napkins, fans, a parasol, and a couple curious square objects Deliverance later found out were called a laptop or computer, and a cellular telephone.

Mrs. Potter turned out to be a kind and patient instructor. Between her and Eleanor's keen eyes, Deliverance learned about formal table etiquette, how to fan oneself, and how to dial a cellphone. That was the most fascinating part — the computer and the cellphone. People could talk to each other and even see each other's faces like some kind of scrying mirror across hundreds, even thousands of miles! Each laptop was like a million books compiled into one tiny pocket, and information could be brought up at will on some sort of spider's web, which Deliverance understood was an invisible network. The most fascinating part was these were not powered by magic, as Deliverance would have assumed, but by something called technology. She understood it to be innovation harnessed for its sole merits without the spark of magic. Even the men on Nar would be able to operate a cell phone. Well, if they had the chance or inclination. Some of them were rather resistant to change of any kind.

"Electrosity is like the circulatory system in a person, then? Only for light or power?" Deliverance asked.

"Electricity. Yes, that is a good way to understand it!" Mrs. Potter praised her.

Deliverance beamed. She rather liked pleasing the elderly, warmhearted woman. And Fades! The advancement these people had at their fingertips! It was amazing.

"We'll have to gird your speech. Any expressions like Fades or Gods' teeth will be dead giveaways," Mrs. Potter warned. "But picking the Southlands as your cover origin was smart on Jack's part. Your throaty drawl will be thought to be Southish. No one from Lontown society has really ventured down there anyway so they will not know the difference."

"Is Southland far away?" Deliverance inquired, making a note to learn more about this nation she supposedly was from.

"It's across the world! I shall show you on a map in the library. We are almost finished for the afternoon, aren't we, Mrs. Potter?" Eleanor said, jumping up.

"Well I had meant to...," Mrs. Potter protested, but Eleanor had already bounced out of the room. Deliverance shrugged and Mrs. Potter waved her on, indulgent smile on her crinkly, kind face.

***

A short while later in the immense, magical room called a library, Ellie showed her that Southland was a colony of Arcanton at the bottom tip of the world. It was considered both foreign and in higher society, backward.

"It's unfortunate people think of Southlanders like that. I would like to visit there someday myself. I want to visit everywhere!" Eleanor exclaimed, turning the globe absently on its spire. Around them sat two stories of nothing but books, stacked in shelves, with the top level reachable by a spiraling staircase and the top shelves each accessible by sliding ladders. Deliverance had never seen so many books in all her life.

"Oh, look, this is where you are from!" Eleanor pointed to a map she had rolled out across one of the many generously sized tables in the library.

Deliverance studied the map and realized that Nar was not all that far, in relative scale, from Arcanton's shores, which must be why they claimed political responsibility for it. She also realized, with an unsettling stir in her chest, that Nar was labeled "Narisi Restricted Zone," not "The Island of Nar" or even just plain "Nar" as she would have expected. As she stared at the miniscule blot on the map, her intuition nagged her. Her entire world up until this point was nothing more than an ink blot the size of a small housefly in relation to the rest of the world. Sometimes she enjoyed the mountains surrounding her homestead back on Nar because they would make her feel so small in relation to them. Now, here in the library at Hathaway, she did not enjoy the feeling so much.

The rest of the manor house also had this effect on Deliverance. Eleanor described it as "just their city home," and went on to tell her of their country home on the seaside.

"There is an even larger garden there than this one," Eleanor said as they wound their way around the laurel hedges outside. "And you can hear the waves crashing along the sea cliffs. It's simply magical! I imagine you will feel right at home there, when we take you."

"You are optimistic like your brother, I see," Deliverance commented, fingers brushing along the leafy structures absentmindedly.

"Yes…" Eleanor said, her face dropping in seriousness, "But that is rather the point of it all. Besides, Jack always gets his way. He will squash any resistance in parliament, you'll see."

Deliverance was not entirely sure what the entire ordeal was about, but she was beginning to understand there were large powers at play. It would not be as simple as getting help for her mother and Effie from this Lord Asher fellow, as she had previously thought.

"Ah there is Mrs. Potter over there!" Eleanor said as they rounded a corner and came into a rose garden. She waved and pulled Deliverance over to where a floppy sunhat was tending the luscious blooms. She did not seem to notice their presence at first, but instead was intent on the suffering bush before her.

"Hmm. Powdery mildew, as I suspected," the greying lady murmured, caressing the plant carefully, avoiding its thorns.

Then with a wave of her hands, a green light settled over the ailing plant, and it almost seemed to sigh in relief. Fresh, green leaves sprouted, causing the rotted ones to fall to the ground. The entire bush seemed to perk up. "There, that's better."

"Mrs. Potter is a hedge witch," Eleanor explained. "It means she's good at growing plants."

"And little girls, it seems," Deliverance joked.

Eleanor smiled. "That too. You should see her at the country house. She has whole rows of different types of lavenders, lemon and bee balm, various kinds of mint. It smells divine."

"Aye, I do favor the herbs more than these fussy roses. And they tend to be more useful besides," Mrs. Potter said, wiping the sweat from her brow.

In the pouring sunlight, the elderly lady's normally watery grey eyes took on a soft, bottle green tinge. The autumn afternoon was unseasonably warm. "An Indian summer," Deliverance remarked.

Eleanor twisted her mouth. "It's funny how you have some turns of phrase in your English that...well you really aught'n know about. Like Indian summer. Where do you suppose Narisis even learned of Indians?"

Deliverance was taken aback because Eleanor was right. She really had no idea what, or who as it turns out, an Indian was. How had that phrase managed to settle itself into Narisi phraseology? There were so many mysteries she had yet to unravel. But she intended to pick at the gnarled web of information as a knitter methodically unknots her yarn.

***

It was well past dinner before Jack returned. Mrs. Potter, Eleanor, and Deliverance were sitting by the fire in the parlor, playing a card game Eleanor called "swap widget." Deliverance found it immensely fun and was caught up in a victorious moment when Jack swept into the room, still in his coat and garters. He seemed to have brought the chill in with his brooding attitude.

"You do not seem pleased, brother," said Eleanor, not looking up from her cards.

Jack seemed to switch instantaneously to a better mood, and came over to give his customary affections to his sister. "I am always pleased to see my favorite ladies," he said charmingly, and added when he met Deliverance's eyes, "You as well."

"You sure your Aunt Claude is not included on that list, sir?" Mrs. Potter said dryly. Jack made a harrumpf noise that Deliverance assumed was an emphatic no. After handing his jacket off to a manservant and thanking him, he joined them by the fire.

"Good day ladies?" he asked, warming himself.

"Yes. The best! We taught Deliverance all about electricity and soup spoons, and how to waltz," Eleanor gushed, forgetting her cards.

"How to waltz, eh? Who played the gentleman?" Jack asked, amused.

"I did, silly! I can waltz both roles. You know that," Eleanor retorted.

"It's true, she used to make me play the lady," said Jack, a sparkle in his eye.

"It seems I am good at neither." Deliverance laughed.

"Do not worry overly, love. Those stodgy bastards at my aunt's stuffy ball will not expect a Southlander to be able to waltz anyway," Jack said ruefully.

Deliverance wondered why Jack did not seem to be overly interested in his own social class of people. Were they really that frivolous? After all, Eleanor was of the same class, and Deliverance found her most entertaining and also intelligent.

"Still, I'd like to be able to. I want to drink up everything here! It's fascinating. Electrosity…electricity! And indoor plumbing! And cellular telephones! It is all amazing."

"Then let's waltz!" Jack said, springing to his feet.

Mrs. Potter smiled and rang for the ballroom fireplaces to be lit. "My Jack has fire in his shoes," she said of his antsy nature.

They ventured to the ballroom together, and Eleanor disappeared in a small side room before reappearing. She held a small remote and at a click, a waltz started playing over the speaker system in the room. Another feat of science Deliverance could hardly believe. To have an entire orchestra at one's fingertips!

"Do you never sit still?" Deliverance asked as Jack took her in his arms, to begin the waltz.

He smiled a rakish smile at her. Deliverance was a tall woman but she still had to look up to regard him. "Hardly ever. Although I get the sense you are a woman of action yourself."

She chatted with him easily as they moved across the floor. "Yes, I suppose I always favored the more athletic chores—wood chopping, hunting, or tending the animals. I am rubbish at knitting," she admitted.

"You know what you are not rubbish at?" Jack asked coyly.

"What is that?"

"Waltzing."

Fades, he was right. As soon as she was distracted she had stopped overly thinking every movement. They had been gliding elegantly together.

"You knew distracting me would help," Deliverance said when the song came to an end.

Jack did not relinquish his hold on her, his hand still seated firmly at her waist. "Sometimes we have to venture out of ourselves to truly find our rhythm," he said finally, eyes locked on hers. After a pause, he dropped his arms and stepped back.

"Jack, it is late. Did you have any dinner yet?" Mrs. Potter interjected, breaking the trance.

"Oh...no, I suppose not. You ladies probably would like to retire soon," he said reluctantly, then added, "Oh, and I have not been able to get a bead on Lord Asher just yet, but I am closing in on him. Damn hermit likes to squirrel himself away. Can be a difficult bastard to get ahold of."

"That's okay, Jack. You will find him tomorrow," Eleanor said, and took Deliverance's hand. "Come on, Deliverance, let's head up to bed." She stifled a yawn. With her lack of hair, it reminded Deliverance a bit of a baby lamb's yawn, all pink and new.

Over her shoulder, Deliverance heard Jack question Mrs. Potter, "Did you give Stevens a taser, for Christ's sake?"

"Oh, aye I did."

"He nearly shot our heads off."

"Don't be daft, sir. It might drop you but it would not shoot anyone's head off."

"Still, why did you think it was a good idea to give Stevens a taser?"

"Well, I was not going to give him my sawed-off shotgun!" Mrs. Potter replied, as if that were the most ridiculous question in the world. There was a beat, and then a rumbling of laughter. Apparently, Mrs. Potter was a woman to be reckoned with.

Deliverance smiled at the exchange and followed Eleanor down the hall.

Later that night, as Deliverance lay amongst the fluffy bed linens, she wondered if perhaps that was what it was like to have a little sister. Holding hands, and teaching each other about things, and walks in the garden? It probably involved fights and wiping sick brows and all the other things Deliverance knew from her family life with Cat went along with being close to another female. Still, she would take it all if it meant that little girl was there.

CHAPTER 15

Jack

Jack really had no appetite when he had so many irons in the fire. Still, he obliged Mrs. Potter by grabbing an apple from the kitchen on his way out to the garden. He disliked the city manor's garden, preferring the expansive one at the country house. It had no imposing walls. He hated walls. Thoughts kept churning in his head, making him restless as he wandered aimlessly through the hedge maze.

He had inquired at Oxdale about Lord Asher's whereabouts and his faculty colleagues at St. Andrew's were less than helpful.

"He's on extended sabbatical."

"Yes, but where?"

"He's ON EXTENDED SABBATICAL."

Or, "You know how he is. He could be in Antarticus for all we know. He was the last time, actually. He is secretive about his research."

Yes, Jack knew he was secretive partly because he had to be. That had been one of the reasons the St. Andrews fellows had selected him initially to work on the Nar Project—his discretion. Also, his expertise in dealing with remote cultures. When Jack had initially approached Oxdale, they vetted him very carefully. Oxdale had a long history of thwarting the government in its radical research, and still retained its charter. Which meant they had a long history of discretion and good judgment in character. Finally, deciding Jack was genuine in his expressed interest in aiding their Nar Project efforts, they had paired him with the lead researcher, Lord Asher.

From what he understood, Lord Asher had been a firebrand in the academic community. Not least amongst his most controversial standings was his unequivocal support of Narisi freedom. When Jack finally got a hold of him, all that fire had seemed extinguished. Jack could tell a fire burning out when he saw one, after all. It was not until he got the full story that he could see why Lord Asher had all but given up, relegating himself to various hidey-holes throughout the planet to do "research." Jack was pretty sure his research involved a detailed description of the bottom of numerous scotch bottles.

Still, he was able to ferret out the name of a student who might be able to get a hold of him. He would try the student tomorrow. He had obtained the student's class schedule from a very helpful, very flirtatious ladder-climbing coed at the registrar. Jack was not above putting on charms when necessary. He did not find it necessary very often.

But damn. It would be this coming week. That blasted ball...although it might be a riot to dance the night away with Deliverance right under all those stuffy aristocrats' noses. He rather liked the idea, honestly. That and Deliverance deserved a night of dancing and feeling beautiful and receiving all the attention she deserved. She deserved all the nights she wanted doing whatever she wanted. He hoped...no, he prayed he would be able to make that happen for her. It was going to be very hard though. There were those in high places who would rather that dream never came to fruition.

✳✳✳

Deliverance

The next day Eleanor and Mrs. Potter insisted on taking her to the dressmaker.

"There are large department stores you can go to for every day clothes, but when one is of a certain social standing, one must look the part," Eleanor said. "Honestly, I do not see what all the fuss is about. I rather like my jeans and hoodies. We shall get you some of those too. You'll see what I mean." Eleanor

Several hours later, in the stuffy dressmaker's shop, Deliverance did see what she meant. She eyed the bags of comfortable, practical clothes they had bought previously at what Eleanor had called a "mall" enviously, as she stood as still as she could on the seamstress's pedestal. She had been standing there for what felt like hours, having traced all the lines of all the bolts of fabrics lining the walls more than once while the dressmaker poked, pinned, and prodded. High society clothes were a nuisance. Not only did they take forever to tailor, but they were impractical.

When they first came in, she'd sized up Deliverance with a quick critical eye, and went to work. All Eleanor had to do was describe what functions she needed the dresses for. That was it. Mrs. Lucinda knew exactly what she wanted to see Deliverance wearing after that. She became a flurry of fabric tossing mania, selecting and discarding this material and that. Finally she settled on deep autumnal and jewel tones in velvets, chiffons, and silk.

"More petticoats!" the dressmaker, Mrs. Lucinda, declared. She had an odd accent, that one. When Deliverance asked, she explained she was a Frankish immigrant. Apparently all the best designers were.

"Why are these coats petty?" Deliverance whispered to Eleanor, who stood next to her assessing. She had donned a cheerful headwrap today, hiding her baldness.

"We shall have the coats that are not petty, please!" Eleanor demanded, laughing. Mrs. Lucinda, whose first language was not English, did not get the joke.

She stared at Eleanor for a beat, then repeated, "No. More petticoats." More petticoats it was.

Mrs. Lucinda was Frankish force of nature. The dresses were more elaborate than anything Deliverance had ever worn, and Eleanor informed her Mrs. Potter would have to help her dress.

"It's been ages since Mrs. Potter was a lady's maid, but she insisted on doing the honors for you," Eleanor explained. Deliverance was still a little hazy on all the household roles, but understood Mrs. Potter and Stevens held the ranking positions in the hierarchy of staff, and for good reason.

Deliverance quickly decided bustles and corsets, as well as high heels, were completely incomprehensible and also reprehensible. Of all the ridiculous fashion machinations!

Eleanor gave a sigh and fingered the dress being constructed on Deliverance's figure. "I wish I could go to the ball. But this one is for debuts and I am not old enough. I am only 14. I have four years before my debut…but thanks to modern science, I will get to see my debut!" She said, brightening.

Just then the tinkling of the doorbell indicated the shop had more customers. A group of three, finely clothed young women came sauntering in.

"Be with you in moment!" Mrs. Lucinda called in her thick, syrupy accent.

The women wandered around, perusing the fabrics before one of them apparently spied Eleanor's headscarf and put together who she was. The ringleader of the group, a petite blue-eyed girl with caramel colored tresses, zeroed in on them.

"Eleanor Quentin! How good to see you out!" she cooed. Her dark brows arched as she regarded Deliverance, still ensconced on the pedestal.

"Mallory. Lovely to see you as well," Eleanor replied politely, if not slightly coldly. "Bess, Emily. A pleasure."

"And this must be the talk of the town!" Mallory exclaimed, regarding Deliverance boldly. She felt like a piece of cattle for auction, the bidders eager for the Sunday slaughter.

"This is my future sister-in-law, Lady Deliverance Von Hattern," Eleanor introduced her, smoothly inventing a Southish-sounding last name. Deliverance repeated it to herself several times in a row to affix it in her memory. It would not do to forget her own last name.

"Ah, Lady? Jack is marrying up then," Mallory exclaimed, a hint of irony in her voice. "Oh, but you both hold titles as well, so then he isn't." There was something baiting in the other young woman's tone, like a turtle's tongue luring in unsuspecting fish.

"Pleased to make your acquaintance," said Deliverance. "I would do my introductions properly, but I cannot disrupt Mrs. Lucinda amidst her craft."

Mallory considered Mrs. Lucinda fluttering around Deliverance for a moment. "I stopped in to see how the alterations were going on Bess's and my gowns. But we shall not interrupt this transformation process."

"I told you before. They will be finished by Thursday. I am never late." Mrs. Lucinda gruffly threw over her shoulder as she kept pinning.

Mallory sidled around Deliverance, her lady friends in tow, not leaving yet.

"Mrs. Lucinda…I think for her the best color would be purple…royal purple. You should definitely make all her outfits in it," Mallory said after a beat, and her friends tittered at some unknown joke. "Well, bye for now." And they left in a flurry of petty-coats, clearing the air with them.

"Fades…I meant Christ! Who were they?" Deliverance asked of Eleanor.

"Society women. Mallory, the little ladder-climbing trollop, has had her eye on Jack even before her debut. It must have been a grave disappointment to her to learn of you. Not that Jack would ever think of her twice. He hates society women and all that fanfare with a passion."

Mrs. Lucinda snorted. "Also, grave disappointment when she too fat to fit in her dress. Maybe I make one oopsie." Eleanor giggled. "Purple, my ass," the older woman muttered.

"What is wrong with purple? I mean, it's not my favorite color but…" Deliverance asked.

"She meant it as an insult. Purple is a colonial color. It is not a color you would catch a Southlander wearing. It reminds them of their status as a sub-state. Things are much improved now, but there is a long history of bad blood between Arcanton proper and its colonies." Eleanor informed her.

"Ah, I see," Deliverance said finally. How underhanded.

"Mallory Trenton—she is pain in the rear," Mrs. Lucinda summed it up and Eleanor burst out laughing. Deliverance could not help but join in. But a small part of her fluttered with concern. Would she be able to handle herself at the ball with all these vipers?

CHAPTER 16

Deliverance

Deliverance's integration lessons continued over the next couple days. Eleanor took her on sojourns to the sites of Lontown. The most impactful was the tour they took through the old Tower gaol. Its thick, gritty walls left a knot in her stomach, reminding her of her own mother and friend's likely imprisonment. While this gaol was different—it was above ground and Effie and Cat would most likely be sentenced to labors in the mine, it was just as chilling. This gaol, like the one back home, was meant for people to enter but not leave. The difference was this gaol was now just a tourist attraction, but the one back home was very much active and very likely contained her loved ones. It took all her willpower to tamp down the panic at the thought of the cold, sickness, or even madness that accompanied gaol labors. Cat would not be able to heal herself or Effie without her herbs. It would not take long for them to perish, even if someone were kind enough to bring them food and water. Deliverance swallowed. In order to save them, she would have to focus on the task at hand, her infiltration of this foreign society.

Wars, innovations, leaps in human understanding...these were all fresh discoveries for Deliverance. Some of it delivered to her fingertips with the flat changing book device called the laptop computer, some of it from oral lessons from Eleanor or Mrs. Potter, some of it read from fading plaques at museums. There was so much more to the world than Deliverance would have ever expected, in what she now considered her previous life on Nar. Not that she did not feel the immediacy of rescuing her mother and Effie—it just felt like a world away, when in reality they were only several score miles out to sea in a westerly direction.

"My hair is beginning to come back in," Eleanor announced one evening by the fire. She had been trying to teach Deliverance how to play the pianoforte, but they both decided it was a lost cause after a bit. "See? Feel it!"

The girl bent her head over Deliverance's lap. Low and behold, Eleanor was right. There was a fine dusting of new dark hairs emerging from her scalp.

"Aye, 'tis there!" Deliverance said, forgetting to disguise her Narisi lilt.

The girl sighed, being prone, like her brother, to rapid mood swings. She gestured for Deliverance to sit in front of her by the fire. Deliverance complied, and the younger girl began to fuss with Deliverance's own hair, combing her fingers through the unruly locks.

"Is it hard for you to block my power stealing like that?" Deliverance asked curiously. She tried to turn her head, but

Deliverance

Eleanor firmly turned her face back forward when it interrupted her braid work.

"Oh, no not at all. See, hair is dead actually. So, none of my power feels wanton to leak across to you," Eleanor said.

Deliverance frowned. "If it's dead, then how does it grow?" There was so much to science she still did not understand. It almost seemed an insurmountable task to catch up to the understanding of a fourteen-year-old, much less an adult. Granted, Eleanor was a precocious fourteen-year-old.

"Your scalp puts together these complex proteins and then pushes them up out of the hair follicles…at least that is my limited understanding." Eleanor

"And you lost your hair…because you were sick?" Deliverance asked, hesitantly. She did not know if it was a sensitive subject.

"Yes," the girl said with a sigh, then continued, "Cancer. I had a form of cancer in the blood called Leukemia. Which is why I was not allowed to use my gift for so long. They had no way of knowing how it would affect me or others while I was sick."

"Cancer…I am not familiar with that term. For us Cancer is a crab—a constellation in the stars," Deliverance replied uncertainly.

"It's like…when the cells of the body mutate into unusable things. The body attacks itself. Sometimes people develop tumors or growths, and the growths metastasize or spread, eventually killing the person," Eleanor replied with academic coolness. For her it was water under the bridge.

"That sounds like wasting disease," Deliverance said finally. She had watched over thirty people die from it in front of her eyes, and knew before her time many had as well. It was incurable, at least for Cat's skills as a healer and herbalist. "I never knew it was fixable."

"Sometimes it is not. But modern medicine, along with dedicated doctor-healers with strong gifts, has made it possible. Well over 90% of childhood cancer is curable now," Eleanor said, still tugging at her bushy tresses.

Deliverance lapsed into a silence. Some of the thirty people she had watched pass into the Fades were children. She wished those children could have had the same chance…the same access to medicine that Eleanor did. And then her thoughts grew into consternation. Why should the children on Nar not have access to such medicine? The consternation was imbued with the unfairness of it all. Why had her people not tried to leave the island before—constructed boats and went into the Outside and found these wonders? Were they so hobbled by their own ignorance that they were killing themselves off slowly, rather than venturing out to gather what the world had to offer? The utter ridiculousness of it all incensed her.

She sat there brooding until Eleanor announced, "Voila!" and handed Deliverance a looking glass to inspect the intricate braid she had fastened Deliverance's locks into. It was complicated and made her hair look rich rather than wild.

"Thank you!" Deliverance said, smiling. "I do not have a sister, but I imagine if I did, I would want her to be like you."

Deliverance

Eleanor flushed with pride. "If I were your sister, I would want whoever endowed you with such hair to be so kind to me as well. I shall be stuck with this forest of short stubble for quite some time," the girl said wistfully, running her fingers along her work one last time.

Staring into the mirror, Deliverance suddenly had an idea. She sprang to her feet, startling Mrs. Potter, who had dozed off over her embroidery. With a single-minded purposefulness, Deliverance strode across the room to the sewing cabinet, where she had seen Mrs. Potter retrieve her embroidering hoop and bits of thread earlier. As she rummaged through the cabinet, she was aware Stevens had sidled into the room. Perfect. Eleanor and Mrs. Potter looked at her strangely, like they didn't understand her odd burst of energy, and Stevens' greeting to them was cut short. They had to be used to such action though, living with Jack, Deliverance reasoned. Aha! She found the item she was searching for.

Grasping the pair of shears in one hand, and her thick braid in another, Deliverance shore off the thing with a few decided snips at the nape of her neck. Triumphantly, she held the braid out in front of them like trophy.

No one moved. Mrs. Potter's mouth fell open. They stared.

Deliverance dropped the shears back into the cabinet and strode across the room to Stevens.

"Here!" she said, thrusting the braid into his stunned hands. "Miss Eleanor shall have her hair. Take this to your wig maker. Then she shall have hair just like mine, as she wishes." Stevens, to his credit, did take the braid from Deliverance blinking, although he and Mrs. Potter were still speechless with shock.

It cannot be that unusual, thought Deliverance. Women wore wigs on Nar. Did they not here?

Finally, Eleanor broke the silence with a squeal and bounded up to wrap her arms around Deliverance's waist. "Oh, that was bloody brilliant!" she cried. "And thank you sooo much. Stevens, would you have one of your men find a wig maker for it? I'm ever so grateful! I just love you!"

Deliverance felt her heart melt. She just loved this little girl, too.

✼✼✼

The rest of the evening, Eleanor was on Cloud 9, a new expression Deliverance had learned. Jack had not returned before they retired.

However, a small knock came at her door later that evening. She was in her dressing gown, but it was decidedly modest, so she bid whoever it was to enter. She had been gazing at the new moon slicing its way across the sky. The stars were obscured, though, by the lights of the city around them. It was like a live thing, humming with lifeblood even at night.

Jack slid into the room, quietly closing the door behind him, still in his tweed coat. He came to join her outside.

"Nice night," Jack commented, then slid his eyes sideways. "But are you not cold?"

"No, it's actually quite a warm night," Deliverance replied, not taking her eyes from the stars.

Jack barked a laugh and said, "I meant your neck, silly." Deliverance flushed, drawing a hand to her now very exposed neck. "I heard all about your antics from Mrs. Potter and Eleanor. The girl is still too excited to sleep. She says you will look just like sisters…and I am pretty sure Stevens is too dumbfounded to speak for a week!"

Deliverance gave a small smile. "I was glad to make her happy. I had no need of it anyway. It is just dead stuff after all."

Jack continued to chuckle. "I applaud your rationale, madam. Mrs. Potter says she can clean up the ends and fashion it a bit tomorrow…I rather like it." As he said this, he reached a hand up and grazed the nape of her neck, where short, wispy hairs wafted in the night breeze. She had to stifle a pleasure-filled shudder. A man had never touched her one way or another before, and any other man, she would have broken a riding crop over their heads. But not Jack. Jack was different.

He cleared his throat and turned back to the stars. "I've had quite a few breakthroughs today. First things first, I was able to track down that lout Lord Asher. He shall be back in town the Monday following the ball this weekend…which means we are still roped into going. Sorry, love."

"That's good you found him though!" Deliverance said, filling with hope. Perhaps she would be on her way to sorting this mess out and procuring the safety of her mother and friend soon.

"Also, I received a communique from your mother," Jack added.

Deliverance turned to him abruptly, her eyes widening in wonder. He'd heard from her mother? How? When? But the most important question was— "What did she say!?"

"She and Effie are imprisoned in the mines," Jack began, but had to catch a hold of Deliverance's arm as she started to feel faint and nearly lost her balance.

"Oh no! There is so little time then! They will starve!" she cried, panic curdling in her stomach.

"Her message says they have sustainable access to food and water though," Jack told her quickly, searching her eyes. "Deliverance. They are alive and they will stay alive for the near future."

"You're sure?" she croaked, almost disbelievingly. Her problems from home still roared in her ears, threatening to cause another bout of lightheadedness.

"Yes, I've had it confirmed. The drones caught successive imagery of a pair of women visiting the mines regularly carrying baskets," said Jack.

Deliverance stared at him a few moments longer, at the certainty in his eyes. She could trust him, couldn't she? Why would he lie to her about this? Slowly, she allowed her shoulders to relax—but only a little. Even if her mother and Effie were alive, they were still far away. Still at the whims of the Abbot and other Narisi men. Relief and apprehension tangled together in a ball inside her stomach. Who found it in their hearts to take food to her mother and friend, she wondered? Charity or Amity, she suspected. Both girls had been blessed with caring natures, whether it be by magic or personal will. Would they be able to bring Cat herbs if she or Effie were to fall ill? How much freedom would the Abbot allow them to bring supplied to them, or would it be just meager bare rations? The questions swirled in her head like a potion not yet ready to be bottled.

"What is a drone?" she asked, realizing Jack had used that unfamiliar word.

"I believe you call them hoverbirds. They're the high-flying silver so-called birds you often see circling the island but never landing there. They're actually machines used to take pictures," Jack explained.

Deliverance considered this. She and her mother had always assumed the high-flying shiny, grey birds were similar to the hummingbirds that liked to nurse the honeysuckle and trumpet vines that blossomed on the island. Narisis would have no knowledge of what a machine was and the birds were too high to see very clearly.

But they were...spying on them!

"Listen, love. This is a good thing! They are safe for the time being and we will be able to get a hold of Lord Asher. I've been planting seeds all throughout the political elite in Lontown to accomplish our aims. It is coming together," Jack said, taking her hands in his. "Look, you can even control taking my powers. No flames!"

Deliverance looked down at their joined hands. It was true. They were making strides.

Jack cleared his throat. "Also, I wanted to bring you this." He reached into the pocket of his coat and pulled out a small clasped box. Thinking better of it, he pulled the entire coat off and wrapped it around her. She pulled it closer gratefully.

He creaked the lid of the box open and inside was an exquisitely designed moonstone ring.

"My mother never was much for convention. She insisted my father buy her something other than a diamond. 'It's just wasted money on a lump of rock,' she used to say. My father picked the moonstone because it is said to represent feminine power, and he always said my mother had an eerie amount of power over him," Jack said, his voice becoming hoarse with emotion. He took her right hand and gently slid the ring over her ring finger.

Deliverance looked into his eyes, alarmed. "I can't wear your mother's engagement ring!" she exclaimed, horrified.

Jack laughed at her expression and replied, "People will expect you to be wearing one, especially at the ball."

"Can't you just find any old ring? Does it have to be your mother's? What if I damage it or lose it!?" Deliverance cried, looking at the ring like it was a leaden responsibility, dropping her to the bottom of the sea.

"'Fraid not, Love. Those old society buzzards have been on the lookout for this ring and the girl who will be sporting it for a long

Deliverance

time. Can't disappoint," Jack said carelessly. "Besides, I like the idea of you wearing it."

At that, his pupils dilated with something Deliverance thought looked like hunger. He firmly grasped the lapels of the tweed coat and pulled Deliverance against him, his mouth finding hers. He kissed her deeply, and Deliverance felt a small, traitorous groan of pleasure wheedle its way up her windpipe and escape before she could tamp it down. This was her first kiss...besides Effie. And it was warm and searing at the same time.

He pulled away for a brief moment, searching her eyes for permission. His expression asked, was that all right?

Her reply came in the form of crashing back into him, wrapping her arms around his neck and finding him again. She felt insatiable cravings in places she never knew there could be cravings, blood coursing through her body.

She pulled away suddenly, panicked. "I..." she stammered and looked around her. She suddenly felt a very immediate need to escape.

"Shhh," said Jack with a warm smile, which slowed her down. "It's all right, love. That's all I wanted. It will go no further than that, I promise."

What had come over her? Deliverance realized she must have been reacting to the nature of the embrace. Jack was right...she only wanted a taste for now. Thank the Gods he was a gentleman. Effie's stories of men overcome with lust must have spooked her subconscious. But looking into Jack's gentle face, Deliverance calmed. He would not take forcibly what was hers to give, regardless of what the men on Nar were like.

Seeing she had stilled, he wrapped her back up in his arms again, warming her with his body. His chin rested lightly atop her head. She buried into him further, smelling the pine-and-salt scent of him, letting it wash over her like a relaxing bath.

"You are the most singular woman I have ever met," Jack murmured into her now decidedly shorter hair.

When he bid her good night, he said over his shoulder, "Wear the ring. You will breathe new life into it. My mother would have liked that." And with that, he clicked the door softly behind him.

CHAPTER 17

Deliverance

Deliverance stretched languidly as sunlight poured through the floor to ceiling windows. She had slept well, and a small smile could not help but affix itself to her mouth. Someone had brought a tray with coffee and biscuits in, unbeknownst to her. She must have either been dead asleep or it was one of the servants who, Deliverance had learned, had the gift of stealth. They could slip in and out of places almost entirely unnoticed. Mrs. Potter told Deliverance she insisted on thorough background checks for anyone in her employ who had this type of gift. Deliverance could see why…but also how it could be useful as well. She dressed quickly, starting to get the hang of petticoats and the various layers. Grabbing a scone from the tray, she nibbled a bit as she made her way downstairs.

As she drew near the morning room, she picked out the voices of Mrs. Potter and Jack. At first, she was going to announce herself, but the raised pitch of Jack's tone made her hesitate.

"Damn the bloody parliament and damn those stodgy aristocrats who fill its halls. To hell with them all!" Jack fumed. Deliverance paused, listening, although a small voice in her conscience twitted she ought not to.

"I am just saying do not lead the poor girl on. It is not fair to her. Or to you," Mrs. Potter replied, even keeled in contrast to Jack's raging.

Lead her on? Was he just fooling with her last night!?

"I…I am not leading her on. I care for her deeply. I intend to give her the world."

"Intentions and delivering on those intentions are two separate matters," Mrs. Potter pointed out, though her tone was kindly.

"Christ…I know," Jack relented, sounded despondent.

"She has a heart of gold. Try not to put it through any more heartbreak than she is already in for," Mrs. Potter gently advised.

Deliverance heard a noncommittal grunt from Jack, and decided it was probably time to pretend she had just come down. She backed up a few steps, as if that would aid in her pretense of not overhearing their conversation, and then went forward again, knocking and entering. She arranged her face like nothing was amiss.

"You heard the whole thing," Mrs. Potter said after one glance at her.

Damn! Was she so easy to read?

Deliverance

"I'm afraid you have an honest face, love. Never play poker," Jack advised, whisking by and planting a small kiss on her cheek. What did fire pokers have to do with her face? Nothing Deliverance wanted to know. The Arcantons had such odd expressions.

After he left, Mrs. Potter said to her, "I'm sorry you had to hear that."

Deliverance schooled her face, trying to tamp down the emotions bubbling within. "It's all right. I know...we've a long road ahead of us, and I must fix my attentions exclusively on my friend and mother's welfare. It is hard not to get distracted in this world though...there is so much to discover!" she admitted.

"My Jack has never been able to combat what his heart believes is right," Mrs. Potter answered, then held out her hand to Deliverance. "Come. We shall clean up that hasty haircut of yours."

Deliverance took the sun spotted, callused hand, a gardener's hand no doubt, and focused on blocking her gift from prodding into Mrs. Potter's.

"Ah, the missus's ring!" Mrs. Potter exclaimed, laying eyes on the moonstone creation resting on Deliverance's ring finger. After a pause, she added, "It suits you, my dear." Deliverance felt a swell of affection for the elderly lady.

They set about dealing with her hair next. Over the next hour or so, Mrs. Potter, with Eleanor supervising, was able to shape

Deliverance's hack job into something Eleanor assured Deliverance was quite fashionable.

"All the girls at uni wear their hair like that...well, not ALL of them. But a lot," Eleanor bubbled. Apparently, Stevens had taken the braid and commissioned a wig maker that morning. The girl was over the moon over the whole ordeal. Deliverance could see the beginnings of the girl's eyebrows attempting to reclaim their place upon her face. The stubble seemed a bit longer atop her head too. It might seem like a long time to a fourteen-year-old girl, but Deliverance knew it would not be long until she had no need of a wig. Still, she smiled at the girl's enthusiasm.

"There, that's better," Mrs. Potter announced, setting down her scissors and comb. She handed Deliverance a looking glass.

It did have much more of an intentional shape now. Deliverance had no concept of what short hair on a woman should look like, and she really did not much mind as long as it stayed out of her face. Lush waves fell past her cheekbones, with the back cropped in shorter wisps.

"You have the most gorgeous eyes!" Eleanor declared. "This cut makes them stand out even more. Speaking of making your eyes stand out—your gown has arrived, pressed and ready to go for tonight!"

Deliverance felt a flutter in her stomach. The dreaded charade was closing in on her. She was not looking forward to spending an evening in a den of vipers like those she had met at the dressmaker's.

"But we have the whole day before you must get ready. What shall we do?" Eleanor mused, but did not pause to wait for an answer. "I know! I shall take you to the museum! Wait until you see what a dinosaur is!"

***

Eleanor was a master at getting Deliverance to forget her anxieties. She had been right, too, about the dinosaurs. She gave a bone-deep shudder. She was thankful those monsters were not alive today, although she had no wish to encounter something called an alligator any time soon either.

Despite Eleanor's bubbly nature, she was intuitive. She was careful not to overload Deliverance, letting her wander the exhibits slowly, touching display plaques and glass enclosures, absorbing, taking in everything at her own pace.

When Deliverance told her as much, the girl preened. It was like watching a flower blossom in the sun when Deliverance praised her. How amazing it was to have such an effect on another person, especially one so young and promising. It was truly validating.

"I would like to volunteer and help the others too, when they get here or we go there." Eleanor remarked as they took in a display about pirates. It struck Deliverance as funny, now, that she had thought Jack was one…although Finley most definitely was about some nefarious business or another.

Deliverance considered the girl's comment. "I suppose I did not think of what was next other than freeing my mother and my friend Effie. But you are right. Changes are coming." She admired the girl for wanting to be on the forefront and to help people.

"Come along! I want to show you the mummies!" Eleanor squealed, quickly changing gears.

✸✸✸

Mummies, it turned out, were not mothers. Deliverance could not stop shuddering about them, even after they left the exhibit and returned to the manor to get ready for that evening. She could not stop picturing those gauzy corpses wrapped like solstice presents and on display for all the see. Lurid!

"You must hold still, madam." The lady's maid behind her had spent the better part of an hour pulling various substances through Deliverance's hair and dabbing concoctions on her face. She felt like a painting. A painting with very stiff hair.

Eleanor lounged on a chaise nearby, adding comments as she saw fit while Mrs. Potter fluttered around, messing with the dress on the hanger. The dress…it was more ornate than anything Deliverance could have imagined. Its silk was a deep emerald green, brocaded with gold-threaded lace in intricate flowery patterns. It had long rows of decorative buttons like little candies in lines all the way to the floor.

After the lady's maid helped her into the infernal contraption called a corset, Mrs. Potter advised the maid to not tighten it so bindingly. "It's inhumane. And she has such a lovely figure anyway."

Deliverance

There was much ado in rustling and lifting and lacing and fastening, but finally Deliverance was ensconced in the lavish dress.

Eleanor clapped her hands in delight. "Go and look in the full-length mirror!"

Deliverance toddled over, still becoming accustomed to dancing shoes on the soft carpet of the bedroom. She was almost afraid to look. After so much pasting and primping and preening and plumping, she was certain she would look like a trussed-up cupcake. Unwillingly, she slit one of her eyes open to take a peak.

No. Not a cupcake. Where she was expecting to see an awkward girl playing dress up with her mother's extra fabrics, she instead saw a woman. A tall, graceful, lithe woman. The lacey shoulders of the dress came just below her collarbone in a sweeping line across her chest, exposing milky décolleté. At the dressmaker's she had expressed concern it would be too bawdy or inappropriate, but the dressmaker assured her it would be tasteful. It was. Deliverance smoothed her hands down the rippling planes of jade. For once in her life, she felt…beautiful. It was rather nice, although in hindsight she was not sure it was worth the hours of effort.

"Here, Miss. Do not forget these," Mrs. Potter said, handing her a pair of satin, elbow length gloves dyed to match the green of the dress, and of her eyes. "It would not do to have a…transgression when you are not on guard."

Eleanor hopped up once Deliverance had donned the gloves and took her mother's engagement ring from the dressing table.

She slipped it over the appropriate gloved finger and beamed her approval.

"Okay, now you wait a few minutes for us to get downstairs first before you come down," Eleanor instructed her. "I want to see the look on my barmy brother's face when he sees you in that dress."

Deliverance acquiesced, hoping she would not tumble down the stairs while everyone was watching her.

And watch her they did. Deliverance paused at the top of the main stair landing. The whole household had apparently turned out to see her butterfly-like transformation. Jack, messing with a cufflink at first, did not notice her until she began to descend the staircase.

"Oh, it's like a movie!" Eleanor sighed romantically. Jack rolled his eyes at his sister, but then stood transfixed. They locked eyes, and Deliverance could see the heat in his stare.

"Ladies and gentleman, I give you the first ever sight to render our Master Jack speechless. Lady Deliverance Von Hattern," Stevens drawly announced.

Jack did not take his eyes off her, ignoring Stevens and the ensuing titter of laughter, but came forward to meet her at the bottom of the stairs. She took his arm, self-consciously, heat blossoming in her cheeks.

Eleanor came up and tumbled along in their wake. "Remember every detail! Every single one!" she instructed Deliverance and added wistfully, "Oh, to be a fly on the wall!"

Deliverance regarded her. Being a fly did not sound pleasant, nor very safe. Especially from ponytails and frogs. Such odd turns of phrase they had here.

Jack still had not said anything as they both took their seats in the back of the motorized coach. Apparently, these were relics of the past, but it was traditional for the elite to break them out for special occasions such as balls. Stevens sat in the drivers' seat, fiddling with the controls.

Intensity pooled in Jack's eyes as he finally broke the silence between them. Deliverance sighed in relief. It was becoming quite awkward.

"You look stunning," he said, but then added after a beat, "You always look stunning, though. You do not needs all these bits and bobs to distract from your true beauty."

"You like me just as I am, then?" Deliverance asked, relieved he was not enamored with this odious primping routine.

"Just as you are," he confirmed with a nod. With that they sat back and chatted easily as the coach glided through the city.

"Aunt Claude's estate is on the other end of the borough, not as close to Kensington or Hyde Park…a point she loathes," Jack remarked dryly.

"You do not hold them in high regard," Deliverance noted, although she knew some of why that was.

"No. I have found some of the most honorable people are the lowliest, like Finley, or my fellow soldiers I served with in the conflict. Not that there are not honorable people in high society…it just seems to breed less of them, I'm afraid. My aunt and her progeny are…manipulative and self-involved," Jack said.

Deliverance had nothing to add to this. It had been her assessment as well.

"Gird your loins, Master and Mistress. We are about to pull into the drive," Stevens called back to them in a tone too jaunty for the occasion. Deliverance wondered if he enjoyed the thought of her squirming under the microscope of all those people, but pushed the thought aside.

"It will be okay," Jack reassured her, and squeezed her hand, then he alit from the carriage in front of another imposing manor house, brightly illuminated with activity. He held out his hand to her. She swallowed, sucked in a deep breath, and took his hand.

CHAPTER 18

Deliverance

"The Honorable Senator Jack Quentin and Lady Deliverance Von Hattern!" The doorman announced them as they entered the buzzing ballroom. Deliverance clutched Jack's arm more tightly.

The cavernous room, with its sweeping ceilings and relief-laden walls, was humming with activity. The area would have been warm with the press of rustling people despite the cheerful fires lit in each marble hearth in the room. Glittering chandeliers dangled above the fray, throwing diffracted rainbows across the parquet floor. It was not as large as the ballroom at Hathaway, but Hathaway's ballroom, in Deliverance's mind, remained only partially lit…sleeping. This ballroom was anything but sleeping.

The din of chatter threatened to overcome Deliverance and she clung with even more vigor to her faux-fiancé's arm. A string quintet sang in the background and smells of flowers and champagne hung in the air, humid with breath and gossip.

Jack expertly guided her into the throng. "Relax. You are lovely. It will be fine," he reassured her. "Come, I will introduce you to some of my associates in parliament...but only the ones whose politics I approve of." He said this overly loudly, and then pretended to overlook a stately man standing directly in front of them, as if waiting. "Nope. Not seeing anyone over here," he added with a glint of mischief in his eye.

"Senator Quentin, you jest!" The man called jovially, coming forward to take Deliverance's hand. "And this must be the mysterious bride to be. Since your fiancé is so lax in his manners, I will introduce myself. I am Senator John Ribald."

"Pleased to make your acquaintance," Deliverance responded, allowing the elder man to plant a kiss on her glove.

"You wouldn't be if you saw the bill he put forward on the floor last month," Jack said dryly, but quickly dropped his charade and smiled warmly. "This is my intended, Lady Deliverance Von Hattern."

"Von Hattern? Southish then, eh?" the elder man inquired. Deliverance nodded. "Jack has been traveling quite a bit. Bring me back one just as pretty next time!"

"I'm afraid I do not deal in tea, diamonds, or women, Senator Ribald. But I shall take note of your request."

"He's a funny one, your intended," Senator Ribald told her. They exchanged a few more friendly words with the senator and then moved on.

Deliverance

That went smoothly, Deliverance thought. Perhaps this will not be so odious.

Jack escorted her around the ballroom, introducing her to various parties, a whirl of names threatening to drown Deliverance. Some regarded her warmly, others distantly. She was aware there were threads of politics woven into the fabric of conversation here, of which she was only slightly aware. That made it dangerous. But she did the best she could.

"Ah, I see Senator Smithson over there. I need to press him on the Nar issue a bit. Feel him out. But I'd rather do so without a Narisi standing right in front of him…but where to put you? I do not feel like leaving you alone in this shark tank," Jack said, stretching his neck to catch a glimpse of the man with whom he desired an audience.

"Go!" Deliverance insisted. "I am not inept nor in any danger of being eaten alive. I shall be fine on my own for a while. Take care of your business."

"You're sure?" he asked uncertainly.

"Positive."

Jack had not been gone three minutes before the sharks descended. Deliverance mused perhaps he had some shark repellent quality he had developed over many years of dealing with this class of people. Mallory—whom Deliverance recognized from the uncomfortable exchange at the dress shop—was flanked by a cotillion of bottom feeders in petticoats and closing in fast.

There was no way for Deliverance to gracefully escape in the crush of bodies.

"Lady Deliverance!" Mallory cooed sweetly to her. "Lady Deliverance! Over here!"

She arrived with her cronies in front of Deliverance in a swirl of perfume and ill intentions.

"Lady Mallory. How delightful," said Deliverance, her tone indicating she was anything but delighted.

"Actually, it's Miss." She sniffed. "Some of us have yet to marry into titles. But then you haven't either…yet."

Deliverance caught her drift immediately. What a wormy little thing she was!

"I see you decided against the purple. Pity," she added, eyes running up and down Deliverance's outfit critically. "Your people do look good in it."

"Do you know many Southlanders?" Deliverance asked, eyes casting for a suitable way to escape. Drat. None presented itself.

"Oh no," another of the spiteful hens chimed in. "We only associate with suitable company."

Well, that went mean quite quickly, Deliverance thought dryly. "Well, I must be off to…" Deliverance tried, but Mallory cut her off.

"Oh, do stay and chat with us. It is quite a novelty for us to see what exactly Jack sees in you."

"Mallory rather thought she would be able to land him," one of the other hens clucked. Mallory cast her friend a disgusted look.

"Must you be so crass, Gertrude?" she complained.

"What? You said it was only a matter of time. Until SHE came along," the other girl replied, annoyed as well. Deliverance was quickly tiring of this little game.

Her savior came in the form of an elegant young woman perhaps a few years older than Deliverance.

"Miss Mallory Trenton," said a voice from behind Deliverance's shoulder. Perched there was a blonde in an elegant periwinkle blue ball gown, her corn silk tresses gathered into an elaborate braid atop her head. Her intelligent eyes mirrored the color of her dress and were affixed upon Deliverance's would-be foe.

"Ah, Lady Pennington." Mallory greeted the woman, and the circle of intrigue expanded to allow her in.

"Actually, I prefer Doctor," the woman corrected Mallory, and turned to Deliverance, offering her a handshake. "Doctor Adelaide Pennington. Some of us prefer the titles we earned rather than those we stole or married."

Deliverance gratefully shook the blonde's hand, not quite certain she was not another foe, but definitely certain this new addition to the party did not like Mallory. The enemy of thy enemy, and all that, thought Deliverance.

"Well, lucky for you that you did not have to marry your title," said Mallory with syrupy sweetness. "I admit I did not expect to see you tonight. This is a debut for the younger girls, after all."

Doctor Adelaide, the picture of grace, remained entirely unruffled by Mallory's rude insinuations. She again turned to Deliverance and interpreted, "She means to call me a spinster. An old biddy if you will."

The woman's directness flustered Mallory and her flock. "Well, I meant no offense!" She blustered.

"Of course not. Just like you meant no offense when suggesting Lady Deliverance here wear a color denoting subservience in her culture. Never you fear, Miss Trenton, we all know exactly what you meant," said Doctor Adelaide smoothly, never raising her voice above a graceful lilt.

Doctor Adelaide had turned her back to the women almost entirely now, looking as if she intended to address Deliverance alone. And yet the flock did not disperse. She cast an annoyed glance over her demurely laced shoulder.

"Oh, and Miss Trenton? Whoever does your brows should receive a stern word. She missed an entire patch right in the middle of your brow. You should really see to it," Doctor Adelaide cooed, and did not bat an eyelash as Mallory smacked a hand to her forehead and ran away gasping in tears, her entourage in hot pursuit.

"There. That is better. One can breathe again," Doctor Adelaide said with a small smile on her pert mouth.

"Thank you for the rescue," Deliverance said earnestly.

"Do not mention it. These social obligations can be frightfully dull or frightfully aggressive. I tend to avoid them as often as I can. Besides, any friend of Jack Quentin's is a friend of mine," Doctor Adelaide replied, pausing to swipe a couple glasses of champagne from a passing waiters' tray. "There, that should be medicinal...I would know. Doctor and all that."

Deliverance smiled gratefully and took a sip of the fizzing liquid. It tickled her sinuses but did take a bit of the edge off. "You're a friend of Jack's?" Deliverance inquired.

"Ah yes. We are old childhood friends. I knew Jack when he was still in nappies," Doctor Adelaide said, stepping out into the room. "Here, if you move like you are deep in conversation and do not stand still, you are less likely to attract interceders in your conversation." Sage advice, Deliverance noted, as they adeptly made their way around the room.

Eventually, Jack caught back up with them.

"Ah, Addie, love!" he said brightly, kissing both of Doctor Adelaide's cheeks warmly. She greeted him in kind. "Thank you for saving my damsel in distress," he added cheekily.

"You know I am a sucker for a damsel," Doctor Adelaide replied jokingly.

"She would never submit to playing the maiden when we were children," Jack told Deliverance, a glint of something like pride in his eyes. "She was a knight or else! You look ravishing, by the way. I've always liked that color on you."

"I prefer my lab coat," Doctor Adelaide admitted rather wistfully.

They conversed easily for a while. Deliverance noticed how Jack's demeanor relaxed in Addie's presence—she insisted Deliverance call her Addie as well. It filled Deliverance with a feeling she could not quite put her finger on...not unease exactly. Addie had done nothing to warrant an uneasy feeling, after all. But there was something about the familiar way she touched his arm or he elicited a laugh from her that was disconcerting.

Jack broke through Deliverance's thoughts, asking her to join him on the dance floor. He had asked Addie, but she declined with polished reserve.

Deliverance gulped. "Don't worry. You are quite graceful," Jack assured her, leading her out onto the floor.

Deliverance became increasingly aware at the stares they were garnering. Some sneering and some approving. Everyone had an opinion about Senator Jack Quentin's love life, apparently.

As the waltz began, Deliverance moved stiffly in his arms. After a beat, Jack whispered to her, "Look at me...no, ignore them. Just look at me."

At first, she resisted for some unknown reason, but relented, reaching up with her eyes to find his stare enveloping hers. With his quiet reassurance, she began to relax and move more fluidly.

"There. See? Not so bad now, is it?" said Jack as they twirled across the floor. Deliverance admitted she was having quite a bit of fun. The champagne helped as well, a tonic to release the burning of the prying eyes and hissing of malevolent whispers. They danced several more together…more than Eleanor had instructed her was appropriate for one dance partner, but neither she nor Jack cared.

After a while, the crush of people was beginning to wear on Deliverance, though. Jack, ever his intuitive self, picked up on her waning.

"Come, let's grab some fresh air," he said, leading her off the dance floor and outside toward the terrace and the back garden. "I will say one thing. Aunt Claude does buy good champagne," he quipped, but then something caught his eye. "Ah, darling, I see one more senator I have to goad. Would you mind terribly if I go prod him for a few minutes?"

"Prod away!" Deliverance replied. He looked at her as if asking with his eyes if she was sure she was fine being left to take air on her own, but she shooed him away with a kiss on his cheek.

After he loped away to catch his next political target, Deliverance turned to enjoy the breeze. The night air hung solidly, puffing only at broad intervals. The darkened gardens were, however, quite cool compared to the press of the ballroom. From out of the thickets in the gardens, Deliverance caught snippets of giggles and hushes from lovers absconding for some privacy in the dark.

"Lovely night for it." The voice came too close to her ear, startling her.

Behind her stood a man, about her equal age with age, to whom she had not been introduced. He stood with the casual air of a man who knew he was handsome and was used to capitalizing on that fact. "Ned Turner. And you must be the exquisite pearl Jack Quentin brought back from the Southlands."

Deliverance was not sure why being referred to as hardened clam spit was supposed to be flattering, but she assumed by his tone it was. She nodded briefly, replying, "Deliverance Von Hattern."

"Ah, but soon to be Deliverance Quentin, I see," the man remarked, grabbing Deliverance's hand and eyeing the ring upon her finger.

She was starting to become uncomfortable with the intensity in the man's stare, and grew more so when he did not release her hand.

"Yes, quite soon," she replied, looking around for an escape.

It was not until the man put his hand upon her bare shoulder that she felt his gift. It was unlike any gift she had seen before, even in her careful observation of life in Lontown these past few days. The sparkling green of his hand against her skin made her feel ever so drowsy. Like her consciousness was being drained like a swirl of water down a bathtub drain. Hazily, she thought she should take his power and reverse it on him, but she found her head too cloudy to think.

Her head lolled back just as she heard Jack's angry cry, "What the devil do you think you are doing, Ned!?" In a fog, she realized the man had wrapped his arms around her and was making his way for the dark maze of the garden.

"Ah, Jack. It's about time you shared your imports." A detached voice floated over Deliverance's head.

Then suddenly the earth was tilting and she was being swept up in a familiar scent—sea and pine. Rapidly, her vision cleared. What on earth had that man been doing to her!? She found herself in Jack's arms, as he resolutely started away from the intrusive man.

"I was not finished with her yet," snapped the man—Ned, Deliverance remembered. Deliverance could feel Jack's skin begin to simmer beneath his coat and tails. Carefully, Jack set her down on the first terraced step he came to. She had not realized Ned had led her so far out until Jack brought her back within view of the house. Curious onlookers began to gather at the topmost steps of the terrace.

Deliverance could feel the rage building, like steam pressure beneath Jack's skin.

"It's all right, Jack. I am fine." She tried to calm him, and for a second she thought it had worked.

He brought his hand to her cheek and replied, "It is most definitely not all right." With that, he whirled and clocked the other gentleman in the face.

Ned staggered back from the force of the blow. Deliverance scrambled to her feet and heard cries of outrage and excitement coming from the onlookers above. God's teeth! They were causing a scene.

Ned, cheek already purpling with a bruise, put his hands up in a show of mock defeat.

"Hey now, hothead. I only meant to sample the wares before they were sold," Ned said in fake contriteness. Jack rounded on him, still spoiling for a fight. "If you aren't going to share her, at least bring that pretty little sister of yours out once she's grown back some decent hair." With that comment, it was Deliverance who snapped.

She almost involuntarily grasped the root of a potted rosemary plant and swung it with the same force she swung her axe whilst chopping wood. Ned collapsed like a rag doll in a shower of herbs and terracotta fragments. Jack looked at her in awe as she panted with rage. She started forward with the intent of kicking the man's rotten carcass down the stairs before Jack caught her in his arms. The man groaned and turned over. Not a carcass yet then, she thought ruefully.

Suddenly, Deliverance became aware that the music had ceased, and the entire guest list of the ball were spectating the events. Addie broke through the crowd with determined elbowing and skittered down the stairs toward them.

"Come on!" she called to them, reaching for Deliverance's hand. "Let's get out of here!" And just like that, the three of them absconded into the night.

***

Addie's apartments were not far from Aunt Claude's estate. They were able to hoof it on foot, clambering over fences awkwardly and skittering across some darkened lawns. Both Addie and Deliverance tore generous rips in their finery, but the freedom of the escape was well worth it. They were breathless and giddy by the time they let themselves into her apartments.

"Oh, the looks on their faces!" Addie hooted, tears of laughter streaming down her heart-shaped cheeks.

"I think Mrs. Wentworth might have peed her pants!" Jack bellowed.

Deliverance was laughing as well. In retrospect she was rather glad that wretched Ned fellow was still alive. But only a little bit. She had not felt her temper flare so wildly in quite a while, but she realized after studying Jack that he and his whole family had gotten under her skin, rooting themselves firmly in her heartstrings.

"I heard Lord Crandle declare you two a perfect match!" Addie added, still howling with laughter and aching ribs. Perfect match indeed! Two brawlers, Deliverance thought amusedly.

After they spent themselves laughing, Addie removed herself from their seated circle on the carpet in front of the fire Jack had lit with a flick of his wrist.

"Let me grab my medical bag and I'll have a look at your hand, Jack," Addie said as she left the room in search of her medical supplies.

Jack had been painfully flexing the hand he had used to wallop Ned. He felt Deliverance's eyes upon him, and scooted closer. With his good hand, he smoothed an errant lock of dark hair from her face.

"You…" he said, gazing at her intensely.

"Are trouble? Scandalous? Base? Violent even?" she offered playfully.

"No. Beautiful." And he kissed her slowly, deliberately. A cough let them know Addie had returned. "Go away, Addie," Jack said, kissing Deliverance again. When Addie did not go away, he groaned and sat back. He handed over his broken hand to her in a resigned way.

She cleaned the cuts with alcohol and salve, then studied his hand for a second. "Does this hurt?" she asked, and Jack swore. "Yep, must hurt. I'm afraid it's broken."

"I should probably stop finding my fist attached to other gentlemen's jawbones," Jack replied wryly. "In my defense, this one attracts trouble." He nodded at Deliverance.

She was about to protest when Addie said, "Nonsense. You just repel the masses. It's a skill you have been exacting against your own kind since we were children. When you stepped away, the unsavory lot simply filled the void." Her voice brokered no argument and Jack shrugged.

"All right, do your worst, Doc." Jack nodded at his decidedly swollen appendage.

"Do not tempt me. I might remove it altogether," Addie warned, but then took his damaged hand between her two, finely fingered good ones. She sat for a moment with her eyes closed, flicking beneath her lids. Then warm, vibrant green light shot from between their fingers. Addie kept her eyes closed, concentrating.

Jack sucked his breath in.

"Does it hurt?" Deliverance asked.

"A bit." He wheezed.

"Shhh. Let me concentrate unless you are not overly fond of all your fingers!" Addie hushed them, eyes still firmly closed. After a while, her celeste eyes awakened and she released Jack's hand. The magic light dissipated, leaving them with only the natural glow of the hearth again.

"How does it feel? Can you flex this way and that?" Addie asked with almost clinical detachedness. Jack showed her his hand flexing and no longer swollen. The cuts along his knuckles had knitted themselves back together neatly under a series of white, creviced scars.

"Addie, you're brilliant!" Jack exclaimed, rubbing his hand. "It's completely healed!"

She tut-tutted at him. "Not completely. Give the nerves in your hand a few days to calm down. I could not fix those without an MRI."

"Still brilliant. There are not many with Doctor Pennington's magic skill AND academic prowess. She's the reason Eleanor is still with us." Jack praised his friend. Addie, seemingly unflappable, did blush at this.

"You treated Eleanor for her cancer?" Deliverance inquired. Addie nodded. Jack must truly feel a connection with this woman, Deliverance decided, although part of her came to this conclusion unwillingly. She brushed these unwelcome feelings aside though, and they enjoyed each other's company well into the wee hours of the morning.

Finally, all yawning, Jack rang Stevens to come retrieve them, laughing when he told him no, they weren't at Aunt Claude's anymore.

"What are your plans tomorrow?" Addie asked Deliverance as she was showing them out.

"We are going to the university…Oxdale…to meet someone," Deliverance told her.

Addie's eyes glittered. "Ah, the den of miscreants!" she exclaimed but added, "Oxdale has a long history of thwarting the government with its politics and research. It's a bit of an Arcanton cultural tradition. They battle back and forth and prevent one from becoming too powerful over the other, and the rest of us profit...I suppose. Although Jack never does tell me what he does over there all the time."

"If I could tell you, love, I would," Jack said, pecking her on the cheek in goodbye.

"The day after, though, Deliverance, let us go riding!" Addie called, and Deliverance agreed as they stepped out the door.

"Difficult night?" Stevens inquired, eyeing Jack through the rearview mirror of the automobile.

"Highly entertaining," Jack replied, putting his arm around Deliverance, who was wearing his jacket.

Stevens drove for a few more minutes before suggesting, "The next time you decide to have an entertaining evening, sir, might I offer you the use of my taser?"

CHAPTER 19

Deliverance

Despite the lateness of the hour in which they retired, Deliverance was awake at dawn. She rubbed the sleep from her eyes as she stood, sipping a mug of coffee on the balcony of her room. She pulled the blanket wrapped around her closer as she regarded the new day. The watery ale of the morning light sunk the shadows slowly into the neighboring structures and the flowers in Mrs. Potter's garden cloaked themselves yet again in color. What would this day bring her?

Today they were to meet Lord Asher. However, Deliverance now knew that finding him was merely the beginning of some greater problem, some complex task that she and Jack would have to navigate together. His fixture at her side seemed a constant, although Deliverance was not entirely sure why. Whether altruism, ideals...even love was the causation of his steadfastness, or some other motive she had yet to understand. It was hard to wrap her mind around the entirety of the issue when so much was still shrouded in darkness, an object not yet focused, like the camera Eleanor had shown her the other day.

A small wren flitted down to join her on the balcony, torqueing its curious head this way and that.

"I've nothing to give you, little friend, unless you'd like some coffee. Something about your manner makes me believe you do not need any, though," Deliverance murmured absently to her little impromptu companion bouncing along the stone balustrade, singing for her. Behind her, the inner door to her chambers clicked open and Eleanor let herself in. "I will see if I have any leftover toast for you later, friend," Deliverance said to the bird and turned to go inside.

Eleanor demanded a full account of the evening, which Deliverance promptly gave her. By the end of the telling, Eleanor was sprawled out, flabbergasted across the chaise.

"I can't believe you could get into so much trouble from the time I went to bed until now!" the girl exclaimed. The shadow of hair reemerging from her scalp was a cool slate grey, making her eyes glow a shade just darker than amber in the morning sunlight.

"Will it…cause trouble, do you think?" Deliverance asked her.

Eleanor lifted her head from her flopped out position and replied, "Probably not. Jack is rather untouchable. He seems to skate along however he pleases, society be damned. And so far he has been none worse for the wear." Then Eleanor abruptly switched gears, another expression Deliverance learned from her study of the Arcantons. "Let's see, today you shall be going to university. How shall we dress you today?"

Deliverance ignored the fact that Eleanor seemed to regard her has her personal, life-sized doll and focused on the fact her advice was indeed quite helpful.

"We could go with the typical pullover and jeans...but no. You're going to Oxdale. Not some local place," Eleanor mused.

With the discarding of the jeans and pullover idea, Deliverance felt a pang of wistfulness. She rather liked that style of dress. It was comfortable and versatile — she could climb and move freely without worrying about tears.

After rummaging through the armoire, eventually Eleanor selected a sweater, jacket, tall boots and some stretchy blue pants. The soft leather boots cradled her feet and the plaid scarf provided a bit of extra warmth. Deliverance was satisfied with Eleanor's selections and Eleanor seemed to approve as well, although their criteria for selecting outfits did seem to be at odds more often than not.

Jack knocked, coming to collect her.

"Good morning, Fuzzhead," he greeted his sister and then Deliverance. "Good morning, Gorgeous."

"I don't see why I can't come with you today." Eleanor pouted, playing with the buttons on the chaise upholstery.

"Because you're our ace in the hole, and we have to keep you in the hole for a while longer," Jack replied.

"That's really not an explanation," Eleanor argued. Deliverance agreed she had a point. What did that even mean?

"It is if I say it is," Jack retorted, and his sister relented. Apparently, Eleanor knew more about holes and aces than Deliverance. Before they left, Deliverance remembered to leave a bit of toast out on the balcony for her wren friend. And then they were off.

"It's a little over an hour's drive from here," Jack said as he took the wheel of one of the cars. Deliverance considered the relative size of Arcanton, which was really a large island, like Nar, with a series of outlying islands, and tried to put the scale into her brain. She was struggling though. Jack arched an eyebrow at her.

"The Outside is so…vast," Deliverance explained.

"Indeed, and this is just a small day trip. Someday I will take you to the Indus plains, the Egyto-Levanine valley, the Kathmalu mountains, the Carib islands…everywhere and anywhere you desire," Jack said animatedly as he drove. Deliverance did not feel like squelching his good mood and so kept the thought to herself that Mrs. Potter had warned him against making overreaching promises. Jack was a dreamer. He needed his dreams to fuel the fire, so to speak.

As they left the city, the panorama of the car windshield took on green rolling hills, gently changing into autumn color. The climate here seemed much the same on Nar, although perhaps Nar was a bit harsher. Jack assured her the winters here brought

Deliverance

snow as well, although not in the abundance to which she was accustomed.

"You are very well traveled," Deliverance commented as she watched the pastures roll by.

"Some of it is from my days in the military, although they hardly ever sent us anywhere pleasant. Some of it is from my work in the Senate. Some of it is just plain old academic curiosity," Jack replied. "St. Andrew's, the college we are going to in Oxdale today, has one of the best cultural anthropology programs in the world. It's been really quite a privilege to work with them…well, most of them. Some of them are a bit odd…academic sorts, you know." He glanced at her. "Well, I guess probably you don't know. Some of them are a bit eccentric, Lord Asher included…just so you are prepared."

Deliverance nodded, digesting this warning. Why would her mother send her out to find a crazy person? And what could he possibly do for her and her situation?

Some parts of Arcanton looked a lot like the farming plots on Nar. Although the occasional mechanized tractor dispelled that notion. Cows were still cows though, Deliverance mused.

Buildings were not, however, still buildings in Arcanton. As they pulled through the outer historic gates of Oxdale city, Deliverance was swept away by the grace of the architecture.

"Most of it is Gothic, although there are still some medieval buildings standing, and a few more modern ones sprinkled here and there," Jack said as they exited the car park. The sweeping sandy-colored blocks were punctuated by flying buttresses and dark-paned windows, spires reaching up to the sky in intricate repeating patterns. The green lawns stretching in between the structures seemed opaque in comparison.

"That's the Bedlam Library over there. I'll take you in there later. If you think our private library is expansive, you're in for a treat," Jack said, pointing out this structure and that as they walked along. "Ah, here we are. This is St. Andrews' main hall."

Jack held open an imposing, ratcheted door, and Deliverance felt she had been blown into another world. Here, inside, the lines were modern and clean. Students and faculty walked around not in the Edwardian dress of the English posh society, but a mixture of tweed jackets, pullovers, and lab coats. All carried stacks of books, satchels, and reems of paper. Others carried thermoses of coffee, or wore smart looking eyeglasses, and earbuds playing music floated by. Deliverance could almost smell the learning in this place, the budding of mind, the exchange of ideas. She looked around in wonderment as she followed after Jack. They went up a couple flights of stairs, dodging distracted looking students and muttering professors as they went and ventured down a long hall. Jack disappeared behind a door for a minute.

He came back out scratching his head in confusion.

"What's wrong?" Deliverance asked.

"I think he's moved his office spaces. Damn, it was here the last time I worked with him, but he's become something of a recluse. Wait right here. I am going to see if I can sort this out. I *know* he is back today and they certainly have not fired him with

Deliverance

his boatload of completely unearned tenure under his belt," Jack said, shaking his head and frowning. "I'll be right back."

Deliverance wandered up and down the hallway with it speckled, shining floors and cork bulletin boards for a while, but Jack still had not yet returned. As she passed one of the back doors of a lecture hall though, a single phrase jumped out at her, arresting her complete attention.

"The Restricted Zone of Nar," a disembodied voice intoned into a voice microphone. Deliverance froze, not daring to move for a beat. They were lecturing on Nar in this hall! She looked around furtively, and then, making her decision, slipped into the back of the stadium-like lecture hall.

A smartly dressed woman in pumps and a lab coat stood at the very bottom on the stage with a light upon her. The rest of the hall was darkened, but Deliverance could see it was more than half full of students in various states of awake. They all, however, sat up a bit straighter when the lady at the front mentioned Nar. Deliverance silently slipped into one of the padded lecture hall seats in the very back and waited with abated breath.

"Also known as the Island Nation of Nar, or what once was the Kingdom of Nar," the woman continued, flicking through images on the overhead projector. Deliverance caught her breath. They were drone images of her island! "This course is about the morality of anthropology and the issues surrounding it. None is more famous than that of the Narisi Restricted Zone. Can anyone tell me why that is?"

| 239 |

A tremulous student braved to raise her hand in the front and when called upon answered, "Because everyone wants to know about it, but no one is legally allowed to go there. Not even anthropologists. And no one has ever been off the island."

"Almost correct, Ms. Herrera," the professor replied, and then flicked the slide again.

Deliverance's heart almost stopped. Upon the screen a spotty black and white image of her mother, in a small boat alit upon the screen. She looked younger and cast an expression of apprehension over her shoulder at the photographer, who must have been in the boat with her. What in the Fades were they doing with a picture of a much younger Cat?

"Everyone knows about the plague and the exodus to the island in 1483. Let's fast forward to 2087. Twenty-three years ago. This woman, a Narisi native, was photographed aboard a boat. Who can tell me why this is odd?"

This time a young man in a smart blazer raised his hand, more confidently than his predecessor. "Because the phycological narrative fed to the Narisis has discouraged their use of boats to keep them captive on the island. All the boats were to be burned, as per the accord with Queen Arwen the III and her husband King Daniel the Red. Memory stealers later sent spells via messenger bird to wipe the idea of boats or the concept that people could float on water on vessels at all from the minds of the people."

"Correct, but not entirely complete, Master David," the professor answered. She flicked back to the slide of Deliverance's mother. "In the mid-1700s, there was an attempt by a Narisi faction to flee the island. In an effort to quell this type of action, the Arcanton government, which regards the island of Nar as occupying its sovereign waters, came up with a solution. Does anyone know what that solution was? No one? Come on, people. This is central to the whole lecture!" Deliverance's face burned with fury and indignation. This group of academics was discussing her people like they were some sort of insect, a curiosity to be catalogued and prodded in experimentation!

The professor paused, taking a swig of water from a nondescript plastic bottle before continuing, "All right, I will help you out on this one. Governments in the mid-1700s were not renowned for being the most ethical. The idea of human rights was only just beginning to be explored in various pockets throughout the planet at that time. The rights of an actively plagued people with a potentially magically dangerous disease did not rank high on the rights priority list for the leaders of Arcanton at the time." She flicked through some photos of past senators of the era.

"Therefore, they used magic, one more time, to install a rogue faction amongst the Narisis. Enter the informant line. A daring mother-daughter duo volunteered for the task of emigrating to Nar and upholding Arcanton's objectives on the island. Perseverance Magne and her daughter Lana, who was later renamed Solitude, when they were chosen for the mission to Nar. With the help of some of the most genius memory changers in the known world at the time, Perseverance and Solitude were smuggled into the very fabric of the island life. The natives' memories were altered so that they had no idea Perseverance and her daughter had not always been there in their little homestead on the outskirts of the isle." The lecturer flipped to an aerial shot of Deliverance's homestead.

Deliverance gripped the armrests of her chair violently. Luckily, no one was sitting as far back as she and took no notice of her.

"They were the first in a long family line of Narisi informers who worked with the Arcanton government to shape the narrative on Nar. This responsibility was handed down from generation, from mother to daughter, until the 2080s. Does anyone know why there was a break in the tradition?"

Another sharply dressed, Frankish-braided student raised her hand and was called upon.

"Because the University of Oxdale managed to obtain full control over the informant program from the Arcanton government in a gesture of good academic will a decade before and then...well, the picture happened."

"Precisely!" the professor exclaimed, pointing at the braided girl, who looked smartly around at her peers. "The Oxdale-Senate Treatise of 2079 gave control of the informant program over entirely to the university, whereas before we just had an advisory role. It was meant as an olive branch between the government and the university—as you all know, we have a long history of butting heads."

Deliverance

This comment garnered a few chuckles from the crowd. Deliverance did not chuckle. How could they be sitting here, discussing her home as if it were some kind of science experiment!?

"Now we get into the modern morality of it all," the professor continued. The slides became generic pictures of various technological innovations. "Modern medicine. Xrays, MRIs, vaccines...cures for horrible diseases that used to plague our society. They have been all but eradicated...but not on Nar. Forget your cellphones, your internet, your languages, your education. We're talking about mere survival here, people!" Deliverance could tell the professor was getting a rise out of the students. They sat forward. "So, is it moral to keep all that from these people?" she asked. "Well? Let's hear some opinions!"

A girl with ebony skin and fluffy pigtails raised her hand this time. "The government seems to think so, in order to keep their plague—which was proven in the 80s to still be active—quarantined."

"Ah, yes. That is what the Arcanton government thinks. And they are prepared to enforce such with military power. But what do you think?" The professor prompted.

"No?" a girl with slick, shiny black hair and almond shaped eyes answered tentatively. She gulped, then continued, "No, because they should know what the outside world is. We have been lying to them for generations!"

"Yes, but that is to preserve the quarantine without violence or the spread of disease," another student chimed in.

"Is death by gunfire or fire breathing any different from death by early childhood illness?" Yet another challenger piped up.

Visions of stillbirths and dead infants Deliverance had personally swaddled in their grave clothes flashed before her eyes.

"But we read all about their culture last semester. It's positively medieval how they treat their women! Totally barbaric!"

The voices swirled around Deliverance like fireflies on a summer's eve.

"Yes, you there in the back. Do you have something to add?" the professor said, squinting against the overhead lights. Deliverance realized she had raised her hand.

"Yes…I…why is the disease considered so dangerous?" she stammered, aware of eyes registering she was one more student in the room.

"Now that is the fundamental question now, isn't it Miss…?"

"Deliverance."

"Miss Deliverance has asked a pertinent question. Why is it we fear the Narisi plague so much?" the professor asked her students.

"Because they can steal magical powers?" answered one student while another called out, "Because the men are totally impotent of magic and no one wants to risk that."

"Again, partially correct. The men are considered genetically incapable of any magic. But is magic so necessary in today's society? Show of hands, who has actually used their gifts today?" The professor polled the crowd. Only a couple students raised their hands. "It seems modern technology provides a certain amount of gift-spanning equality, does it not? Okay, so let's assume our problem is not with the men, but the women."

"Because we don't know?" One student hazarded after a lull of silence.

"Bingo! That is precisely why the Narisi problem set is considered so dangerous. We do not have enough data to make informed decisions about how their magical malady would affect us on a large scale. Which is one reason this incident," the professor flicked back yet again to the image of younger Cat a sea, "caused such a scandal. People fear what they do not know. And fear is a very dangerous thing indeed. And time's up for today. Study up for the next lecture. I do not want to have to pull answers out of you, people!"

Deliverance blinked as the lights flickered on, and the crowd began to filter out of the room.

"Deliverance?" Jack's voice came to her from somewhere behind. Had he been there the whole time? She sat rigid as a board, shaking with fury.

"Deliverance, come on. We have to go," he said gently, placing a tentative hand on her shoulder.

"Is that what you meant!? By Nar being a complex problem!" She whirled around, trembling with rage. "We're prisoners! Kept there on that island, isolated from everything, oppressed and sick and dying young all because of people's fear! And my family has helped secure that terrible legacy for hundreds of years!"

"Hey, come on. Let's get some fresh air," Jack coaxed her, but Deliverance was not having it.

"And you! You are a part of the Arcanton government! Are you a supporter of this so-called quarantine?" She zeroed in on him with pent up rage.

His eyes flickered darkly. "No. I am not. If you have forgotten in the past half hour, I am on your side. YOUR SIDE. Now, let's get out of here before you attract unwanted attention."

She wanted to argue. To scream. To beat her fists. But he was right. They could not stay here.

The midmorning air was a tonic to her nerves. She pulled in deep gulps of it, resting her hands on her knees.

"Hey..." Jack prodded her gently.

She looked up at him. No, he was not the target of her ire. At least, she was fairly certain he was not, although she had little knowledge of the inner workings of the Arcanton government.

"It's all right. I'm fine," she said, straightening.

"Well that's amazing. 'Cause I wouldn't be if I were you," he said. She regarded him, feeling something in her putting emotional distance between them...a protective barrier.

"It was all very…jarring. But I will manage. I've made it through being lost at sea, kidnapped by pirates, skydiving, and a ball at your aunt's. This is just one more hurdle," she answered resolutely.

He smiled approvingly at her. "That's my girl."

No, I might not be, Deliverance thought silently to herself as she fingered the ring still on her finger while she followed him across the mall.

CHAPTER 20

Jack

It had been a shock to find her squirreled away in the back of a lecture hall listening to a lecture on Nar, no less. It must have been more of a shock for her. He did not regret standing silently by while she absorbed the lecture. The better the picture she had, the better off she would be. He could've strangled the lecturer though...Dr. Phillips. Self-righteous academic sort. Thought she was too smart for the normal people who made their way in the real world, not surrounded by the fortress of the academic ivory tower. She made the Arcanton government out to be one big entity, an all-consuming blob that smashed the world under its heels.

Granted, the unflattering parts of their history had been accurate. And there were still many — a slight majority in fact, of all the damnable obstacles — who were stuck in their old ways. Ways of fear and oppression. Jack was certain Deliverance did not have a good concept of how the Republic was run, and he was determined to show her the process. Checks and balances, parties, freedom of the vote, elections…these were all concepts foreign to the girl.

There were two sides to every story though. In this case Lord Asher represented an entirely other side, which would not improve Deliverance's outlook. Jack frowned grimly. Events had not unfolded in the way he'd hoped they would today, but at least they were getting the worst out of the way. Then they could begin the real work. He slid a glance over his shoulder and saw Deliverance trodding gravely behind him, mouth set in a firm, thin line. He felt her pull away instantly, armor herself against him and against the world. Hopefully he had not lost her entirely. His heart gave a painful squeeze at this thought, but he soldiered on. That was, after all, what he was.

✳✳✳

Deliverance

Tucked away in the corner of the expansive kelly-green mall, mowed in checkered patterns, was a Victorian era house with gables and gingerbread trim. It was not, however, a living quarters but another of the school's offices.

"Apparently Lord Asher has confiscated the building entirely for himself and his research," Jack remarked dryly as they climbed the creaking steps to the veranda. The glass doors entering into the house had been inscribed with another professor's name and credentials, but someone had taken red spray paint and blotted the etched lettering out. Under it was a hastily taped sign in handwritten marker stating: "Office hours: never! Go away!"

Jack grunted when he looked at the sign and as they passed through the door, surreptitiously swiped the sign off the door and crumpled it. As he tossed it into the bushes he said "Oops" in an innocent tone. They must have a complicated relationship, Lord Asher and Jack, Deliverance thought.

The entryway of the old structure had been well maintained, but its contents were now covered in a thin layer of dust. There were no lights other than what was leaking through the grimy windows.

"Now where could he be..." Jack mused. All of a sudden, a loud crash came from overhead. "Ah...that's where he be. Come along."

They took the double flight of stairs to the second level of the house and followed the racket to a closed door. The sound of smashing glass ricocheted out from under the draft in the oaken door.

Jack traded a look with Deliverance and then said, "Maybe you should wait here for a second." She nodded in agreement.

Jack squared his shoulders, rapped twice on the mottled glass of the door, but did not wait for a call to enter. He let himself in and shut the door behind him. Deliverance could hear their conversation clearly.

"What! Who's there…? Oh, it's just you, Jack. Why the devil do you have to sneak around like that?" A gravelly voice arose.

"I knocked. You probably couldn't hear it over all this racket. What on earth are you doing, man?"

"What? Oh, this is research."

"Right…it looks like a bloody mess."

"All part of the scientific process."

"Is denying office hours part of the scientific process as well?"

"As a matter of fact, it is. Need time…and quiet for research. All those damn students are so noisy. Did you take my sign down again? You did, didn't you?"

"Even with all your tenure, you ought to at least attempt having office hours at some point."

"Why? My students are doing just fine."

"That's because you never hold class…and you give them all top marks for effort."

"See? The system works fine. Now unless you have something pertinent to say, Jack, I really must—"

"Pertinent? Pertinent! Have you bloody well forgotten about your responsibilities on the Nar project!?"

"What…no…it's just…it is at an impasse. You know that. Unless you can persuade more senators to see your view then there is not a whole lot to be done. Now, Antarticus…there is a geographic region prime for research...no bloody restrictions and no politicians interested in it. Perfect. No offense, Jack...well maybe slightly some offense."

"So, you just abandon all interest because of a small road block? I've been hard at work on my end persuading and wheeling and dealing. With my calculations I just lack the backing of one senator. Do you hear me, Asher? One! We're almost there!"

"Ah...that is nice."

"Damn it, man. Stop avoiding this issue! In fact, you cannot avoid it. Not anymore. Your damn escapades have come back to bite you in the ass and the biter is waiting just outside these doors!"

"What do you mean?" A note of panic hit the other voice in the room.

"Come on in!" Jack called cavalierly to Deliverance, through the doors.

Intrepidly, she stepped into the room. Jack was right. It was a bloody mess in here. Papers and books were stacked floor to ceiling throughout the lab space, broken glass littered the floor, and a Bunsen burner was spewing some odd purple concoction out all over the exposed floorboards. In the back of the room entire library shelves were filled with identical looking glass jars, labeled, with green, luminescent swirls flitting about inside them like the swirls of freshly poured cream in tea. Behind one of the tables stood an imposing man. Or at least he would have been if he did not have spectacles on which made his pupils absurdly huge. He looked like a Great Horned Owl with his salt and pepper locks standing at all ends and his stained lab coat disheveled. He had a curved, aristocratic nose, and Deliverance could see tufts of slate colored chest hair peeking out from under the man's rumpled collared shirt. So, this was Lord Asher.

He had been attempting, unsuccessfully, to shoo Jack away when Deliverance made her entrance into the room, clicking the door softly shut behind her. When the stormwater blue eyes, with their enormous pupils fixed upon her face, though, they became impossibly larger. The man griped the sides of the tall table and swayed like he might swoon.

"Impossible!" He gasped. "Cat?"

Deliverance paused a beat. He thought she was her mother.

Jack chimed in, sounding almost cheerful at the man's discomfort. "Wrong again, old man. This is Deliverance…your daughter."

CHAPTER 21

Deliverance

Deliverance then understood the man's propensity to stagger.

"WHAT?" They both bellowed at the same moment.

"Well, it's not like you were going to be any more graceful at breaking the news to her." Jack shrugged, hoisting himself up to perch on one of the tabletops that was not covered in debris.

Deliverance felt drained all of a sudden, sparks flitting across her vision. Jack shifted like he might rush to her side, but she straightened and took a deep breath. Fainting would not do at a moment like this.

"Is it true?" she asked quietly of the man before her. Studying his face, she could see how paternity might be possible.

The man did not answer, but instead rounded the table and stared at her intensely, as if looking at a specimen through a microscope.

"Oh, for God's sake!" Jack said, reaching over and swiping the man's spectacles off his nose.

"Ah, yes that's better," the man said, his pupils now of regular proportion. "No...not Cat. But the resemblance is remarkable."

"Really? That is all you have to say?" Jack cried, throwing his hands up in the air. "Try...hi, my name is blah blah Asher—or, I am really sorry I was not a father to you?"

"Oh. Uh—" Lord Asher stammered but Deliverance cut him off.

"Jack, really, there is no need," she said crisply. "I did not have a father for twenty-three years. I certainly do not require intricate explanations now. I've been perfectly fine without them." Who cared who this man was? All she needed from him was to help her mother. She was seriously doubting his ability to do so, though.

"That's not entirely true," Lord Asher replied quietly.

"What, that I am twenty-three or that you were never there?" Deliverance challenged him.

"I was there," he answered softly. "In the beginning. Before... the scandal. You just do not remember."

"I think I would remember a man living in my house!" Deliverance cried. What on earth was this addlepated man getting at?

"No, not necessarily," Jack said, entering into the conversation again. "Lord Asher here is a memory stealer...meaning he can take memories from people. I assume that is what you did to your daughter so she would not remember you?" The last sentence was tinged in acid.

"I...I did it so she would not feel the pain of separation! I did it out of love! It was really quite impossible to go back, after they discovered Cat had left the island. They shut down all my winter visits. They would have murdered Cat and the baby to cover their tracks!" Lord Asher protested.

This drew Deliverance up short. "Who would have murdered us?"

"The Arcanton government for one — those idiot village people for another. They are really quite devolved," Lord Asher answered.

Jack coughed. "You said the term 'devolved' was not academically correct or appropriate, as per one of our previous interactions that you would call conversations but I would call inane lectures."

Lord Asher regarded him coolly. "In this particular case, it is rather fitting. Those men are barbaric. The things we catch them doing on the drones...their style of so-called justice..." He shook his head in contempt.

"And yet, you seem to have left my mother and I to their mercy," Deliverance remarked with acid in her voice.

"I...your family has been on the island for hundreds of years. Perseverance and Solitude Magne were the first narrative shapers commissioned by the Arcanton government on the island of Nar," Lord Asher began.

"Oh, she knows. She was treated to a lecture by that showboating Professor Phillips," Jack cut in.

Lord Asher looked at a loss for a minute, staring dejectedly as his hands, as if by the sheer weight of his gaze he could will them into effectualness. "Wait!" he piped up. "I can show you!"

He leaped from the stool he had slumped into a minute before and trotted to the back of the room where the shelves of eerie, glowing jars were kept. He perused them, muttering to himself, fingers trailing in the fine dusty film coating most of them. "This one…and perhaps that one, to be fair." He gingerly grasped one of the jars, tucking it carefully in the crook of his elbow as he reached up a bit further and plucked another down from a higher shelf. Then, cautiously, he brought them back over to one of the lab tables. Less cautiously, he swept everything clear off the table with his other arm, letting books, papers, inkpots and the like crash to the foreground.

"Here. These will show you," he said, gesturing at the two jars.

"Ummm… what are they?" Deliverance asked uncertainly. Briefly, she wondered if madness ran in the family, and if so, was she at risk?

"They're memories, darling," Jack answered for her.

"What!?"

"That's right. Doctor Asher here uses his magical gift to pull memories from a mind. Then he stores them in these little pots, like a serial killer stores people's fingers and toes in his freezer." Judging by the wryness in Jack's voice, Deliverance was gathering he rather loathed her father.

"These...these are all people's memories!? Surely you've no right!" Deliverance cried, eyes widening, taking in the row upon row of jars collecting dust in this hermit's den.

"Huh? Oh, those. Most of those the people wished gone," Lord Asher replied meekly.

"Most..." repeated Jack.

"Really, must you be so sanctimonious?" Lord Asher bit back.

"I am a politician after all," Jack returned in kind.

"A rotten one at that. When will you ever get a majority to back the Nar project? It's politicians' fault we are at a standstill on Nar and politicians' fault I could not go back to see my daughter!"

Jack snorted. "Sure, blame someone else for your lack of trying."

"Not everyone can steal an airship and get away with it."

"Wait, Jack, you stole an airship?" Deliverance cut in, trying to stop the back and forth.

"It was just a small one...I gave it back!"

Deliverance was developing an acute headache. "So, what do we do with these creepy little jars?" she asked.

"Here, let me show you." Lord Asher lifted the lid and coaxed the sprite-like light from the jar. Without warning, he touched Deliverance's temple, and the light shot through his fingers like a conduit into her brain.

※※※

It was frigid sailing navigating the North Sea in November. John tucked his chin down farther in his fisherman's sweater and anorak. He was cutting it close—the ice would not be navigable in a few days. It had been unavoidable though, after the previous memory-stealer appointed to the Nar Restricted Zone had an unfortunate stroke. John Asher had been called to fill in for him, as he was the only other anthropologist and memory-gifted of the Oxdale staff at the time. It took him a few weeks to get up to speed on the project. It was particularly important to get to Nar before the winter stuck its deep, treacherous fingers of ice into the sea because the informant line was down to one. Catalyst's mother Independence had succumbed to influenza not a few weeks ago. The girl had to be brought up to speed in order to keep the Narisi narrative alive and safe.

He knew exactly where the hidden cove was from the briefings. He had not expected, however, for Catalyst to be waiting for him on the beachhead.

As he drew nearer, he realized she was not waiting on him. No, she was dancing! There was a large pyre built in the hidden alcove, its flames licking at the craggy mountain ridgeline. The girl was swaying and twirling, circling the fire like a whirling dervish or a rain dancer. Her arms spun an intricate story.

As his vessel drew nearer the shore, the girl's eyes, a glowing green as if her magic had been activated, locked on his. But she continued to dance. Even as he pulled his boat ashore, boots mired in sand and surf, she did not cease her dance. The hypnotic gyrations and the wildly akimbo limbs continued on until finally she halted, her lithe body in the position of a giant X. As though she were Atlas and the weight of the world rested upon her, she pushed up and out, releasing a cloud of green into the atmosphere. Finally, when she was ready, she turned to greet him.

"You are John Asher," she stated, head up almost defiantly. A priestess in her own right.

"I am."

"I am Catalyst, daughter of Independence, granddaughter of Reliance, great granddaughter of Quickening, heir to the burden of Solitude nee Perseverance Magne. Welcome to my island."

***

Deliverance gasped for air, hands clutching the sides of the lab table, encrusted with suspect unknown substances.

"What did you just do to me!?" she cried, eyes wide.

"I let you see a memory," Lord Asher replied.

"You invaded my brain!" Deliverance accused him, eyes flashing.

"Not for the first time!" Jack added cheerfully, although he shut his mouth with a click when both Deliverance and Lord Asher eyed him.

"I took the memory back. It's mine, so you saw it from a third person perspective. Really quite interesting how it works," Lord Asher explained academically.

"But if you took it back, then how come I still remember it?" Deliverance asked uncertainly.

"I didn't wipe it from your mind. It will leave a trace, like an imprint. But it won't affect your subconscious or your personal thoughts. I could erase it, but then we'd be right back where we started."

"Back before you leapt into my head!" She rubbed her temples as though she could smear away the invasion.

"Yes…I am so accustomed to my own gift, I forget others find it…unsavory?" Lord Asher tried.

"Creepy?" Jack suggested. "Violating? Psychotic even?"

"Jack, you're not helping," Deliverance snapped.

"All right…but to be fair, I'm actually the only person who has helped you since you found yourself afloat at sea," he said. This was true, Deliverance thought, heart softening a bit.

"You were afloat at sea!? What on earth were you doing? And where is Cat?" Lord Asher yelped, eyes bulging.

Deliverance

"Shall we catch the old man up, since he has had his head stuck up his arse for the last twenty-some years?" Jack said to Deliverance.

She rolled her eyes at Jack but turned to her...father...and recounted her tale from the beginning.

It took several hours, and so Lord Asher sent one of his minions (his word, not Deliverance's) for coffee and refreshments. They retired to the study downstairs, which was at least somewhat less chaotic than the lab, but Lord Asher brought along the second swirling jar and set it on the table. It seemed to stare at Deliverance like a bird of prey from its perch on the end table. Jack lit a fire in the fireplace and Lord Asher accused him of being good for party-tricks and little else. They were about to descend into another quid pro quo before Deliverance intercepted.

"Gentlemen, please! Focus!" Deliverance clapped to get their attention. They both looked at her like naughty schoolchildren. This was going to be a long day.

"So, if I am understanding this correctly...Cat is imprisoned and you are here. You would likely be arrested as well if you were returned to the island," Lord Asher reasoned aloud.

"Most definitely," Jack replied grimly.

"The informant line is compromised and so is the narrative that keeps the islanders...well, on the island. Parliament will have to act," Lord Asher declared. "But I do not trust them to do the right thing! More than likely they will incinerate the whole island or put up a military line of demarcation and murder anyone who attempts to leave the island. The narrative was preventing such action before."

"You mean the lies you concocted and fed my people to keep us prisoner?" Deliverance retorted, crossing her arms.

"It was only to keep the plague at bay, the contagion contained," said Lord Asher. "It was still alive in your mother when she tried to make her escape to Arcanton. They…did experiments on her then after they captured her. It is the only solid scientific data we have about the disease. Then they sent her back and removed me from the project."

"Is every man so frightened of not having magic and of women whose gifts may change?" Deliverance sighed, exasperated.

"If the plague were to spread on a mass scale—and likely it would given globalization—it could cause mass chaos," Lord Asher explained gently. "There would be no checks on powers; people could change and discard gifts at will. There would be no way to track and record who has what gift. Criminals would wreak havoc with that. It is a magical illness, Deliverance. It is not the way things are meant to be."

"God's teeth! You're one of them!" Deliverance cried.

"You look a lot like your mother when you're angry," Lord Asher commented, as Jack talked over him, saying, "No, he's not one of the government technocrats who wants to either wipe Nar off the map or find a permanent imprisonment method. He's just ineffectual and fell into a bottle when they took him off the Nar Project."

"Oh, unlike you who is so radical you can't get a single senator to side with you on the issue?" Lord Asher shot back nastily. "If it were up to him," he said, thumbing at Jack, "anyone with a magical illness could just walk around willy nilly infecting everyone else until the apocalypse happened! It seems to me you are just as ineffectual!"

"Actually, he said he has almost a majority lined up to support us. Just one more, right?" Deliverance said in defense of Jack. Jack nodded gravely. That one would be difficult.

"But what are you going to do with all those people once you have rescued them from the 17th century? Put them in a shoebox? Oh, I know! Let's just unleash them on the world having no concept of how it functions now and watch them go mad! And in the meantime, they can infect everyone else!" Lord Asher fumed.

"I didn't go mad," Deliverance protested quietly. "And I haven't infected anyone."

"No, not yet. Not until you have children. That's what the damn ring on your finger is about, isn't it? Good God, Jack! You're going to make the same mistake I did!" Lord Asher replied savagely.

"You would rather I act the broodmare, so you can continue your little farce on my island? Sorry, but I seem to have screwed up your plans!" Deliverance shouted back.

"Now you listen here, you washed up old man," Jack growled, heat beginning to radiate off him in waves. His teacup was tremoring in a boil before he set it aside. "We have a way to cure them. You hear me? Cure them all! I have a magical malady healer strong enough to heal anyone who wants to leave the island. And I intend to put that solution before Parliament. Where I need you to get off your useless duff and help is by recording the results of Deliverance's healing. We need everything recorded and documented just so, so that when we go before Parliament, our case will be airtight. You have the knowledge and the facilities to do that…to do that for your daughter. And that is what you WILL do. And furthermore, if you ever refer to Deliverance as a mistake again, I will start charring your internal organs one at a time until your insides look like the pit of a volcano. Am I clear?"

Lord Asher was silent for a long moment, lost in thought. Without looking at Jack, he nodded his assent. Before he got up to retreat back to his offices, he shoved the second jar at Deliverance, saying, "Here. This is actually yours. Just dip your finger in and touch it to your temple."

"Why do you keep your own memories in a jar then?" she asked pointedly.

"Because sometimes it is easier to live with oneself if one can forget." And with that, he swept out of the room.

CHAPTER 22

Deliverance

"You're not saying anything," Jack said, eyeing Deliverance sideways as they drove home.

"There's a lot on my mind," she replied, watching the wheat fields that were now ginger with the tinge of sunset.

"Like…?"

"Like I am beginning to see why everyone thinks Lord Asher is a nut."

Jack chuckled at that.

"And," she continued, "I think politics is much more complicated than I understand. And it makes me nervous. And…I thought for a while that perhaps you were one of them…those men who would keep us on that island for all eternity."

"You thought I was a technocrat!?" Jack yelped. "I do not believe I have ever been so insulted. Even by your father. And he's pretty insulting." Jack was kidding with her, Deliverance realized, and cast a grateful smile at him for lightening the mood.

"He is rather that, isn't he?" Deliverance mused. She was not about to let a man who had abandoned her and her mother, no matter the reason, get under her skin. "What do you think I should do with this?" she asked, holding up the unsettling little jar he had bid her take.

"Well…that is entirely up to you, my love. But those memories are rightfully yours," Jack advised and would say no more on the subject.

They lulled into a companionable silence for a while as they traversed the countryside. Then, unthinkingly, Deliverance reached over and placed her hand overtop Jack's to give it a squeeze. Immediately, she was rocketed into a memory.

✱✱✱

"Medic! Medic!" The desperate cries rang out. All around was chaos and death. The air stank of flesh in all stages of life—fearing death, dying, and dead. An explosion rang out, causing a deafening, piercing ring to block out all the noise. In front of her, Deliverance could see a much younger Jack, carrying a fellow soldier over his shoulder, attempting to navigate the perilous chaos. His charred fatigues were covered in the filth of war, grime, blood, and fire.

"Hang in there, old chap!" Jack shouted to his friend, as he struggled up the sides of an embankment. His fellow soldier groaned and then grew silent, limply dangling as Jack fought his way up the steep, silty mound. He stumbled, and almost collapsed once he reached the precipice.

Deliverance

Giving a frustrated shout of effort, he carried his companion the last several meters to the perimeter line.

"Medic!" he shouted desperately as he navigated his way through the reinforced defenses. Finally, unable to go any farther, Jack collapsed with his back to an entrenchment.

"We made it, buddy," he said, heaving. Rivets of sweat drew channels down the sooty grime of his face. "There! A medic is on his way...Roger?" His voice grew tremulous, and with shaking hands he flipped his friend over, face to sky.

When the medic arrived, he confirmed what Jack saw — Roger was dead.

"I'm sorry," the medic said breathlessly. "I have to get back to the others." Then he paused for just a second, adding, "That was a brave thing you did, Sergeant. Carrying him all the way back here."

Jack had slumped back down, back sliding down the chalky sand of the trench wall. He waved the medic away wordlessly.

Emotion threatened to overtake him, eyes tearing up. He put a hand to Roger's eyes and shut them for their final sleep. Shock, grief, disbelief played across Jack's younger features, each emotion overtaking the next. Finally, he settled on anger.

"DAMN!" He cursed, leaping to his feet and punching the earthen wall. "DAMN! DAMN! DAMN!" With each punch, Jack's skin began to smolder a bit more, building heat.

"Sergeant!" barked a voice. Jack paused in his assault of the wall, rivers of red-hot blood still snaking their way under his skin, the veins *causing little spots of charring where they brushed his uniform. "Compose yourself!"*

Shoulder heaving, Jack relented and dropped his fists. He turned to eye the other sergeant, a man of equivalent age, a prowess-gifted he recognized but did not know personally. He worked in reconnaissance though — a brave capacity. Highly dangerous even for one as gifted with stealth and agility as a prowess-gifted.

"And just how do you propose I do that?" Jack snarled, his power still threatening to take off.

"What three things cannot long be hidden?" the other sergeant countered.

"Huh?"

"I said what three things cannot long be hidden?" the man calmly repeated. He had an air of tranquility about him even in a warzone.

Jack cursed, then said "What?" to placate the man.

"The sun, the moon, and the truth," the even keeled sergeant replied.

"Are you a Buddhist?" Jack said, eyeing him.

"No, I saw it on a TV show about werewolves," the man replied, breaking into a grin. "But you see, it worked."

Jack glanced down at his hands. His forearms were no longer glowing with lava rivers in his bloodstream. The magic had retreated, taking his rage with it.

"I'm Niles," the man introduced himself, offering his hand when he was certain Jack would not singe it to a crisp.

"Jack," Jack said in kind, shaking the man's hand. He looked down at his dead companion, unnaturally peaceful in his hollowed form, and grief welled up inside him. "But, really, how do you do it?" he whispered.

Niles looked at him thoughtfully and then answered, "That rage you have?" Jack nodded. "Use it. Burn down the whole world around you. But do it with calculation and control. Burn it down, then rebuild it again in a better image."

***

Deliverance gasped, jolting out of the memory. It took her a moment to realize Jack had pulled over to the side of the road. He was patting her face, trying to get her to come to.

"Oh, thank God!" Jack breathed. "What was that!?"

"I...oh. I had forgotten Lord Asher touched me," Deliverance replied.

"Jesus. Your eyes rolled in the back of your head and there was no reviving you. I nearly had a heart attack!" Jack exclaimed, putting both hands on the sides of her face and examining her, as if to reassure himself she was cognizant and with him.

"I must have absorbed his power. I saw a memory..." Deliverance reasoned.

Jack stilled. "Of mine?"

"Yes, it was a battle. There was blood and chaos everywhere...your friend. Roger. He died," Deliverance choked, the emotion swelling up in her chest, threatening to crush her.

A grimace pulled down Jack's face. "I'm sorry you had to see that," he quietly said, after a moment.

"Oh, Jack, no! I am sorry!" Deliverance said, unable to stop the tears from rolling down her face.

Jack gathered her close, and comforted her. "Hey now. Easy there. It's all in the past," he murmured, rocking her. He had unbuckled her seatbelt, and pulled her into his lap.

"But it just happened right in front of my eyes," Deliverance said into the collar of his shirt where she had buried her face.

"Makes one almost want to cut Lord Asher a little slack. His gift is bound to rock someone's stability after a while," Jack commented. "Almost," he added, not quite willing to give the man an inch.

They sat that way for a long while, until Deliverance had collected herself. When she had, she removed herself to the passenger seat, wiping her face, her cheeks warming with embarrassment.

"I feel silly. It was you who should be upset. It was not even my memory," Deliverance said, as she refastened her seat belt.

"I've learned to come to terms with my past," Jack said evenly. "But it fuels me all the same today." Deliverance nodded, understanding Jack just a bit better now.

He started the car with a thrum, and they drove in silence for a while, each mired in deep thought.

Then Deliverance said, "Jack?"

He hmmmed at her in reply, so she continued, "When we get home, we are most definitely going to need another family meeting."

CHAPTER 23

Deliverance

Normally she would worry her long, thick braid when faced with a decision of this magnitude. In its absence, she ran her fingers through her choppy ends repetitively as she paced the length of her bedroom. The jar, swirling in its effervescence, was perched on a lacy pillow case on her four-poster bed. She would walk to it, then think better of it, and begin to pace again. Pretty soon she would wear a tread in the pastel, vined rug beneath her stockinged feet.

She blew out a breath. "Bloody hell. I've never been a coward before!" she reasoned, finally settling onto the bed and reaching for the jar. Her hand quivered slightly as she reached for the stopper, but with thick determination she quelled her misgivings. Knowledge was always better than ignorance, she thought, and plucked the stopper from the jar with a thunk. Carefully, with still trembling fingers, she coaxed the green thread of wispy magic from the jar. With another deep breath she plunged the magic into her temple.

The memories were hazy at first, as though viewed through a wide-angle lens out of focus. They were not all sights, but mostly sounds, smells, and feelings. The sound of a rumbling Arcanton lilt and her mother's own tinkling laugh. The smell of cinnamon and pipe tobacco, of maleness and the scent of safety. The feeling of tickling chest hairs and the purr of a hum not her mother's, but deeper. Security. Attached. Content. Safe.

Then the memories began to evolve, take more shape. The excitement for winter to arrive. The million questions she would pepper at her mother while they waited for the ship to come ashore. The splash of water as her daddy... Her daddy! Daddy would wrap her up in his arms and toss her high over his head like a little bluebird. He called her Del. No one ever called her that but him.

"Here," he said. "A gift for my lovely Del. Someday this is where we will go." He pressed a cool, round object with a heavy base into her chubby little fingers. "Watch," he said and shook the ball. Snow fell all around the magical fairy city inside.

Then the winter night fighting would begin.

"I'm tired of waiting!" Del would snuggle down deeper into her blankets but she could hear Mommy and Daddy arguing still. "We have to wait three seasons just to see you! And even then 'tis not safe! If one of the villagers decided to brave the snows to check on us, they would sooner murder you than welcome you!"

"No one ever comes here in the winter."

"But they could, John. They could."

"All right, but I will need this next season to plan. Be ready with Del after the Autumn Equinox."

Deliverance

Then another warm season without Daddy, tending the garden. But Mommy sold all their animals that September. Del was sad about her favorite pony but remembered Daddy had said he would buy her a new pony when they got to the new home. Del did not know what this meant, but it sounded exciting.

Terror. The boat felt wrong to every fiber of her being. Daddy said it was the magic of the narrative working its way into their minds, but Del did not know what this meant either. Rocking, cold, salt, wet, shivering. Mommy clutched her close.

"It's all right, Del. Come over here and sit with Daddy."

The warm, sturdiness of his knees.

"Would you like to play with Daddy's camera?" *She nodded. She loved the flashy box that made pictures.*

"John, really?"

"What? It's keeping her distracted. Del likes Daddy's toys, doesn't she?" *Del poked her tongue out of her mouth in determination to hold the shot still and snapped. The picture showed up on the screen — Mommy looking over her shoulder apprehensively at her and Daddy from her seat at the prow of the boat.*

✳✳✳

Tears poured freely down Deliverance's cheeks, plopping in ugly splatters upon the coverlet. With a cry she heaved the damnable jar at the wall and it shattered into inefficacy.

She had taken the Fades-fated photo of her mother on the boat that she had seen in the lecture hall that day. How could her father steal all that from her? To protect her? Instead she had spent her life wondering, ignorant, a cog in a machine whose purpose she'd only just revealed. She shuddered, wracked with grief. Maybe it had not been such a good idea to try to put the memories back into her mind tonight. But she figured it was late. Everyone had gone to bed. She would have some privacy. She was not prepared for the onslaught of emotions that came with the returned memories.

Her door softly opened and closed again with a click. Deliverance did not have to look up to know who it was. Soft pine and sea enveloped her before his arms did. Jack held her all night as she cried, until she fell asleep. And even though she was sad at the loss of her father, she felt safe again.

***

John Asher

The fire crackled in a vivacious commentary. It was as if that damnable Jack Quentin had never left. John sat back and stewed, ruminating over his second glass of smoky scotch. His comfortable, careworn chair by the fire in his shabby apartments beleaguered his staunch bachelorhood. Everything in the tattered scholar's room spoke of austere function. The piles of manuscripts, the curled maps with notes scribbled haphazardly in the margins, stacks of dust-filmed tomes, propped open to this page and that, were the only evidence a person actually dwelled

Deliverance

here. Otherwise, the cobwebs in their gossamer filaments would have taken over the few areas he moved about as well.

The ephemeral, delicate cobweb silk reminded John of the memories he took, from others' minds and his own. Upon the coffee table, laid out in front of him in several jars were such memories, lissome in their flotation in their milky jars. John sat back, rubbing his hands across his scruffy face, and considered the jars. He had retrieved them after Jack and Deliverance left.

Deliverance. The girl's image sprang to his mind unbeckoned. If he could have, he would have taken this afternoon and its painful reunion from his mind as well. That was how he had been coping these past almost two decades. At first it had been a poignant moment, a profession of love or the act of lovemaking with Catalyst, memories that resurfaced over and over again, causing him unbearable anguish. Those went first, sliding easily into their compartments, offering ease for his grieving mind. Others, eventually, took their place. A little dark-headed girl's giggle, the infant smell of milk and lavender. A flash of green eyes, glinting in the midwinter sun. These went as well.

It was not as if he forgot who they were. The idea of them was still ever present, haunting him. But these little details he spared himself…they spared his sanity as well. He was well aware others thought him eccentric. The therapy of relieving his mind and conscious of his once wife and daughter, however, had saved him from breaking over and over. His futile efforts to regain them had been like water crashing against stone. After years of attempting everything within his perceived power to go back to them, he relented. He never forgave himself for relenting.

Now, this brash Jack fellow may have actually figured out a way — succeeded where he had failed. He took a healthy swig of the amber liquid in his glass. This stung more than he would ever allow. He saw now his failing was in acting within the law. Jack Quentin never concerned himself with what was actually legal, only what he thought was just. An odd trait for a man entrusted with lawmaking. John grimaced, thinking of the younger man's smug expressions, his irritating bravado. He hoped to God the man did not fail his daughter as he had failed her mother.

Carefully, he set aside his glass and considered the jars before him, winking in their firefly way, twisting like silky cream in tea, the green ribbons giving off a scintilla occasionally. Before him in life lay an opportunity — one he could not afford to waste. He had a chance to succeed where before he had failed. Perhaps it was time to retake these memories.

As he considered the jars, though, he was daunted by the number that had accumulated over the years. Had he really taken that much out of his own head? To put it all back in one fell swoop could possibly drive him mad. No, it was better to reintegrate them into his brain slowly. He sat back, fingers poised at his lips for the longest time, considering. Finally, he selected one of the jars, slowly coaxing the lid open.

Inside, he could hear the sigh of the memory, as if it were relishing the contact with open air. He coaxed the memory up, so that it was floating on his fingertips, swirling gently in the warmth by the fire. For a moment, he considered putting it back. Shutting it back in its place or worse, smashing the jars to bits on the floor, and having the choice irrevocably out of his reach.

No, he determined. This time he would not fail them.

And he plunged the memory through his temple back into his mind.

***

"How is that even legal?" John asked Cat as they sat on the ridge overlooking the beachhead. They had built a fire and were enjoying the stars for as long as they could before the bitter cold drove them back indoors.

"'Tis how it is done," she replied simply, sitting back on her hands, eyeing him challengingly.

"No records? No witnesses?" John scoffed. "Can't possibly be that simple."

"No, 'tis not a simple thing, marriage. It binds two people by their souls for life. But that requires not the eyes of others, only the gods. If I say I be married to a man, then my word is all I need. I have no use for the assumptions of others," Cat replied seriously.

"Then marry me. Perform the handfasting," he demanded, sitting up and searching her face. She was like a priestess, this wild woman he had found and fallen in love with. She carried herself with the bearing of a tribal queen, reigning over her section of the world, this remote piece of island. Once she had taken him, into her bed and into her heart, he knew he would never be rid of her. She was written in his blood.

She regarded him thoughtfully, then reached down and with a yank, ripped a section of cloth from her linen tunic. With the scratchy, tawny fabric, she bound both their hands.

"'Tis about time ye asked me, Lord John Asher. We have a little one on the way. She needs a father," Cat told him.

John's eyes swam. What? Had she just said…there was a baby on the way?

"Now repeat after me you daft man."

"I take thee, Catalyst nee Independence Magna, body and soul, before all gods…"

✳✳✳

It was some time before John resurfaced, gasping. He was reeling with the familiar demons he had closeted away. But one at a time, he would have to challenge each one and win this time. There was no avoiding it. Any small sliver of information he could remember from his days past on Nar could prove useful in the battle to come.

It was a battle he meant to win.

CHAPTER 24

Deliverance

She was warm and relaxed...so relaxed a small dollop of drool eased its way out of the corner of her mouth onto the pillow. No, not a pillow, she realized as she grew more awake. Jack.

Carefully, she lifted her head from his chest, trying not to disturb him. He was so animated when he was awake; she wanted a chance to study him while the calm of sleep was upon him. He looked so much younger, lips parted, breathing softly, tranquil. Jack awake was entirely different, a storm of energy ready to take on the world. Deliverance loved that Jack, but this one was attractive as well. She attempted to commit to memory the line of his brow, the curve of his throat where his Adam's apple lay, the graceful, powerful fingers subdued with sleep.

Despite her attempts to let him sleep, he stirred and pulled her closer. After a minute he grunted.

"Good morning," he said simply in a gravely, sleep-ridden tone. He eyed her, and she turned to rest her chin on his chest. "Sleep well?"

"Yes, actually. I am accustomed to sharing a bed with my mother. I did not know I missed having the company until now," she answered, careful not to jab her chin into his chest as she talked.

"Well...hmm. I'm not sure how I feel about being your surrogate mother," Jack said playfully, rubbing his face with the arm not around Deliverance.

"You know what I mean!"

Just then the door opened, revealing one of the serving girls with a tray of breakfast who promptly squeaked. "Oh! Oh my goodness! I am so sorry!" She dropped the tray on the nearest surface that would hold it and scampered away.

"Well, now you've done it," Deliverance said to Jack. "The whole house will be a flurry with gossip."

"Dear me. How scandalous," he said in an entirely unconcerned tone. "Let's give them something to talk about then." And he pulled her even closer.

❋❋❋

Oh my, Deliverance thought to herself, blush raging in her cheeks as they descended for breakfast much much later. That was entirely pleasant after the first initial coupling. Jack was a gentle lover, watching her face, reading her body. It was not entirely unlike how Effie described her more enjoyable encounters, although Effie's descriptions lacked something. They were so carnal, almost crude. Perhaps it was the heart-pounding surge of emotion, the love that Deliverance felt when she was with Jack that was lacking in Effie's accounts. Deliverance felt a surge of pity for her friend. Perhaps here in this more accepting world, she too could find something more.

Eleanor read her face, being somewhat of a master people reader like her brother, and tittered. Great, Deliverance thought. It was already afoot.

"You're up late…or are you?" Eleanor said to her brother.

"Hush you." He scolded her and dropped his customary kiss upon her crown, entirely indifferent about whatever gossip might be flitting about the house.

"You're to meet Doctor Pennington this afternoon," Eleanor said to Deliverance through a mouthful of toast. "Riding in Hyde Park." The girl gave a sigh. "I am well enough to go riding again, brother." She petitioned her brother.

"Yes, of that I am certain. However, this particular invitation was for Deliverance. If you would like to take your pony out, I am sure Stiles would accompany you," Jack told her. Stiles was the head stable hand.

"What about you? What are you up to today, my scandalous brother?" She prodded him.

"Trying to cause more scandal. So, I must be off. Behave, you two! Actually, I find it rather more interesting when you do not.

Go forth and wreak havoc, my ladies!" He laughed and headed out the door.

"So," Eleanor said, fixating her pixie stare on Deliverance, "tell me everything about yesterday."

After Deliverance finished her account, Eleanor sat back, hand to her forehead.

"Holy jiminy Christmas!" She swore. "What a load to swallow!" Deliverance nodded. It had been a lot. "And to think, Doctor Asher is your father! That must have been a shock."

"It was. But this whole experience has been one after the other. I am learning to roll with the punches, as you would say," Deliverance replied, taking a sip of her coffee.

"Do not worry, though. I can do my part! I am certain I can fix you…and all your friends. It is my personal crusade!" Eleanor declared with the melodrama of a young teen girl.

Deliverance smiled at her bravado. "I know you can," she said.

"Well, you have to be off soon to go riding with the good doctor. Let's get you dressed in some breeches!" Eleanor announced, pushing away from the breakfast table.

Deliverance had become used to being Eleanor's personal fashion project by now. Riding clothes, as it turned out, were a combination of comfort, durability, and flair. The breaches were of a soft, stretchy tan fabric, reinforced in areas, and the boots, tall, guarding the calves. The jacket had gusseted arms, allowing for free range of motion, although the tweed was a bit showy.

Deliverance

"I had thought at one time that Doctor Pennington and Jack would get married. They were such good friends even after Jack came back from his military service," Eleanor commented as she surveyed her work.

Deliverance felt her stomach drop, annoyingly. "Oh?" She managed casually.

"It never did come to fruition," she went on, and added brightly, "And now he has you!"

Ah, but what would the future bring? Deliverance pondered darkly. If she were cast back to her island, would he find comfort with his old friend? She was ever so much more polished and elegant than she, and beautiful as well. She realized such thinking would do no good, however, and tried to cast the thoughts aside.

✽✽✽

"This is Horace. He is a gentle soul, but eager to please," Addie introduced Deliverance to the horse she would be riding. He was a lanky chestnut with a smart, white blaze upon his kind face and three white stockings to match. Deliverance stroked his elegant, curved neck. Their horses were so different here…so tall! They were nothing like the stocky ponies on Nar.

"He is beautiful. And so shiny!" Deliverance murmured, running her hands along his glossy coat.

"Yes, I have a new stable master, but I believe he is doing well so far. And this is Curie. She's my personal mount. I named her after one of my favorite scientists." Curie was a dappled grey, almost azure in hue with her legs descending into cobalt socks. Her generous mane almost reminded Deliverance of the wild manes of her island ponies, as it fell in lush, generous waves over the horse's elegant neck. The horse whuffled softly into Addie's hand, evidently pleased to see her.

A stable hand had led the horses out for the waiting ladies, and they now each grasped their mounts' reins in their hands. Addie's stables were not far from the riding park. She assured Deliverance they could ride the horses there along a path. The stables themselves were immense and airy, light filtering in from all sides.

"We have twenty-seven horses here and another hundred or so at my family's country estate. My father was something of a horse enthusiast, although my uncle and I really share the passion for the hunt. It is a family tradition if you will, although I have forced him to start using a drag instead of hunting an actual fox. I cannot bear the thought of the poor creature being tormented. My uncle is stuck in his ways but I have my influences. He relents to my whims if I am insistent enough," Addie chattered as she bent over and checked the horses' hooves for stones.

"I love horses as well…but these are quite a bit different than I am used to," Deliverance admitted.

"Oh? How so?" Addie said as she finished running her finger along the crevice along the frog of the hoof.

"They're…" Deliverance was not sure what Southish horses looked like and did not want to give too much away, so she avoided noting how much taller they were. "They have an odd seat on them is all."

"What? Oh, the saddle?" Addie asked, pointing to the foreign looking pad of leather attached to the horse. It had odd dangling elements and different belt attachments.

"Yes, I'm afraid I've never ridden with one," Deliverance said, looking at the saddle skeptically.

"All right then!" Addie remarked brightly. "We shall go without! Might as well give those Hyde Park biddies something else to talk about. There has been nothing but tongues wagging since you rather flattened Ned Turner at the ball. It's been delightful."

Addie circled Horace, and popped the large belt, called a girth, on his saddle and slid the contraption off the horse. She set it, propped on its front against a stall and did the same for her horse. "It's been ages since I've ridden without a saddle. It will be like being a little girl again! Let's go!"

She clipped her velvety helmet in place on her head and Deliverance copied the motion. Then Addie, in a graceful movement, leapt, swinging her leg around, and mounted Curie. It took Deliverance a couple tries, but with a fistful of Horace's generous mane, she managed to haul herself atop her steed. It was much farther from the ground than she was used to. Luckily, the journey to the park was at a walk, so Deliverance could adjust to the rocking gait of the much larger horse.

The leaves about them were changing as the God of Horizons slowly began to bring about winter. Autumn was in full bloom; crimson, saffron, amber, and carrot floated all around them, occasionally dropping in swirls to the path below. Stretching limbs arched over the wide, well trodden pathway, giving the illusion of arcs along the promenade. The sweet, tannin smell of decaying leaves wafted on the sunny afternoon breeze. As they made their way into the park itself, Deliverance noted the popularity of the location. Other equestrians dotted the expansive green and trails throughout. Groups of mothers pushing lacy prams ambled along passing walkers enjoying a sojourn in the warmest part of the day, parasols lazily perched on shoulders. Men in tails and tweeds smoked cigars and gestured as they discussed this matter and that, and older ladies perched upon benches, feeding the flitter of birds. Occasionally the flock would rise up, startled, and then settle back to the ground to commence nibbling the scattered seed again.

Deliverance breathed in the fresh air, glad to not feel so enclosed as she often did in the city proper. As they passed a group of well-heeled men, Deliverance could feel the stares upon them.

When she looked at Addie questioningly, her friend replied, "They are not used to seeing women of our station ride without saddles...or women in the city at all ride without saddles. I'm afraid our wildness is offending their delicate sensibilities." Addie's tone belayed she was not at all concerned about offending their sensibilities. She must be secure in her station,

Deliverance

Deliverance reasoned, as was Jack, to not care a whit what society thought. It was a luxury, she decided, not everyone could afford.

As they road, Addie regaled Deliverance with tales of Jack as a child. Addie was an eloquent storywinder, and Deliverance found herself enjoying her company. In the back of her mind, however, Eleanor's comment lingered. Why had Jack not fallen for this lovely, engaging woman?

"You have an excellent seat," Addie complimented her as they ambled along.

"Oh, thank you. I must admit I am not accustomed to riding horses like this. Although I find their gaits to be much smoother than I am used to from my own horses back home." Deliverance told her.

"I would imagine so. Wherever your home is," Addie replied nonchalantly.

"I'm from Southland," Deliverance protested, her heart giving a leap into her throat. Addie suspected something!

"My dear, unlike most of my class, I am well-traveled. I have been to Southland many times. You are most certainly *not* Southish," Addie declared. Deliverance struggled for a cover but Addie continued before she could make an excuse, "Do not fret, my dear. Your secret is safe with me. I shan't reveal you to anyone, nor shall I question you upon it."

Deliverance relaxed a little.

"You've known for a while?" she asked curiously, studying the other woman with renewed eyes.

"I've suspected for a while. But I am a master at keeping secrets. Ask Jack," Addie answered her, steering down another path.

Screwing up her courage, Deliverance finally asked, "You and Jack have been close for a long time…why have you never…?"

Addie turned to her and gave a gay laugh. "I was wondering when you would work up the gumption to ask. No, Jack and I…we have never been lovers. Nor will we ever be."

"Oh."

Addie's eyes sparkled. "My dear, I am a lesbian."

***

Addie was, as it turned out, good at keeping secrets. Deliverance asked her why she had never married. It was, as Jack had explained, allowed in Arcanton after all.

"In Arcanton, yes, but our class, in all its infinite luxury, is, I'm afraid, the slowest to adapt to new social conventions," Addie explained to her. She added ruefully, "It seems those of us with the most to lose are the least accepting of change." When Deliverance looked at her not quite understanding she expounded, "It is not done in our society. I have not had a chance to meet anyone suitable who shares my…preferences. And so, I am the dedicated spinster."

Deliverance

"You are hardly a spinster!" Deliverance cried, indignant for her friend, remembering Mallory insinuating such at the ball.

"I am twenty-eight, unmarried, and perfectly happy to spend my inheritance as I see fit, doing whatever I damn well please. It is a lonely existence at times, but nonetheless fulfilling. Besides, I have my work as a healer," Addie informed her.

By the end of the day, Deliverance was glad she had accepted Addie's invitation. She had a whole new perspective on one of Jack's oldest friends and was delighted to know her.

Before she left in the car with Stevens to go back home, Addie called to her, "If you ever need my help in any way, you let me know."

"I may at that," Deliverance replied gratefully and waved goodbye.

***

That night, over dinner, Jack seemed preoccupied. It was not until he called everyone into the drawing room for a family meeting that Deliverance understood why.

"I have yet to secure the last vote we need, but apparently Doctor Asher," Jack said his name with acrimony, "has let the cat out of the bag." Deliverance wondered why Doctor Asher would keep a cat in a bag, but then decided he was obviously deranged. Someone should stop him from being cruel to animals, however.

"He maintains he had to tell the relevant people in order to secure the facilities and proper equipment to document

Deliverance's healing process. Apparently, that involves telling everyone associated with the Nar Project about our visitor. The man is a menace!" Jack fumed, raking his fingers through his rooster's crest of hair. The motion stood his hair even more on end than it normally did.

"Wait, so how many people know about me!?" Deliverance asked, panicked.

"At least twenty. They have a history of government subversion, though, so hopefully they will keep their traps shut long enough for me to somehow weasel that last vote out of one of those stodgy technocrats in our way," Jack admitted gravely.

Mrs. Potter chimed in, "This foreboding." Stevens nodded his agreement.

"That being said, they are reading to proceed...which means tomorrow. If you are ready, Deliverance. We can have a go at trying to heal you. Are you ready?" Jack asked, hesitation in his voice.

"I am," Deliverance asserted, no hesitation in hers. Who knew how long the food bringers would continue to support Effie and her mother? Time was of the essence.

✳✳✳

"Are you really ready?" Jack asked her, that night, when they were wrapped up together in her bed.

"I have to be," she replied, sinking her face into the front of his shirt. He smelled like Mrs. Potter's lavender laundry soap and his own sea-and-pine musk.

"Just remember how you got control when you absorbed my gift. You will have to do the same thing when Eleanor restores your rightful gift. And it will probably be violent, since she will be restoring you to your full adult power." Jack cautioned her.

"I know," Deliverance said, and to add emphasis to her point, she grabbed a little of his gift from his skin and lit a small flame, dancing it from finger to finger until she extinguished it. Jack smiled down at her.

"Getting pretty good at that," he remarked, and began playing with the short, wispy locks at the back of her head.

"Does it not unsettle you? Me absorbing your gift?" Deliverance inquired curiously.

"Nothing you could do would unsettle me, love. Although you do drive me rather crazy." He growled and they fell into each other for a while.

Later, exhausted, Deliverance lay with her back to Jack as he traced lazy circles across her skin with his fingers.

"Sun, moon, truth," he murmured. Deliverance turned to him.

"Come again?" she asked.

"What three things cannot long be hidden? The sun, the moon, and the truth," he answered cryptically. "It a mantra—something people repeat to themselves to help them focus."

"Ah yes! I read about this. Buddha, yes?" Deliverance replied, pleased she knew something of his culture finally.

He chuckled. "Yes, I believe so, although I saw it on a television show about werewolves."

Never mind, Deliverance thought. There was still an overabundance to learn about his culture.

CHAPTER 25

Deliverance

No one spoke at breakfast the next morning; a pall enveloped them all. Even Eleanor was silent, for once her bubbly nature dampened. Her amber eyes stood out starkly against the slate-colored crop of hair growing on her scalp. They were intense with concentration, with preparation.

Before they got in the car, with Stevens at the wheel, Mrs. Potter pulled Deliverance into a strong embrace. She smelled of baby powder, roses, and cardamom, the pillow-y softness of feminine age. "You be brave, Miss," she said, fighting tears in her watery eyes. She cleared her throat, in her Arcanton-ness unaccustomed to strong shows of emotion, and let Deliverance go. Deliverance slid into the car, with Eleanor between her and Jack, and they pulled out of the drive. Deliverance cast a glance over her shoulder, taking in Hathaway and Mrs. Potter standing resolutely outside waving them goodbye and had the sinking feeling she may never see the place again.

"We're going to the auxiliary facility, Stevens," Jack instructed, breaking Deliverance's dark thoughts.

"Yes, sir," Stevens replied, obviously already knowing where they were going.

Jack seemed distracted as well.

"Hey," Deliverance called to him softly above Eleanor's bristly head, "Sun, moon, truth."

Jack smiled at her gratefully. "Sun. moon, truth," he said back to her.

✼✼✼

When they arrived, they swung into a secured car park of a massive, hulking square of a building. There did not seem to be any windows, and the structure stood out with its crisp, no nonsense lines, against the gentler, swaying autumn trees. It was as if the building were uninterested in the irrelevant chatter of the leaves rustling in the breeze.

Inside the austere yet clinically clean lobby of the building, their party was greeted by Dr. Phillips. She strode right up to Deliverance, examining her as though she were a cow for sale or a piece of art on display. Up close, Deliverance could see the professor was just beginning to show the signs of age in her lightly lined, pale skin. Her blonde hair was brushy and trailed with the vestiges of beginning grey. Her cerulean eyes were devoid of emotion; it was unsettling. Jack coughed to get her attention.

Deliverance

"Hmm, there are no outward signs that she is Narisi. Interesting," Dr. Phillips noted of the subject with clinical coolness. Then she turned to Jack. "I am excited to be included in this research. It is utterly fascinating."

"She is looking at Deliverance like she's a guinea pig in a cage," Eleanor whispered to Stevens, although Deliverance heard her quite clearly.

"Right...shall we?" Jack said, clearly not enthused to be yet again in Dr. Phillips' presence. The professor led them through a series of hallways and into a large conference room. The entirety of one wall was lined with windows facing out into the expansive room, almost like the gymnasium Eleanor had shown her earlier in one of their tours of Lontown...except for the thickly padded walls. Septic bright lights illuminated the space both in the conference room and the large area on the other side of the thick windows.

Assembled in the conference room was a team of people in lab coats, including Lord Asher. Deliverance was surprised at the tug of emotion she felt when her eyes landed on her father, but quickly tamped it down. From behind the sea of crisp, white coats popped a curly blonde head and familiar cornflower blue eyes.

"Addie!" Deliverance cried, greeting her new friend.

"I asked her to be here. I trust her," Jack informed her as the women traded embraces. He eyed Dr. Phillips when he said the last sentence. Eleanor received a warm hug from Addie as well before Lord Asher broke in.

"All right, well let's get started," he said, taking control. Dr. Phillips, Deliverance noticed, cast her father an annoyed glance before schooling her features. That was troublesome, but her attention was soon needed elsewhere.

The first part of the process was to document her, for lack of better words, Narisi-ness. They had to prove first that she was from Nar and then that she had an active magical malady. This included long recorded interviews with video. The team of coated minions, as her father rudely called them, interviewed first Deliverance, then Jack, and finally her father, who confirmed her heritage. They also asked Deliverance all about life on the island, including the name-curse and how women were treated.

"It's to add an emotional appeal to our cause," one of the minions explained.

When that was completed and everyone was adequately refreshed with tea and coffee, the next exercise began. Lord Asher led Deliverance and Jack into the large gymnasium on the other side of the glass. The leaden door to enter the space was sturdy and locked from the outside. The space seemed even larger as they walked in. The ceilings appeared at least two stories up, the walls generously padded in gaffer-tape colored mats. The only incongruous wall was the one with the wide observation windows.

"The glass is high impact, bulletproof. The walls can take a ballistic impact. But don't worry, we will be able to communicate through the two-way intercom system," Lord Asher said as he pointed out various features of the room.

Deliverance swallowed. They were prepared for a violent transition.

"Now remember, the easier you can make the transition into your healthy, adult powers, the better. It will help in convincing Parliament it will not be as chaotic as they think."

Deliverance nodded, her palms sweating.

"I will leave you two in here to begin the first part of the process. Just listen to the instructions coming from the intercom…" Lord Asher said, then paused. "Good luck," he said finally, patting Deliverance on the shoulder awkwardly, and left the room without another word.

Jack rolled his eyes after her father. "Hey," he said, reaching out to squeeze her hand. "It will be okay, love."

Deliverance nodded, wanting to believe his words, needing to believe his words.

The intercom crackled to life. "Can you hear me?" Lord Asher's voice came over the loudspeaker. Jack gave him a thumb's up. "Brilliant. Let's begin."

He had Deliverance walk through showing the camera how she could not mimic powers by touching Jack through his clothes or hair first. Then he had her show the camera how once they pressed their hands together, she could light a flame in her palm, a twin to the one Jack now displayed.

"Yes, very nice. See how it is nice and controlled?" Lord Asher noted for the video. Deliverance and Jack traded a glance. The audience did not have to know they had practiced.

Deliverance made a show of manipulating the flame, keeping it carefully under control. After a bit of this, Lord Asher called that part of the data collection a wrap.

"We're going to continue straight into the healing phase. It's best if you do not have anything in your stomach," Lord Asher said over the intercom. "Jack, if you could?"

Jack looked reluctant to leave the observation room. He squeezed Deliverance's hand tightly.

"Just remember, Sun, Moon, Truth," he said, and she smiled what she hoped was a reassuring smile at him. Then, after one more moment of hesitation, he left the room, trading places with his younger sister.

Eleanor, for her part, looked entirely more assured. She had donned one of the crisp lab coats the minions had given her, and it looked smart on the girl. Eleanor stood beside Deliverance as introductions were made for the video and a detached voice explained Eleanor's gift for the recording.

"Okay, it looks like we're ready. All the diagnostic sensors have been turned on and are reading properly. You can commence, Eleanor," the voice instructed.

Eleanor turned to face Deliverance and asked her, "Ready?"

Deliverance nodded, certain. "Ready."

Deliverance

At first it was just the same as Eleanor had done before. Her eyes began to glow green as she elevated off the floor, palms upon Deliverance's. Suddenly, though, her entire head snapped back at an unnatural angle and came forward again, mouth agape. Deliverance felt herself being lifted slowly off the ground, as if the very marrow in her bones was magnetized. Green light poured from Eleanor's mouth into Deliverance's, which involuntarily was pried open by the force of Eleanor's gift. Deliverance could feel the regurgitated magic circulating through her bloodstream, entering her cells, prodding.

Then with a gasp of blinding pain, she felt the magic latch on. Her organs screamed, crying out at the intrusion. Her very blood felt like it was boiling. Deliverance bit her lip hard, but kept her palms upon Eleanor's, although she found through a haze of pain, she could not have removed them even if she wanted to. They were locked in place. Deliverance could barely bear the wrenching pain and detachedly, she heard a scream. It took her a moment to realize it was her own. Then, when she thought all the bones in her body might disintegrate into dust, Eleanor's head reared back at that terrible angle once again. Deliverance felt the magic seeping back out of her mouth, being pulled toward Eleanor's impossibly gaping one.

As the force left her body, a great white light flashed before Deliverance's eyes, followed by a deafening ringing in her ears. The world tilted impossibly. She could not hear anything above the ear-piercing tone. Vaguely, as her vision cleared slightly, she became aware Eleanor was being rushed from the room. Everything shuddered. Suddenly, her vantage point was different. She was looking down on the room from above, then suddenly she was staring at the ceiling from the floor. Her vision would not still—frames jolted around her as she felt a sickening thud through her bones.

As she tried to focus, the ringing in her ear lessened enough she could hear a voice over the intercom. "Try to calm yourself!" it yelled, causing her head to spin. Then the world was spinning again…or was she spinning? She could not tell.

"Oh for Christ's sake, give me the damn mic!" another voice said. Jack's voice.

Deliverance tried to focus on that sound, and the ricocheting world began to slow.

"Deliverance. Love. Focus on my voice," Jack's voice came in over the loudspeaker. She was trying but everything was so disorienting. The world kept flipping upside down then right side up again. "Hey, over here by the windows."

Deliverance screwed her face in concentration. Yes. The windows. She could see them. She could see Jack there. Her eyes zeroed in on his face. And the world began to settle. Slowly, she realized she was clinging to the wall, like a squirrel almost a story up. She tried to descend but the world became shaky again.

"Easy does it. That's my girl." Jack spoke to her through the microphone.

Step by laborious step, she detached herself from the wall, concentrating with all her might on her lover's face behind the thick glass. As she neared him, she held his gaze. Mossy green to near black.

"Breathe, darling," he said, and put his hand up to the glass. "Sun, moon, truth."

"Sun...moon...truth," she repeated, touching her hand to his through the glass. She felt a stilling in her as her body seemed to wrap around itself, pulling its new power under her control. Sun...moon....truth. And finally, the world stopped gyrating.

"Good! Beautiful! Now, do not be alarmed. There will be a man entering the observation chamber. His name is Niles. He's here to help," Jack said to her. Deliverance nodded weakly.

The sound of the air escaping the door as it opened caused Deliverance to careen haphazardly against the far wall with impossible speed. She heaved a great umpf sound.

The man who entered did so with great calm. He had a kind expression upon his strong face. He wore a simple linen tunic and pants over his cappuccino-colored skin. His head, like Eleanor's used to be, was completely bald, but he had eyebrows, so Deliverance assumed he was not sick but had just chosen to shave his head. Small constellations of freckles dotted his nose and he smiled a great, white smile. He looked so familiar...then Deliverance remembered Jack's memory. This must be the same man.

"Jack had a feeling you might be a prowess gift," Niles said. "My name is Niles. I teach at the kinesiology department here at

Oxdale. He had a number of us on standby depending on what your gift showed itself to be."

"Prowess gift?" Deliverance asked, her throat gravelly.

"Yes. Physically gifted. Athletic. Here, I will show you," Niles said, and sprang backward with impossible speed, flipping once and landing in a graceful crouch. When he looked up, his eyes, which used to be a soft, light brown, glowed magic green.

"That's...amazing," Deliverance breathed, then winced as she grabbed her ribs.

"Yes, I'm afraid you took off on quite a tear after your powers were remedied. We will get Doctor Pennington in here to look at you as soon as I determine it is safe. You cannot run into her like you did those padded walls, after all, right?" Niles said, smiling broadly. The green faded away from his eyes, returning them to his warm brown. Deliverance nodded.

It was hard to concentrate above the pain that was starting to make itself known all over her body. Blood dripped from her face and down her arms, but she willed herself to pay attention to the task at hand.

Niles was an excellent instructor—direct, clear, and calming. Deliverance followed him through a few basic drills before he was satisfied she was in control enough to not endanger anyone.

"Great!" he said enthusiastically. Deliverance slid down to the floor along the back wall of the gymnasium. "I will go get Dr. Pennington now."

As soon as he said the word, Jack, Eleanor, and Addie all flew into the room.

"Careful now," Niles warned. And the three attempted to slow their steps. Jack reached her first and gathered her up in his arms.

"Owww," she complained hazily, then noticed she was bloodying his shirt. She started to say something but forgot what it was she was about to say. He stared back at her, his eyes intense with worry. "Shhh. Let the good doctor work, love."

"She's got a concussion, three broken ribs, one of which is attempting to puncture her lung but has not yet, and a sinus hemorrhage," Addie announced after laying her hands over Deliverance's form, resting on the floor, propped up against Jack. Eleanor remained quiet, sitting by closely, watching. "Hang in there."

Deliverance began to feel numb. "I can't feel my feet," she said.

"I'm sedating you. This would be terribly painful otherwise," Addie said.

Deliverance looked down and realized Addie had stuck a needle into the vein in her elbow and plucked it back out again. She felt a prickly tingling as Addie began her healing work, but could hang on to consciousness no longer.

Chapter 26

Deliverance

She must not have dozed for long. When she came to, she was still in Jack's arms in the same place.

"Hey, easy there," Jack said, smiling at her. "Addie said you would not be out long."

Deliverance glanced down at her body. Besides the stains upon her clothing, she could not tell she had ever been injured. Testing, she poked her ribs. No pain.

"Did I do okay?" she asked, fearful of his answer.

"Love, you did beautifully. The science geeks in that room were expected you to bounce around the room like a ping pong ball for weeks." Jack laughed.

"I'm glad I did not. That was terribly disorienting," Deliverance said, sitting up.

"I bet. It looked painful."

"That too… Jack, how did you know this might be my magic gift?" she asked.

"Just a hunch, love. Just a hunch. Come on. Let's get you out of here," Jack said as he helped her to her feet. She sprang up lightly, but was careful not to let the magic go wild and fling her to the ceiling again.

As they were about to leave the room, Jack paused and turned, looking thoughtfully around the room. Then with a flash of green, he threw a giant fireball at one of the padded walls. It sizzled into the mats, melting it into a stinking black smudge.

The intercom crackled on and Lord Asher's voice rang out, "What did you have to go and do that for!?"

Jack shrugged nonchalantly and answered, "You said the walls were flame retardant. I wanted to see if you were right." A string of expletives followed over the loudspeaker until someone with a cooler head disconnected the sound.

Inside the conference room, the team was abuzz.

"That was amazing!"

"Great work!"

Lord Asher ventured up to Deliverance, flashing blinding light in her eyes.

"Hey! Stop that!" she cried, rubbing her eyes.

"Just wanted to test your neural reflexes," he said sheepishly. "All that's left to do is have Eleanor retest you for any sign of magical malady, and we should have all the documentation we need to make a case with the Senate—"

Just then the doors to the conference room crashed open, and heavily armed men in uniforms poured in.

"EVERYONE PUT YOUR HANDS UP AND STEP AWAY FROM THE GIRL!" one of the men, yielding a semiautomatic weapon shouted.

Everyone in the room looked panicked...except Dr. Phillips.

"Her. She's the one," Dr. Phillips called out, pointing at Deliverance.

"What on earth?" Lord Asher bellowed.

Jack positioned himself in front of Deliverance, heat already radiating off him in stifling waves. Deliverance's heart lept in her throat as she calculated their odds and realized they were far outnumbered, even with Jack's barely controlled fire seething beneath his skin. Her skin tingled as she came to the conclusion that even if they tried to fight their way out, it would be too much risk to Eleanor, not to mention Addie, Lord Asher and the rest.

From behind the armed thugs, a man without a uniform stepped forward. Ned Turner, the despicable senator from the night of the ball. Deliverance's dread coupled with fury, a beast in her skin. She had to struggle to maintain control of her new magic gift, concentrating on not flying at the reprehensible man's throat.

"Well well well. Little troublemakers making more trouble. Imagine that," he taunted as he walked around to stand by Dr. Phillips.

"How could you?" Jack hissed at Dr. Phillips.

She shrugged noncommittally. "I got tired of watching her father bumble around as head of the department. Waste of good tenure. Senator Turner here offered me a promotion I could not refuse."

"Senator? He's a senator!?" Deliverance hissed at Jack.

"Yes, unfortunately," Jack replied, not taking his eyes off his adversaries.

"A senator…with the majority. I hate to brag but that seems to be a problem for you, doesn't it, Jack?" Ned said with a sly smirk as he walked around the room. "All of this, it's very good. But it will not do you a lick of good. By the time we put this to a vote, I will have all of Parliament convinced to level your little island hovel."

Dr. Phillips, apparently having had enough of the display, simply turned and left the room.

"You thought it was a good idea to bring that little back stabber onto the team!?" Jack cursed at Lord Asher.

Lord Asher, for his part, simply shrugged. "She was good at research."

"You're impossible."

Deliverance

"Are you two quite finished?" Ned broke in. "Deliverance Asher. You are hereby arrested on the accounts of violating the restricted zone of Nar, of trespassing, of endangering the lives of civilians, civil disobedience, and felony assault on a member of Parliament."

Two armed men came forward to take Deliverance into custody, but Jack barred their way and with a hand to each of their chests, dropped them, sizzling and screaming. Another came at Deliverance from behind, but she easily avoided his grasp by twisting to the side.

"Enough!" she shouted. Jack was snarling like a caged animal, ready to burn down the whole facility. "Jack, please. It's all right. I'll go with them." Her voice firm, though small she felt. There was no use in fighting. It would be futile at this point, but they still had a chance on the Senate floor. And she could not watch Jack consume the whole room in flames for her sake.

"What? Don't be silly," Jack replied, panting and his voice cracking.

"Get the data to the Senate floor. Get them to vote with you. I believe in you," Deliverance said, placing a hand on his chest. It had a dowsing effect, as all the fight seemed to leave him.

"Please. Don't. We can find another way," Jack pleaded with her.

Stevens, this time, stepped forward. He pulled a trench coat around Deliverance and said, "We will see you soon, Miss. Sir, she is right. Let's solve this on the field of battle otherwise known as the Senate floor."

Deliverance stepped away from Jack. As the armed guard came upon her though, she held up her hand. "Do not presume to touch me or I will break every bone in your bodies. I said I would go with you. I do so willingly." She threw one last glance over her shoulder, catching the horrified looks on Eleanor and Addie's faces, and the tormented one on Jack's as she left the building with the unsavory men.

CHAPTER 27

Deliverance

The gaol in Arcanton was not unlike the gaol on Nar. It was cleaner, but the bars were the same. A cage. Deliverance always hated to see a caged animal. Now she was one.

At first she was restless...then she was bored. Time passed tediously slow, although she had no real idea of how long she had been here in this windowless cell. They had deposited her here quickly, and without ceremony, leaving her to her own devices. She pulled Stevens' coat closer around her. It seemed like the past few weeks had all been a futile effort to avoid this—imprisonment. She wondered if Effie and Cat felt the walls of the mines closing in on them the way she felt the dour block walls of this cell pressing against her aura. Were they even still alive or had cold already taken them in their sleep, or sickness already ravaged them with deadly fever?

"Oppressive, isn't it?" A snake-like voice awoke her from her reverie. Ned Turner stood outside the door to her cell, smoking a cigar and leaning on the wall just out of arm's reach.

"What do you want?" Deliverance sniffed.

"Hmm...what do I want? I want to replace Jack in the Senate with someone who will vote my way. I want to keep your nasty little disease from spreading." Ned blew smoke her way. Deliverance turned her nose up in disgust.

"I see," Deliverance said. "You are so frightened of being impotent that you would isolate an entire population of people away from the world and from life saving technology. It makes me wonder how else you are impotent, to be so entirely insecure?"

"Isolate?" He laughed. "No. I would bomb the entire place off the map. Make it a smoking cinder. Kind of like the one your boyfriend burned in the wall back there at the research facility. I had Dr. Phillips erase all your data, by the way. It will not be going to any Senate hearing any time soon."

Deliverance felt the blood rush to her head. All the data...all the work they had done to meticulously document her transformation and the healing process—it was all for naught!? She fell back, sitting on the bench seat with a thud. How could all their data just be gone, wiped away like fog from a windowpane?

"What are you doing here, then?" Deliverance asked in a resigned, gravelly tone, still processing the blow. Ned Turner stood up and scuffed his cigarette out on the gummy floor, fixing his stare on her.

For a moment he didn't speak, simply staring at her with a level gaze. "I find myself in an odd position," he began finally. "On the one hand I am more powerful, more privileged, and more connected than Jack Quentin could ever hope to be. And on the other..." He paused for a second, swallowing what looked like distaste in his gullet. "Well, on the other hand, this Jack Quentin fellow, the man who did everything backwards, who thwarts authority, who scoffs at society, who spits in the face of law and order, *he* always seems to get everything handed to him on a silver platter. Popularity, favor, a blind eye to his transgressions with that idiot privateer Finley...women." With this last word, his grey eyes zeroed in on her green ones.

A flash of dread spun its way through her veins as she saw the keys produced in Ned Turner's hands. Surely the guards would not give him the keys to her cell?

The spider web of dread became a thicket when the tall man reached for the doors and slid a key into the lock, clicking with terrible certainty as it undid itself for him.

"Ah, I see," Deliverance stammered, trying to stall Ned Turner's advance into the cell. "You're jealous of Jack...you covet his reputation."

He snorted. "Jealous? No. I would liken it more to annoyance than anything else. He's like an annoying pest that the public refuses to stop feeding." He paused for just a moment at this, and Deliverance had the wild thought that perhaps he only meant to talk with her without the hindrance of the bars in between their view. Ned Turner was not an ugly man, not remarkable but with squarish features that could have been pleasant were the man not so dreadfully full of venom. It dripped off his soul like Spanish moss.

"But I do admit," Ned Turner began again, sidling closer to Deliverance, who stood and inched backward until her back bumped against the concrete wall, "I rather like taking what is his."

Her delusions of simple talk vanished as the sinister man reached for her with those toxic fingers of his, capable of sapping the consciousness from a being in seconds. What he would do to her, once he had stolen her awareness, she didn't need Effie to explain. It was clear in his licentious stare what he planned to take from Jack. Scrambling backward, Deliverance looked for something, anything to help her. She could not simply use her new gift to evade his grasp—the quarters were too tight and she would end up just careening around until she bumped into him and he touched her anyway. *Think, girl!* She screamed silently to herself, eyes wildly roving for a solution.

That was when she felt it. The lump in the pocket of Stevens' jacket, the jacket that still smelled of his mint tobacco and cinnamon candies.

Without hesitation, Deliverance pulled Stevens' taser from her pocket and dropped Ned where he stood, twitching and pissing his trousers.

Deliverance

***

Apparently, one could be charged with felony assault on TWO accounts. Who knew? Deliverance thought ruefully. The clunky uniformed guards carted Ned Turner off swearing, while Deliverance waved goodbye. Apparently the guards Ned Turner had paid off to let him have his way with Deliverance had left their shift. The fresh shift did not look too pleased about lugging the wobbling senator who smelled of urine from the cellblock, but they did it expediently, leaving Deliverance alone, yet again.

The hours began to crawl by, yet again.

"If your face gets stuck in with that dejected look, I shan't be able to remedy it." A voice broke through Deliverance's stare into empty space.

"Addie!" she cried, springing to her feet.

"Hello, darling." Addie greeted her, and another fuzzy head poked out from behind her.

"And me too!" Eleanor exclaimed.

"Come along. We have a Senate session to attend," Addie said as a buzzer sounded in the cell and the door lock clicked open.

"Addie, how on earth did you manage it?" Deliverance said, finding the cell door to be indeed unlocked.

"Oh, it was brilliant! You should have seen her!" gushed Eleanor. "Addie strode right into the police station and demanded that nasty Ned Turner drop all the charges. When he laughed at her, she began naming names, one right after another of women he'd been fresh with or worse. By the time she was done stringing him up, he was begging HER not to bring charges against HIM. What with #MeToo Revival and all that, he was keen to avoid a scandal."

"What's a hashtag? Is that like hash browns?" Deliverance asked. She rather liked hash browns in their salty tastiness but saw little relevant connection here.

Eleanor giggled and replied, "No, silly. Not even close to like that."

"Here are some different garments. It would probably be best to show up looking more like a lady and less like a war casualty," Addie remarked, handing her a bundle.

After Deliverance returned from changing in the restroom, she thanked Addie heartily.

"Don't be silly. It was what needed to be done. Now we all have parts to play in this upcoming Senate hearing, so let's make haste to the gallery where we will watch until called upon to do our parts." Addie took Deliverance's arm in hers and linked her other with Eleanor's.

Together the three women left the police station and headed toward the Parliament building.

CHAPTER 28

Deliverance

"How can anyone possibly get any law making done here?" Deliverance shouted above the din at Addie. They had seats perched in the uncomfortable gallery surrounding the Senate floor below. Over a hundred men and women stood on the Senate floor shouting at each other at the tops of their lungs, shaking their fists.

"It's always like this at first. You'll see!" Addie replied back, unconcerned.

"Look, there's Jack!" Eleanor said, pointing out her brother. As usual, he was right in the thick of the fight.

"Have I missed anything yet?" Another voice came from behind them. Lord Asher appeared and took a seat on the end of their bench, next to them. He had cleaned himself up with a shave and was wearing tails.

"Not yet, they're just getting warmed up," Addie replied.

Deliverance leaned over and said despairingly to her father, "Ned Turner said he had all our research destroyed!"

"Did he now?" Lord Asher answered, not looking the least bit worried.

"Does that not concern you?" Deliverance cried. Confound this blasted man! Maybe Jack was right. Maybe he was addlepated from removing too many of his own memories.

He shrugged. "I suppose it would if I did not have a digital backup on a remote server."

Deliverance paused. "What does that even mean?"

"It means we have a copy of everything," he said simply.

"You...you did that?" Deliverance asked incredulously, not believing it at first.

"Yes, of course. I'm not batty after all!" Lord Asher said, looking at her sideways and smiling a knowing smile. "Well not entirely so at any rate."

Eleanor, Addie, and Deliverance all broke out into huge grins. They would, after all have some ammo for the upcoming fight. Below, a churlish Ned Turner sat nursing his wounds, not joining the fray, and looking decidedly sour in his fresh trousers.

"For God's sake come to order already!" the speaker bellowed, slamming his gavel on the lectern. The end popped off and rolled down the aisle, and the man looked defeated until someone handed a fresh gavel. Eventually, the Senate floor quieted enough for the speaker to call out the business of the day.

"We originally had another land tax on the docket, but apparently the honorable Senator from Cornwall has yet again upset the order of things. We find ourselves in the midst of an emergency vote. The subject: The Narisi Restricted Zone."

This caused another uproar on the floor and it took the Speaker a good ten minutes to call everyone to order.

"Let the man speak!" a shout came from the floor. "Speak! Speak!"

Finally, Jack took the lectern, and everyone fell silent.

"Senators, ladies and gentlemen of the Parliament of the great Republic of Arcanton. We find ourselves today in a unique position. A position to secure ourselves a page in world history books as a nation of enlightenment."

"Are we not already?" a naysayer called out.

"Ah. Yes, the nation of modern medicine, of electricity, of steam ships and dirigibles. But are we not also a nation who was one of the last to abolish slavery, who still demands subservience and high taxes from our colonies...who still imprisons the people of Nar?"

This garnered more shouting, and Jack waited for them to quiet before he continued. "The island of Nar. 408 people, the last time we did a drone count. What do 408 people matter in the grand scheme of things? I would pose to you those 408 souls matter the world. What we do with the information I am about to present to you and the bill I am about to put forward to you for a vote could very well enhance the reputation of the Republic of

Arcanton, or put it down in the books as a scourge on humanity. Think wisely, ladies and gentlemen."

"What could you possibly tell us that we don't already know, or are you just filibustering with your warm fuzzy cockamamy like usual, Senator Quentin?" An older, distinguished looking senator called out.

"Ah, that is an excellent question. Get comfortable. Over the next couple hours, I shall call forward witnesses to testify to what we now know—new information and research on the state of Nar and its plague. Then I will propose to you a solution to the problem at hand. I suppose I should begin by telling you that the population of Nar is now 407, and the cause is not a death." With that, Jack began to present his case.

"Isn't he a charismatic speaker?" Eleanor sighed, watching Jack as he went through the facts, point by point. Deliverance could not help but agree. He seemed in his element down there, standing up for a cause he believed in wholeheartedly. She wondered why she ever doubted him.

The knowledge that a Narisi was among them, alive and well, caused much consternation in the crowd. Murmurs of discomfort rolled through the room like waves breaking on a coastline.

"For the research evidence, I am going to call Lord John Asher, PhD in Biochemistry, Forensic and Cultural Anthropology, and three-time award winner of the Cranston Prize for Science, to assist in the presentation," Jack announced.

"That's me," Lord Asher whispered to the ladies and turned to find his way down onto the Senate floor.

"Good luck...Fath...John." Deliverance hiccupped. Lord Asher's seat was taken by Mrs. Potter and Stevens, who came in with a flurry of cold still upon their backs.

"Did we miss much yet?" Stevens asked Eleanor, as they took their seats on the teak benches.

"Jack's opening remarks, but Lord Asher is about to take the stand," Eleanor replied, talking sideways.

"Thanks for the coat," Deliverance added mischievously to Stevens.

"Aye. I heard it was confiscated," Stevens replied.

"Why would they confiscate your coat?" Mrs. Potter asked.

"No, my taser."

"Oh, good God."

"I heard you got a good shot off though," Stevens added. "Bully for you."

Lord Asher took command of the stage then. He called for the lights to be dimmed and a large computer screen descended for all to view. After a pause, he began to speak. He did not appear like the offish, flaky man Deliverance was now accustomed to associating with her father. When he took command of the stage, he did so with ease and magnetism. The hall hushed to hang on his words. This was a man who had ages of wisdom, years of research, and was accustomed to presenting the facts. This was a man who charmed lecture halls full of coeds and symposiums full of world leaders. This was a man who, through the careful, precise presentation of fact, always won his way. As he laid out his indisputable findings, he drove the nails of logic with a tremulous force into the railway that would take them to Nar.

"As you can see here, the subject is still exhibiting the symptoms of the plague. Now this is before we treated her. Do note how in control she is of the mimicked gift. Also note the subject her magic imitates does not lose any power of his own. It is a mirroring effect, not a parasitic one," Lord Asher said and continued on with the video documentation.

"Now see in this later clip — note the time date stamp — the subject is entirely without symptoms. No detectable magical maladies remain. This of course triggered the inevitable onslaught of the subject's birth gift in its full adult form," Lord Asher lectured.

Murmurs rippled through the crowd as they watched the violent video of Deliverance coping with her new gift.

"Now this may seem like a chaotic transformation, especially if you consider going through over 400 of such situations," Lord Asher lectured, "but we have plans to mitigate the risk to both the Outside world and the citizens of Nar. In fact, we expected the coping mechanisms to take quite a bit longer to develop, but this research shows the powerful capability of the human body to adapt." He droned through the statistical readouts given by the sensors in the room and expounded upon other research in

Deliverance

similar cases...of which there were not many, but he was setting the stage for Eleanor to confirm their findings.

"Let's get ready, Deliverance. They are going to call us next," Eleanor murmured, and tapped Stevens on the shoulder. He had been wrapped up in the proceedings and startled a bit at the prodding. But he quickly recovered and realized what Eleanor was after.

"Here you go, Miss," he said and handed her a soft mass of something wrapped in velvet. "Straight from the wig maker."

In the rippling folds of crimson velvet lay a wig, just below shoulder length, of what Deliverance assumed used to be her hair as it was the same color and texture.

"If the senators do not already know I was treated for cancer, they do not need to know now," Eleanor explained to Deliverance and donned the wig. After she straightened it for the girl, Deliverance was struck speechless. So, this was what young, healthy Eleanor must have looked like before the ravages of disease stole the color from her cheeks and the hair from her head.

"Does it look all right? Not fake?" Eleanor asked, biting her lip in concern at Deliverance's stare.

"No, it looks real enough...it looks perfect. Good thinking, Eleanor," Deliverance answered, and they turned their attention back to the ending of Lord Asher's presentation.

"The ability of magical illness detectors has never been refuted. They are rare, but the few cases we have had the privilege of studying throughout history have indicated no less than a 100% detection rate. In our lifetimes there have been thirteen confirmed magical malady detector gifts and only 4 of those were also able to cure said maladies. We have one, which you witnessed in the video, to be powerful enough not only to cure our test subject, but many more." Lord Asher finished by stating, "And now I shall hand the floor back to Senator Quentin, representative from Cornwall."

For a moment, while Lord Asher was in the throes of speaking, Deliverance could almost see what her mother saw in the man... almost.

"As you can see from the evidence carefully documented by some of the world's finest research teams from Oxdale University," Jack began, but his mention of the controversial academic institution garnered some mutterings, "the girl from Nar has been completely cured of her magical malady and is no longer contagious. To put to rest any doubts you may have, ladies and gentlemen, I will be calling various witnesses to testify, starting with the most compelling. Miss Deliverance Magne and the magical illness healer, Lady Eleanor Quentin, will you please take the stand?"

Deliverance sucked in a breath. It was now or never. Eleanor took her hand firmly in her own, and adeptly led the way out of the gallery and down to the Senate floor. Deliverance could feel each burning stare prickly at the collar of her dress. The eyes she managed to meet either looked at her with curiosity or outright animosity. There seemed to be no middle ground. She swallowed a gulp and grasped Eleanor's hand like a life raft.

It struck her as odd, how loud the clacking of her shoes sounded as they walked down the planked center aisle and took a position on the front dais where all could see.

The Speaker, a harried-looking, portly man with a generous waist and not a generous hairline, looked to Deliverance. "Can you introduce yourself for the assembly, ma'am?"

"My name is Deliverance..." she began.

"LOUDER!" one of the senators jeered at her.

She cleared her throat, squared her jaw, and cast a reproving gaze around the room.

"My name is Deliverance. I did not know until recently my surname might as well be Magne. I was born and spent my entire life until a little over two weeks ago on the island of Nar. What you would deem to be called the 'Restricted Zone of Nar.'" Deliverance spoke with clarity. She would not be made to cower by these senators any more than she would cower before the bullish men on her home island. "I am told you have questions for me. Ask."

She stared down each of them, mostly graying old men in various states of decay, but a few were professionally dressed women spanning several decades in age, and there were a few younger, energetic looking men like Jack.

"If you are Deliverance Magne, then why are you not at your post keeping us all safe from the narrative faltering?" one old, crotchety-looking man called out.

"I am indeed Deliverance Magne. My father, Lord Asher, took blood samples to prove it," Deliverance answered directly. This first part of her answer caused a stir. "I am not 'at my post' as you deem it for several reasons. The first is that there was a problem on Nar in which my mother and I both would have been cast into prison for no fault of our own. My mother sent me off the island to send word and find help. She, herself, is imprisoned, and the narrative along with it. The second reason is that she refused to inform me of my duty to uphold your precious narrative. Until a couple weeks ago, I was ignorant of the whole affair." This caused more consternation in the crowd. "The third and final reason is that I, Deliverance nee Catalyst Magne, am no man's subject whether he be Narisi nor Arcanton." She stared back at the old man defiantly. She could almost hear Stevens groan of dismay in the gallery and did not need to look at him to know he was wildly waving her off, to temper her combative responses. But she could not. Looking around the room at these...dictators, she could no longer hold her tongue silent.

She noticed a thoughtful looking Senator somewhere in her late fifties regarding her with interest, rather than revulsion.

"Does this mean Catalyst Magne never meant to teach you how to hold the narrative?" another senator piped up.

"I do not know," Deliverance answered truthfully. "She may have when I got older, but I am twenty-three years of age, and she has not yet chosen to enlist me in your decree that by birth my family is somehow beholden to your false weavings."

The thoughtful looking senator stood up and quietly walked to the other side of the room where Jack was standing and took a seat.

"What is she doing?" Deliverance whispered to Eleanor.

"She's taking her stand. She's decided for us. That is how they show their allegiance or if they want to switch sides. Once everyone has stopped moving, the Speaker will ask for a final standing and then it will be decided. Whomever has the most senators on their side of the hall wins," Eleanor explained.

Deliverance cast a grateful look at the female senator who was now firmly planted on Jack's side of the aisle. Ned Turner's side, directly opposite him to the left, Deliverance assumed, was the opposition.

"Those false weavings keep us safe and they keep the Arcanton military from using force to keep your people on that island! Who are you to endanger us all?" accused a droopy-eyed senator from Sussex. He did not wait for a reply, but took a seat behind Ned Turner, who smirked at her.

"Is it for you to speak of danger, Senator Trenounen, when your grandchildren sleep safe in their beds, vaccinated against polio and a myriad of other diseases, assured against blight, and famine?" Jack shouted, jumping to his feet. "While these poor people, through no fault of their own, must suffer in ignorance as we block the world from them?"

This caused an uproar that took the Speaker a while to quell. "Let's continue with the pertinent questions, please!" he instructed, wiping his brow with a kerchief.

"How do we know this little girl is capable of actually curing anyone?" one of the opposition called out.

It was Eleanor's turn to puff out her chest. "That is Lady Eleanor Quentin to you, sir. Not little girl." She began dressing the man down systemically. "I am one of four people in the entire world who possess such a gift. I apprenticed under the fifth, The Honorable Tifia Ben Abnezir, until I was twelve years of age, at which point I fully cured three documented cases of magical illness. I am fully capable of handling the Nar project, as evidenced in the video documentation Lord Asher presented earlier."

"And why is The Honorable Tifia Ben Abnezir not stepping forward now to help us with this problem?" one of the other senators called out.

"Because she's dead. She stepped on a leftover landmine from the Arcanton-Plaedes conflict leftover in her hometown of Acrasis. The other three live in remote parts of the world not sympathetic to Arcanton causes...nor do they have my power aptitude," Eleanor replied coldly, enunciating precisely.

"Can you show us the girl has no markers of illness anymore?" another senator requested from the back.

"I can," Eleanor stated simply, and turned to Deliverance, pulling at the stretchy fingers of her gloves. Deliverance did the

Deliverance

same and held out her palms, sweating for Eleanor. Eleanor's hands, in contrast, were cool and dry with confidence. She readied herself, took a breath, and closed her eyes. Seconds ticked by as the entire hall fell under a spell of absolute silence.

Eleanor opened her eyes and just for a moment gave Deliverance the most bizarre look, before masking her face in calm collection again.

"There, you see, ladies and gentlemen? No magic spark. No green indicators. Nothing," Eleanor said, without a shade of doubt in her voice.

"And can you, young lady, now control your gift without hurting anyone?" asked a shaky, elderly senator with blue lips.

"Aye," Deliverance responded and did a quick spin around the room, pausing next to the Speaker. Her actions had been almost too fast for the eye to catch, so she made sure to stop in a different spot. Whispers washed over the hall like a summer rain.

"As you can see, Miss Deliverance is a prowess gifted and is in complete control. She is not in any danger of hurting anyone," Jack asserted, gesturing.

Deliverance gave a look of apology to the startled Speaker and popped at magical speed back down to her place by Eleanor on the floor. A couple more senators, including the blue-lipped man, who needed assistance in moving, crossed over to Jack's side. By Deliverance's count, they were still lacking a majority.

Eleanor must have caught her counting and pulled her sleeve. Deliverance lowered her ear and Eleanor whispered, "Jack still has yet to present the plan and then there will be bartering on the terms. We have time." Deliverance nodded grimly. But how many of these stodgy people, set in their ways, would stand and move?

"In fact, I have a whole team of people assembled to ensure no one is hurt on this endeavor. I have a powerful doctor-healer, several elementally gifted, a prowess gifted, and a few mind gifted volunteers ready for our mission," Jack said, segueing into the next part of his plan.

"And what mission is that, pray tell Senator Quentin? Hopefully nothing brash!" Ned Turner mocked Jack.

Jack's mouth hit a thin line, hesitating before deciding to plow forward. "This mission," he said, clicking on the overhead computer to a different slide presentation. "Operation Liberty."

The speaker bid Eleanor and Deliverance to resume their seats in the gallery. Deliverance walked away frustrated, feeling as if there were things left unsaid. There had to be something more she could have expressed in order to win more to their cause. Maybe she should not have been so confrontational.

Jack managed to outline the proposed mission despite the upsets and a couple Senators walking back to Ned Turner's side. Deliverance could feel her future slipping away like grains of sand in the surf. It was all completely out of her control now. She found that feeling deplorable.

"So, let me get this straight." Ned Turner sneered at Jack after he managed to gain the floor. "You want to sail to Nar and cure everyone on the island, then open the island up to the rest of the world? Sounds a little farfetched."

"No, that's only if everyone wants to be cured!" one of the senators on Jack's side chimed in. "Otherwise they are only going to cure the ones who want to leave and take them with them."

Jack outlined provisions for an encampment where they could conduct the healing process then coach the newly healed people in their gifts safely before boarding transport back to Arcanton.

"It's entirely possibly no one will want to leave the island!" someone shouted.

Another rebutted, "No, there are at least a few!"

"All this trouble for a handful of people?" Ned Turner jeered, but his comment had the opposite effect he had intended as a couple more senators gave him a disgusted look and switched to Jack's side.

"What if hundreds want to leave? Where will we put them? What will we do with them?" another voice rang out.

"Oxdale University has a team on standby ready to receive them, house them, and ultimately help them assimilate into society. A lot of grad students are set to do their theses on Narisis," Jack answered cheekily, and this garnered some chuckles.

A few more senators switched sides. It was getting close!

Deliverance grabbed Addie's and Eleanor's hands in each of hers. Eleanor grabbed Mrs. Potter's, who grabbed Stevens', who looked at Lord Asher and shook his head. Together they watched with bated breath as the Speaker called for closing remarks.

Jack took the floor again. For the longest moment, he did not speak. But when he did, there was fire behind it. "Ladies and Gentlemen of the Senate. What I proposed to you today was radical. I know, I have a reputation." A few more chuckles here. "But what I am asking you to consider is not radical but fundamental. For hundreds of years the government of Arcanton has stolen from the Narisi. For hundreds of years we have kept them in the dark, bound them prisoner on their island. Some would say it was for fear and others a necessary evil to contain the spread of contagion.

"Now, however, things are different. Not only do we now have a way to cure the illness, but we ourselves are different as a people. We are making strides each generation for a better, kinder, worldlier, more humane Arcanton. How can we take up that mantle when a couple hundred miles off our own shore we are keeping people enslaved? We are letting people pass away of curable diseases, mothers die in childbirth, children grow wracked with illness, women remain enslaved to a tyrannical culture we created, aided, and abetted! It is hard to admit one's mistakes. We can try to wash them away with excuses of historical context. Or..." Jack paused for dramatic effect. "Or we can begin to remedy our wrongs, take responsibility, and showcase the seat of Arcanton governance as it rightfully should be, as an enlightened nation of liberty and humanity!"

Deliverance held her breath as she counted...

"Now is the final call for standing!" the Speaker announced. No one moved. Deliverance's heart plummeted to the floor. They were one short! Eleanor groaned, but Addie remained cool and collected as usual, her heart-shaped face belaying no worry.

"Then, unfortunately I must—" the Speaker began before a gravelly voice rang out from Ned Turner's side.

"Wait!"

There were gasps, and whispers undulated through the crowd like wind over wheat.

A stately, older gentleman with a stern face and bushy brows stood, one hand in the pocket of his waistcoat. He gazed around him, as if everyone's attention on him was a given right, and refused to speak until there was absolute silence in the hall.

"I have been told," the senator said finally, "by my niece that I need to learn to change with the times. So, let the change begin." With that he stood and walked purposefully over to Jack's side of the floor.

"Senator Pennington cedes sides to Senator Quentin's cause. Motion called in favor of Operation Liberty!" the Speaker called out and rang his fresh gavel.

Deliverance jumped to her feet with joy as the crowd erupted.

CHAPTER 29

Deliverance

After much squealing, hugging, and dancing up and down, Deliverance's new family broke apart to find Jack on the now adjourned floor.

"Senator Pennington?" Deliverance asked pointedly of Addie.

Addie smiled a knowing smile. "Ah yes, my dear uncle. He has a bit of flair for the dramatic." Deliverance pulled her into yet another embrace.

"Thank you," she whispered through tears of joy. Addie produced a handkerchief from her sleeve and handed it to Deliverance.

"Dry your eyes, my dear. We have a lot of work ahead of us."

As the group waded through the crowd, Deliverance noticed the number of eyes on her had not lessened but there were many more sympathetic and friendly looks to be had.

"Jack! You did it!" Eleanor squealed as she darted through the crowd and attached herself to Jack's side, reminding Deliverance rather much of a tree frog clinging to a branch.

"We. We did it," Jack corrected her wrapping one arm around her and reaching the other out to Deliverance. "Tonight we celebrate! Tomorrow we sail!"

"Jack...we're not sailing until the day after tomorrow," Eleanor told her brother.

"I know...it just sounded better that way." Jack replied cheekily and they all laughed.

✻✻✻

Everyone gathered at Hathaway that night. Addie and her uncle were among the first to arrive, followed by a grinning Niles, and a now rumpled again Lord Asher. Mrs. Potter and Stevens were relieved of their duties for the night and bade to join them as well, which they did albeit somewhat uncomfortably. They were used to running the gatherings from behind the scenes, not being waited upon. The champagne flowed along with the laughter. The energy level in the room was high—they were all anticipating the next steps, the challenge to come.

"I was not, obviously, a fire breather," Niles explained to her about their military days over a glass of bubbly. "Jack was a force to be reckoned with back then...after watching him today, he still is. Just a bit more focused and refined."

Deliverance

Deliverance snorted. "I doubt Jack would consider himself refined."

"Compared to the wildness of his younger years, he is an absolute pussy cat now." Niles laughed, a catlike grin of his own upon his face. "Although this mission is unpredictable in nature. It will be good to have him on our side."

Deliverance frowned. "Do you think there will be violence?" It was a thought she had considered.

"It's possible," Niles said thoughtfully. "We're dealing with people who have, for all intents and purposes, lived in the 17th century. We're offering a one-time chance to rip the life they knew away from them with promises of something better. It is a risky proposition."

Deliverance's frown deepened into a scowl. "Yes, I was annoyed they insisted on enforcing the military restricted after we leave the island. Anyone who attempts to leave afterward…well…"

"They'll be shot," Niles answered for her grimly. But he added, "It's a one-time shot for now. Politics change. Minds change. With Jack in the Senate we may get another chance later to do another rescue mission."

But would the Narisis view them as a rescue party? Deliverance pondered, sinking into her own thoughts. Or would they see them as dangerous interlopers?

Her reverie was broken when she heard Jack call out, "Serves her right!" She wandered over and took his arm. Jack had been chatting with Lord Asher with surprising amicability.

"Serves who right?" Deliverance inquired, looking up at Jack. The triumphant flush of victory suited Jack—his face was animated with vigor.

"That little back-stabber Dr. Phillips. She got canned from the university for her little stunt!" Jack crowed.

"Yes, the university does not look kindly on jeopardizing research subjects. She was told to look elsewhere for a teaching position…without a reference," Lord Asher informed her. He seemed to be eyeing Deliverance's hand upon Jack's arm, but his face was inscrutable, betraying nothing of what he thought of their courtship now. For Deliverance's part, she did not much care what he thought about it other than curiosity's sake.

As the evening carried on it struck Deliverance deep in her core, as she watched this group of people whom she had come to regard as family, that Hathaway was a second home to her. These were her people. Addie laughing merrily as Eleanor did an impression of Senator Turner, Mrs. Potter warmly smiling upon them all, Stevens in an animated conversation with Niles and Lord Asher—his thin arms gesticulating wildly, and Jack…passionate, resilient, stubborn Jack. Jack who had been her stalwart companion and her constant ally. She realized she was far closer to these people than she had ever been with any of the villagers on Nar save her mother and Effie.

But it was time to collect the rest of her family and bring them home.

✳✳✳

Jack and Deliverance held each other later that night, wrapped up in each other's limbs. Together but silent. Eventually, Jack cleared his throat.

"Deliverance?"

She hmmed at him.

"I want you to keep the ring," he said finally.

Deliverance propped herself up on her elbow and regarded him. "Are you asking me to marry you for real?"

"If you'll have me I am," Jack replied earnestly, his eyes open and searching her face. He looked so vulnerable.

"Jack Quentin. I love you," she began but paused, rapidly searching her mind for the words.

"...but?" He asked like he was dreading the response.

She sighed. "But everything is so overwhelming right now. Everything that's happened and everything that has yet to happen." She could see the disappointment flare in his eyes. "I do love you, Jack! I want to marry you someday! I do."

"Just not right now?" he asked.

"Just not right at this moment," she confirmed, her heart twisting painfully.

"But someday?" he asked again, hope still lingering.

"Absolutely someday," she replied, kissing him enthusiastically. His body responded in kind, rolling her into his arms and kissing her deeply.

"I thought that might be your response," he said unexpectedly, then shot out of bed for a second, rummaging in the pocket of his shirt, which had been discarded in their hasty passion earlier that night. "Ah, here."

He sat back on the bed and handed her a metal chain, meant for a necklace.

"Keep the ring with you. Keep it until you decide you want to marry me or until you've regained your sanity," he joked and slid the delicate ring from her finger and then threaded the chain through it.

"Oh, Jack, what if I lose it?" she cried, looking at the necklace with the ring attached doubtfully. "I'd never forgive myself if something happened to your mother's ring!"

"This chain was forged by a gifted metal worker. It shan't break. I promise. He used magic to sure up the links," Jack explained.

"Then I accept if that is the case," Deliverance acquiesced and allowed Jack to fasten the chain around her neck from behind. He did not stop with the fastening of the chain, though, his lips and hands finding more and more interesting purchase upon her. And they fell into each other once more, the world falling away until the only thing left was she and he.

CHAPTER 30

Deliverance

"Ready, troops?" Jack barked at them two mornings later cheekily. Deliverance, Eleanor, Stevens, and Mrs. Potter were lined up with duffle bags, ready to depart.

When questioned as to why she and Stevens wanted to go, she looked almost offended. "You might need my healing herbs and I can help comfort the new ones on the ship! And Stevens is a fine air bender. He can hasten sails like nobody's business. You shan't leave us behind, no sir!" Deliverance loved her all the more for her plucky spirit.

They were all to meet Niles and Addie, who would be the head doctor on the mission, at the docks. The heady sent of salty fish and suspect river algae hung in the morning air at the James River docks. The brackish water was already full to the brim with vessels going about their mornings. The docks rose early, already hard at work bustling when the sun crested the horizon, illuminating the stately sandstone artifices on the banks.

Seeing Addie and Niles waiting a little farther down on the docks, Deliverance sped around moving crates and leapt over a wheelbarrow or two carting fishnets with supernatural grace.

"Very good, Miss Deliverance," Niles greeted her approvingly.

"Aye, I am thinking I like this gift very much!" Deliverance said with a grin. She found the increased speed and agility to be exhilarating and fulfilling at the same time.

"It suites you," he replied and turned to greet Jack with one of those complicated handshake jives only soldiers and pirates seemed to know.

The two women exchanged warm hugs as the rest of the party caught up. Before them, looking unusually more still on the river water than it was accustomed, was the *Daedalus*.

"Finley!" Jack called out in greeting, arm held high as they ambled up the slipway onto the deck of the ship. While the *Daedalus* dwarfed many of the small fishermen's vessels tossing about, there were still larger, more imposing ships anchored in the riverway.

"Aye, Master Jack! The last of your crew came aboard about half an hour ago. Let's be off. I am not at ease in these brackish waters," Finley crowed in his swarthy drawl.

"You mean you are not at ease being legally docked and with actual documentation," Jack retorted.

"Aye, that might be true also," Finley admitted with a grin.

"Let's get this show on the road then," Jack commanded.

Deliverance shook her head. Just when she thought she was getting the hang of Arcanton expressions, a new one would crop up and puzzle her. They were most definitely not on a road!

Navigating the James River in the heart of Lontown apparently required a lot of swearing on the part of Finley and his helmsman, but soon the vessel had breached the estuary and gained speed out into the open waters. It was a little like déjà vu, watching the crest of waves from the stern of the ship, Deliverance thought.

Then she spied Lord Asher on the same deck, just a bit off, fumbling with some piece of equipment. She ventured over to him to watch his efforts.

"What is that?" she asked, accidently startling the man. He bumbled around, trying to catch the contraption in his slippery hands, but managed to secure it before it leapt overboard. "Oh, sorry," she said as an afterthought.

"This? This is a set of infrared binoculars…it allows one to see heat signatures at greater distances. It helps you see at night," Lord Asher explained.

"But…it's daylight," Deliverance said, unsure.

"Yes…which is why they are not working. Same with my astrolabe," he replied cryptically.

"You have an astrolabe?" Jack said, creeping up behind him. Lord Asher gave another start.

"What? Yes of course I do! Any self-respecting cultural anthropologist understands the workings of an astrolabe!" Lord Asher cried indignantly.

"Uh huh," was Jack's unimpressed response. Great, Deliverance thought. They were back at each other's throats.

"Good to get this business over, so I can go back to my research on Antarticus," Lord Asher mumbled, fiddling with the binoculars.

"You're an anthropologist!" Jack stated.

"Your point?" Lord Asher replied snidely.

"There are no people on Antarticus," Jack replied incredulously.

"Precisely."

Both Jack and Deliverance rolled their eyes. One too many memories stolen or just plain eccentric either way, Lord Asher was a character. Jack left to go do a roll call of his team, leaving Deliverance with her father.

"Lord Asher?" she prompted, after a minute, having secured a position at the rail to watch the horizon. "It's rather formal to call someone that who shares half of one's DNA," she remarked.

"Ah, you learned about DNA! Good!" was his reply.

So she continued on, "But it does not seem to sit right to call you father…at least just yet. Can I call you John?"

Lord Asher stilled for a moment, then replied, "I would like that very much, Del."

Deliverance nodded. They spent some time in companionable silence before Deliverance gathered the courage to ask, "Are you nervous? About seeing my mother?"

"Oh...ah," John stammered, blushing rather prettily for an older gentleman. "I am dreading it, to be honest. I have not had direct contact with her since they captured her and took me off the Nar Project. Scientists are not supposed to get involved with their research subjects, according to Oxdale." Deliverance detected a note of irony in his voice.

"That must have been hard," Deliverance allowed.

"It was. We had such plans. We were going to travel the world. Escape from all this silly nonsense and raise you with your feet dancing in Morakech, running across the sands of Meldina, surfing in the Southlands. We were going to go anywhere and everywhere. But it was not meant to be. Someone somewhere must have betrayed us or detected us. I still do not know who or how. But they were waiting on the coastline for us as we pulled the boat in and ambushed us as soon as we set foot on Arcanton soil. I tried for a while after that to get put back on the project or to bribe the new project managers to slip notes through to Cat. But after a while, I grew despondent. I fell into a pit and rationalized it with research in other areas and a healthy dose of scotch...I am sorry." John had a quake in his voice at the last sentence. Deliverance regarded him carefully, as he stared at his hands, a man at a loss.

"The past is done," Deliverance said finally. "There is no undoing it. Let us move forward from here. I never would have been able to come this far without your aid, John. Leave your apologies behind us and let us start anew." She added wryly, "As for my mother, I will let you figure that one out on your own when you reunite."

John nodded, looking both relieved at Deliverance's answer and foreboding at the idea of seeing Cat again. She decided to leave him with his thoughts, and ventured below deck to find Eleanor, Addie, and Mrs. Potter. On the way she passed Stevens on the quarterdeck, pushing air into great billowing sails of the ship. He looked entirely content being of use in this capacity, so Deliverance did not disturb him.

Below the deck, Deliverance found Mrs. Potter had ousted the ship's head chef and was directing the kitchen staff to the suite. She smiled to herself at the woman's gumption.

"If we have all the spices and provisions and necessities, why not combine them to make an appealing meal? The sludge that man was preparing tasted like pig slops!" Mrs. Potter declared, gesticulating with a rather sharp looking butcher's knife. Deliverance was not about to argue the point with her either.

Deliverance found Eleanor helping Addie arrange her field medical supplies in one of the bays. Addie was showing Eleanor the suture kit and where to put each type of accouterment, so they would have ready access if they needed it. Deliverance swallowed. She hoped they would not, but she knew better than any of them the violent, unpredictable nature of the de facto leaders on Nar.

She squeezed Addie's shoulder as she walked by and began to help the ladies with the preparations. There was nothing else to do between now and then but ready themselves as best they could.

✷✷✷

Their plan was to free Cat and Effie first, and then engage with the villagers. Deliverance described where the gaol was in the mineworks on the Eastern side of the island. If they landed under the cover of darkness, they would have enough time to gather Cat and Effie before anyone realized the large ship was anchored off the coast. They would have to take the smaller landing craft into the island, though, and climb the cliffs to gain access to the mine. The rest of their party would wait aboard the *Daedalus* for the signal to come ashore on the more exposed beachhead. It was decided Niles, Jack, and Deliverance would be the forward leading team.

It was dark when they sailed into the vicinity of the island, but Deliverance could smell she was home, could feel it in her bones. Thanks to Stevens' airbending they had made impeccable time to Nar, far quicker than the journey away had been weeks before.

"Be careful," Eleanor whispered to Deliverance, grasping her around the neck in a wringing hug.

Deliverance put a hand to her cheek. "We will be back before you know it. Get ready and listen to Doctor Addie!" she instructed. Then she swung her legs over the side and landed softly in the dingy. Jack and Niles were already preparing to cast off.

They all three held a look. "Ready?" Jack said, green fire sparking in his eyes.

"Ready," they both agreed.

CHAPTER 31

Deliverance

The slap of the oars on the cobalt cresting waters sounded deafening to Deliverance, even though she knew they would not likely be detected. Perhaps her nerves increased her sensitivity to the creak of the boat joints or the breathing of her companions. The shore seemed impossibly far, but distances in the dark were deceiving.

She was awash with energy when the boat hit sand, and her feet were immediately in the surf, helping to pull the dingy ashore. The scrape of the boat along the cove grated on Deliverance's nerves and she was shaky by the time they readied themselves to start surmounting the cliff face in front of them. In the daytime the cliff would be a wash of white, creamy stone, creased with iron and jutted with pines and scraggly brush. The moon overhead, though, gave the rock a bluish tint, which faded to soot grey up close.

Niles led the ascent, being an experienced climber. Deliverance was in the middle and Jack, now being the slowest, took the bottom position. Despite the looming height of the cliff face and the dark, they climbed steadily up. Deliverance thought she would have to wait longer for Jack to catch up and clip in at each interval, but he was proving himself full of his own brawny prowess, although his was entirely natural, not magical. The thought sent a hot flash through Deliverance in unmentionable places, and she quickly stuffed that thought to the back of her mind.

Niles held his fist out to order a halt, just before they crested the cliff. Deliverance could see him peeking above the edge, checking to make sure the coast was clear. Satisfied, he dropped his fist, and they hauled themselves up over the edge of the precipice, Jack a tad more winded than Niles and Deliverance.

Deliverance sprung to her feet, gathering her ropes and coiling them as she padded quietly toward the gaol entrance to the mine just above. There was no light emanating from inside the cave or from anywhere around, but Deliverance expected Cat and Effie would have nothing to light a fire with to warm themselves. Had they been much later, the two women could have passed out from the cold at night. Deliverance shivered at the thought. She hoped they were not already too late.

She rounded the last part of the climb up the hill to the tall bars drilled into the cave entrance. It was dead quiet.

"Mom?" she called quietly. "Effie?" Her heart was pounding so hard she could scarcely hear herself.

For the longest time there was no reply. Nothing. Not even the wind. Just the cold rebar grating Deliverance's sweating palms.

Deliverance

Then, "Deliverance!! God's teeth!! What in the Fades be ye here for?" Effie cried, running to the entrance and embracing Deliverance through the bars. Deliverance tried to shush her but both women had burst into tears.

Cat appeared behind Effie, a specter at first. "Deliverance?" she asked almost incredulously. Her eyes too watered with unshed tears.

"I've come back! I've come back for you all!"

Effie's eyes landed on Jack and Niles, who'd just appeared behind Deliverance, and she startled away from the bars, stumbling and landing on her rear.

"And who in Fades be these men?" she hissed, scrambling backward.

Deliverance had forgotten Effie had probably never seen a man like Niles before, but then she may have been startled by the strange men in general.

"It's okay Effie! These are my friends. They are here to help," Deliverance reassured her. Effie only looked marginally less alarmed.

Jack strode forward and stuck his hand through the bars toward Cat. "Jack Quentin. Pleased to finally meet you."

"Ah, so you are Jack Quentin. The studious senator determined to upset the world with your radical ideas. The narrative developers mentioned you often," Cat said coolly, regarding Jack.

He let his hand drop. "Right, well I suppose there is more time for introductions later. Let's get you out of here."

"And just how do you propose to do that?" Effie asked. "I've scoured every inch of this place looking for a way out. There tisn't one."

"Like this," Jack said with a spark of mischief in his eyes. "Oh, by the way…stand back."

Effie scrambled back, eyes the size of saucers, as magic roared to life in Jack's hands. The green flame rocketed into orange then deep, searing blue as Jack grasped the bars of the gaol.

"God's teeth, what in the world are you!?" she yelped, although Cat looked only vaguely surprised.

Deliverance caught her mother's eye. "You and I have much to discuss, Mother."

"Yes," she said airily. "I suppose we do."

Jack bent the metal bars back, some of the metal sloughing to the cave floor in red hot, molten puddles. Once the opening was large enough, Effie and Cat scurried through, careful to avoid the hazardous beads of molten metal and scalding, bent bars.

"They probably saw that little display in the village," Cat remarked to Jack as they hastened down the path to the shoreline on the other side, where the bigger beachhead would be the site of their landing.

"If they did not, they will definitely see this," Jack replied, holding his arm straight up and sending a billowing, roaring flame ball into the air. The signal to come ashore. It had begun.

"Criminy, what is wrong with that one?" Effie asked under her breath to Deliverance, eyeing Jack like a three-headed toad.

"There is so much to explain, Effie. But I am so glad you and Mother are all right!" Deliverance replied, squeezing her oldest friend's hand.

"Aye, Charity and Amity attended to us so's we dinna starve," Effie informed her. "I dinna expect them to be so decent, and yet...I suppose people surprise ye. We're alive because of them."

"Then we shall try our best to help them in turn," Deliverance replied.

By the time they made their way, slipping on the sandy path, down to the beach, a number of dinghies were already visible floating atop the moon-dappled waters. The first boat to arrive had John standing in the front. He leapt into the waters and strode straight forward. Deliverance saw her mother converging on him to meet him in the ankle-deep water.

Cat reared her hand back and with a resounding thwack planted a cracking slap across John's face. He stumbled in the tide and almost lost his balance. Cat did not wait a beat, though, before grabbing both the man's lapels and forcibly pulling him to her in a hungry, impassioned kiss. Deliverance looked away, slightly embarrassed.

"I see you come from a long line of socially adept people," Jack said to her, tongue in cheek. She eyed him at first, then chuckled. Cat was also most decidedly not a people-person. "Well, I will help the others get the supplies ashore while you…have some explaining to do to your mum and your friend." Jack sounded like he was ever so pleased to schlep equipment rather than face Cat.

Deliverance found Effie on the edge of all the landing activity, staring blankly and shivering. She cast around for a second before grabbing a blanket off a pile of supplies being carted in.

"Hey," she said to her longest friend, wrapping the blanket around her shoulders. Effie's eyes snapped to hers.

"What…what is all this, Deliverance!?" she cried, tears of shock creating small channels of clean on her otherwise sooty face.

She gathered her friend in her arms and hushed her soothingly. "This, my friend, is change. But do not fear. This time, it will be for the better."

After Effie gathered herself together, they went in search of Cat and John. As they passed Niles, Deliverance stopped and asked him, "Have you seen any sign of the villagers yet?"

He shook his head. "Isn't that odd? Don't you think they should be here by now?"

"I would have thought so…do you think it's wise to make camp here without encountering anyone yet?" Deliverance asked Niles, grateful for his military expertise.

"It won't matter either way. Between Jack and I, the camp will be safe from any threat. It is odd, though, there has not been a greeting party yet," Niles replied grimly. Deliverance nodded in agreement.

By the time Cat and John were found...decidedly more disheveled than Deliverance could have believed possible for either one of them, Addie had managed to get her medical tent erected in the clearing on the plateau above the shoreline. Others were working diligently to put up more infrastructure.

"Come, let me introduce you to some of my new family," Deliverance said. Cat cocked an eyebrow at her word choice but said nothing.

Inside the medical tent, Addie and Eleanor were hard at work arranging cots and sorting through their medical packs. Deliverance hailed them to come meet them.

"These are my good friends Doctor Adelaide Pennington and Eleanor Quentin. Addie and Eleanor, meet my mother Catalyst and my best friend...well we never use her given name, but everyone calls her Effie." Deliverance introduced them.

"It is truly an honor," Addie said and stuck her hand out to Cat.

Cat eyed Addie for a second before extending her own hand in friendship. "Cat. Sorry, we do not get many visitors here. I am out of conversational practice."

"She weren't never good at it ta begin with," Effie interjected and smiled tentatively at Addie. "I'm Effie."

"Charmed! Call me Addie. And this is Eleanor, Jack's sister. Jack is the gentleman who helped you escape your imprisonment." Addie replied, putting an arm around Eleanor's shoulders. Eleanor for once looked a tad shy.

Effie eyed the fuzzyheaded little girl with suspicion. "You aren't as tetched as yer brother, are ye?" she asked accusingly.

This brought a smile to Eleanor's face. "No indeed. Although I'm told my gift is much stranger to behold."

"God's teeth. It gets stranger than shooting fire out of yer hands!?" Effie cried, consternation written across her fey-like face.

"Come, there is much to tell," Addie said, inviting them in. And so they all sat in a circle on blankets on the forest floor, the canvas of the newly erected tent flapping and crinkling gently in the sea breeze. And Deliverance started to speak.

✱✱✱

"Fades," Effie whispered in awe after Deliverance, with the help of Eleanor and Addie, had finished her recounting of the last few weeks.

"'Tis rather a lot to take in," Deliverance replied, noting the Narisi lilt coming back into her speech.

"And you mean to bust out our actual gifts from wherever they're hiding inside us?" Effie asked Eleanor, looking at the girl with intense curiosity.

Deliverance

"Yes, that is rather the idea." She giggled in return at Effie's description of the healing process.

"What if we want to keep our gifts we already have?" Effie demanded.

"You want to keep your gift?" Cat remarked dryly.

Effie shrugged. "I'm used ta it. 'Tis familiar."

"It is something someone else saddled you with," Jack said, ducking as he ambled into the tent. "Wouldn't you rather be who you were meant to be, rather than struggling along being what someone else decided for you?"

Effie sat back and considered this for a spell. Finally, she said, "All right, but I hope I get ta shoot fire from my hands. There are a few heads in the village which are needing a little less hair...and some other body parts as well."

Eleanor giggled, and Deliverance smiled. Her friend, for her part, had not changed a wick since she had been away.

"I suppose you've come to add your two cents in, Senator? To lecture us on how we aught to be?" Cat accused Jack snidely, just as he had made himself comfortable on the floor next to Deliverance.

Jack regarded her coolly. "I do not presume to dictate to you, madam, on what choices you should or should not make. I am not like your island men here. However, if you are asking whether I judge you in your part of keeping the false narrative alive...well, I cannot. I was not here in your shoes, with a family to protect and limited means to survive. I suppose your mother must have brainwashed you into believing the necessity of the whole bit."

Cat leveled an equally cool gaze at Jack. "'Tis good you do not judge me as you really have no idea what it was like here, nor my mother's motivations." She turned to her daughter. "There is a reason you had no idea about the narrative weaving." Cat, it seemed, also had a story to wind.

"So, let me get this straight. You purposefully did not tell me of our familial obligation because you knew this would happen!?" Deliverance said incredulously after Cat finished piecing together the plan her mother, Independence, and she had hatched decades before.

"Not precisely this, but I knew something would happen. Something earth shattering. Something large enough to rock the very earth beneath our feet. Why do you think I named you Deliverance?" Cat asked her.

"I have never had any idea, mother. You know this," Deliverance replied with annoyance.

"Look about ye, girl," Cat told her simply. So Deliverance did as her mother bade, and then she saw.

"I delivered this opportunity," she said, awestruck.

"Aye. Without you, we wouldna be here, on the precipice of change." Her mother confirmed, pride glinting in her usually enigmatic eyes.

"And what of your name?" Eleanor inquired of Cat.

Cat smiled deviously then. "Aye, most think my name Catalyst made me good at chemistry and herbs. Which is true for the most part. But a catalyst...now that is a strong word. Catalysts enable elements around them to bring change. My mother, Independence, was a shrewd woman."

Deliverance sat back, slapping a hand to her forehead. Of course!

"So, you are not a subversive bent on keeping prisoners on tiny islands then," Jack said dryly.

"No, indeed. I tried to leave with Deliverance once," Cat said, snaking her fingers through Johns and meeting his eyes. "But it was not written on the horizon yet. Now, we have a chance, a better chance. And I mean to convince as many Narisis to come with us as possible."

Jack nodded approvingly, a silent truce brokered between them.

Just then a shout rang out across the camp.

Their party had to shoulder their way to the front of the crowd gathered at the forest's edge. When they got there, they were met with a line of men from the village. Their torches cast deep shadows across their faces, accenting the already deeply evident distrust and fear.

The Abbot stepped forward, seconded by the Fishmonger-Reave.

"Who are you? And why do you trespass here?" the Abbot called, his voice cracking though he was attempting to sound brave. Cat and Deliverance exchanged a glance and stepped forward. "You!!" he hissed, upon recognizing them. "How did ye escape the bonds of the gaol!?"

The men assembled behind him rumbled suspicious murmurs.

"With my help," Jack said, casually ambling forward to look at the Abbot in the eyes. The Abbot shifted uncomfortably.

"We have not had visitors to this island. Make your purpose known," the Abbot demanded, in a watery tone probably less forceful than he intended.

Jack circled the Abbot, sizing him up. "My purpose," he called, so all the men could hear him, "OUR purpose. Is to offer you freedom." This caused quite a stir.

"What do you mean by that, intruder?" the Abbot replied.

The entire village had not turned out, Deliverance noticed. It seemed only the men had. That meant the women, children, and elderly would not hear Jack's words uncolored by the prejudice of these brutes. Out of the corner of Deliverance's eye, she saw Eleanor and Effie come panting up, having disappeared for a while into the woods. Odd, she thought, but turned her attention back to the events unfolding before her.

"The Republic of Arcanton has granted a one-time reprieve. A chance to leave the island, to see the Outside, to have access to improved lives! Better medicine, more technology! Your children will no longer waste away with whooping cough and polio. Your wives and brothers will no longer succumb to consumption and cholera." Jack spoke with clarity and authority, his proud features catching in the firelight.

"And why have you never come before?" the Reave piped in.

"We have not had a way to safely remove you from the island until now," Jack replied.

"What is that supposed to mean?" the Abbot shot back.

It was Cat who stepped forward now, staring down the men of the village, daring them to not allow her to speak. Under the forcible intimidation of her green stare, they let her have her say.

"It means you and I...all of us, for generations as far back as the Exodus, have been stricken with a magical plague. It lives in our blood. It binds the gifts of your wives and sisters in the naming ceremony and it renders your magic null," Cat declared, chin up, shoulders back, unafraid of these men who for so long had intimidated her into hiding.

The Abbot scoffed. "Do not be absurd, woman! The Naming God made us so—men have no power. It is only born of the intrinsically evil vapors of a woman!"

"Is that so?" Jack replied casually, walking down the line of men. With a flick of his wrist, a ball of dancing flame hovered in his palm. The whispers amongst the men grew almost to a sea-crashing roar.

"Unnatural!" the Abbot cried out, shying back away from Jack, pointing.

"Nay, friend. It is you who is unnatural. You all have an illness in your blood. You have passed it to your children for generations. But we have a way to cure it," Jack called out so everyone could hear him.

"And wield the feminine powers, like you?" the cartwright's voice rang out.

Jack laughed. "Everyone has a power on the Outside. Men and women. Some are like me, fire bringers. Some call the rain. Some have mental powers, or gifts of extreme agility and strength. If healthy, one comes into their powers as they grow into adults."

"And we would also have powers?" the Abbot asked. Deliverance could see the oil-slicked gears in the man's evil mind turning.

"Aye, ye all would. Men *and* women," Effie called, stepping out from behind the shoulders of those in front of her. Her appearance caused another stir in the crowd. Deliverance caught snippets of, "Thought she was in gaol," "slut," "whore," and "unnatural."

Effie walked slowly, eyeing every one of her accusers, each one of her gaolers, challenging them to take her freedom again. Then, when she hit the center of the line, she looked the Abbot straight in the face. Raising both her arms high over her head, she sneered at the Abbot. Then she called forth a firestorm from her hands. The rolling flames shot up high into the night sky with a searing vengeance. The Abbot stumbled back, terror rising in his eyes at the sight of Effie's unbridled power.

Deliverance

That must have been where Eleanor and Effie had gone off to, Deliverance reasoned. Effie must have shed her fear of the transformation and Eleanor must have just cured her. One look over her shoulder at Eleanor confirmed her suspicions.

"I figured she'd be a fire bringer. She rather looks the part," Jack said in an aside to Deliverance.

"There was no doubt in my mind," Deliverance whispered back.

"Do not be afeared, Abbot. I willna hurt ye," Effie cooed at the Abbot. "That is…as long as ye have stayed away from my friend Tobin while I was rotting in your cursed gaol."

The Abbot swallowed, taking several more steps back. "We have much to discuss amongst ourselves."

"Aye. We shall be here at this encampment, waiting for any and all who wish to be cured and start a new life. It is worth it, I promise you all," Jack declared, his clear voice ringing out so the whole crows could not miss the offer. The Abbot's Adam's apple jumped in his scrawny throat, and he turned and retreated. The rest of the crowd left as well, albeit more slowly, curiosity ringing in their stares.

Once the torchlights from the villagers had disappeared, Effie turned to everyone and declared cheerfully, "That went well, did it not?"

"No," Jack said quietly, thoughtfully. "I do not believe it did." He was the politician amongst them, after all. He would know.

"What are you thinking?" Niles asked as he took a place in their group.

"I'm thinking I don't trust that slithery bastard. There's no telling what he might do."

Deliverance, Cat, and Effie had to agree with his assessment.

"What is our next move then, sir?" Stevens asked Jack.

Jack paused for moment, considering. Thoughts flitted rapidly through his mind, displayed upon his open face. "Niles," he said after evidently coming to a decision. "Care to bust out those reconnaissance skills of yours?"

CHAPTER 32

Deliverance

Deliverance, Jack, Niles, Effie, and Stevens gathered at the top of the crest of the ridgeline overlooking the village square. The group of men had returned from their rendezvous with the party on the beach and appeared to be gathering outside the town hall. With the binoculars John had given them before they left, they spied on them from afar.

"It looks like they're arguing," Stevens assessed, handing the binoculars down the line. They had lined up, flat on their stomachs, watching the dance between the village men unfold below them.

A large swath of the men planted themselves in front of the hall, facing off with a small offset standing behind the Abbot. The Reave stood in the middle, gesticulating wildly, pulling his hair, looking as if he were distressed and shouting.

"Want me to pop down and see if I can glean any more info?" Niles asked Jack. As soon as Jack nodded, Niles disappeared, leaving a puff of pine needles in his wake.

"Wow, he's really fast," Effie breathed. "Are you sure they won't see him?"

"No, he's an old hand at this. As stealthy as they come," Jack assured her, not taking his eyes off the scene below. It was impossible from this distance to tell what was unfolding between the men, although whatever it was, there was a schism between the two groups.

When Niles returned, covering an impossible distance in a few short minutes, he was gasping for breath. "The Abbot wants to burn the hall! I think there are people barricaded inside!" He gulped, urgency ripping in his voice. Sweat cascaded down his shiny brown scalp.

"No!" Effie and Deliverance both cried. "Jack, we have to stop him! He might have the entire village in there!" Effie sobbed, grasping his arm in panic.

"GO!" Jack shouted without hesitation. They sprang to their feet and took off in the direction of the village, careening down the steep ridgeline path. Deliverance and Niles were the first to arrive, although Stevens landed in a puff of dust, having catapulted himself with his gift through the air not far behind them.

The moment of their arrival caused all heads to turn, startled, in their direction and the Abbot stole the advantage. Quickly, he heaved his heavy torch onto the thatched roof of the hall. Then he snatched the cartwright's torch from his grasp before the man could pluck it away from him and threw that one as well. The thatch of the roof went up in flames almost immediately.

"NO!" Deliverance screamed and flung herself against the barricaded doors. Hands grasped her from behind and ripped her away from the doors. She twisted painfully, before focusing on her gift and flipping back to unseat their hands.

She landed in a crouch and surveyed the scene around her. Several men had turned on the Abbot's group and were bent on violence against the man and his followers. Others circled Deliverance with the look of mountain lions about to pounce, their predatory stares maniacal in the firelight. She realized they would not let her or Niles break the barricade, while they were standing.

"Here!" Niles said, tossing her and Stevens each an unlit torch. They grasped them like clubs but did not dare to wait to size up their opponents before launching at them. The fire was spreading too quickly.

Stevens bowled over a score of men trying to take their flank and walloped the last man standing in the head, while Niles took rapid swinging arcs with his torch, knocking down swaths of men. Deliverance focused on the three men standing in front of the door.

"Why are you doing this?" she cried, as she launched herself at them.

"They cannot be allowed such power!" One of the men heaved, before Deliverance knocked him on his rear with a fist to the jaw. She swore, feeling the minuscule bones in her hand crack.

"Who?" she yelled back, evading another man's attempt to grasp her by rolling to the side and sweeping his legs out from under him.

"The women...the children," gasped one of the men, whose ribs Deliverance was sure she'd pummeled into a pulp.

"You mean to take the power for yourselves," she realized, eyes widening in terror.

"What did you think would happen, unnatural girl? Bringing a cure to the island like that?" A snaking voice hissed over her ear. The Abbot rounded on her, battered, arm hanging limply at his side. "We will find the cure and use it for ourselves. It is better the women see the Fades than be tempted in their evil ways with new powers. You saw Mistress Effie. It was horrid—that spiteful, disgusting girl wielding such power. It cannot be allowed. We must save their souls before they corrupt them past the point of achieving the Fields in the afterlife." The Abbot's eyes glowed with the raging conflagration, both on the roof of the hall and from the madness within.

"And so you mean to burn them alive!?" Jack puffed, he and Effie finally arriving.

"Jack! Help me! Hold them back while I tried to break down the door!" Deliverance screamed.

Effie stalked around the Abbot like a wild animal, her eyes crazed with vengeance. Deliverance did not have time to pull her back from that abyss.

Jack positioned himself back to back with Deliverance, watching as a group of men descended upon them, war on their faces, clutching pitchforks and machetes.

"Break down the door!" Jack shouted to her. "I will hold off this bunch."

The men started to converge on Jack, assured in their large numbers against one man. Jack looked up at them, a strange, almost ecstatic expression alighting his features. "You will stand down," he commanded. The men, looking around at their superior numbers, chuckled to themselves and started to advance on him.

"YOU SHALL STAND DOWN!" Jack commanded again, both his arms reaching out to the sides. From his hands shot the most intense fire Deliverance had ever seen him produce, roaring from his palms in either direction, creating a wall between the men and her.

Deliverance wasted no time, heaving herself against the tall double doors. They were stout and locked with a chain lock. Inside she could hear cries of fear and pain. She heaved against the doors harder, the metal on the doors growing hot and searing her shoulder through her tunic. Still it did not budge. Again and again she careened against the door, hearing her bones crumple and snap with each blow. Still, she persisted as Jack held everyone off with his wall of fire. Over and over she struck the door, heaving with all her magical might. But it did not budge. Rage and tears threatened to overcome her as she began pummeling the wood with her bloodied fists.

Suddenly, she became aware of Niles at her side. "Stop," he commanded her. When she did not cease, he grabbed her from behind, pinning her arms down. "Calm yourself. We shall try again, together. But you must concentrate. Build your power up inside you before you release it in a burst of speed."

"How!?" Deliverance cried.

Niles spun her to meet his eyes. "Sun...moon...truth," he repeated the mantra. Slowly, Deliverance gained control of herself. Sun...moon...truth. "Feel it growing in you. Feel it circulating in your blood, blooming like a lotus flower. Feel it gathering...gathering... gathering. Breathe and let it build."

Deliverance breathed with him and felt it. She felt her blood singing, a magnetic pull drawing energy into her. The more she steadied herself, the stronger the pull became. It grew, swelling like the rising tide.

"Now we shall try in unison," Niles instructed her. "On three. ONE...TWO...THREE!!"

They both shot forward like rockets, fueled by the gathered energy between them. In the slowed moment in which Deliverance actually sped up, but the world seemed to still, she felt the devastating impact of the solid door. For the smallest portion of a second she despaired as she thought it would not give way. Sun...moon...truth. She focused as she gave every ounce of herself in that last push. The door groaned, and as the world came back into real time splintered and cracked off its hinges, dropping inward.

Deliverance

Several of the village men fighting on their side rushed forward through the doors, shouting for their loved ones. Effie was amongst them.

"TOBIN!" she screamed. "CHARITY! AMITY!"

Niles and Deliverance did not waste another second, but sped into the building, dragging people out. Soon the entire group was working in unison, attempting to pull the rest of the survivors from beneath the caving wreckage of the roof. It wasn't long before only Jack and Effie would withstand the heat of the fire, but they kept going, carrying badly burned victims out rapidly, handing them off, and going back for more.

It was hours before they stopped trying. No one left in the hall was alive and the roof had fully collapsed in, a smoldering, ember-ridden wreckage.

Reinforcements had arrived, carting the casualties off to the field hospital where Addie, Cat, and Eleanor were waiting with a score of recruits to do triage.

Deliverance, Jack, Effie, Niles, Stevens, and the handful of men who had opposed the Abbot and were not tending to loved ones sat slumped on the hill watching the hall finish its burn to the ground. No one spoke. No one had the energy or the will to move. They simply numbly stared at the ashes and carnage. They sat there as the light of morning began to work on the blackness of the night sky, turning ink into indigo, stars stubbornly refusing to give up their posts.

Finally, one of the relief workers came and tapped Jack on the shoulder. "Doctor Pennington is ready to see you now," she informed him. "Does anyone need mobility assistance?"

Jack shook his head and sent the girl on ahead. Slowly, the group gathered themselves. As Jack lifted Deliverance from the dirt, his touch broke through the din of her shock.

"Oh, Jack!" she cried, and clutched him to her, burying her face in his chest. His strong, sure arms wound around her, and the tears came. "How could anyone be so heinous...so entirely evil?" Her sobs came with big hiccups. Effie and Stevens joined in the embrace, sharing the sadness only Deliverance was ready yet to express. They would come to terms with their grief and shock at the events in their own time.

Finally, they dropped their arms. And one by one, their group started to amble in the direction of the beachhead and the camp.

Jack took Deliverance's hand, lightly squeezing it, careful not to exacerbate the already swollen joints. "Come on. Let's let Addie clean you up."

As they walked across the knoll together, they came upon a body, staring lifeless up into the sky. Around his throat, the charred flesh blackened perfectly in the shape of two, feminine hands. The Abbot. Both of them knew who had dispatched him, and neither commented, as they stepped around him.

When they reached the large hospital tent, Cat swept Deliverance into a fierce embrace. "Ye were so brave, my love! I'm already hearing tales of your deeds."

Deliverance

"Oww," she replied, wincing at the pressure.

John was also there but patted her in a far gentler hug. "Have Doctor Addie clean you up, Del. I am already detected some internal bleeding. It needs to be tended to as soon as possible," John assessed, ever the clinical observer.

Deliverance nodded. "Thanks, Dad." And walked on before her choice of words could be registered.

When Addie spied her over the tops of heads, relief scrawled across her face. "There you are!" she exclaimed, collecting her friend and leading her to an empty cot. Eleanor was following at her heels with a tray of medical supplies.

"Wait," Deliverance said. "Where is Effie?"

"Oh she's fine, but gosh you took a beating!" Eleanor declared, setting her tray down on the table beside the bed. "She's just over there." The girl pointed out a scarlet head several cots down.

Next to Effie stood Tobin, the abused orphan from the trial, covered in ash but appearing none worse for the wear. Charity sat on the cot next to hers, holding Amity's hand. Charity and Amity both had suffered some minor burns, but none too severe from what Deliverance could gather from her vantage point. The group of friends was leaning together, giving each other solace and comfort.

"I need to treat you now," Addie said, snapping her fingers in front of Deliverance's face to grab her attention away from the moving scene.

Deliverance nodded her assent. And Addie began a thorough examination of her dozens of injuries. She called out conditions to Eleanor, who attentively scribbled them down on a notepad as she went. With each proclamation, Jack's frown deepened. He hated seeing her pain, Deliverance realized, and reached out to squeeze his hand. He was truly heroic, the evidence mounting daily. Of course, the stark contrast between her fellow islanders and him aided in this thought process.

"She must have used blunt force at a level so much higher than her body could withstand," Addie told Jack as she poked and prodded Deliverance.

"Aye, if it had not been for Niles and her, they never would have broken the door down and rescued the people we could save," Jack replied grimly, his jaw clenched in empathy and worry.

"Deliverance, I am going to have to sedate you again. Are you okay with that?" Addie said finally. Deliverance could tell by the look on her face that she'd confirmed what John suspected. Her internal organs were bleeding, and it would take all of Addie's skill to remedy them.

"Do what you need to," Deliverance replied, lying back on the cot. Jack took her hand and clasped it in both of his.

"I'll be right here the whole time," Jack told her, and Deliverance did not doubt him.

Blackness overtook her suddenly. The last image she saw was a handsome face stretched in worry, dark eyes filled with concern.

CHAPTER 33

Deliverance

She did not dream, thankfully. If she had, it would have been filled with fire and screams. But Addie's drugs kept her mind blissfully blank. Emerging from that comfortable nothingness took effort. She did not want to leave the peace behind. It was so enthralling in its tranquility, not cold like one would expect but warm like a familiar quilt. Begrudgingly though, her traitorous body began to rebel, pulling her back into the world like a fisherman pulls in a large catch on his line, slowly and into the light.

Deliverance groaned before she blinked blearily, trying to make sense of the hazy world around her. It did not come into focus readily, but her eyes adjusted in their own time. She was not in the hospital tent anymore, but a different, smaller one. Hers was the only cot in it, she realized as she attempted to sit up. Ensconced around her were all her friends — Effie, Eleanor, Stevens, Mrs. Potter, and her mother and father. The only two missing were Jack and Addie, although she quickly realized Jack was behind her, asleep in a chair with his head propped on his hand. All the others were sound asleep too, taken with fatigue from their vigil.

Jack's eyes popped open as his head slid forward, and he blinked.

"Oh thank God!" he whispered and gathered her in his arms. He sat on the cot next to her, holding her, rocking. Soon, Deliverance realized he was fighting back tears.

"Whatever is the matter?" she asked him, in a low voice, careful to not wake the others.

"What is the matter?" Jack whispered back incredulously. "My love, you've been out for three days. No one could revive you. Addie said your body needed time to come to terms with the extensive healing she had to accomplish. We nearly lost you." His voice dammed up, croaking.

"I really did all that damage to myself, trying to open that blasted door?" Deliverance asked him, once she thought he might have control of his voice again. It did not seem possible now, after the fact.

"Aye. You were bound and determined to get those people out. You're a hero…heroine. Whichever you prefer," Jack replied, taking her face in both his hands and kissing her forehead tenderly. "Please never ever be a heroine like that again." He pulled her back to him, Deliverance guessed so she could not see the couple tears she felt land on her shoulder. And he held her like that for a very long time, reassuring himself she was alive and well.

There was much rejoicing when everyone awoke to find Deliverance sipping on a mug of "instant" coffee, chatting with Jack. Hugs and laughter abounded.

"I am very proud of ye, daughter," Cat said, squeezing her shoulder.

"I as well," John seconded, which Mrs. Potter and Stevens echoed.

Deliverance pulled her knees up to her chest. "I wish we could have saved more people... The death was..." She choked. She could not continue putting the brutality into words. So many had perished, either fighting against them, or in the fire.

It was Effie who broke the melancholic silence. "Aye. 'Tis a terrible tragedy we will all never forget. But we've work ahead of us now. People to cure. Lives to rebuild."

"When did you become so wise, friend?" Deliverance teased her.

"Ah, I've always been wise. It twas just all that pent up fire wanting ta escape that masked it!" Effie replied cheekily and the rest of them laughed. It felt good to laugh. To breathe. To be alive. To love.

✳✳✳

Over the next few days, Eleanor readied herself and then began the healing process. She would tire after several cases and have to rest. Though the girl grumbled about having to take respite, she was dogged in her determination to heal the villagers.

"Come on, love," Jack called to Deliverance, once she was rested enough to get up and walk around. "There's not much for us to do here, but I know a chore that needs to be sorted."

Deliverance followed him, curiously, as he walked out of the camp. He strode purposefully north for a few steps, before turning to her.

"Actually, I have no idea where we are going. You'll have to lead," he admitted, grinning at his own folly.

"All right. But where are we going?" Deliverance agreed, coming up to take the lead.

"Home," Jack replied simply. "Your home."

Home…it felt odd upon her tongue now. The idea of it had altered so much in the past weeks. But Jack was right. He wanted to take her to the homestead, to see if there was anything they wanted to bring along, and also, he admitted, because he wanted to spy her childhood home.

"I want to see where baby Deliverance was raised. Where the feral girl roamed the woods. I want to have a picture in my head of you and yours," Jack told her, as they ambled along. It would have been faster astride a pony, but if Charity were telling the truth, the ponies were all safely pastured on her family's

Deliverance

homestead south of the village. They would have to be collected for boarding the ship.

When Jack had told Finley they were bringing their farm animals, the man had exclaimed, "What am I? Noah? And this is my ark?"

Deliverance had replied insouciantly, "If Noah has a ship full of ponies and pigs, then yes. You are Noah." And that settled that.

She did not mind, she found, walking along with Jack. They chatted easily, freely, about the future. Where they would go, what they would do.

"I've commissioned a relief team at the ready at our estate in Cornwall," Jack told her as he swung a pilfered stick along, carefree.

"This is your country house you speak of?" Deliverance asked.

"Aye. There is room enough for everyone. The relief team is ready to help with gift coaching and to teach everyone usable skills. I have a few farm tenancies vacant as well, for those who would wish to retake up farming," Jack informed her. He turned to her, radiance shining from within. "You will love Morwenchase. It's large and open, and right on the sea, just like....oh."

He stopped talking when they finally came into view of the homestead Deliverance had shared with her forebears for hundreds of years. It was no longer.

"Someone must have burnt it to the ground whilst Cat was imprisoned," Deliverance commented, picking through the wreckage. The once cozy house, sprouting like a benign tumor from the mountain wall, was no more than a few charred timbers on the ground. The inglenook where she and her mother shared their many evenings over their cups and tales was reduced to cinders. A great black blight on the otherwise picturesque hill.

"Are you so very upset?" Jack asked her, apprehensively searching her face for signs of sadness.

Deliverance stood back on her heels and considered for a moment. "I suppose I will miss it in a way. The days of my youth spent here in what I thought was relative freedom. But I've learned that home is not a place. It is wherever you are, and my loved ones."

Jack grasped her hands, bringing them to his lips. "I feel exactly the same. I love you, Deliverance."

"And I you, Jack…oh!" Deliverance exclaimed, reclaiming her hands from Jack. She felt tentatively around her neck and brought the chain he had given her forth. From it, dangling like a bronze berry, was his mother's ring. "You were right! The chain did not falter! Even through the whole ordeal."

"If you had lost it, I would not have cared," Jack told her. "All I care is that you and Eleanor and everyone are alive and safe."

"Well I care!" Deliverance exclaimed with mock indignation. "I mean to wear it!" And with that she slid it from its chain and onto her ring finger.

Deliverance

"Does this mean...?" Jack asked, not daring to believe. She nodded and he grabbed her up in his arms, swinging her around and kissing her until she was dizzy.

"I do not think there is much to salvage here. Shall we go back and tell the others?" Deliverance asked, turning to leave.

But Jack stopped her. "Wait. Didn't you say you had a cache beneath the floorboards?" he asked her, and she nodded. "Shall we see if anything survived there?"

Indeed, he was right. The cache was low enough in the floor the contents had escaped relatively unscathed. After casting aside the singed floorboard, she first plucked out her snow globe of Arcanton, sooty, but cleanable, the miniature city now familiar under the thick, marred dome. Then her mother's grimoire, the cover warped with heat, but her healing recipes on the parchment pages inside intact. A folder with the names of her ancestral line had been charred beyond recognition, but Deliverance knew Cat could recite it from memory anyway, so it was no great loss. Most of the other books crumbled past saving when Deliverance sifted through them, until she came to the last one at the bottom. The Odyssey. The cover curled in heat damage at the edges, but the book itself was intact. Deliverance lifted it carefully, cradling it against her.

It was then she noticed the page affixed to the front cover had come unglued slightly from the heat of the fire. Fiddling with it, she realized there was something behind it, something almost plasticky, glued between the cover and the first page of the manuscript. As she pried it free, she realized it was a polaroid of her family. In its time-warped colors, there she sat between both her parents on a winter morning, John's arm stretched out to its full length to collect them all in the shot. They were all grinning ear to ear, enjoying one of their winters together as a family.

It was here all along, Deliverance mused, and she never knew. He was here all along.

CHAPTER 34

Deliverance

Their newly obtained carefree state, however, was short lived. When they returned to camp, it was evident there was a problem. Tensions were palpable as they passed through tent structure after tent structure.

"Where is everyone, do you think?" Deliverance asked, a suspicious feeling snaking up her spine.

Shouts over in the direction of the field where Eleanor had been conducting her healing operations indicated they should head that way.

"It's not my fault!" Eleanor's cry came to them over the top of a sea of heads. Jack and Deliverance elbowed their way to the front, though once the crowd realized who was doing the elbowing, they parted of their own accord.

Eleanor stood with Addie and Effie on either side of her. The baker had his finger pointed at Eleanor's face, in the appearance of giving her a good dressing down.

"Think very carefully about whether or not you want to lose that finger," Jack said dangerously as he rounded the man's field of view.

The baker, a portly man resembling a potato, had thunder in his face. He quickly brought himself into check once he saw Jack, however.

"She says there ain't nuffin wrong with me!" he accused Eleanor, scowling at her.

"I fail to see the problem, or why that would cause you to verbally accost my sister," Jack replied smoothly.

"That's just it, Jack..." Eleanor said to her brother, tugging his sleeve. "There IS nothing wrong with him." Jack raised his eyebrows at his sister, not comprehending.

"What she means is," Addie broke in, explaining for the flustered girl, "is that there is no malady for Eleanor to cure. There is nothing at all. The man has no magic to latch onto and nothing in his bloodstream indicating he even has the ability to do magic."

Eleanor regained her words. "It's been like that with all the men I've tried to treat today! This is the first day I've attempted to treat any of the males. Up until now I have only cured a few dozen females."

"She's doing it on purpose!" An indiscriminate voice rang out from the crowd. Jack whirled on them, prepared to do violence on his sister's behalf, but Deliverance caught his sleeve.

"What about Tobin? Have you tried to cure Tobin?" Deliverance asked Eleanor. She nodded and the lad appeared, ducking through the crowd to come stand with her and the others.

He took Effie's hand and affirmed "Aye she did, Miss. She tried but there weren't nuffin there for her to fix."

"We love Tobin," Deliverance called out, her voice ringing clear. "Effie went to gaol on the boy's account, for Fades' sake. If Eleanor cannot cure him, then she is telling the truth."

Deliverance let her words settle over the crowd. For the longest moment, nobody spoke, lost in a quagmire of possibilities.

Addie cleared her throat. "It seems, and we would not have known this before, having only had female test subjects, that the magical illness is hereditary and passed through a double X chromosome combination...females. The males on the island must have been rendered magically obsolete centuries ago as a result of the spells it took to bind the island. Due to...inbreeding," she coughed slightly at this, "the men here have never regained any magical aptitude or genetic markers to carry magic in their blood." She let them digest her speech for a moment before declaring, "They are, for all intents and purposes, magic-less."

The crowd stirred. A group of girls sat in a line along the edge of the activity, having been cured earlier that day. They shuffled uncomfortably as they felt a mix of glares and considering stares upon them. Mrs. Potter had been serving them each tea before the ruckus ensued, and glared back at the crowd, daring them to make one jealous move against the girls who had just now regained their rightful powers.

"Well, what are we supposed to do now?" another voice from the crowd rang out.

The baker chimed in, "Aye—my wife has already been cured! What am I to do?"

The baker's wife emerged and looked at his crossly. "Well I'm not bloody well giving up my powers now. Especially not for you, you faithless lout," she declared primly and marched off toward camp. The baker looked terribly at a loss. Deliverance did not blame his wife...especially not after the warts issue.

"I love my wife and daughters!" the Reave called out. "Can I still come with them? I want them to be cured and have a better life!"

Addie, the expert on genetics, considered the issue, cocking one fey head to the side, running through the variables in her mind.

"It should not be an issue," she said finally. "You are not contagious and are not in danger of spreading it to future generations. I confirmed this with blood samples when we first tried to cure Tobin."

"But, we'd have to go into a world full of magic when we've none of our own to defend ourselves," the cartwright protested. This caused a stir of consternation amongst the crowd. "What about our sons? Are they to be left impotent?"

It was Jack who fielded his concern. "Aye. It would be a brave undertaking. There are some in our world who go their entire lives without really using their powers. Our technology is so great we've come not to rely on our powers. There are many among us who still choose to, but it is not the norm. Plenty of people spend their lives with little to no magic in it, content to rely on the mind and its innovations instead." He let this settle in before continuing, "But it is your choice. You can choose to stay here. Here are my two warnings. The first is that your wives and daughters will be allowed, free of any interference from you, to choose for themselves whether they wish to leave Nar or not. The second is that once we are gone, so is your chance to leave. The Arcanton military will begin patrolling the waters outside Nar. Any attempts at fleeing after we are gone will be met with deadly force. Eleanor has several days of healing left ahead of her. Make your choices, and may you choose wisely."

With that, Niles dispersed the crowd and they went about their business, some grumbling and some deep in contemplation about the choice before them. It was, Deliverance thought to herself, a daunting one. Stay in the familiar world with little more than a quarter of the island's population left alive or risk everything, venturing into a new world that promises great rewards but could also hold great danger? Be potentially defenseless against other men with powers like Jack's? She shook her head. It was a conundrum.

※※※

Eleanor carried on her healing, with Addie, Cat, and Mrs. Potter to support her. She revealed many hedge and kitchen witches, some healers, and many soothers. A few were elemental benders like Effie, though none wielded fire like her. Air and water. No earth movers among them. A couple had mental gifts such as object levitation or telekinesis, but none as eerie as Eleanor or John's powers, thank the gods. She worked with a single-minded determination through all hours, only pausing when she was depleted and could carry on no further without respite.

In the end she cured over fifty women. The rest had either perished in the fire or decided to remain on Nar with their families. Deliverance scanned the crowd readying to pack up camp and depart after Eleanor had declared she was finished and all the final tests confirmed those who were to depart were disease-free.

They seemed so few, and yet they were able to save many, Deliverance thought. Not as many as she had hoped, though; her heart weighed heavy, sinking into the charred soil of the island with those who had lost their lives. It was such a waste and for naught but ignorance and hate. The casualties of war, Jack had called it, shaking his head in disgust.

"Are many wars like this? Undeclared, without law or regulation?" Deliverance had asked him.

"Most, unfortunately, are. There are all kinds of battles, love. Many are violent or have violent consequence. But it does not make the aim less chivalrous or the cause less valid," Jack told her, wrapping her in his arms as if he meant to soften the blows of the world by shielding her from them bodily.

When they were ready to depart, Jack broke through the tearful and sometimes angry farewells, offering those staying one final chance.

"You can still come. We will stop everything, cure your women, and take you with us. Just say the word," Jack pleaded with those who remained, the paltry few families determined to stick it out on a now almost deserted island. None took his offer, however, and after they loaded the last of their ponies onboard, they pulled the dinghies up and secured them in their holdings.

A pall fell over those onboard the *Daedalus*. No one waved. No one called farewell. The eerie silence permeated with only the lap of the water on the belly of the boat to break the hush. In this moment, their freedom seemed pyrrhic. Everyone stood still as Plaedic statues, watching the few fated families lined up along the shore as they grew smaller and smaller upon the horizon. Eventually, the Island of Nar, itself, was no more.

CHAPTER 35

Deliverance

Several Weeks Later

The roar of the sea on chalky cliffs, pushing flotillas of aquatic birds eve closer to sandy surfs, soothed Deliverance as she remembered the events on Nar. Sometimes she would awaken, crying out in terror in the middle of the night, until Jack soothed her back to sleep. Here, in the Arcanton countryside by the sea, she could almost pretend she was back home on Nar...almost. The spaces were vaster, the sunbaked coastline more rolling and yellow than the piney-craggy ridges of Nar. But the smell of the salty sea was the same, the crash of waves upon cliffsides, the feeling of being able to stretch one's arms and reach tip to tip without a soul to judge.

As she continued her daily constitutional along the coastline, she shielded her eyes from the sun and regarded Morwenchase in the distance. It stood out upon the horizon, even from afar. Its wings stretching out over a generous lawn. Deliverance could spy from here a group of ladies playing a game in the garden. She knew Mrs. Potter would be hard at work there as well, teaching a new group of hedge witches which herbs to use for head colds, and how to coax the deepest blooms from a rosebush. Stevens, likewise, was coaching new airbenders through various drills, strengthening their grasps of their gifts with patient words and a jovial smile.

Just beyond the steepled stables of the estate, a herd of wild ponies thundered over the rolling hills, kicking their heels and frolicking, enjoying the last of the autumn sun before the winter had the countryside in its clutches. Deliverance knew it was one of the last days of decent weather they would have before torrential rains came and then eventually turned to sleet and snow. Even so, she pulled her thick, woolen shawl closer to ward off the fingers of cool air seeping down her collar.

In the distance, Deliverance heard a whoosh and saw flames leap into the sky. Jack was hard at work clearing back some of the overgrown farmland for his newest tenants, trying to get as much done before the weather turned. Effie gladly aided in these efforts, a new carefreeness settling on her friend, the likes of which Deliverance had never seen before. She smiled to herself, running a finger along her lips. These were among the happiest days she had ever known. Cat had gone off to Antarticus with Lord Asher, but they promised to return by spring. Addie had taken up residence close by, monitoring the new emigres progress and health, although Deliverance secretly thought it might have something to do with Effie as well. Eleanor was already whipped up into an excited flurry about getting to celebrate *both* Christmas *and* Yule this year.

Deliverance's life now, despite the trials to achieve it, was filled with joy. Soon it would be filled with handfasting feasts and wedding bells.

As she turned to walk back toward Morwenchase, she glanced around her, assuring herself she was entirely alone. Then, with a smile upon her lips, she brought her hand up and with a flash of green, lit a small scintilla of fire on her fingertips. She delighted in dancing it from finger to finger for a moment, before extinguishing it with a giggle. It was her little secret. No one had to know, for now.

NOTES

"The oldest and strongest emotion of mankind is fear, and the oldest and strongest kind of fear is fear of the unknown."

~ H.P. Lovecraft

Uncontacted peoples are a source of fascination not only amongst anthropologists but the world in general. These are the last tribes of people who, generally through choice of their own, reject contact with the outside world. Most of these peoples live in extremely isolated pockets of the world, like the deep, dense jungles of South America. The Sentinelese are a hostile island people who live on an island in archipelago of India's Great Andaman Island Chain in the Indian Ocean. Anthropologist estimate from what little they could garner of their language they have been living in isolation for over 60,000 years.

Efforts to contact the Sentinelese have been met with hostility and Indigenous rights groups insist on their right to choose isolation. The Indian government and the local Andaman Administration have adopted a "hands-off eyes-on" approach to keep interlopers from harassing the island.

The controversy over the issue of uncontacted peoples sparked inspiration for Deliverance. While in reality these peoples have little immunity to outside diseases and have displayed every signal of not desiring contact, so a hands-off approach has been the safest for all concerned. Some like the idea of preserving these uncontacted cultures like they are an endangered species. Others are dying to bring them modern medicine and technology, to help improve their lives. Overtures of aid have been met with violence. But it does beg the question—what if they fully understood what the outside world had to offer? Would they still choose to remain in isolation? Who amongst them decides? What if some of these isolated people would, if offered a different choice, choose to step off into the outside world?

Thankfully, the Indian government has held the Sentinelese in much higher regard than the fictitious people of Nar. After the tsunami in 2004 the Indian Coast Guard was able to drop food off on the beaches for the people. They were promptly shooed away with spears and arrows.

I hope you have enjoyed reading about Deliverance's adventures. The next in her adventures will be coming out soon!

ACKNOWLEDGMENTS

I would like to acknowledge my lovely editor Stephanie Diaz for her help in revising the (extremely) rough draft and for her expert guidance. My mother and brother also deserve my thanks for being my stalwart beta readers and suffering through all my novels as they come into fruition.

Samantha Schinder

AUTHOR BIO

Samantha Schinder is a military veteran and a PhD student at Capella University. She has Bachelor of Arts degrees from Indiana University in Italian Language and Literature and Near Eastern Languages and Cultures as well as a Masters' degree from American Military University. She was honored to be one of the first Legacy Fellowship recipients from A Room of Her Own Foundation. She has also had her work published in the Paragon Press's Nabu Literary Review. Her popular dog-and-travel blog, sammythedogtrainer.com, is one of her main writing passions. She owns a small dog training business and is an avid skydiver.

Made in the USA
Middletown, DE
26 May 2022